SECRETS NEVER DIE

ALSO BY MELINDA LEIGH

Morgan Dane Novels

Say You're Sorry
Her Last Goodbye
Bones Don't Lie
What I've Done

Scarlet Falls Novels

Hour of Need
Minutes to Kill
Seconds to Live

She Can Series

She Can Run
She Can Tell
She Can Scream
She Can Hide
"He Can Fall" (short story)
She Can Kill

Midnight Novels

Midnight Exposure
Midnight Sacrifice
Midnight Betrayal
Midnight Obsession

SECRETS NEVER DIE

MELINDA LEIGH

Montlake
Romance

Published by Montlake Romance, Seattle

www.apub.com

Amazon, the Amazon logo, and Montlake Romance are trademarks of Amazon.com, Inc., or its affiliates.

ISBN-13: 9781542040181
ISBN-10: 1542040183

Cover design by Eileen Carey

Printed in the United States of America

To Anne Walradt,
writing teacher extraordinaire, mentor, and friend.
For (gently) shining a light on what my writing lacked
and showing me how to be better.

Chapter One

Why was the house dark?

Sitting in the passenger seat of his friend's Honda Accord, Evan checked the time on his watch. Twelve thirty a.m. His mom's car wasn't in the driveway. She must still be at the urgent care where she worked as a nurse. Evan's stepfather, Paul, always left a light on for her.

But there weren't any lights on tonight.

Every window was black. Even the lamppost at the end of the front walk was out.

Unease crept up the back of Evan's neck. His pulse kicked up a notch. A small punch of adrenaline countered his current overall state of exhaustion like a can of Red Bull. He hadn't slept in days, not since the last court-ordered visitation with his real—no, biological—father. A real father would care about Evan, and Kirk never had.

"Are you getting out?" Jake blew smoke out the driver's side window.

"Yeah." Evan opened the car door. A gust of wind almost ripped it out of his hand. He caught it and held on as he climbed out. "Thanks for the ride."

Jake waved his cigarette. "See ya."

Evan shut the door. Jake backed his car out of the driveway, leaving Evan alone.

He glanced up and down the suburban street. Past midnight, light from streetlamps pooled in shiny yellow circles on the blacktop. Overhead, thick clouds obscured the night sky. A storm system was on its way across upstate New York, and the air seemed charged with electricity. The weather report had warned of high winds and heavy rains, maybe even hail and tornadoes. He hoped his mom's shift had ended so she could get home before the storm started.

A hot, humid wind lifted the hair on the back of his neck. He suddenly felt as if he were being watched. Despite the heat of the June night, a shiver shot through his bones. His gaze fell on the windshield of a dark-blue sedan parked across the street, but he saw no one behind the wheel.

Now he was being paranoid. Lack of sleep must be making him stupid. Maybe a fuse had blown. That would explain the lack of lights.

Using his flashlight app to navigate the walkway and front steps, he slid his key into the dead bolt, but there was no resistance when he turned it. Had the door been unlocked? Nah. He must have imagined it. Paul would never leave the house open.

Evan was making excuses. He just didn't want to go inside the house and face his stepfather. Evan was two and a half hours past his curfew, he'd been a complete asshole to Paul that afternoon, and he'd ignored Paul's concerned texts about his being late.

Not that Paul would yell or anything. Paul was cool. But he'd want to talk about Evan's shitty behavior and the root cause. Getting grounded wasn't a big deal, but Paul's disapproval hurt.

Evan might as well get it over with. Better to do it now, before his mom got home. Unlike Paul, she would lose her shit, and Evan didn't want to deal with her freak-out. He opened the front door and went inside.

He heard voices that sounded like the TV coming from the back of the house. Definitely a fuse. The den, aka the man cave, was on a different electrical circuit from the front lights. A couple of weeks ago, Paul had shown Evan how to reset the switches in the electrical box in the garage.

Evan walked down the hall, his steps slowed by dread. Paul had waited up for him even though Evan had been a complete dick. Now Evan felt twice as bad.

Why did he let Kirk get to him?

Why was some fucking judge forcing Evan to spend his Sunday nights with the asshole?

Anger curled Evan's hands into fists.

His father didn't just bring out the worst in him. Kirk also cultivated anger and resentment. His father played him to get even with his mom. Kirk was a pro. He found a way to get to Evan every time.

Evan was an idiot.

"I bet moving out to the sticks was his idea," Kirk had said. "He was the one who made you move away from your friends. He probably had his eye on your mom while she was still married to me. She's his meal ticket. He quit his job as soon as they were married, right? He's set now."

But Kirk had twisted the facts. Paul had retired from his job as a sheriff's deputy months before, and he did all the stuff around the house, even cleaning, something Kirk would never do. But Kirk had gone on and on, picking at all of Evan's scabs until he'd found one that bled. Then Evan turned around and took out his anger on Paul, just like Kirk had planned all along. Evan couldn't wait until he turned eighteen, when he would be able to tell Kirk—and that asshole judge—to fuck off.

"Everyone makes dumbass mistakes," Paul had said last time. "But you have to own up and apologize."

Evan was going to make it right. He was not going to turn into his father.

He walked toward the den and stopped just short of the doorway, bracing himself for the talk his apology would initiate. But a loud pop brought him up short. What was that? His instincts said gunshot, but at the same time, his brain told him that was crazy.

Still in the corridor, he peered through the doorway. Paul lay on the floor. Blood saturated his T-shirt and spread to the carpet around his body.

So much blood.

Evan couldn't even register the horror. What he was seeing was beyond comprehension. He couldn't move, and he couldn't look away. His eyes were locked on Paul, the pain and fear on his stepfather's face.

Move! Do something! Help him!

Shaking himself out of his paralysis, he started forward. Paul saw him. His eyes widened. His head shook, almost imperceptibly, and he mouthed, "Run."

But Evan couldn't leave him there. His feet were rooted in place, as if the carpet had turned into ten inches of thick mud. He couldn't do anything. Paul's eyes shifted to the coffee table. Evan followed his line of sight to where Paul's handgun lay next to gun-cleaning supplies set out on a newspaper. Paul's fingers crawled along the carpet toward the table, but there was no way he'd be able to reach. He tried to roll, but the movement sent blood gushing onto the carpet, and he fell back.

Then a man walked into view and stood over Paul. He had a gun in his hand and wore a suit that didn't seem to fit him very well. When he lifted the gun, his suit jacket opened, revealing a gold badge clipped to his belt. A cop? He pointed the gun at Paul's face. The cop wore purple gloves that looked like the ones Evan's mom used at work. Panic grabbed Evan by the balls as he realized what was going to happen. The man was going to shoot Paul again. And Paul was going to die. Paul's legs twitched, almost in a running motion. He knew what was coming too, but he was too badly wounded to move anything except his feet.

And what did Evan do?

Fucking stood there, frozen, staring and shaking like a coward.

"What do you want from me?" Paul hissed, his voice weak as a breath.

"I want you to die." The man pulled the trigger. The gunshot blasted through the room.

Evan jumped. His heart skipped a beat. Panic tightened his lungs until he couldn't draw a breath. Paul's legs went still, and Evan knew he was gone.

Dead.

Evan felt the choking gasp tear from his throat, yet he didn't recognize the guttural animal sound as coming from his own mouth. His gaze was locked on the horror in the den.

Paul lay dead on the carpet, his body an island surrounded by a lake of blood.

Evan inhaled. At the rush of oxygen, his heart stuttered and kicked back into rhythm. He took one step forward, toward Paul, on reflex, before his brain put on the brakes.

But Paul was dead. Shot in the head by the man who now stood over him.

No. Not shot.

Executed.

The man turned, his eyes fixing on Evan, his gaze dumping pure terror into Evan's bloodstream. It flowed into his veins like ice water. His bowels cramped. Gooseflesh rippled up his arms. He turned toward the back door, but the dead bolt was locked. Afraid of easy break-ins, Paul had had the turn lock replaced with a keyed dead bolt when they'd moved in. Where was the key?

He turned and ran the way he'd come. Equal parts anger and terror fueled his steps and scattered his thoughts. Evan tore into the kitchen, his feet sliding on the tiles. He slammed into the sideboard. A stack of dishes slid off and shattered. Framed wedding pictures fell from the wall, the glass breaking as they hit the floor. Evan went down on his ass.

His tailbone rang with the impact on the tile, and his legs went numb for a few seconds.

"Where are you?" a voice called.

Scrambling to his feet, Evan ran toward the front door. He had to get out of the house. He was one of the fastest players on his hockey team, both on and off the ice. Once he was out in the open, he could outrun almost anybody.

"You can't get away." The voice was in front of him.

While Evan had been picking himself up off the kitchen floor, the killer had circled around through the dining room, beating Evan to the front door.

Evan stopped and tried to be silent. But his knees shook, and his breaths came fast and hard enough to echo in his ears. He fought to slow his breathing. The killer would be able to hear him.

He was going to die. Shot in the head like Paul.

His pulse sprinted in terror.

"You might as well give up now. I'll make it easy on you and kill you quickly." He was closer.

Evan backed through the kitchen. A piece of glass crunched under his foot. Sweat poured down his back. He was trapped. He needed the key to the back door.

He's going to get me.

"Know this: no matter what you do, no matter where you go, I'm going to find you and kill you." The sentence was delivered with the same cold-blooded calm that had been in the killer's eyes when he'd shot Paul.

The faint squeak of a floorboard in the hall nearly made Evan's bladder give way. He concentrated for a second until it passed. Then he stepped over the glass, easing his way back into the corridor that led to the den.

He slipped into the room. Paul's eyes stared blankly at the ceiling. Tears and snot ran down Evan's face as he skirted the bloodstained carpet. Standing next to Paul, he searched his pockets. Keys. He pulled them out, wrapping his fingers around them to keep them from jingling.

"Where are you?" the voice called, irritation clipping the words. "You're just dragging this out."

Evan eased to the back door. He held Paul's keys in his palm, his shaking fingers finding the right key. He held the rest of Paul's keys quiet as he unlocked the dead bolt. The hinges groaned as he began to open the door.

"I'm going to kill you. You can't get away from me." The man was in the doorway between the kitchen and rear hall. He raised his gun. "You're a dead man."

Evan flung open the door. The gunshot rang out. A lick of hot pain sliced through Evan's arm. He grabbed his bicep, automatically feeling for the wound. His hand came away wet, but his arm had gone numb. He felt nothing.

"Don't think anyone can hide you," the man called out the door. "I will find you. I will hunt you down."

Evan sprinted across the backyard, grabbing the top of the tall fence and swinging his legs up and over. He landed hard on the other side.

Was the killer chasing him?

Evan didn't stop to find out. He bolted away from the house, crashing through the underbrush like a panicked deer. He couldn't see the ground in front of him in the dark. Sticker bushes pulled at his feet and legs. His foot snagged, and he went down on his knees. He felt no pain as he shoved himself back onto his feet and kept moving.

After a short sprint, he hit the game trail he and Paul had used to hike to the lake. It was the same path that the deer and other wild animals used to access the water. The open trail let him turn on some speed, though the ground was uneven. He tripped twice but regained his footing without falling. He didn't know how long he ran, but he didn't slow until he thought his lungs would explode.

The physical movement was a relief. Like every coward, he was more comfortable with flight than fight.

He stopped in the center of the trail. Darkness closed around him. Something rustled the branches. The wind? He scanned the woods, but the sky was overcast, emitting little natural light. He strained for additional sound but heard nothing.

His hands patted his jeans pockets. His phone, which had been in his back pocket, was gone.

Did it matter? Who would he call?

The cops?

Paul had been a former cop. He'd been trained and armed. And this man had killed him. Evan remembered the flash of a badge at the man's belt. Evan couldn't trust the police to keep him safe.

The killer was a cop.

And Evan could identify him. He couldn't call his mom. She'd try to protect him, and she'd become a target too. There was no way he would endanger her. He had to stay far away.

The trail spilled onto the road. Evan came to a stop and stood still, lungs heaving, trying to listen for footsteps over the sound of his ragged breathing.

He didn't hear anyone behind him.

Evan debated. If he crossed the road and continued on the trail, he would end up at an abandoned campground. He and Paul had hiked through it a few weeks back. There had been a few canoes and kayaks. One of them might float. Evan could get away faster on the water. But where would he go?

On the other hand, if he followed the road, he would eventually see a car. He could get help. His arm throbbed in rhythm with his pulse, the pain strong enough to nauseate him. His wound needed treatment. But who could he trust at this point?

The sound of an engine approached. But as the engine came closer, he backed into the shadow of the trees.

Headlights appeared. The vehicle approached too slowly, as if the driver were looking for something.

Or someone.

He was afraid to move. He didn't want to draw attention. The vehicle crawled by. It was a dark sedan. Was it the same one that had been parked across the street from his house? Evan's pulse kick-started. The sedan stopped. His heartbeat scrambled inside his chest like a fawn trying to gain traction on icy ground.

Behind him, he heard the sound of a car door opening and closing. He'd been seen. As he turned to run, the killer's words echoed in his head.

I will hunt you down.

Chapter Two

Morgan Dane woke to the buzz of a cell phone. Raising her head, she glanced at the clock. One thirty-nine a.m. As a defense attorney, she occasionally received middle-of-the-night calls. People were arrested twenty-four hours a day. But a stomach virus had been making the rounds at the grammar school, and the two oldest of her three daughters had suffered through the bug. This was the first night in four that all her children were sleeping, and her head was as heavy as a bowling ball from lack of sleep.

Her hand was halfway to the cell phone charging on her nightstand when a second vibration, clearly from the other side of the bed, told her the call was for her fiancé, private investigator Lance Kruger.

Nudging Lance, she let her head drop back to the pillow. He was already reaching for his own phone. He swung his legs over the side of the bed and sat on the edge of the mattress.

"Lance Kruger." His body stiffened. "Did you call 911? Do that now. I'll be right there."

The alarm in his tone roused Morgan. She levered up on one elbow.

Lance set the phone back on the nightstand, switched on the bed-side lamp, and stood. Cotton pajama bottoms rode low on his hips. Morgan's French bulldog, Snoozer, burrowed under the covers. Dog number two, a bulldog mix named Rocket, raised her head and pricked her ears at the activity.

Morgan sat up. "Who was that?"

"Evan Meade's mother, Tina." Lance rushed for the adjoining bathroom, grabbing a pair of pants from a chair on the way. "Do you have anything important on your calendar this morning?"

"Nothing I can't reschedule." Morgan tossed back the covers.

Lance coached a hockey team of at-risk youths, a role that had started when he'd been an officer with the Scarlet Falls PD. Even after a bullet had ended his career on the police force, Lance continued as coach. More importantly, he was a mentor to the troubled kids. Since she and Lance had started dating last fall, Morgan had handled most of the boys' legal issues. "Is Evan in trouble?"

Zipping his black cargo pants, Lance hustled out of the bathroom. His blond hair was short enough that brushing one hand across the top was enough to settle it into place.

"What happened with Evan?" Assuming the boy had gotten himself arrested for something stupid, which was the usual reason one of the hockey parents called Lance, Morgan hurried past him and took a quick turn in the bathroom. Thirty seconds later, she opened her closet, grabbed a pair of black slacks, and stepped into them.

Lance tugged a gray T-shirt over his head. Tall, jacked, and grim-faced, he wore the tactical look well. "Tina came home from work. She found Paul shot to death and Evan missing."

"Paul is dead?" Shock froze Morgan's fingers for a heartbeat, then she continued buckling her belt. She'd briefly spoken to Tina's new husband a few times during hockey games or when he'd picked up Evan from the rink.

Lance sat on the chair to put on his boots. "Yes. That's all she said. When I told her to call 911, she hung up."

"She didn't do that first?" *Odd.* Morgan put on a white cotton blouse and shoved her feet into a pair of black pumps.

"No. She was upset." Lance retrieved their handguns from the safe in the closet.

If Morgan had found a dead body, her automatic reaction would have been to call the police.

He holstered his gun at his hip and tucked it under his shirt. "I'll start the Jeep."

Morgan took her Glock and did the same. She grabbed her black blazer from the closet and her giant tote bag from the dresser. "I'll be out in one minute."

Her live-in nanny slept in the room down the hall, across from the bedroom that Morgan's three little girls shared. She tapped on the door. At Gianna's sleepy "yes," Morgan poked her head into the room and gave her the news.

In an attempt to isolate the youngest from her contagious siblings, Morgan had put three-year-old Sophie in Gianna's room. Morgan had made a bed on an inflatable mattress, but the little girl had climbed into bed with her nanny and stolen most of it. For a small and wiry child, she could take up a surprisingly large amount of space. Poor Gianna slept on her side in the remaining eight inches.

The dogs slipped through the open door, jumped onto Gianna's bed, and curled up around Sophie's sprawled limbs. Gianna responded to Morgan with a nod, rolled over, and tried to pull the edge of the blanket over her shoulders, but the child and dogs weighed it down and she gave up.

Closing Gianna's door, Morgan turned and went into the girls' room. Five-year-old Mia slept in a pile of stuffed animals, her loyal zebra tucked under one arm. Ava, at age six, barely moved in her sleep. Her covers were as tidy as when she'd gone to bed. Even her teddy bear was neatly tucked in. Morgan pressed a light kiss to each of their foreheads to check for fevers. Both were cool. A rush of love filled her chest and blurred her vision. She wiped a tear from her eye. She really needed some sleep.

Satisfied that both children were well, Morgan strode past the clear plastic sheeting taped over the demolished kitchen, which was in the gutting phase of a major renovation project. She went outside, locked the door behind her, and pressed the button on the key fob to reset the security system.

A hot gust whipped Morgan's hair around her face as she rushed to the Jeep. The air felt heavy and damp. Thunder rolled, low and threatening in the distance.

Lance was waiting for her in the driver's seat. She climbed into the SUV and fastened her seat belt as he backed out of the driveway.

"Would you call Sharp and let him know what's going on? He knew Paul too. He's going to want to help."

Private investigator Lincoln Sharp, Lance's boss, owned Sharp Investigations. Morgan called him and relayed the few facts they knew. Before he'd opened Sharp Investigations, Lincoln Sharp had served on the Scarlet Falls PD for twenty-five years, most of that time as a detective. Paul Knox had been a retired sheriff's deputy. Limited staffing in rural jurisdictions often required law enforcement agencies to cooperate, and the two men had occasionally worked together.

Sharp digested the information in a second. "On my way."

Morgan lowered her phone to her lap. The country road leading out of the neighborhood was dark and empty.

Lance rolled through a stop sign. "I can't believe Paul is dead."

"It's horrible." As a mother, Morgan's thoughts immediately shifted to worrying about the missing teenager. "Poor Evan."

"I don't know how he's going to react. He's a good kid, but he's already had his share of troubles. A few years ago, his father went to prison on an assault charge, and his parents divorced. Evan lashed out. He was arrested for underage drinking, vandalism, mostly stupid stuff." Lance turned left. "He was becoming a frequent flier at the station, but he settled down over the next year. His grades started to recover. I expected even more improvement when his mother married Paul Knox last fall. I thought Paul's presence in Evan's life would be a good thing."

But Morgan sensed the situation hadn't panned out the way Lance had expected. "It wasn't?"

"I don't know," Lance said. "Evan has seemed extra moody the last couple of months, but he won't talk to me."

Tina and Paul lived in the neighboring town of Grey's Hollow, near the border with Scarlet Falls. At 1:53 a.m., Lance turned into a residential neighborhood of older homes built on large lots.

"Looks like we beat the sheriff's department." Lance pulled to the curb a half block away from Tina's house. No doubt he didn't want the Jeep to block access to the street for first responder vehicles. He and Morgan climbed out of the SUV.

Morgan's house was closer to the Knox residence than the Randolph County Sheriff's Station was, so being the first to arrive wasn't a surprise. But that left one major question wide open.

Is the shooter still in the house?

They jogged along the sidewalk. Morgan had a long stride, but she worked hard to keep up with Lance. They approached a quaint two-story home at the end of the street. A white vinyl fence enclosed the backyard. The Knox residence was on the periphery of the development and abutted the woods.

Lance drew his weapon. "If I asked you to wait in the Jeep until I cleared the house, would I be wasting my breath?"

"Yes."

They turned and ran up the driveway.

Morgan pulled her Glock and followed him to the front stoop. "You're not going in there without someone to watch your back."

The death of Morgan's first husband had left her in a very dark place, one she'd climbed out of less than a year ago. Her daughters had already lost their father. Now that she and the girls had been blessed with Lance in their lives, Morgan would not allow him to take an unnecessary risk.

Her pulse accelerated as adrenaline surged through her. The door was closed but unlocked. She positioned herself at Lance's left flank as they went into the house. It appeared as if every light in the house was on.

Lance glanced into the dining room on their right. An archway opened to the kitchen as well. "Clear."

They withdrew back into the hall and approached a set of French doors on the left side of the foyer. Lance opened one door. He swept his weapon from corner to corner. Morgan covered the hall at their backs.

"Clear," he said.

They continued down the corridor. Morgan's heart thumped against her ribs. Her lungs burned as she fought to quiet her breathing. They emerged in the kitchen. Broken glass and shattered plates littered the floor. They detoured around the shards. Lance led the way through the room to another doorway. They stepped into a short hallway.

Lance hesitated for a few seconds as they passed a half bath and laundry room. "Clear."

The next door was open.

Lance crossed the hall to stand behind the doorframe and peer around it. He lowered his gun. "Tina?"

Morgan followed him into a den. Paul lay in front of a square wooden table, his legs sprawled out. His shirt was soaked in blood. His hands clutched his abdomen, where he'd clearly sustained at least one devastating wound. A bullet hole pierced the center of his forehead.

Morgan pulled her gaze from the body. Tina knelt on the floor at her husband's side. Blood streaked her hands and smeared the side of her face, as if she'd forgotten her hands were wet and brushed her hair away from her cheek.

Tina turned stunned eyes to Morgan and Lance. "I can't find Evan."

"Stay with her while I check the rest of the house." Lance turned and disappeared.

"I tried to save him," Tina said in a detached voice.

One glance at Paul told Morgan he'd died quickly. Her gut twisted as she pictured Tina desperately attempting to resuscitate her dead husband.

Morgan angled her position until she could see down the hallway. She kept watch, gun raised, sweat trickling down her back, listening to the squeaks of floorboards overhead. As much as Lance would like to find Paul's killer, Morgan hoped the murderer was not in the house.

Chapter Three

Lance crept up the stairs. His heart galloped in his chest as he went into the master bedroom. Crouching, he swept the beam of his flashlight under the bed. Nothing. He opened the door to the walk-in closet. Tina's clothes hung in a neat row on one side, Paul's on the other. Shoes were lined up on shelves. The floor was clean. He checked the en suite bath and backtracked to the upstairs landing to poke his head into the hall bath. *Clear.* Then he moved into the home office and ended in what was clearly the bedroom of a teenage boy.

When he was certain the house was secure, he paused on the landing and listened. The faint sound of sirens approached. He didn't have much time. The police would be here in a few minutes, and Lance's opportunity to search would be over.

He went back into Evan's room. Dirty clothes spilled out of the hamper and were strewn across the floor. Empty cups and plates covered the dresser, and his sheets and blanket were pulled half off the bed to pool on the floor. An electric guitar stood in the corner, and posters covered the walls: Guns N' Roses, Rush, Jimi Hendrix. A *Game of Thrones* banner for House Stark hung above the bed.

Lance scanned the tops of the furniture. He searched the floor for the black Converse sneakers that Evan always wore but didn't see them. He used a pencil to open the top nightstand drawer. No wallet or phone in sight.

The sirens drew closer. Lance closed the drawer and hustled his butt down the stairs. Grey's Hollow was the territory of the Randolph County Sheriff's Department, and Sheriff Colgate would not be pleased to catch him snooping. He made his way to the back of the house. At the doorway to the den, he hesitated, his gaze locked on the back door—and the bloody handprint on the white paint just above the doorknob.

He returned to the den. When he and Morgan had entered the room, he'd been focused on the body and the potential for danger. On this second look, Lance absorbed the details. Paul had been shot at least twice. One bullet had hit him in the lower torso. That injury had bled heavily. A second bullet wound, to the center of his forehead, had not.

Tina knelt next to her husband, her face dazed.

Lance scanned the room. Besides the blood and the body, there were signs of a struggle in this room as well, though they were subtler than the broken glass and dishes in the kitchen. A remote control lay in the middle of the room, as if flung there. Next to it, a ceramic cup rested on its side. Its dark contents had spilled on the carpet. The brownish stain suggested coffee.

The low table was covered with newspaper. On it, a black case filled with gun-cleaning supplies lay open. The room smelled faintly of solvent and lubricating oil. But there was no gun in sight.

He heard the front door open. Someone yelled, "Police!" Footsteps sounded in the hall. The deputies were here.

Morgan slid her gun into its holster and lifted her hands away from her body. Lance did the same. It was understood that the deputies' duty was to neutralize all threats until they had secured the situation.

A sheriff's deputy rushed into the room, gun drawn. "Let me see your hands!"

Lance recognized Deputy Todd Harvey. When he'd been a cop with the SFPD, Lance had worked with Harvey a few times. In addition to his duties as deputy, Harvey volunteered with the local search and rescue.

The deputy's eyes lit with recognition. "Kruger, what are you doing here?"

"This is Mrs. Knox." Lance pointed. "She found her husband's body and called us. We're friends of the family."

Harvey stopped short at the sight of the body. "Oh, my God. It's Paul."

"You need to find my son," Tina begged, emotion edging into her voice as the shock began to fade. "He's missing."

"Yes, ma'am. First, I need to make sure you don't have any weapons on you," Harvey said. "Please extend your arms to the sides."

When she complied, he patted down her pockets. "How old is your son?"

"Sixteen," she answered in a strained voice.

Harvey stepped back and holstered his weapon. "I'll need a description and a recent photo."

"He's six feet, three inches tall and a hundred ninety pounds. I have a photo on my phone." Tina lifted her phone. Harvey gave her his number, and she texted the photo to him. "His name is Evan Meade."

"When was the last time you saw Evan?" Harvey checked his own phone, nodding when he received the text.

"Right before I left for work at two thirty this afternoon." Tina raised a hand as if to touch her forehead but then stopped and stared at the crusty blood on her fingers. "I'd like to wash my hands."

"I'm sorry, ma'am. I'm going to have to ask you to wait for just a few minutes," Deputy Harvey said with sympathy.

Footsteps sounded in the hall. A few minutes later, thumps overhead indicated more deputies were searching the upstairs. Morgan listened as men's voices called out as they cleared rooms, just as Lance had done.

A young deputy strode into the den. "The house is secure."

With a nod, Harvey escorted Morgan, Lance, and Tina into the formal living room, instructing the young deputy to stay with them. A soft-looking sofa and two overstuffed chairs faced an old-fashioned brick fireplace.

Deputy Harvey left the room and returned in a few minutes. He wrote the case and collection information on a white swab box. Then he put on a fresh pair of gloves and opened a prepackaged set of sterile swabs. He used swabs dampened with sterile water to sample the dried blood on Tina's right hand. After he put those swabs in the labeled swab box, he changed his gloves and repeated the procedure on Tina's left hand.

"I'm almost done." Harvey changed his gloves again. He opened a GSR kit and swabbed Tina's fingers and palms for gunshot residue. "I'll let you know when the forensics team has finished with the bathroom. Then you can wash up. I'm sorry it's taking so long."

In Lance's opinion, the GSR kit was a waste of time. Tina could have picked up gunshot residue if she had touched surfaces in the direct vicinity of where the firearm was discharged. GSR could be deposited onto any objects in close range. Morgan could invalidate the presence of residue on Tina's hands in two minutes in a courtroom. But from the deputy's perspective, prosecutors liked to dog-pile evidence on a suspect, and it was now or never to collect the samples. On the bright side, from the position of a defense attorney, a GSR residue test couldn't hurt. The presence of residue could be easily dismissed, but its absence would support innocence.

Outside, lightning flashed and thunder cracked, the boom much louder than earlier.

"The storm is closer." Lance paced the small room. "We need to look for Evan."

"The sheriff will be here any minute." Deputy Harvey cast a worried glance at the wide window that looked out onto the street. He turned and gave Lance a pointed look. "Please stay in this room. No wandering."

Lance nodded, and the deputy withdrew, closing the door on his way out and leaving the younger deputy to watch over them.

Tina Knox perched on the edge of a sofa cushion, her elbows resting on her thighs, her hands clenched together. Her head remained bowed over her joined knuckles, as if she were praying. Morgan sat next to her, but neither she nor Lance assured her that they'd find Evan or that everything would be all right. Empty promises were worthless.

Fifteen minutes after the first deputy had arrived, Sheriff Henry Colgate walked into the den. His white hair was mussed and seemed even thinner than it had been the last time Lance had seen him. At sixty, Colgate had stepped into the position when the previous sheriff had died. He was ready to retire, though, and had made it very clear that he would not be running for the position in November. He was a decent man, albeit a reluctant and inflexible sheriff.

Colgate turned to Lance. "Why are you here?"

Lance explained.

Colgate accepted the story with a slightly skeptical twist of his mouth. He turned to Tina. "Now tell me about tonight, Mrs. Knox."

"I was supposed to be off today, but there's a stomach virus going around. The urgent care has been swamped with vomiting kids. I was called in to work the evening shift. I don't like to turn down extra shifts, not with the new mortgage. When I came home, the house was dark. It shouldn't have been dark. Paul always leaves a light on for me." Her words stumbled over each other as she recalled finding Paul's body in the den. "I wasn't thinking. I'm a nurse. I knew Paul couldn't be saved. As soon as I stopped trying to bring him back, I ran upstairs to find Evan, but his bed was empty. He's supposed to be home by ten p.m. on school nights."

"Where was your son when you left for work?" the sheriff asked.

"He was in his room," Tina said. "Evan's friend Jake was picking him up at seven. They were going to the talent show at Scarlet Falls High School."

Sheriff Colgate took a small notepad and a pen from his chest pocket and made a few notes. "I'll need the name and number of Evan's friend." The sheriff poised his pen over the paper. "A list of his other friends and their phone numbers would also be helpful. We'll call them all and see if they've seen Evan tonight."

Tina reached in her pocket and pulled out her phone. "His best friend is Jake O'Reilly. He had a few other friends in Scarlet Falls, but he hasn't seen them much since we moved. I should have thought to call Jake." After giving the sheriff the information, she pressed the heels of both hands to her forehead.

"Yes, ma'am." The sheriff ripped the paper from his notepad and handed it to the deputy with the command, "Start with Jake."

"Yes, sir." The deputy left the room.

Tina chewed on her nails, and Morgan soothed her in a low voice. Unable to sit, Lance paced. He hated being on the sidelines. He wanted to be searching the house and looking for Evan. He kept one eye on the French doors, watching activity in the hallway through the glass panes.

The medical examiner arrived, along with the crime scene techs dressed in PPEs or personal protective equipment coveralls. Harvey appeared at the door and motioned to the sheriff through the glass. Colgate went into the hall, spoke with the deputy, and then returned to the living room.

Tina's spine snapped straight. "What have you found?"

"Please sit down, Mrs. Knox." The sheriff angled an overstuffed chair to face her and sat.

"What is it?" she asked, her eyes widening.

"Deputy Harvey just spoke with Jake O'Reilly. Jake said that he picked up Evan around seven o'clock last night and dropped him back home at approximately twelve thirty. He wasn't sure of the exact time."

"He was supposed to be home at ten." Tina clasped her hands together in her lap.

The sheriff hesitated. "The medical examiner estimates that Paul was killed between midnight and one a.m."

"So Evan was here when Paul was shot." Tina pressed a hand to the base of her throat. Her breaths came faster, until she began to wheeze.

"We don't know that for sure," the sheriff said. But it seemed likely.

"You're hyperventilating." Morgan wrapped an arm around Tina's shoulders. "Take a breath and hold it for a few seconds."

"I'll get a paper bag." The sheriff ducked out of the room.

A few minutes later, he returned and handed Tina a brown paper bag. She put it over her nose and mouth for a minute.

"I know this news is upsetting," the sheriff said. "We're doing everything possible to find your son. Alerts have been sent out to every law enforcement agency in the area."

Tina lowered the bag. Her breathing had returned to normal, though her face was still white as chalk. She clenched the paper bag in her lap.

Thunder boomed, and wind rattled the living room window.

Tina jumped. "Evan could be out there, and there's a storm coming."

"We're not wasting any time. We're going after him." The sheriff paused. "But first, I have a few more questions for you."

Tina's nod was stiff.

"Do you know what kind of guns Paul owns?" the sheriff asked.

"He has a rifle for deer hunting, a shotgun, and a Glock handgun," she said. "He kept his guns and ammunition locked in the safe in the master bedroom."

The sheriff leaned forward, resting his forearms on his knees. "His gun-cleaning kit was on the table in the den."

"He does—did—little chores like that if he couldn't sleep," Tina said.

The sheriff hesitated. "The safe is open. The long guns are in it. We haven't found the Glock."

Lance tried a scenario in his head. Paul was up late. He confronted an intruder. The intruder shot him first. Evan walked in on the shooting. Maybe Evan ran away. The boy was fit and fast. He would be a difficult target in the dark. But where was he? Why hadn't he come home or gotten help?

"What time did Paul usually go to bed?" the sheriff asked. "We're trying to piece the timeline together."

"He had insomnia," Tina said. "He often stayed up late or got up in the middle of the night."

Deputy Harvey opened the door. "Sheriff, I need to speak with you."

The sheriff went out into the hall, closed the door behind him, and conferred with Harvey again. When Colgate returned, his face was grim. "We've found a cell phone on the other side of the back fence. Does this look familiar?" He held up a plastic bag. Inside was a cell phone in a black case with a wolf on the back.

"Yes!" Tina perked up. "That's Evan's phone."

"Do you know your son's password?" the sheriff asked.

Tina's voice shook. "3-3-0-3."

The sheriff wrote the code down and shoved his notepad and pen back into his chest pocket.

"So maybe Evan got away?" Tina searched the sheriff's face, clearly looking for hope.

"It's too early to draw conclusions, ma'am, but we hope so," the sheriff said vaguely. "How well does he know the woods behind the house?"

Lance had worked with the sheriff enough to recognize his *holding back* tone.

"A few weeks ago, Paul took him camping out there." Tina pointed in the general direction of the back of the house. "They've gone fishing a few times too. Paul was teaching Evan to shoot."

"Can you tell me what kind of shoes and clothes he was likely wearing tonight?" the sheriff asked.

"He has a brand-new pair of black Converse sneakers," Tina said. "When I left for work, he was dressed in jeans and a black T-shirt with a direwolf's head on the front. It says WINTER IS COMING." She closed her eyes for a second. "Evan is a huge *Game of Thrones* fan. We binged six seasons when he had an emergency appendectomy over the winter." A tear rolled down her cheek. She wiped it away, the gesture almost angry.

The sheriff nodded. "You hang tight, Mrs. Knox. We're going to do everything possible to find Evan."

But on his way out of the room, the sheriff avoided eye contact with Morgan and Lance. Behind Colgate's carefully schooled expression, his eyes were worried.

The cops had found something they didn't want to share with Tina.

Chapter Four

Lance followed the sheriff into the hall. He closed the door behind him. "What aren't you telling her?"

Colgate grimaced. "This is an active investigation. You know I can't divulge the details."

"I'm going to find out." Lance crossed his arms over his chest. "I will not stop until I find Evan."

Colgate's jaw sawed back and forth. Some cops worked with PIs. Others refused. Colgate shared only if it suited his case.

The sheriff sighed. "We would like to keep some details from the media."

"Understood."

"We found blood on the back of Evan's phone. We also found a bloody handprint on the top of the fence in the backyard, just above where we found the phone. There are footprints in the dirt at the base of the fence as well."

"Where someone landed after climbing the fence."

"Yes." Colgate frowned. "The soil is soft back there from the recent rains. The impressions are very clear. The tread has Converse written across the sole." The sheriff brushed his hand through the wispy white hairs on his head. "We're trying to process the outside of the house first, before the rain starts. The tech was able to pull prints from the fence. But matching them will take time, as will getting a DNA analysis on the blood."

"And until the DNA test comes in," Lance said, "we won't know if Evan touched Paul and transferred his blood to the doorframe and fence, or if Evan is bleeding."

The boy could be injured. Maybe even shot like Paul.

He was well enough to run and scale a fence, Lance reminded himself. To the sheriff, he said, "We also don't know if the shooter went after Evan."

"That's right," the sheriff agreed. "We're going to work with the worst-case scenario—that Evan is hurt and whoever killed Paul is after him."

"We're running out of time if we want to follow his trail." Lance glanced out the window at the end of the hall. Outside, tree branches swayed violently in the wind. "That storm will wash away all the tracks."

"As much as I don't want to, I agree." The sheriff rubbed a hand down his face. "I called for a K-9 team from the state, but they can't get here for two hours."

"That's too long to wait," Lance insisted.

"Yes." The sheriff propped a hand on his belt.

"Sheriff?" a young deputy called from the entryway. "There's a man named Sharp here. He wants to talk to you."

"Have him wait outside," Colgate answered, then turned back to Lance. "Tell your boss that no one else gets into this scene."

Lance nodded. "Will do."

If Lance and Morgan hadn't arrived before the cops, they'd both be out on the sidewalk too.

"I'd like to go on the search." Lance held up a hand. "Before you say no, let me sum up why you should let me. First, Evan might run from your deputies. He's been arrested before. He does not have a positive association with the police in general. Evan and I have a relationship.

He trusts me. Second, Mother Nature is about to dump a ton of water on your outdoor crime scene areas. You need every available person combing the grass. Third, you can't send SAR volunteers into those woods if there's a possibility they will encounter an armed shooter."

The sheriff nodded. "All right."

The quick agreement was the last thing Lance expected.

"I want this boy brought home safe," the sheriff said. "I don't particularly care who finds him or how. His mother has already lost her husband. I do not want her to lose her son too. I'm fine with you going along, as long as you're ready when the team goes in and you follow orders."

"I've participated in plenty of searches." Lance didn't mention that he wasn't as skilled in following orders.

The sheriff lifted a hand. "Be ready in fifteen minutes, and don't get yourself shot or struck by lightning. The department can't afford to get sued. If you can't keep up, my men will not wait for you." The sheriff walked away.

Lance wasn't worried about keeping up. Coaching hockey—on skates—had strengthened his bad leg. He went back in the living room and relayed the situation to Morgan and Tina. "I have to run out to my Jeep for my gear."

"Thank you," Tina said. "I knew you'd help."

Morgan followed him to the door. She cast a worried look out the window, where lightning flashed. A boom of thunder shook the glass panes. "You'll be careful?"

"I will. You'll stay with Tina?" Lance and Morgan shared a pointed look. Tina would need more than emotional support. As Paul's spouse, she would automatically be a suspect in his death. Evan would also be on that initial list. Hopefully, early evidence would eliminate them both, but having Morgan there to protect Tina's interests eased Lance's mind.

"Of course." Morgan touched the center of his chest and said in a low voice, "I love you."

"Back atcha." Lance gave her a quick kiss, then hurried from the room. On the way out of the house, he passed a fingerprint tech crouched next to the front door, swirling black powder onto the door-knob with a small brush.

Lance went outside. The property had been transformed into a crime scene. A young deputy stood at the bottom of the driveway. He held a clipboard on which he would be recording the name of every person who entered and exited the crime scene. A tech was setting up floodlights. The portable generator that powered them hummed. Randolph County Sheriff's Department SUVs, the medical examiner's van, and a county crime scene unit clogged the suburban street. Crime scene tape had been strung around the perimeter of the property. News vans lined up farther down the road.

Sharp was standing on the sidewalk. In jeans and a T-shirt, he tapped the toe of one running shoe impatiently on the concrete. Lightning flashed across the sky, blinking like a strobe light. The boom of thunder that followed was close enough to rattle Lance's teeth.

"Follow me," Lance called to Sharp. Then he turned and jogged toward the place he'd parked his vehicle. He threaded his way through clusters of neighborhood gawkers, dodging an older couple huddling on the sidewalk in their bathrobes. When they had broken free of the crowd, Lance filled Sharp in on the case so far.

At the back of his Jeep, Lance opened the cargo hatch and grabbed a waterproof jacket and his Go Bag, a small backpack he kept filled with emergency supplies, including protein bars, water, a first aid kit, a Mylar emergency blanket, a flashlight, and spare batteries.

A spare magazine and extra ammunition.

He grabbed his Kevlar vest. After their last case, they'd invested in body armor.

Sharp frowned. "I'd like to go on the search with you, but I don't want to hold the team back."

The admission had clearly hurt him. On their last big case, Sharp had suffered a serious abdominal wound. Before he'd been hurt, Sharp had been one of the fittest people Lance knew. Thanks to a green, crunchy lifestyle, his fifty-three-year-old boss had been in better shape than most twentysomethings. Given the seriousness of his injuries, his three-month recovery had been astonishing, but he wasn't in marathon-running condition just yet, which irritated the hell out of him.

"Tonight's search is going to be ugly," Lance said. Lightning, thunder, and a blast of wind punctuated his statement.

"I know."

Lance slung his backpack over one shoulder and turned back toward the house. "You'll be running half marathons again by fall."

"But I'm not there yet." Sharp looked miserable, but he would never jeopardize the search. "I'll see if I can be useful to Morgan."

"Send her a text or call her. The sheriff doesn't want you on scene."

"I understand." Sharp nodded, obviously depressed. "Text me if there are any major updates."

"Will do."

They separated at the bottom of the driveway. Lance headed for the sheriff's vehicle, where the sheriff and two deputies gathered around an electronic tablet. Both deputies wore rain gear.

The sheriff motioned to Lance. "Kruger, you already know Todd Harvey." Colgate gestured toward the other deputy, a wiry man in his late thirties. "This is Jim Rogers. Rogers is a hell of a hunter and tracker."

"Glad to have you on board. I hear you know the boy." Rogers extended a hand.

Lance shook it. "I do."

The sheriff nodded at Harvey. "Todd's in charge."

Harvey pointed toward a satellite image of their general location displayed on the electronic tablet in his hand. Forest dominated the screen.

Lance glanced at the image. "What's on the other side of those woods?"

"A couple of roads. More woods." Harvey moved the image. "There's an abandoned campground to the south, at Deer Lake. To the north are farms, individual homes, and a residential development. It's three thirty. Evan could have as much as a three-hour lead on us. Is the boy familiar with the woods?" Harvey looked to Lance.

"He's been out there a couple of times, and he's damned fit. Unless he's badly injured, he's going to be able to move faster than the average person." Lance believed in conditioning drills on top of conditioning drills. Hockey was an exhausting sport. Fit players made a better team— and tired teenagers got into less trouble.

"We're coordinating with patrol vehicles from the state police and neighboring townships. Normally, I'd limit the search to a six-mile radius, but I'll expand to nine. It's easier to tighten the scope of the search than expand it later."

"Seems you all know what to do," Colgate said. "Keep me updated." The sheriff walked away.

Rogers tapped the screen and shifted the map image. "I'm worried about the Deer River. It's already high from the rains we had last week."

A fat drop of water landed on Lance's head. "Won't take much to reach flood stage."

More rain pattered on the pavement.

"We'd better get moving." Harvey stowed the electronic tablet in the car and grabbed his own Go Bag. He led the way around the side of the house. The neighbor's rear yard was not fenced, and they walked through it to reach the area behind the white vinyl fence that enclosed the Knoxes' backyard. A fifty-feet-wide swath of tall weeds and grass separated the fence from the forest. A floodlight had been set up at the base of the fence, where the two clearest footprints had been found. Under a tarp strung up to protect the area from the rain, two crime scene techs were casting the prints. Closer to the woods, two deputies searched the weedy ground with high-powered flashlights.

Lance scanned the ground, tracking a line of smashed grass and weeds that led from the fence to the woods. Along the same path, three yellow evidence flags poked above the grass.

"Those flags mark partial shoe treads." Harvey pointed. "All the tread marks look like they were made by Converse shoes, men's size 13, which Mrs. Knox confirmed is Evan's shoe size."

"No second set of footprints?" Lance asked, thinking of the shooter.

"No. There are no additional tracks to suggest someone followed the boy." Harvey walked toward the woods, parallel to Evan's tracks.

Rogers hefted his AR-15 and gestured for Lance to go next. Rogers brought up the rear. They trudged through the wet, knee-high weeds and entered the forest. Once they were under the canopy, overhead branches provided some cover from the drizzle, but they all knew they had to move fast. The light rain falling now would soon become a downpour.

Thick, dense summer foliage also blocked some of the wind. The air became muggy, oppressive. Beneath his body armor, sweat broke out between Lance's shoulder blades and dripped down his back. He continually scanned the surrounding forest, looking for signs that they weren't alone and ignoring the swarms of gnats buzzing around his face. He listened for sounds of movement under the patter of rain on leaves.

Rogers bent to study the soft earth, eyeing the distance between tread marks. "He's moving fast. Running through here at top speed. Not concerned with anything except putting distance between him and whatever he thinks is chasing him."

Evan had run in a straight line for the woods during the initial stage of his flight.

Lance let Rogers and Harvey study the ground while he continued to watch the woods. The trees were dense, and the darkness pressed in on the men from all sides. Lance moved a few feet away from Harvey and Rogers. Instead of using his flashlight, which would show him only a small section of forest at a time, he allowed his eyes to adjust to the dimness.

Lightning flashed, illuminating the forest. In the split second of brightness, Lance scanned their surroundings. The woods were green from recent heavy rains. The lushness would provide plenty of cover for a shooter who had already proven himself capable of committing an execution-style murder.

Just because they hadn't seen the killer's tracks didn't mean he hadn't been there. Or hadn't circled around in an attempt to intercept the teenager.

A person capable of executing an experienced cop might also be skilled enough not to leave a trail of footprints through the woods.

Rogers straightened, and they moved forward. It was impossible to move silently through the dense underbrush. Prickly plants snagged at Lance's pants legs, and twigs snapped underfoot. For the first half mile, they were able to follow Evan's flight by tracking freshly broken foliage and the occasional partial shoe tread in the earth.

They emerged from the underbrush onto a game trail.

Rogers crouched to study three shoe prints. "Looks like he took the trail from here. These prints are still far apart. And see the way he's digging in with the balls of his feet? He's still running at top speed."

Lance hoped that meant the teen wasn't injured too seriously, but he knew adrenaline could mask pain. Evan would be in panic mode. His bloodstream would be flooded with it.

Rogers stood, and they moved on. The trail was wide enough to open the canopy above their heads and expose them to the storm. The rain increased, now falling in a steady sheet. Wind whipped through the woods, blowing water droplets into Lance's face. Each gust held a fresh chill as the temperature dropped. Soon, the storm would wash away all traces of Evan's flight. On the game trail, there was no clear path of damaged underbrush, and his route was harder to track.

A road bisected the trail. Rogers surveyed the muddy shoulder and found a few broken twigs and one deep footprint in some thick mud on the opposite side of the road. "Looks like he stuck to the trail instead of taking the road."

They picked up their pace. The rain became a downpour, hitting the ground faster than the already saturated soil could absorb it. Water puddled under their feet, washing away any remaining footprints that might have been in the earth. There would be no more tracks to follow. Lance hoped that the teen had stuck to the trail. Since they were no longer looking for tracks, they were able to move faster. Lance broke into a jog, his boots splashing in the mud, the rain lashing his face.

Rogers and Harvey wore brimmed hats, which gave their eyes some protection from the torrential rain. Lance was bareheaded. He didn't raise the hood of his jacket. He didn't want the nylon to impede his hearing. Water invaded his collar, ran around his neck, and trickled down his back.

They kept moving. The wind howled, its force pushing against Lance's body. He leaned into it and pressed on. The rain shifted to hail, the hard beads stinging his face. He gave up trying to hear anything, raised his hood, and tightened the chin strap to keep the wind from blowing it off his head. The short brim provided his eyes some protection from the ice pellets peppering his face.

Where was Evan? Had he found shelter? Visions of the teenager, bleeding and shivering, the violent storm raging around him, flashed through Lance's mind. Worry fueled his steps, and he plowed forward.

As long as the trail was passable, he would not give up. Neither Rogers nor Harvey showed any signs of wanting to stop either.

Lightning flashed, the thunder booming while the sky was still flickering. The trees swayed, branches whipping and waving as the wind thrashed around them, but they kept going, moving as quickly as the slippery ground and poor visibility would allow. A bolt of lightning streaked across the sky. The thunder was deafening and felt like it was right over Lance's head. The next gust of wind nearly took him off his feet.

Crack!

The sound of wood splitting echoed over the noise of hail and wind. Lance caught movement in his peripheral vision—a tree, crashing toward them.

"Look out!" He reached out, grabbed Rogers's and Harvey's arms, and hauled them backward.

The three men fell onto their asses in the mud. A huge oak tree crashed to the earth a few feet in front of them. The ground shook with the impact.

Lance climbed to his feet and shone his flashlight on the felled tree. On either side of him, Rogers and Harvey stood. The mature oak lay over the trail. Its trunk was too wide for Lance's arms to reach around it.

Heart hammering, Lance climbed over the downed tree. He checked his watch. They'd been on Evan's trail for nearly two hours, but Lance estimated they'd covered barely a few miles. Evan had a significant lead on them, but maybe they could catch him if the boy had taken shelter from the storm.

Gradually, the wind and downpour eased, allowing the men to pick up the pace. The storm broke with the dawn. The rain tapered off, and the sky brightened. Lance and the two cops emerged from the forest at the abandoned campground at Deer Lake. A run-down, rickety dock extended out over the water. Broken branches, leaves, and other storm debris littered the ground and the sandy beach that edged the lake.

"Maybe he holed up in one of the buildings." Harvey shook the water from his jacket and unzipped it.

Lance did the same. "We'll have to search each building."

Which would take time.

Rogers walked in circles, scanning the ground. "Any tracks the boy might have left are long gone."

Lance surveyed the old campground. A campfire ring ten feet in diameter occupied the center of a large open space. A dented canoe lay in the middle of the ring, as if dropped there by the storm. Cabins surrounded the clearing. A few squat cinder block buildings were nestled in the trees. He spotted restrooms, shower facilities, and a main office. Closer to the water was a boathouse with a hole in its shingled roof.

"Let's start clearing buildings," Harvey said to Rogers, then pointed at Lance. "Stay behind us."

Weapons drawn, the deputies moved toward the cabins, entering doorways and securing cabins as a well-drilled team. Lance drew his gun and watched their backs. Most of the wooden doors were broken or hanging on their hinges. The cabin interiors were in ruins. Beneath collapsed roofs, dead leaves and animal feces were piled in corners. They moved from the cabins to the bath facilities. More substantially constructed of cinder block and metal roofs, they stood intact, but all were empty. Hypodermic needles, empty cans, and other trash littered the concrete floors.

As they emerged from the final restroom, they approached the boathouse near the lakeshore. The door stood open, revealing a dented aluminum canoe and a fiberglass kayak with a hole in its hull.

"Looks like blood." Harvey pointed to a few dark spots on the floor. "I'll have the sheriff bring the K-9 team to the campground." Harvey lifted his handheld radio. "Maybe the dog will be able to pick up the boy's trail from here." He turned and walked away.

The clouds broke apart, exposing the sunrise. Light poured over the treetops and onto the lake, its reflection flowing across the surface like spilled blood. Lance walked out onto the beach.

Where are you?

The lake was long and narrow. He could see the opposite shore a hundred yards away, but to the south, the lake doglegged to the right and disappeared behind thick forest. Beyond the bend, the lake fed the

Deer River. Looking for a better view, he crossed the sand and walked onto the old dock. The weathered boards creaked under his weight.

He scanned the shoreline. *Could Evan have found a boat in good enough condition to paddle away?*

He walked to the end of the dock and stared out over the water. The southern end of the lake remained out of view, and no boats marred what he *could* see of the lake's perfect surface.

Lance's mind's eye returned to another lake, another missing teen— and the body he and Morgan had found lying in the reeds the previous autumn. He could see her clearly, but his imagination replaced her face with Evan's.

He pivoted to return to the beach. Something scraped under his boot. He looked down. A silver key chain lay on the dock at his feet. Lance used the sleeve of his jacket to pick it up. He dangled it in front of his face. A silver wolf's head shone with the reflection of the bloody sunrise.

Chapter Five

In the Knoxes' living room, Morgan balanced a notepad on her knee. Next to her, Tina perched on the couch, her posture rigid, her phone open in her hand.

Morgan jotted down Evan's email accounts and passwords. There were only two—one issued by the school, the other personal. "He doesn't have any other accounts?"

"Not that I know of." Tina turned grief-stricken eyes on her. "Do you think they'll find him?"

"They're doing everything possible," Morgan reassured her. "Are you working on the family timeline?" She had asked Tina to list everything she could remember happening during the previous week.

"Yes." Tina kept a family calendar on her phone. The sheriff had already taken a copy of the last week's agenda. But now Tina was interpreting abbreviations, adding notes, and listing phone numbers. She'd also given the sheriff access to Evan's cell phone records.

"When you're finished, we'll work on a list of Evan's social media account information," Morgan said.

"OK." Tina coped better when she was kept busy.

Morgan closed her eyes and rested her head against the back of the sofa, willing Lance to call with an update. Her gaze strayed to the window, bright with dawn. The storm had raged for nearly three hours. She prayed that he was all right, and that he'd found Evan.

Alive.

Morgan crept through the darkness, the reeds surrounding the lake waving in the night. Her feet splashed in the shallow water at the shore's edge. The reeds parted, and a flashlight beam fell on the body of a dead teenage girl. Horror filled Morgan. Her stomach rolled into a tight ball.

Morgan's body jerked. She glanced around, disoriented. She must have dozed off, only to have a nightmare about her first case as a defense attorney. They hadn't found the victim in time. Sickening dread gathered behind her sternum.

The sheriff walked in. "Mrs. Knox?"

Tina's eyes filled with fear.

The sheriff held up a hand. "I'm sorry. We didn't find him, but I need you to look at a picture." He pulled a chair to face her, sat down, and showed her his phone screen. "Do you recognize this?"

"Yes." She nodded. "That's Evan's house key."

"Kruger found it at the Deer Lake Campground." The sheriff pocketed his phone. "We're sending a K-9 unit to see if the dog can pick up Evan's trail there."

Tina exhaled. She blinked rapidly, as if light-headed. "But he was alive when he reached the campground. Why isn't he coming home? Could the person who shot Paul—" She stifled a sob behind her fist, then took a deep, shaky breath and pulled herself together. "Could whoever shot my husband be holding Evan captive?"

The sheriff hesitated. A full thirty seconds ticked by before he finally said, "We don't have enough information at this point to answer those questions."

He knew more than he was saying.

"Have you determined how the intruder gained entry into the house?" Morgan asked.

"No, but the crime scene unit isn't finished with the house yet." The sheriff turned back to Tina. "We have the list of Evan's friends that you gave us earlier. I'll send a deputy around to talk to them."

Tina frowned. "I thought you already called his friends."

"We did." The sheriff stood. "But maybe seeing a deputy in uniform on their doorstep or being brought down to the station might encourage them to cooperate more fully with us."

Morgan thought the opposite was more likely. Kids with previous legal problems did not rat out their friends to the cops.

"Do you have any reason to believe these kids are not being forthright?" she asked.

"Nothing specific." Sheriff Colgate shrugged. "But you know how these kids are."

Morgan didn't. "What do you mean by *these kids*?"

The sheriff met her gaze. His face hardened. "None of these kids are honor students," he said, as if that one statement was explanation enough.

Morgan didn't let it go. Did the sheriff know that Evan wasn't an honor student either? And more importantly, did that make him less important? "I don't understand."

The sheriff's jaw tightened. "Kids with prior arrests are less likely to be honest with us."

Morgan didn't respond, but her mind was busy. Evan had prior arrests. Was the sheriff making similar assumptions about him?

Sheriff Colgate scratched his head. "Do you have Evan's email account information?"

"Yes." Morgan handed the sheriff the paper, glad that she'd made a copy for herself. The stubborn set to the sheriff's shoulders gave her an uneasy feeling that she and Lance could be shut out of his investigation. Paul had been a deputy. His retirement was recent, and the sheriff's department still considered him one of their own. All of these factors might make the sheriff want to keep the case details to himself.

"What are you doing to find my son?" Tina's voice had toughened. She was no longer begging, and her tone was more defensive. Clearly, she had also noticed the sheriff's change of attitude.

"Law enforcement has been notified statewide." The sheriff looked up from the list he was scanning. "Officers are trolling the teenage hangout spots in Randolph County. The Scarlet Falls PD is looking for him there in case he went back to visit his old friends. I've put out a press release with his photo. We're reviewing his phone history, and we'll go through his social media accounts to see if he had any new or strange contacts." Colgate paused, his mouth flattening into a grim line. "We won't stop looking for him, Mrs. Knox."

Tina studied the sheriff with an intense expression. "What about an AMBER Alert?"

"We can't issue an AMBER Alert unless we confirm that Evan was abducted," he explained.

"Have you talked to the neighbors?" Morgan asked. "Surely someone heard the gunshots."

"We have. The neighbor over there"—the sheriff gestured toward one side of the house—"is away on vacation. The neighbor on the other side is deaf and was in bed without her hearing aids. No one else heard anything except thunder, which could have masked the sound of the gunshots."

"Paul was a deputy for a long time," Morgan said. "He must have put away some nasty criminals. Have any violent offenders been let out of prison recently?"

"We're looking at Paul's old cases." The sheriff nodded. "Mrs. Knox, did Paul say anything recently about being threatened? Was he getting unexplained calls or texts? Was he acting strangely, or did he seem particularly worried about anything?"

"Paul is—was serious about home security. He changed all the locks when we bought the house, and he was going to install a security system. We didn't have the money for a professional company. Paul was going to do it himself. He was worried about my ex-husband. Kirk was in prison for assault for the last couple of years. He was released on parole a few months ago."

"Has your ex-husband ever threatened you or Paul?" Colgate asked.

"No, but he hated Paul." Tina's fingers worried the seam of the sofa cushion. "Paul was the deputy who arrested Kirk for assault. It's how we met. Although we didn't actually get together until months later when Paul came into the urgent care. Kirk blames Paul for the divorce. Kirk had zero interest in Evan when we lived together, but the minute Kirk was paroled, he sued for visitation. He just wants to get even with me. Can you believe he even tried to get alimony? Thank goodness the judge turned around and asked me if I wanted to countersue for child support."

Did Tina's bitter ex kill Paul?

Tina paused for a breath. "Kirk lives in a group home. Visits with Evan are supposed to be in a public place. We agreed that they would have dinner every Sunday night, but I still can't believe the judge granted him visitation, even community supervised. Anyway, two months ago was Evan's first scheduled meeting with Kirk. Evan isn't happy about it, but he goes."

A sixteen-year-old did not have the authority to refuse a court order, and the custodial parent was obligated to foster a relationship between the child and the noncustodial parent. A strained relationship was not enough justification to refuse visitation. Generally, the court's opinion was that the relationship could not improve if the child and parent did not see each other, and that it was in the best interest of the child to know both his parents. Since the visitation was community supervised, in a public place, Tina could not argue that Evan was in any physical danger. In short, she had no grounds to petition the court. Judges did not like to terminate parental rights.

"But to your knowledge, your ex-husband never communicated directly with Paul," the sheriff clarified.

Tina shook her head. "Not that I know of. Kirk called me or texted Evan if he needed to cancel."

"Do you think Evan might go to his father for help?" the sheriff asked.

"I doubt it," Tina said.

"We'll pay him a visit anyway. Can I have your ex's full name and contact information?" The sheriff clicked his pen over a tiny notepad.

"Kirk Meade." Tina also provided a phone number and the address of the group home.

"Thank you, Mrs. Knox." The sheriff stuffed his notepad into his pocket, rose, and walked out the door.

Morgan followed him into the hall. "Are you looking at Paul's phone records too?"

"We're looking at everything." Sheriff Colgate pointed at Morgan. "I know Kruger wants to find the boy, but you will stay away from the murder investigation. Paul was one of ours. We do not need you and your partners muddying up this case."

Morgan met his gaze without yielding. The sheriff blinked away. He had been the one who'd *muddied* the last case they'd simultaneously worked, and he knew it. He'd followed the physical evidence to a suspect and had been unwilling to accept any other theories.

"Mrs. Knox will need a place to stay." Morgan did not want Tina alone in the house where her husband had been murdered. Also, since the sheriff personally knew the victim, he would be in no rush to release the scene.

"It would probably be best if she stayed with family or friends," the sheriff agreed.

"She'll need to pack some things," Morgan said.

"Make a list of what she needs," the sheriff said. "I'll have a deputy pack a bag for her. Also, before she leaves, I need her to walk through the house and see if any valuables are missing."

Robbery gone wrong would be the simplest explanation for the murder. Without waiting for a response, Colgate walked away.

Morgan returned to the living room and relayed the information to Tina.

"I'm not leaving my house." Tina's chin lifted, and her jaw tightened.

"You don't have a choice," Morgan said. "Your house is a crime scene. It might not be released for a few days."

The forensic unit would need to sift through the evidence they'd recovered from the scene and decide if any experts needed to be called in. At the very least, Morgan would assume they'd request a blood spatter analysis. A rural county did not have every expert on staff the way a large city might. Colgate would have to utilize state police resources or cooperate with neighboring counties. All of these requests took time, though all agencies would prioritize a case involving a missing child and the murder of a former deputy.

"A few days?" Tina's voice rose. "But how will Evan find me? He doesn't have his phone. He won't know where I am."

Morgan's heart bled for her. The mere thought of one of her daughters going missing made her physically ill. She touched Tina's forearm. "I doubt very much that Evan would come back here, not after what happened."

"Maybe you're right." Tina covered her mouth with her hand, stifling a sob. She fought for control for a few seconds, then lowered her hand to her lap. "Then what can I do?"

"Try to think of anywhere Evan might go to hide. Does he have any favorite places? Where does he hang out with his friends?"

Tina clenched her hands together. "There are only a few places. Most of them are in Scarlet Falls. He hasn't made any new friends since we moved to Grey's Hollow."

"I'm sure Evan knows your cell phone number, and we'll reach out to his friends and make sure they have it as well in case Evan contacts any of them." Morgan didn't know a single teenager who trusted adults over friends.

"You're probably right." Tina frowned. "Evan did miss his friends when we moved here, but frankly, those old *friends* were part of the reason I wanted to leave the apartment in Scarlet Falls. I thought he could start fresh in a school where the principal didn't automatically suspect him for every act of vandalism and every new spot of graffiti that showed up on school grounds. I wanted him to make new friends, ones without juvenile records. I have worked my ass off to give him a better life than I had, but I can't make him want it." Bitterness pursed her lips. "But right now, I would give up this house and everything in it just to have him back." She lifted her gaze. Her eyes were filled with grief and desperation. "All I want is to get my son back safe." Fresh tears welled, and her hand clenched into a frustrated fist. "How far could he have gotten in last night's storm?"

Morgan thought of the team's last hockey game. They'd come from behind to win in the last period. The kids on Lance's team were not accustomed to winning anything. They didn't fall apart when the going got tough because for them, life was always tough. They were the underdogs every single day.

Evan was determined, focused, and resourceful. He wouldn't be easy to find if he wanted to stay hidden.

That was, if he was still alive.

Chapter Six

It was late afternoon before Lance parked in front of Sharp Investigations. The PI firm's office occupied the bottom half of a duplex in the business district of Scarlet Falls.

He locked his Jeep and headed for the door. His clothes were still damp from the night's soaking, and he was bone-weary from the weather, the disappointment, and worry. The kid was out in the woods, alone, bleeding, and terrified.

Removing his mud-crusted boots, he carried them inside. The air-conditioning washed over him, the dry chill a relief after a wet and muggy night.

"Lance?" Sharp called from his office.

Lance poked his head in the doorway.

Sharp frowned. "You look like hell. Go get cleaned up."

As much as Lance wanted to discuss the case, he also wanted dry clothes. "Give me five minutes."

"Have you eaten?" Sharp asked.

"I had a protein bar."

Sharp huffed, stood, and left his office. A few seconds later, he was banging around in the kitchen at the back of the building. When Sharp had converted the bottom apartment of his duplex into office space for his private investigation firm, he'd left the full kitchen and bath intact. The facilities were useful when they worked long hours.

Lance walked past his office to Morgan's doorway. With her own criminal defense practice, she often required the services of an investigator, so her renting the extra office from Sharp was convenient for all of them. Plus, Lance got to spend more time with her, even when they weren't working a case together.

He stuck his head through the doorway. "I'm back."

Her desk was clear except for her laptop and notepad. She sat behind it, equally tidy in a silky white blouse, her dark hair twisted into a smooth knot at the back of her head. She must have stopped at home to shower and change.

Lance went into his office and rooted in the closet for fresh clothes. Morgan followed him in.

She moved toward him, reaching to embrace him.

He held up a hand, then gestured to his dirt-streaked pants. "I'm filthy."

"I don't care." She wrapped her arms around his waist.

Lance lifted his boots so they wouldn't touch her.

"I should shower." But instead, he rested his face against her temple. In flat shoes, she was a few inches shorter than he was. Unlike him, she smelled amazing.

"Just give me a second, all right?" She pressed her face into his shoulder. "I'm glad you're OK."

"I'm sorry. I should have checked in more frequently."

"It's all right. You needed to focus." But her eyes were relieved.

"Don't be so forgiving. I might need a little prompting here and there. I tend to get tunnel vision on a case." He kissed her temple. As usual, the contact with her centered him, and he realized for the billionth time just how much he needed her.

"Any more news on Evan?" she asked.

"No."

As if she knew he needed to clear his head, she didn't press him for details. She splayed her hand on his chest. "You look beaten up."

"I just need a shower." He kissed her on the mouth, then went into the bathroom.

Morgan followed him, closing the door behind her. Lance turned on the spray and stripped off his clothes. They'd been together for just nine months, but he could no longer imagine his life without her.

"Have you thought about a date for our wedding?" Lance tested the water temperature with his hand.

"Not really. We've been so busy planning the renovations." She traced her finger on his back. "You have a big scrape here."

"We're always busy with something." Lance stepped into the shower and closed the curtain. "You should call your sisters and brother and see when everyone would be available."

"I should." She went quiet, just like all the other times over the past few months that he'd tried to pin her down about setting a date.

He tried a different approach. "If you want to get married in a church, we'll have to find one and see about availability."

"I know."

He looked around the curtain. She was folding his dirty clothes, her movements slow and deliberate, almost melancholy.

He didn't doubt that she loved him, but was she changing her mind about getting remarried? Maybe she didn't want the girls to think she was replacing their father. He knew he had to force her into a serious conversation, but he was also afraid of what she might say. He was more terrified of losing *her* than he'd been about the possibility of facing an armed shooter in the woods. So he dropped the curtain and the subject. He turned to let the hot water rush down his back. The scrape she'd pointed out burned.

"Where is Tina?" he asked.

"The sheriff took her to a hotel. He says it'll be a day or so before the crime scene is released, although I can't imagine her ever living there again. I volunteered to stay with her or call a friend or family member, but she said she wanted to be alone."

"Tina is quiet. Evan was on my team for months before she ever spoke to me." Lance ducked his head under the spray. "But I don't like that she's on her own. Whoever killed Paul is still out there. Does the sheriff know how the shooter got into the house?"

"They found no sign of a break-in."

Lance looked around the curtain again. "Then how do they think he gained entry?"

"Finish your shower. We may as well review everything with Sharp." She picked up his boots and carried them out of the bathroom.

Something in her tone made him hurry. Five minutes later, he was dressed and walking into the kitchen. He felt almost human in clean clothes and dry socks.

"Sit." Sharp pointed a wooden spoon at a kitchen chair. He stirred something on the stove.

Lance dropped into a seat.

Morgan walked into the kitchen carrying a cup of coffee. "I cleaned your boots and put them on the back porch to dry."

"You didn't need to do that," Lance said.

"I know." She smiled.

"Thank you."

"You're welcome." She dropped into the chair opposite him. "Tell us what happened on the search."

Sharp set a gross-looking green protein shake in front of him. Lance drank it without asking what was in it. He had no doubt it contained all kinds of antioxidants. Sharp's lifestyle was the reason he looked as fit as he did twelve weeks after major surgery. Sharp frowned at Morgan's coffee, but after working together for nearly nine months, he'd mostly given up badgering her about her caffeine and sugar consumption.

"We followed Evan's tracks on a game trail that led to Deer Lake Campground," Lance began.

"Didn't they close that place a few years ago?" Sharp turned off the burner on the stove. He scooped the contents of his cast-iron frying pan onto a plate.

"Yes. It's in pretty rough shape." Lance's mouth watered. Protein bars could sustain him, but his body wanted real food. "After I called you, the K-9 unit was able to track Evan to the boathouse and the public bathroom. The deputies found blood in both buildings."

"How much blood?" Sharp set the plate in front of Lance. Scrambled eggs and home fries with onions were piled high. Everything would be organic, of course, and the eggs free-range as well.

Lance dug in. "Enough to indicate a serious injury."

Morgan's brow furrowed. She gripped her coffee cup in both hands.

Lance sniffed. "That coffee smells amazing."

"I'll make green tea." Sharp shot her mug a disapproving look. He lit the burner under the teakettle, then turned to face them, crossing his arms over his chest and leaning back on the counter. "Did you see any sign that someone was following him besides you?"

Chewing, Lance shook his head.

"So where is the person who killed Paul?" Morgan sipped her coffee.

"I don't know." Lance plowed through the eggs and moved on to the potatoes. "But Evan was running all out, as if he thought he was being pursued."

"He must have been terrified." Morgan's eyes misted.

Lance reached across the table and squeezed her hand. For a woman who'd once been a successful prosecutor, she was a softie. She'd rescued two stray dogs and cared for her elderly grandfather. The young woman who worked as her nanny suffered from kidney disease. Gianna might help out with childcare, but it was clear that Morgan was the one looking out for her. Lance had no doubt that Morgan would work on Evan's case without any discussion of compensation.

Nodding with approval, Sharp collected his empty dishes. "Since you're back, I assume the dog lost the trail."

"Yes." Lance sat back. "He picked up the scent in the buildings, but outside was a no go. We suspect Evan took a boat from the campground. The handler walked the dog along the shoreline, but he didn't hit on anything."

"All that heavy rain and wind messed with the scent trail." Sharp frowned.

"What is the sheriff's game plan?" Lance asked.

Morgan outlined the usual procedure the police typically followed when looking for a missing teen. "He didn't say much else."

Lance stiffened. "Why? Aren't we all on the same side here?"

"The sheriff is holding this case close." Anger flattened Morgan's lips.

"I'm not surprised." Lance's food churned in his gut. "What about all the scumbags Paul put away?"

"Colgate says they're looking at Paul's old cases," Morgan said.

"The bullet between the eyes feels revenge motivated to me." Sharp dropped a metal tea ball into a pot and filled it with hot water. He turned to Lance. "Do you need a combat nap?"

"No. We need a murder board." Lance couldn't be still, not with Evan still missing. The short break, shower, and food had revived him. He stood and headed for Morgan's office, which they used as a war room in major cases.

A long whiteboard spanned the far wall. He hadn't noticed when he'd stuck his head in earlier, but someone had already begun organizing the little data they possessed. Photos of Evan, Paul, Tina, and her ex, Kirk, hung on the board, affixed with magnets. As the victim, Paul held the center position.

Morgan walked in and brewed herself another cup of coffee. She sat at her desk. Opening a drawer, she pulled out a white bakery bag and offered it to Lance. It was full of chocolate donut holes.

"No, thanks," Lance said. A sugar rush would lead to a crash, and he was already strung out.

Morgan ate one in two bites and wiped her fingers on a napkin. "As you can see, Sharp and I started laying out Paul's case. While our primary objective is to find Evan, his disappearance is likely intertwined with Paul's murder."

On the right side of the board, Sharp's blocky print spelled out POSSIBLE MOTIVES. Underneath, he'd listed ROBBERY and REVENGE. Next to ROBBERY, Lance picked up a marker and wrote, MISSING ITEMS?

Sharp came through the doorway carrying two mugs. He handed one to Lance. "Tina couldn't find anything of value that was missing from the house."

"That doesn't mean robbery wasn't the motive." Lance studied the board. "The killer could have been interrupted by Paul, and then by Evan, before he was able to search the house for valuables. Maybe he decided to cut his losses and run. Most thieves are junkies looking for quick cash to buy a fix. They're not typically criminal masterminds."

"But they usually leave traces of a break-in," Sharp pointed out.

"True." Lance added a TIMELINE column on the board. "Paul was killed between midnight and one a.m. Evan came home around twelve thirty. How much did he see?"

"Enough to get hurt," Sharp said. "Enough to make him run like the devil was chasing him. Maybe enough to identify the killer and become the next target."

Lance set the marker down. "Paul's gun-cleaning supplies were on the table. Maybe he couldn't sleep and was keeping busy."

"Evan was two and a half hours past his curfew." Morgan leaned on her elbows and frowned at the board. "If one of my girls were that late, you can bet I would have been awake. I'd have called and texted their cell phone. And if they didn't answer promptly, I'd ping the phone and drive to wherever they were."

"You'd hunt them down," Lance said.

"You bet I would." Morgan didn't blink.

"But Paul isn't Evan's father." Sharp perched on the edge of Morgan's desk. "The whole father-stepson relationship was still new. Paul was feeling his way through it, trying to establish a connection through male-bonding activities."

"So he wouldn't necessarily want to humiliate the boy." As a prospective stepparent, Lance followed his logic. Morgan's girls were younger, but Lance was still sensitive to the fact that he wasn't their father. Their recent illnesses had hammered that home. Mia's and Ava's viruses had overlapped, and both of them had wanted to be with Morgan all night. As much as Lance had wanted to help out, he'd ended up giving the girls his side of the bed and sleeping on the couch. He'd changed sheets, washed soiled pajamas, and scrubbed carpets, but he'd felt useless in comforting them in their misery. The girls were well behaved, but in the future, he imagined that disciplining them would also be tricky.

The reality of being a stepparent was much more complicated than the idea of taking on three young children. Before he'd moved in with Morgan, he had no idea how hard the job would be. He loved the girls. He thought they loved him back. His bachelor optimism had told him that was enough. It wasn't. Parenting was hard work, and he felt unprepared, as if he were jumping into a hockey game already in progress with no stick or skates.

"Maybe he thought his best course of action was to wait up for Evan and talk with him." Morgan bit into another donut hole.

"That sounds like Paul," Lance agreed.

"Maybe Paul left the front door open for Evan," Sharp suggested.

"No." Morgan shook her head. "Tina said Paul was particular about keeping the doors locked. Evan had a key."

"Then we need to know who else might have a key to the house," Sharp said.

Lance wrote the question on the board. "We need background checks on Paul, Tina, and Evan."

"Don't forget Evan's father, Kirk Meade," Sharp added.

"Let's get some information on Evan's friends also." Morgan wrote a note on her legal pad. "Deputies were supposed to pressure Evan's friends for information today."

"That won't work," Lance scoffed.

"Colgate is an honest cop," Sharp said. "But he's old school enough to think intimidating teenagers is the best course of action."

"*We* might have better luck with the kids," Morgan said. "We're not cops, and we're on Evan's side."

"True," Lance said.

"I'll go to The Pub tonight," Sharp offered. "And see if any of *the boys* know anything."

The boys were not teenagers. They were Sharp's old cop buddies. Most were retired. All were older than Sharp. "Maybe one of them remembers the particularly nasty scumbags that Paul arrested. He was a deputy for a long time. He must have been threatened at some point." Criminals were always vowing to get even with the cops who put them away. Most were all mouth and no action, but a few held grudges.

"I'll get my mom started on the background checks," Lance said. "I need to call her today anyway."

His mother was agoraphobic and suffered from crippling anxiety and depression. She was also a computer whiz and often took over the digital searches for Sharp Investigations, particularly on the larger cases when their two-man firm needed assistance.

Lance rarely went more than a day without stopping in to see her, but he hadn't been by her place for a few days. She was physically frail, and he hadn't wanted to risk infecting her with the girls' virus.

Morgan motioned to a stack of papers on her blotter. "Tina gave us access to her cell phone account. I printed out the family's cell phone activity for the last month. I'll review those, then call hospitals and urgent care centers in the area," Morgan volunteered. "Maybe Evan tried to get medical help."

But Lance didn't think so. Evan was on the run. He wouldn't trust any adult.

Sharp pointed to the phone records. "Let me review the cell phone accounts, get Jenny started on the background checks, and call the ERs and urgent care centers. You two should be talking to Evan's friends. They will be able to predict where Evan would go to hide better than anyone else."

"I haven't visited my mother since Mia and Ava were sick." Lance worried about her. He'd spoken with her every day, but a video chat or phone call wasn't the same as seeing her in person. When he'd been in college, he'd neglected to keep close tabs on her, and she'd suffered a major breakdown.

"I'll call her now and give her the list of names, then stop in to see her later tonight." Sharp nodded. "She works fast. She'll probably have some information for us by then."

Lance set the marker on the metal lip of the whiteboard. "Then Morgan and I will talk to Evan's best friend, Jake O'Reilly."

Sharp caught Lance's eye. "You're sure that Evan couldn't have shot Paul?"

"Absolutely." Lance knew it in his heart. "The only person Evan might hurt is himself."

And that worried Lance the most. Evan wasn't the most emotionally stable kid. If he had witnessed Paul's murder, the trauma might be more than he could handle.

Chapter Seven

Morgan read the name on the mailbox and compared it to her notes. "One twenty-seven. This is the address Tina gave us for Jake O'Reilly, but the name on the mailbox says DUNCAN."

"We'll ask." Lance turned into a long driveway. Jake O'Reilly lived on a small farm on the outskirts of Scarlet Falls. Eyeing the muddy barnyard through the Jeep's windshield, Morgan reached behind her seat, grabbed the boots she'd been keeping there because of the heavy rains, and changed out of her nice flats.

Lance's phone beeped, and he answered the call. "You're on speaker, Sharp."

"I'm reviewing Evan's cell records," Sharp said. "He has seven calls over the past two weeks from a mobile number registered to a T. Nelson. No texts. Just calls, while most of his other cell activity is texting."

"Is this the first time that number appears on his phone records?" Morgan asked.

"In the past two months, yes," Sharp answered. "I still have a few hundred texts to read, but I thought you could ask Evan's friends if they know T. Nelson."

"Thanks, Sharp." Lance ended the call and opened his car door.

Morgan stepped out of the Jeep and scanned the property. Dark clouds gathered on the horizon, threatening rain. A two-story white farmhouse faced the road. Behind it, a red barn sat amid a scattering of other outbuildings. The cleared acreage around the buildings was divided into pastures. The smell of manure and freshly mowed grass lay thick in the humid air, and Morgan sneezed.

Hoofbeats approached, and Morgan pivoted to watch three slender horses gallop to the fence near the Jeep. They slid to a stop, prancing and snorting, mud splashing under their hooves.

"Can I help you?" A man led a slim black horse out of the barn. Lance was big, but this man would tower over him.

A rabbit darted out of a bush. The horse jumped, landing with wide eyes and splayed legs.

"Settle down." The man tugged on the lead rope.

"We'd like to talk to Jake," Lance called out.

The horse whinnied.

"Give me a minute. I'll be right with you." He led the gleaming animal to the pasture. Inside the gate, he unclipped the rope attached to the halter and stepped back. The four horses greeted each other, curling their necks and touching noses. Then they spun and galloped away. Mud flew from their hooves.

The man latched the gate and crossed the barnyard toward them. His jeans and work boots were streaked with mud. Hay stuck to his sweat-stained USMC T-shirt. Morgan read the SEMPER FI tattoo on his forearm.

"I'd shake your hand, but I'm filthy." He raised his hands. "We seriously need this rain to let up for a few days. We're drowning in mud."

Lance handed him a business card. "Are you Mr. O'Reilly?"

"Hell no. My name is Steve Duncan." He read the card and frowned. "You're a private investigator? Is Jake in any kind of trouble?"

"No. We just want to ask him a few questions." Morgan looked around for other vehicles or people. An old Honda was parked near the house. "Are either of Jake's parents here?"

Duncan snorted. "No. Why do you ask?"

"We're looking for Evan Meade," Lance said. "He's missing. I'm not just an investigator. I'm Evan's hockey coach. We're worried about him."

"I wish I could help." Duncan shook his head. "But I don't know an Evan Meade."

"Evan is Jake's friend," Lance explained. "We'd like to ask Jake a few questions. Maybe he has an idea of where we could look for Evan."

"I don't know any of Jake's friends." Duncan pulled a cell phone from his pocket and sent a text with surprising speed, considering the size difference between his huge thumbs and the tiny keyboard. A few seconds later, he read an incoming message. "He's in his room doing homework. He'll be right out."

"We'd like to talk to Jake's parents," Morgan said. "Do you know where they are?"

Duncan returned his phone to his pocket. "Jake hasn't seen his deadbeat father in ten years. His mother briefly lived here with me, but she ran out on both of us last year."

"But Jake stayed here with you?" Morgan asked, surprised.

"She didn't give him the option of going with her." Contempt sharpened his voice. "She left while he was in school. I felt bad for him. He didn't have anywhere else to go." Duncan folded his massive arms across his chest. "He's not a bad kid. He used to get into trouble. But then his mother did nothing but drink, scream, and knock him around. He's better off without her. After she left, I told him if he wanted to stay, he'd better get his head out of his ass. If he was going to screw around, he could move the hell out. If he wanted to live with me, I expected him to do his chores, earn his keep, and stay out of trouble. He does, and we've gotten along just fine since."

"We appreciate your cooperation," Lance said. "Do you remember what time Jake came in last night?"

"No," Duncan said. "I go to bed early. Jake's room is at the other end of the house. I didn't hear him come in."

"Do you usually?"

"No." Duncan shook his head. "Getting to school on time is his responsibility. As long as I don't hear from the truant officer, he can do what he likes. It's not my problem if he's tired."

A screen door slapped open, and a tall, gangly teenage boy loped down the back steps of the farmhouse. He slowed when he saw Morgan and Lance, his eyes wary. As he approached, he looked to Duncan for reassurance.

"They're looking for your friend Evan," Duncan explained.

Jake relaxed a little.

"If you'll excuse me, I'll get back to work," Duncan said to Lance and Morgan. He turned to Jake. "Mind your manners. When you're done, you have stalls to muck. Dinner's at six."

"Yes, sir," Jake said.

Duncan walked back toward the barn.

"Hi, Jake." Morgan held out her hand. "I'm Morgan, and this is Lance. We're friends of the Knox family."

"I know who you are," Jake said to Lance. "You're the hockey coach."

"That's right," Lance said. "I'm also a private investigator. I'm trying to find Evan."

"I already talked to the sheriff. He came to the school. The principal pulled me out of class." Jake scowled. "The other kids thought I was being arrested."

"That must have been embarrassing," Morgan said. What had the sheriff been thinking? Humiliating a teenager would not secure his cooperation.

"It was." Jake's nod was tight. "I don't know where Evan is. I haven't seen him since last night."

"Can we ask you some more questions?" Morgan asked. "We might think of something the sheriff missed."

"I guess." Jake shoved his thumbs into the front pockets of his jeans.

"Tell us about Monday night." Morgan started with an open-ended topic. She didn't want yes or no answers.

"I picked Evan up around seven. We went to the talent show at school, but it was lame, so we left." Jake paused. His forehead crinkled. "Evan didn't want to go home."

"Do you know why?" she asked.

"No." Jake shook his head. "He didn't want to talk about it, but he'd been in a bad mood since he'd seen his dad on Sunday."

"How does Evan feel about his dad?" Morgan pressed.

"He hates him, and he's super piss—mad that he has to see him, but he didn't get a say. His dad had already threatened to have his mom charged with contempt and some kind of alienation . . ."

"Parental alienation?" Morgan filled in.

"I think that was it." Jake shuffled his sneakers in the mud. "Anyway, we drove out to the lake and hung out for a while. I dropped him off at home around twelve thirty."

"Which lake?" Lance asked.

"Scarlet Lake," Jake said. "There's a beach near the school."

"I know it." Morgan's girls liked the playground there.

"When you dropped him off at home, did you see anything unusual?" Lance asked.

Jake shrugged. "Like what?"

Lance turned up a palm. "Cars parked at the curb. People outside."

"There are always cars parked on that street. I didn't notice any particular ones."

Lance frowned. "You didn't see any people outside?"

"No, sir," Jake said.

"Is there anywhere besides the lake where Evan might hang out?" Morgan asked. When Jake gave her a blank look, she added, "Where do you go when you get together?"

Jake rolled a shoulder. "Sometimes we hang at the bowling alley or arcade in town. But we're all broke and don't have a lot of time. I work at the grocery store on the weekends, and I have chores here." He glanced at the barn. "Are we done? I have stalls to clean."

"One more question. Do you know anyone by the name of T. Nelson?"

"Not T. Nelson, but Evan has been seeing a girl named Rylee Nelson." Jake shifted his weight again, then checked the time on his phone.

"Where can we find Rylee?" Morgan asked.

"She works at Tony's Pizza in town." Jake took a small step toward the barn.

"Thanks for your help." Lance gave Jake his card. "Call me if you think of anything else."

"Or if you hear from Evan," Morgan added. "I'm a lawyer. I can help him if he thinks he's in trouble for something."

"Yes, ma'am." Jake stuffed Lance's card into his pocket and headed for the barn.

Morgan and Lance returned to the Jeep.

Morgan wiped her boots on a patch of grass. "Evan is very upset about the court-ordered visitation with his father." She changed her shoes and set the muddy boots on the rubber floor mat before swinging her legs into the vehicle.

Lance stomped his boots twice and climbed into the driver's seat, completely ignoring the coating of filth on his treads. "And Evan has a new girlfriend he did not tell his mother about."

"Also, Jake is mostly unsupervised. Duncan has no idea where he is or what he does."

"They might not have a touchy-feely relationship, and Duncan might give Jake more autonomy than normal, but Jake trusts Duncan."

"He does." Morgan knew Jake could have it much, much worse. "But teenagers need supervision. Duncan feeds and houses him, but he doesn't know when or if Jake comes home at night."

Duncan didn't seem to take much interest in Jake at all.

"He seems safe with Duncan, and he has rules. Rules are good for kids. If his mother truly abandoned him, then Jake doesn't have many options."

"I know." When she'd been a prosecutor, Morgan had seen too many kids destroyed by the foster system. She would never suggest a kid be turned over to them unless they were in danger. She wasn't a family law expert and wasn't even sure of the legality of Jake's guardianship. On one hand, Duncan had no formal relationship with Jake. On the other, Jake's mother had left her child in his care, which would imply consent. Did Duncan sign his school paperwork? Did Jake forge his mother's signature? Morgan was probably better off not knowing the answers to those last two questions.

Lance was right. Jake clearly trusted Duncan. And if the boy had truly modified his behavior for fear of having to leave, then he wanted to stay on the farm. Morgan should mind her own business.

Lance reached over and took her hand. "You can't rescue everyone."

Her face heated. "I'm not that bad."

His short laugh said otherwise. "But I love that you want to protect everyone and everything. Now, what do we want to do next?"

"Let's drive into town. We can show Evan's picture around the bowling alley and arcade and see if Rylee is working tonight." Morgan's stomach growled at the thought of pizza. "Then we can cruise by Scarlet Lake on the way home and be home in time to put the girls to bed."

"Sounds like a plan." Lance drove to the bowling alley.

A senior citizen league occupied most of the lanes. The only people under the age of sixty-five were employees. Still, Morgan and Lance showed Evan's picture to the staff at the desk. They all recognized him but said they hadn't seen him recently.

A dozen teenagers worked the machines at the arcade. Morgan approached a blond boy in skinny jeans and sneakers. "Do you know this boy?"

The boy shrugged. "Maybe I've seen him in here before."

"Recently?" she asked.

He shook his head, blond bangs waving in front of his eyes.

She moved on, but none of the kids had anything more useful to say. They went back out to the car.

Frustrated, Lance jerked the gearshift into drive. "I didn't spot any sparks of recognition or obvious signs of lying."

"Me either," Morgan said. "And no one appeared exceptionally nervous. Shall we try Rylee Nelson?"

Lance drove to the pizza parlor and parked. Tony's was busy at dinnertime. Six of the restaurant's dozen tables were full of families. In the back, three tables had been pushed together to accommodate a Little League team.

Employees wore black aprons and red T-shirts with TONY's emblazoned across the front. Morgan scanned the staff. Three young girls waited tables. Three more hustled behind the counter, filling take-out orders, answering phones, and working the register. Morgan could see into the kitchen. A male cook used a wooden board to slide pizzas in and out of the huge oven. On a stainless steel counter, another man topped rounds of pizza dough.

Morgan approached the counter.

"Can I help you?" a girl with a long brown ponytail asked.

"We're looking for Rylee." Morgan smiled. "Is she here tonight?"

"I think so." Ponytail Girl glanced around, then nudged a blonde next to her. "Where's Rylee?"

"I dunno. She was here a minute ago."

"We're friends of her mother," Lance lied without blinking an eye.

Not as proficient at lying, Morgan merely smiled.

"I'm going in the back for boxes. I'll see if she's back there." Blondie hurried away.

Morgan stepped away from the counter to give real customers space. As she sidestepped toward a window, movement in her peripheral vision caught her attention. She turned her head and spotted a girl in a red T-shirt and black apron hurrying across the parking lot, away from the pizza parlor.

"I'll bet that's her." Morgan rushed for the door.

Lance was right beside her. He pushed through the exit and passed Morgan, calling, "Rylee! Wait! We just want to talk to you."

"Don't scare her," Morgan shouted after him.

He ignored her, but it was already too late.

The girl glanced over her shoulder. Panic widened her eyes. She broke into a run, tripped over the curb, and went sprawling onto the concrete sidewalk.

Lance and Morgan jogged over to her.

"Are you all right?" Morgan gave Lance a *stay put* look. He was intimidating, and the girl was clearly afraid.

He stopped, lifting both hands in surrender, and backed away.

Morgan crouched next to the girl. "I assume you're Rylee. Are you hurt?"

"I'm not saying anything." The girl crabbed away from Morgan. She was about sixteen, with spindly arms and legs she hadn't grown into. Her short brown hair was streaked with purple, and a nose ring glinted in the light. "Get away from me."

Morgan froze. "We just want to ask you a couple of questions."

Rylee scrambled to her feet and brushed some dirt off the knee of her jeans. The fabric was torn, but Morgan didn't know if it had been ripped before the girl fell. She didn't see any blood.

"I don't talk to cops." Rylee's tone was hostile. She pointed at Morgan. The girl's arm was covered in intricate blue designs. They did not look like tattoos but ink, as if she'd drawn the patterns on her skin with a pen. "And leave my brother alone."

"We're not cops, and we're not here about your brother." Though he was now on Morgan's list of people they needed to learn more about.

"We're looking for Evan," Lance said. "Did you know he was missing?"

"Everyone knows." The girl took two steps back. "I don't know where he is. Now leave me alone."

She whirled, stomped across the parking lot to an ancient Buick sedan, and jerked the door open. Rusty hinges squealed in protest. The engine started on her third attempt, and she drove out of the lot with a squeal of her nearly bald tires.

"We usually have better luck with teenagers," Morgan said, discouraged.

"We're getting nowhere with this investigation." Lance punched one palm with the opposite fist. "Evan has been missing for nearly eighteen hours. We both know that his chances of being found alive decrease with every hour that passes."

Morgan checked the time on her watch. Five thirty. She and Lance had had two hours of sleep the previous night and hadn't had a full night's rest in a week. She was running out of steam. Lance's face was lined with exhaustion. Even he would need to recharge at some point. Adrenaline and worry were keeping him going.

She glanced down at her clothes. "Let's stop in at the office. I'll change into jeans and sneakers, you can whip us up a couple of shakes, and we'll head over to the lake. It's a hot summer evening. I'm sure there will be teenagers there. We'll show Evan's picture around."

"All right." On the way, Lance called his mother and added Rylee Nelson and her brother to the list of background checks. His phone signaled an incoming call before he could set it down. He pressed it against his ear. "Kruger."

Tina was sobbing loudly enough that he pulled the phone away from his ear. Morgan could hear Tina clearly.

"The sheriff is here at my hotel," she wailed. "They found a body. It looks like Evan."

Chapter Eight

Sharp parked in the lot behind The Pub. Since his accident and surgery, he was barely maintaining his weight, and his energy was still flagging. He'd been adjusting his diet weekly, but nothing seemed to be working. After making steady improvement for the first two months post-op, he'd been stuck at 75 percent recovered for the last few weeks.

He walked across the cracked asphalt. The muggy air wrapped around him. By the time he reached the door, he was sweating. He really needed to get back into shape.

The air-conditioning was a relief. The bar always drew a decent happy-hour crowd. Sharp passed a dozen occupied wooden barstools. His buddies usually clustered at the back of the bar.

"Sharp!" someone yelled. "Get your butt back here."

He spotted Jimmy and Phil at a round table behind the L of the bar. Phil had worked with Sharp on the SFPD. Phil's wife had made him retire the day he'd completed his twenty-five years. Jimmy was a retired sheriff's deputy who'd worked for Randolph County with Paul.

Jimmy used his foot to push out the chair across from him and Phil. "Take a load off."

Sharp slid onto the well-worn seat.

The waitress, Mindy, looked over the bar and asked, "Beer?"

Sharp shook his head. "Just sparkling water, Mindy. Thanks."

She disappeared into the walk-in cooler. A minute later, she walked around the bar with a bottle of sparkling water. She popped the top and set down the bottle. "It was all the way in the back. No one drinks this here but you."

The Pub was a serious watering hole. It was not a place for health nuts or teetotalers, although the bartender stocked an organic ale just for Sharp. But this was not a social visit.

"Thanks." Sharp swigged from the bottle.

"I hear you're back to work, Sharp." Phil sipped a tall draft, then leaned back and folded his hands across a huge paunch. His wife was an amazing cook, and he was clearly enjoying his retirement.

"I'm getting there," Sharp said with more enthusiasm than he felt.

Jimmy squinted at him. "You still look like hell."

"Been a long day." Sharp hadn't gotten much sleep. After he'd been banished from the crime scene, he'd hung around, eavesdropping on the Knoxes' neighbors, striking up random conversations. Unfortunately, none of the neighbors seemed to know the Knoxes very well. A few had met Paul. No one had spoken more than five words to Tina since they'd moved in. No one had seen or heard anything around the time Paul was killed.

"You need some weight. Order a cheeseburger." Jimmy handed him a menu. "That rabbit food you love can't sustain human life."

Sharp ignored the dietary advice and set the menu aside. "Maybe later."

"I can't believe Paul Knox is dead." Jimmy downed the final drops of his Scotch, raised the tumbler in the air, and signaled the bartender for another. "He made it through all those years on the job without getting shot, only to get blown away in his own house after retirement."

Mindy came around with Jimmy's Scotch and an order of fried pickles. They waited until she'd left before continuing the conversation.

"I heard your partner and his girlfriend were at the crime scene before the deputies." Ice rattled as Jimmy shook the amber liquid in his glass. Paul's death would have started a rush of phone calls and conversations. Jimmy probably knew everything about the investigation by now.

"Lance coaches the stepson," Sharp said. "The mother called him and asked him to find her boy."

Jimmy drank more Scotch, his face grave. The worst cases involved missing or dead kids.

Phil took a long swallow of his beer, set it down on the table, and toyed with a cardboard coaster. "I hope they find him."

The *alive* was implied.

"How long has he been missing?" Phil asked.

Sharp glanced at the time on his phone. "About eighteen hours."

They were all quiet for a few seconds, no doubt all remembering kids who hadn't been found in time.

"Morgan and Lance are covering the direct search for the kid," Sharp said. "I'm exploring the relationship to the murder case. Time is not our friend. We can't afford to overlook any angles." Sharp turned to Jimmy. "Paul must have put away plenty of scumbags. Do you remember anyone threatening to get even with him?"

Jimmy huffed. "Sure. We all got our share of threats."

Phil nodded. "I know I did. A few threatened my family too."

"Same here," Sharp agreed. "But you don't remember anyone specific?"

Jimmy shook his head. "No. You should talk to Brian Springer. He worked with Paul the most before Paul retired."

"Are they still close?" Sharp asked.

"I'm not sure." Jimmy swirled the ice in his glass. "They had a disagreement right before Paul retired. But if anyone will remember individual cases, it'll be Brian. Do you know him?"

"His name sounds familiar." Sharp had been on the SFPD long enough to know many of the local law enforcement officers. The sheriff's deputies had backed up Sharp many times, and vice versa.

Jimmy opened his photo app on his phone and scrolled backward. He turned the screen toward Sharp. "This is Brian."

Sharp recognized the face. "I've met him. Do you have his phone number?"

"Sure, I'll text you his contact information."

Sharp's phone vibrated. He opened Jimmy's text to read Brian's address and cell phone number. "Thanks."

"I'll be right back." Phil belched and headed for the restroom at the back of the bar.

Jimmy pushed the bowl of fried pickles toward Sharp. "Try one."

Sharp took one from the bowl and popped it into his mouth rather than let the discussion segue into an argument about Sharp's diet. "Is Brian still on the force?"

"Yes." Jimmy set his phone on the table and ate a pickle. "But he's due to retire soon."

"Do you know what their argument was about?"

"Not the details," Jimmy said in a vague tone.

Sharp lowered his voice and talked quickly. Recently, the sheriff's department had been caught in a huge scandal, and he wanted to ask Jimmy any sensitive questions before Phil returned from the men's room. "Are there any whiffs of corruption around Brian?"

"Nothing major." Jimmy shrugged.

What does that mean?

But Sharp nodded. He really wanted to know what Brian had done, but if Sharp pushed too hard, Jimmy would become defensive and stop talking. However, if Sharp was patient and played along, Jimmy might just blab. He was drunk enough.

Jimmy shook his head. "Some guy they arrested in a bar fight filed an excessive force complaint. He said Brian broke his ribs with his baton. Nothing was ever substantiated, though, so maybe it wasn't true."

"Right." But Sharp wouldn't be surprised either way. Body cameras weren't in the budget for the sheriff's department yet. It would have been the suspect's word against those of the deputies. The incident would have happened under the former sheriff, who had been known for looking the other way if a suspect got roughed up. "Did the complaint have anything to do with the falling-out between Paul and Brian?"

Jimmy lifted a shoulder. "I assumed Paul and Brian were told not to talk about it."

But details would have leaked.

Sharp waited.

Jimmy swirled the ice in his glass and continued. "Paul and Brian were breaking up a bar fight. Paul had the patience of a saint, but Brian . . ." Jimmy wouldn't directly criticize another cop, but the way he trailed off implied that Brian did not.

"Do you remember the name of the case?" Sharp asked.

"The guy's name was Sam Jones." Jimmy looked up. Phil was walking out of the short hallway that led to the restrooms. Jimmy's mouth snapped closed. He wouldn't say anything else about the excessive force case. He probably already regretted what he'd told Sharp.

Phil returned to the table.

And Jimmy returned to discussing general information. "Anyway, Brian is on vacation." Jimmy raised his glass. The waitress knew him well enough to take her time bringing him refills. He was going to drink the booze as fast as she delivered it. "Here's the worst part. Brian likes to go off the radar when he's fishing. The sheriff had to leave a message on his cell phone. Brian doesn't even know that Paul is dead."

"If Brian knows the most about Paul's cases, then I think I'd better try and find him." Sharp drained his sparkling water. The fried pickle had soured in his stomach. Was there more to the excessive force incident? Could Brian be dirty? Had Paul known? The thought nause-ated Sharp. "What does Brian drive?"

"A black Ford Taurus," Phil said.

"Good luck finding the kid." Jimmy shook his empty glass at the waitress again. "Let us know if we can help."

"Thanks. I will." Sharp left the bar and returned to the parking lot. A swarm of gnats attacked his face. He swatted them aside on the way to his car. Once he was behind the wheel, he called Brian Springer. The call switched to voice mail, and Sharp didn't bother to leave a message. He plugged Springer's address into his GPS and drove out of the park-ing lot. On the drive, he washed the taste of the pickle from his mouth with more green tea.

Brian lived in a development of small, well-kept homes on tiny lots. His one-story house was white with red shutters and had a small backyard surrounded by a four-foot-tall chain-link fence. His black Taurus was parked at the curb in the shade of an oak tree. A small shed occupied one corner of the backyard. Sharp parked behind the Taurus and walked up the concrete driveway. The lawn had been recently cut. The landscaping wasn't fancy, but Brian kept it neat.

Sharp pressed the doorbell. He heard it chime inside the house. A minute later, when no one had answered the door, he pressed it again.

Nothing.

He returned to his car and scanned the street. A young couple pushed a baby stroller along the sidewalk toward him.

"Do you know Brian Springer?" Sharp asked as they approached.

The man stepped in front of the woman and baby. "Why?"

"I'm worried about him." Sharp thought about the business cards in his pocket, then decided to leave them where they were. It might be best if the couple didn't know his name in case the sheriff's department came calling. "I'm a friend, and I haven't been able to reach him for days." The lie rolled smoothly off Sharp's tongue. "Have you seen him?"

The man shook his head. "No, I haven't seen him in a couple of days." He turned to his wife. "Have you?"

The baby made a soft bleating sound, not unlike a lamb.

"No." The woman leaned over the stroller. "But you're the second person to ask about him."

"We live next door." The man pointed to the red two-story house on the adjacent lot.

Suspicious, Sharp asked, "Who else has been looking for him?"

"A police detective came by earlier today." The woman lifted the baby, clearly a newborn, from the stroller and began to sway back and forth. The baby quieted. "I don't remember his name. He wasn't in uniform, but he showed me a badge."

"He didn't leave you a card?"

"No." She smiled at the baby and made a cooing noise.

"Could you describe the detective?" Sharp pressed.

She frowned. "I spoke to him through the screen door. He was ordinary looking. Brown hair. Brown suit. He drove a dark-blue sedan."

Sounded like a county detective. The sheriff had probably sent someone to find Brian for the same reason Sharp was here.

The couple took a step away.

"Do you remember the last time you saw Brian?" Sharp asked.

The man brightened. "I saw him on Saturday. He talked about a guys' fishing weekend with his brother, but I'm not sure when he was leaving." He looked to his wife. "Do you remember?"

"No." She shrugged. "But he was going to bring me a key before he left so we could feed his cat and bring in the mail. He didn't do that." She pointed. "His car is still here."

Sharp glanced back at the black Taurus. "Is that where he normally parks it?"

"Yes," the husband said.

"Do you know if he usually fished at a local spot?" Sharp asked.

The husband tilted his head. "I'm not sure. I think the property belonged to someone in his family. His brother or brother-in-law? It's on a lake."

"Thanks for your help," Sharp said.

The baby began to cry, louder this time.

"Excuse me." The wife turned toward the red house.

The husband took the handle of the stroller. "Bye."

"Thanks again." Sharp turned back toward his car. He stopped on the sidewalk and stared at Brian's house. The couple took their baby inside their house and closed the door. Sharp opened Brian's mailbox. What appeared to be a few days of mail was crammed inside. He gave up any idea of hiding his activity. As far as the neighbors were concerned, Sharp was a worried friend.

He stepped into the shrubs, trying to peer in the front window, but the drapes were tightly drawn. Sharp's instincts began to quiver like an insect's antennas, and he remembered another house he'd approached.

There had been two dead bodies inside and a killer on his way out.

This is a different case.

He went to the garage door. Rising onto his toes, he looked through the high row of windows. No vehicle. Sharp walked around the house, trying to see into every window he encountered. But each one was covered. Who kept all their blinds closed?

No one he knew.

In the backyard, he looked inside the shed but found only lawn equipment. A deck jutted off the back of the house in front of a set of sliding glass doors. Sharp jogged up the steps. Vertical blinds covered the sliders, but a few of the slats were crooked. Sharp could see through the open slivers into the kitchen but saw nothing. He considered the lock-picking tools in his wallet. Was there a door he could break into without a neighbor seeing? On a whim, Sharp used the hem of his shirt to tug on the slider handle.

The door opened.

Sharp stepped inside, using his shoulder to part the vertical blinds. Once the blinds settled back into place—and the neighbors couldn't see him—Sharp reached into his pocket for gloves and tugged them on. The house had a vacant air.

Sharp sniffed deeply. Something smelled foul, not like decomposing flesh but feces. When people died, their bowels and bladder often gave way.

Was Brian here somewhere, recently deceased?

Something bumped his foot. Sharp jumped, drawing his gun on reflex and pointing it at . . . a cat.

Sharp breathed, his pulse scrambling. The orange tabby rubbed on his ankle, then walked away, looking over its shoulder as if to beckon Sharp to follow it. When Sharp took a few steps in the cat's direction, it trotted into the kitchen.

Two bowls sat on a vinyl placemat on the tile. Both were empty. One bowl had a few crumbs in the bottom. Brian hadn't delivered the key to his neighbor. Was he really on vacation?

Sharp filled one bowl with water. Then he found some dry cat food in a cabinet and heaped the other bowl high, enough to hold one cat for a couple of days. He made a mental note to check back if Brian didn't turn up.

Leaving the cat crunching at its bowl, Sharp walked from room to room, finding the source of the bad odor: the dirty cat box. But he still checked any concealed area big enough to hide a body. In the master bedroom, the bifold closet doors were open. A few of the dresser drawers weren't fully closed either.

He stopped in the final room, a small bedroom converted into a home office.

An industrial-type desk was empty. Cable and cords trailed along the floor under it, as if someone had taken a desktop computer. Sharp checked the master bedroom a second time. A thirty-something-inch flat-screen TV hung on the wall, undisturbed. Another larger TV hung on the wall in the living room. An iPad sat on the desk.

A robber would not have taken a desktop computer and left flat-screen TVs and an iPad behind. Had Brian removed his own desktop computer? Why? Maybe it needed repairs.

Or maybe Brian had destroyed it. Physical destruction of the hard drive was the best way to ensure no one could recover any data.

Sharp took one more walk through the house, snapping pics with his camera phone. He didn't see anything that gave him a clue as to where Brian had gone.

Sharp left the house and returned to his Prius. He wrote down all the information he had on Brian Springer. Sharp was stopping at Jenny Kruger's house in the morning. Maybe she could find Brian's mysterious vacation cabin on a lake.

Brian's house had given Sharp more questions than answers. Why was the back door unlocked? If Brian had gone on vacation, he would have had the neighbor feed the cat and pick up the mail. He hadn't done either. And why was his computer missing?

No, it didn't look like Brian had gone on vacation, but he'd gone somewhere, presumably with someone else, since his vehicle was still out front. And he'd been in a hurry when he'd left.

Chapter Nine

Grief gathered in Lance's chest as Tina's voice faded into quiet crying.

He heard a rustling sound over the connection.

"Sheriff Colgate here." He must have picked up Tina's phone. "I'm taking Mrs. Knox down to the medical examiner's office."

"Is it Evan?" The words grated in Lance's throat. Morgan reached over from the passenger seat and gave his arm a supportive squeeze.

"The body was pulled out of the Deer River." The sheriff's voice was scratchy and sounded weary. "It meets his rough description, but the ME has not yet officially IDed him. Evan's fingerprints should be on file in AFIS, but they are not. It seems the original ten-print card was rejected by the Division of Criminal Justice Services, with a reprinting request."

The automated fingerprint identification system worked well, but it wasn't perfect. The system depended on good-quality original prints. The sheriff's department had recently switched to using electronic live scan devices to record fingerprints. Until then, the sheriff's department had been using traditional ink and physical cards. Evan's prints had likely been kicked back by the DCJS because one or more of the prints had been smeared. Lance assumed no one ever followed up on the reprint request.

The sheriff continued. "There were several reporters at the body recovery scene. I didn't want Mrs. Knox to hear about it on the news, so I came right over here. I explained that the medical examiner would notify her as soon as he identified the remains. But she insists on going to the morgue immediately."

"I can't blame her," Lance said. "I wouldn't want to wait either." But part of him also didn't want to confirm that Evan was dead.

"I know," the sheriff agreed in a quiet voice.

Lance wouldn't let Tina face the possibility alone. "We'll meet you at the morgue."

The Randolph County Medical Examiner's Office sat in the middle of the county municipal complex. Twenty minutes later, Lance paced the commercial gray carpet in the waiting area. The smell of burned coffee soured his stomach. Morgan leaned on the reception counter, trying to get information from someone on the ME's staff.

"Conference room two," the woman behind the counter said.

A few minutes later, the door opened. Tina and Sheriff Colgate entered. The sheriff walked close to her. One hand hovered near her elbow, as if he were afraid she would fall down at any moment, with good reason. Tina's face had drained to the color of skim milk. Her hands trembled, and her steps were shaky. She looked like she was walking to the gallows.

Morgan went to her side, took her elbow in one hand, and wrapped the other around her shoulders. Without speaking—no words could possibly bring Tina any comfort at the moment—Morgan led her down the hall.

Following, Lance nearly gagged. The air felt syrupy enough to choke him. The staff tried to contain the scents of decomposition and formalin to the autopsy suites, but they seemed to permeate the walls. Lance could smell death, although maybe that was all in his head.

They stopped in front of a door marked with the numeral 2. Lance and the sheriff followed close behind. They filed into the room, the silence as thick as the odors that wafted down the corridor.

Dr. Frank Jenkins came in dressed in clean scrubs. "Please sit down." He waited for Tina to ease into a chair, her hands clenching the armrests. Then Frank angled another chair to face her. When he was at her level, he gave her his full attention. "First, let me say that I knew Paul. He was a good man. I'm very sorry for your loss."

Tina nodded. "What about—" She choked on the words, but they all knew what she'd been about to ask.

Frank nodded. "I'm trying to identify the body that came in a few hours ago. I can confirm that it is a young man in his late teens with short dark hair. He came in wearing jeans, Converse sneakers, and a black T-shirt."

Tina's breath hitched in her throat. "Just show me," she croaked. "I'll know if it's my son."

"I'm not sure you would," Frank said gravely. "And I don't want you to see him like this."

When Lance had been on the SFPD, he'd worked with Frank. Lance had always thought the ME was a cold fish, but Frank had surprised him a few times lately. There was plenty of empathy on his face today. Maybe Lance hadn't given Frank enough credit. Everyone in law enforcement became hardened as a survival technique. It was impossible to work with death on a daily basis without distancing oneself from it.

"I don't understand." Tina's voice was as soft as a child's.

Frank gritted his teeth. The ME needed to say something very unpleasant. "The young man's face is not recognizable." Frank paused, then finished in a soothing voice. "I believe he was hit by a car. We don't have his fingerprints for a match, but we should be able to identify him by medical and dental records, which are on the way, and DNA."

Tina gasped, a desperate sound. She collapsed into herself, weeping.

Morgan wrapped an arm around Tina's shoulders and spoke to her in a low tone.

Lance jumped in. "Do you know how he died?"

"He had internal injuries but also a single GSW to the head." Frank tapped his forehead.

Shot in the head, just like Paul. Grief pierced Lance right through the heart. He pictured Evan, his cheeks red with exertion, practicing slap shots on the ice, arguing about *Game of Thrones* in the locker room with his teammates, smiling when the team had won their first game. The memories overwhelmed him. Lance couldn't reconcile the teenager he knew with a body on Frank's table. His throat filled with a sadness so acute that he felt like he was swallowing sand.

Tina shook herself, straightened, and wiped her cheeks with her palms. Her eyes were bright with pain. "I can do it. I'll still recognize my son without . . ." A sob cut off her words. Her lips flattened, and she took two long, steadying breaths through her nose. "I need to know."

Lance couldn't take it anymore. Tina deserved better than being left hanging about her son's death.

He pushed off the wall. "I'll go in. I know him." He'd coached the teen three times a week for the last year. He'd seen him shirtless in the locker room a hundred times. The last thing Lance wanted to do was identify his dead body, but no mother should have to see her son in such a condition.

Frank got up. "OK."

The sheriff stood. "Ms. Dane, if you'll stay here with Mrs. Knox, I'll go with Lance." The body had been discovered in Redhaven, but if it was positively identified as Evan, the case would be officially related to Paul's murder and transferred to Colgate.

Nodding, Morgan took Tina's hand and held it tightly.

Lance's feet seemed to weigh a hundred pounds each as he followed Frank down the hall to the autopsy suite antechamber. Lance and Colgate donned gowns, booties, and gloves. Lance carried the face shield in his hand. He'd always found the damned things claustrophobic. He wouldn't put it on unless he had to.

Paul's body was back here somewhere, he thought with a sick feeling, probably still bagged in the cooler. Was he still waiting his turn on the table?

The smells that had been faint in the waiting area exploded in Lance's nose as he entered the autopsy suite. Bodies on stainless steel tables lined up in bays. The morgue had had a busy weekend. Acid churned in Lance's belly.

Frank led them to the last table. "He came in about three hours ago, but we've been so swamped, we didn't match him with the description of Evan Meade right away."

The clothes had been removed. Lance saw them laid out on a nearby counter. A white sheet was spread out under them to catch any trace evidence that might fall off the clothing. Evan had been wearing a *Game of Thrones* T-shirt when his mother had last seen him. The shirt on the counter was a concert tee, but he could have changed before he went out.

Lance turned back to the body. A morgue assistant was photographing injuries. The body was long and lean, with the muscle tone of an athlete. Contusions on top of contusions covered the left side of the body.

"Damn," Colgate muttered under his breath.

Lance had no words. Even if his brain could articulate what he felt staring at the young man's corpse, his throat was too dry and clogged with emotion to allow him to speak. The corpse's face was bruised and swollen beyond recognition. Lance stared at the ruined face, trying to match it to Evan's. The shape of the head didn't seem right, but the swelling had definitely distorted the features. And maybe Lance just didn't want to believe it was Evan lying in the morgue.

Lance squeezed his eyelids shut for a second. He was no stranger to death, but he had to do this for Tina. He opened his eyes and scanned the rest of the body.

Frank pointed to the corpse's forehead. "It's hard to see, but there's a bullet hole in the forehead here." He moved down to the chest. "In addition to the facial bruising, the torso suffered serious damage. There's significant bruising to the ribs and kidneys. His external injuries are consistent with being struck by a car."

The sheriff cocked his head. "Someone ran him down with a vehicle, then shot him in the head?"

"We're just getting started on the autopsy, but that's what it looks like to me. I'll call you immediately if the autopsy produces different answers."

"How long has he been dead?" Lance asked.

Frank pursed his lips. "My preliminary window of death is between two and six o'clock this morning, but I'll have to confirm that after I complete the autopsy."

The hours fit the previous night's timeline, and Lance couldn't help but wonder, if he hadn't waited for the police to arrive, if he had gone after Evan immediately, could he have caught up and saved him?

Sheriff Colgate shifted his weight. "Do you think it's him?"

The hair was dark and short like Evan's, although it was coated with mud and lake debris. The skin was pale, and like Evan, freckles dotted the neck and arms, areas where the sun had the most impact. *Wait.* Lance squinted at the belly. Most of the bruising was along the left side. The right was relatively clear. "Evan had an appendectomy over the winter. I don't see his scar."

"Are you sure it was visible?" Frank asked.

Lance pointed to the corpse's abdomen, just below and to the right of the navel. "It was right about there last week."

Frank moved to the table, adjusted the overhead light, and examined the right side of the abdomen. "No appendectomy scar."

"Then this is not Evan." Lance put a hand out to lean on the wall. His gaze returned to the clothing on the counter. Lance moved closer, noticing new details. The sneakers were high-tops, which Evan didn't wear. Lance read the name of the band on the front of the T-shirt. Panic! at the Disco. Evan was all classic rock. He would never wear an emo band shirt. It was definitely not him. Relief weakened his leg muscles for a few seconds.

"I need to go out and tell Tina." Lance turned and fled the room through the swinging door. He ripped off the PPEs and tossed them in a hamper without breaking stride. The sheriff followed, but the much older man couldn't keep pace with Lance.

Lance halted in the conference room doorway, his eyes seeking out and holding Tina's. "It's not him. This body has no appendectomy scar."

Tina sagged against Morgan and began to weep with relief.

As glad as Lance was that the body was not Evan's, a young man had been viciously murdered. Another mother would soon be weeping with grief.

At the sound of the sheriff's voice, Lance glanced back into the corridor. Colgate was on his phone. He saw Lance watching him, turned, and walked farther away. A few minutes later, he lowered his phone and walked toward the conference room.

Lance met him halfway down the hall. "Just because this isn't Evan doesn't mean this murder isn't related to Paul's death."

The sheriff paused, his face confused, maybe even a little irritated. "Why would you say that?"

"The body in the morgue looked very much like Evan, and he was killed in the same way as Paul," Lance pointed out.

"Not exactly. Why don't we wait until the body is identified before we make any associations?" The sheriff brushed past him and continued to the conference room. He avoided eye contact with Morgan as he entered the room.

"Mrs. Knox?" The sheriff stood in front of her. "I'm so sorry for putting you through this. I wish I hadn't had to."

She looked up at him with red-rimmed, bloodshot eyes. "I know, but now what? Has everyone stopped looking for Evan?"

"No, ma'am. I have every available man on the case." He glanced at his watch. "I'd like you to come down with me to the station and answer a few questions. I've just gotten some information we need to discuss before the press conference I've scheduled for tomorrow morning."

Lance glanced at Morgan. Her eyebrow was up, and clearly, so were her suspicions.

"We'll bring her to the station," Morgan said.

"There's no need." The sheriff narrowed his eyes at her. "I'm headed there anyway."

But Morgan clearly wasn't going to cede control. The police could not force anyone to answer questions. "I insist. Mrs. Knox has a right to have an attorney present during questioning."

The sheriff's jaw shifted, as if he were grinding his teeth. "She's not under arrest. We just want to talk to her."

"Then you've completely cleared her?" Morgan asked.

The sheriff said, "We've confirmed that she was working until after one o'clock."

Which wasn't exactly a *yes*. Morgan stood. "Lance and I will bring Mrs. Knox to the station."

The sheriff was up to something. Lance knew it. But what?

Chapter Ten

Evan's body jerked. A blast of pain jolted him awake. His pulse hammered in his ears. He tried to scream, but his throat was too dry to emit anything other than a croak.

He forced his crusty eyelids to separate. Sunshine seared his eyeballs in a blurry haze of light. His body rocked, and agony radiated from his arm. His empty belly roiled. He closed his eyes, swallowed, and waited for the sick feeling to pass. When he no longer felt as if he were going to puke, he tried again.

He opened his eyes and turned his head from side to side. He was lying in the bottom of a canoe. The overcast sky made it difficult to estimate the time. A few inches of water had accumulated in the aluminum bottom. His jeans and sneakers were soaked. Since he'd tied his T-shirt around his arm to stop the bleeding, he was shirtless.

His flight the night before rushed back to him. Images and sensations flooded him as if he were right there, experiencing the night all over again. He forced the slideshow to cut off.

Paul was dead.

His eyes had been empty, staring at the ceiling. No life left inside.

Evan remembered the very last words he'd said to Paul. *I wish you'd never married my mother.* Those were words he could never take back, as much as he wanted to—mostly because they weren't true. He was ashamed that they'd come out of his mouth. When he spent time with Kirk, he turned into his father, as if douchebaggery were contagious.

His stomach turned again, nausea compounding his misery. Tears pressed against the backs of his eyes. He fought them back. He couldn't afford to lose it, not if he were going to survive.

Not that he was even sure he wanted to live. Did he deserve to?

He shoved the memory away. Pain, throbbing and hot, brought his attention back to the present. He'd been freezing all night, but the morning was heating up fast—and so was he.

He was dehydrated, and he needed to do something more with his wound than tie a T-shirt around his arm. The canoe shook, startling him.

He lifted his head and looked over the edge. The canoe was caught on something in the center of a river or creek, maybe the Deer River. Brown water bubbled white, eddying around rocks. Where was he? The storm had been wild. He'd been swept out of the lake, but he had no idea where the water had carried him. Remembering the torrential rain, thunder, and wicked streaks of lightning, he was surprised he hadn't drowned.

Something buzzed near his ear, and Evan startled. A dragonfly cruised past his head. Its long, slim body hovered over the water next to the canoe. Bulbous eyes seemed to stare at Evan for a minute before it zoomed away. He'd better get moving too.

He sat up. The shoreline was thickly wooded, and the river was clearly swollen from the heavy rain. It ran all the way to the top of the bank. Water rushed past his canoe at a speed he'd never seen in the area before. He could hear it roaring downriver. If this was the Deer River, where he and Paul had camped, it looked nothing like the waterway had just a few weeks ago.

His canoe sat amid a pile of broken branches, maybe even a small tree, that had been swept down the river and gotten jammed up at a bend. He reached for the broken paddle lying in the water at the bottom of the canoe. He poked at the branches. The canoe rocked, but the floating debris held him fast.

Evan used the paddle to shift the lighter bits of debris, not an easy task with only one good arm. He moved a fat branch and revealed the wet sheen of a large rock beneath the hull. Pushing with the paddle, he moved the canoe. The metal bottom scraped as it slid off the rock.

The boat rocked and bobbed a few times, then floated away from the logjam.

The current picked up. Evan used the paddle as a rudder to steer toward the shoreline. The glaring sun amplified his thirst, and he desperately wanted to find some clean water.

But the river had other plans. The canoe dipped and shot back into the center. The boat rounded the bend. Evan's mouth went even drier at the sight of white water and large boulders ahead. Sliding through an eddy, the canoe wobbled and nearly tipped. Evan grabbed for the sides and tried to use his weight to balance the canoe. But this wasn't a kayak. The canoe was made for calm water, not rapids.

He reached out with the paddle to catch the branch of an overhanging tree. The paddle caught, but the pull of the current ripped it right out of Evan's hands. With no way to steer, he held on as the canoe slid down a short waterfall and went nose first into a deeper pool. The boat hit the water and rolled, pitching Evan over the edge.

The water closed over his head, shockingly cold after the warmth of the sun. He tumbled, out of control, striking rocks and debris. He broke the surface and spit out a mouthful of mud. Trying to suck in some air, he coughed and sputtered as he was swept along.

The water sucked him down, then tumbled him into a rock. His injured shoulder took the brunt of the impact. Pain blasted through his arm. His lungs burned as he fought for a breath when his head broke the surface. The water sucked him down again, rolling him over and over until he didn't know which way was up.

He floated, suspended in the murky cold, considering what it would be like to simply let the river take him. *Would all the pain go away?*

Disoriented, Evan opened his eyes and looked for the light that would lead him to the surface.

But all he saw was darkness.

Chapter Eleven

Morgan sat in the passenger seat of the Jeep, her thoughts churning. Normally, the sheriff's request to question Tina at the station would not set off Morgan's alarms. But the sheriff had not been up front with them. She had sensed hostility radiating from him, like the hot wind that came before a vicious thunderstorm.

Lance drove beside her, tense. He knew something was up too. Tina sat in the back seat, shredding another cuticle. How did a parent cope with not knowing whether their child was alive or dead? Morgan couldn't even think about being in that situation without risking a panic attack.

They parked and went inside. The sheriff met them in the hallway and escorted them into one of the nicer conference rooms. It contained a wooden table and upholstered office-type chairs. He gestured toward a small table in the corner where a pod-style coffee maker stood. "Help yourself to coffee. I'll be right back."

Tina sat at the table, facing the door. Lance declined coffee. Morgan went to the machine and brewed two cups. She set one on the table in front of Tina.

Without drinking, Tina cradled the Styrofoam cup in both hands. Her demeanor had changed after the scene at the morgue. She seemed less desperate and more determined. The initial shock of Paul's death and Evan's disappearance had settled. She looked like a woman getting her act together to take action.

Morgan sat next to Tina. Lance took the chair opposite her.

The sheriff entered the room, a manila file tucked under his arm. Tina's swollen eyes fixed on the file. "Have you found my son?"

"Not yet." The sheriff settled in a chair at the head of the table. "I have dozens of law enforcement officers in the field searching for him. A K-9 unit is working the woods and shoreline all around Deer Lake. If Evan is anywhere in the vicinity, the dog will pick up his scent. A good dog is worth a hundred men when tracking a person. We have the ground search covered. The most useful thing you can do is give us more information." The sheriff's mouth tightened. He opened his file. "We also talked to all of Evan's friends on the list you gave us. They all denied seeing him tonight or knowing where he is."

Which meant nothing, Morgan thought. Sixteen-year-olds were good at keeping secrets from adults.

The sheriff's chair squeaked as he leaned back. "At this time, we do believe Evan's disappearance and Paul's murder are linked."

Linked was an interesting word choice. Lance tilted his head, one eyebrow shooting up in a *no shit* expression. Morgan touched his foot with hers and gave him a *cool it* frown. On an *ordinary* case, his temper could run short. His close relationship with Evan would slice his tolerance for bullshit in half.

"Did forensics find anything useful at the scene?" Lance rested his forearms on the table, his posture deceptively relaxed. His tension was all in his eyes.

"A few things, yes." The sheriff leaned back and folded his arms across his slight paunch. "The blood on the fence, the back door, and Evan's phone is type B negative."

Tina stiffened. "Evan and I are both B negative."

"Paul was O positive." The sheriff nodded. "I've asked that the DNA tests be expedited, but I can't say when the lab will get to them. However, only about one point five percent of the population has B negative blood. I'd say the chances are good that the samples belong to Evan."

"So he's definitely hurt." Tina wiped a hand under her eye.

"Yes, ma'am." The sheriff reached behind him and took a box of tissues from a credenza. He set it on the table in front of her.

"Thank you." She sniffed and plucked a tissue from the box.

"The front and rear doors of the house were unlocked. The garage door was secure. All of the windows were locked and intact. Does anyone else have a key to your house?"

Tina shook her head. "No, and Paul didn't believe in those electronic keypad or wireless locks either. He didn't trust electronics and said anything accessible by Wi-Fi could be hacked."

"It's not that hard to pick a lock," Lance said. "What about fingerprints?"

The sheriff didn't respond. "So far, all of the fingerprints that we've identified in the house have belonged to family members—and you." The sheriff nodded at Lance. "Unknown latent prints were submitted to AFIS but no matches so far."

This was not unusual. AFIS held the known fingerprints of criminals and unknown latent prints found at crime scenes. Unidentified fingerprints taken from the Knox residence would be kept on file for comparison in the event a suspect was later arrested.

"Now I have a few questions for Mrs. Knox." The sheriff leaned forward, resting his forearms on his knees, his focus narrowing on Tina's face. "Two months ago, deputies were called to your house because Evan and Paul were fighting."

Morgan didn't react, but why hadn't Tina told her about this?

"Arguing," Tina corrected. She shifted her torso, settling back into the chair, distancing herself from the sheriff—or the question.

"All right. Arguing. Important distinction," the sheriff acknowledged with a nod. "Can you tell me what they *argued* about?"

Tina sighed and scrubbed both hands down her face. "Kirk had just won his visitation petition, and Evan had had dinner with him the night before. He told us he wasn't going back."

The sheriff's eyes narrowed. "Why is that, Mrs. Knox?"

"Because his father is an asshole." The skin around Tina's lips wrinkled as her mouth pursed. "Paul said he had to or there would be legal repercussions. Kirk was claiming parental alienation. Kirk said that, while he was in prison, I had turned Evan against him, as if that was even necessary. That was when Evan started yelling. But he was angry in general at the situation. His temper wasn't really directed at Paul. Paul just happened to be the one standing in front of him."

The sheriff lifted a sheet of paper from the table. "The police report says Evan took a swing at Paul."

"He didn't hit him, and Paul wasn't mad." Tina exhaled audibly through her nose. "He knew how much Evan was hurting. I don't know how to describe how upset Evan was that day."

"Their argument was loud enough that your neighbor Mr. Palmer called the police," the sheriff pointed out.

"The windows were open." Tina's tone was more hostile than Morgan expected from her.

Lance's head swiveled around. He and Morgan shared a concerned glance.

Morgan stepped in. "Where are you going with these questions, Sheriff?"

"Just trying to get all the facts that might help us find Evan." The sheriff glanced at Morgan with irritation.

Morgan bit back a *bullshit*. She had established a shaky working relationship with Sheriff Colgate since he'd taken over the department. On one hand, she did not want to jeopardize his cooperation. The previous sheriff had made every aspect of her job as difficult as possible.

On the other hand, she did not like the direction he'd taken with this line of questioning.

He was treating Tina more like a suspect than a victim.

"How have visitations gone with Evan's father since then?" The sheriff set the paper down and steepled his fingers.

"More often than not, Kirk cancels, which is fine with all of us, but this week he actually showed up." She paused for a breath. "Sunday night, I picked Evan up at the restaurant, and he refused to speak all the way home. He went straight to his room. He was still mad when he came home from school Monday. When Paul asked him to mow the lawn, he refused and started yelling. Paul and I could both see that he was hurting from whatever Kirk had said to him. Usually, he doesn't mind helping out. He knows Paul has—*had*—a bad back." She caught herself with a quiver to her breath. "But Evan went to his room and slammed his door."

"Was Paul angry?"

"No. Paul said, 'He had a rough night. Give him some space.' Because that's the kind of man he was." Tina's gaze dropped to the tissue in her hand. "I went to work. I thought seeing Jake that night would cheer up Evan."

"Evan had a record before you married Paul." The sheriff had clearly also worked late gathering background information last night.

"He had a hard time when his father went to prison. Although frankly, that was the best thing that could have happened to us." Tina frowned. "Have you questioned Kirk? He told Evan that Paul was the reason we couldn't be a family."

"Was he?" the sheriff asked.

"No." Tina shook her head. "I would never take Kirk back. He's a thoroughly nasty man. However, he can put on a charming front for a short period of time when he needs to."

"In what way was he nasty?" the sheriff asked.

"He insulted me every day, telling me I was ugly and stupid. He threw temper tantrums and broke things. He screamed and yelled, always stopped just short of physical abuse. I think he knew that's where I would draw the line. Plus, he was allergic to work. He was always scheming to avoid getting a real job. It was ironic that he called Paul a gold digger, as if Paul and I were rolling in money."

"Was money tight?" the sheriff asked.

"Not tight, but we lived on a budget." Tina frowned. "We have Paul's pension and my income. He considered getting a job, but he has a lot of lower back pain from wearing a duty belt all those years. Plus, he really wanted to be at home so he could spend time with Evan."

The extra twenty pounds of awkward equipment on a duty belt could do a number on a cop's back over the course of a career, especially if he spent many hours sitting in a patrol car.

"Why did you stay with Kirk?" the sheriff asked.

Tina lifted one shoulder. "I thought that's the way all men were. But the first couple of weeks after he went to prison were the most peaceful of my life, and I decided Evan and I were much better off alone."

The sheriff tapped his pointer finger on his file. "But you married Paul not long after that."

A tear fell from Tina's face to the table. "As you know, Paul arrested Kirk. But we didn't see each other again until months later. Paul came into the urgent care for a few stitches." She wiped her eyes. "A few weeks later, he asked me to dinner. He was so different from Kirk. Paul wanted to take care of me and Evan." She took a fresh tissue from the box. "Could it have been Kirk? He hated Paul enough."

The sheriff opened the manila file in front of him and flipped through several papers. "His group home has an eight p.m. curfew unless residents are at work. He swiped his card to check in at seven thirty."

Lance craned his head, clearly trying to see the sheriff's papers. "Is there any type of additional monitoring?"

The sheriff rested his arm across the page. "Residents aren't under house arrest. The curfew, along with a list of other conditions, is set by the home. But the supervisor on duty Monday night confirmed that Kirk came in at seven thirty."

"Did anyone see him at the home after seven thirty?" Morgan asked.

The sheriff ignored her question, turning back to Tina, which Morgan assumed meant *no*.

"Tell me more about the relationship between Paul and Evan. Was it rocky from the beginning?" the sheriff asked.

"No. Actually, Paul and Evan didn't argue often. Most of the time they got along well. Paul took him shooting a few times. He wanted to be a good stepfather. Evan needed a good example in his life. They even went camping last month, and Paul talked about finding a couple of used kayaks."

"Where did they go camping?" the sheriff asked.

"The woods behind the house," Tina said. "They left the house on foot with two backpacks."

The sheriff flipped over his page of notes. "And when was the last time you spoke with Evan?"

"Before I went to work on Monday. Why are you asking me this again?" Suspicion narrowed Tina's eyes.

"We ask the same questions over and over again, Mrs. Knox. It's routine. Sometimes witnesses remember more details after the initial shock has worn off."

Morgan thought it much more likely that the sheriff was trying to catch Tina in a lie.

"Is Tina or Evan a suspect, Sheriff?" Morgan cut to the chase. Working relationship or not, she was tired of the bullshit. The boy had been missing for over nineteen hours.

"Everyone involved with Paul is a suspect until they are cleared." But the sheriff's eyes belied his words.

Tina's head snapped up. Anger and surprise flushed her face. "That's ridiculous. Evan is just a boy. He would never hurt Paul. My son was probably shot by whoever killed my husband." Her voice rose, all traces of shakiness gone. "And you are wasting time and resources thinking Evan did it."

"As I said before, everyone is a suspect." The sheriff kept his voice calm. "We can't know Evan's side of the story until we find him and talk to him." The sheriff leaned forward. "Why is he hiding from us? Why didn't he try to get help?"

Tina opened her mouth, then shut it again. Her eyes closed for a second, then opened full of grief. "Maybe he can't."

The sheriff sat back and scratched the gray stubble on his chin. "When was the last time you spoke to your father?"

Tina stiffened. "What?"

"Your father." The sheriff's eyes gleamed with interest. "It should be an easy question."

"I haven't seen my father in twenty-five years," Tina stammered, clearly blindsided by the question.

"How is Mrs. Knox's father connected to Paul's murder?" Morgan asked.

"We don't know," the sheriff answered, then continued to question Tina. "Did Paul know about your father?"

"He did," Tina said. "Kirk and my father were the reasons he was going to put in a security system."

"I'm not following," Morgan interrupted. "How is Mrs. Knox's father relevant to Evan's disappearance or Paul's murder?"

"Joseph Martin was recently released from New Jersey State Prison after serving the entirety of a twenty-five-year sentence for murder and drug charges." Though answering Morgan's question, the sheriff never took his eyes off Tina. He tilted his head. "Is there a reason you didn't tell me about your father yesterday?"

"I didn't think of it," Tina said. "For the first few weeks after he got out, I didn't sleep, and Paul went to bed with his gun tucked under his pillow. But it's been over six months. I haven't received any threats or contact of any kind."

The sheriff flattened his palm on the table. "Do you know where he is?"

"No," Tina answered. "And if Joe doesn't know where *I* am, I'm not telling him. I changed my name when I moved to Grey's Hollow for that very reason."

"How did you know he'd been released?" The sheriff tapped a finger on the table.

Tina's gaze skittered away. "I was notified."

"Through VINE?" the sheriff asked.

"Yes." Tina stared at her clasped hands on her lap.

Victim Information and Notification Everyday was an automated system where crime victims could register to be notified if an offender was released or transferred. Offenders did not know who registered for notification. VINE was created after a Kentucky woman was murdered by her former boyfriend shortly after he was released on bail. No one told her he had been released. He had previously been jailed for kidnapping and raping her.

"VINE is for victims," the sheriff said. "Why were you registered?"

Tina lifted her chin and looked him square in the eyes. "Because I testified against him."

Chapter Twelve

Lance slid his phone under the table and sent Sharp a quick text, giving him the new information on Tina's background. Then Lance copied the message and sent it to his mother. Name changes were public information, like birth and death records, but Lance's mother might have to verify the paperwork with the county.

Lance wanted Tina's entire story double-checked. The bombshell she'd dropped had been a nuke. Her middle-class working-mom persona didn't mesh with that of a drug dealer's daughter.

Across the table from him, her body was a rigid line. Her face was tight, and two angry flushes of pink were the only spots of color on her face. "I was born in Newark, New Jersey. When I lived there, Newark had one of the highest murder rates in the entire country. The whole city was one giant drug market. People were getting shot every other day. Also, Joe wasn't really a father." She said his name with disdain. "My mother was fifteen when he knocked her up. He had other girlfriends—and other kids. He didn't care about any of them. He used the boys as runners and lookouts, grooming them to work in the business—the girls got worse." She looked away, the pain on her face disarming before she completely shut down.

Her eyes went blank. Lance had seen that expression before—one devoid of any emotion—on the faces of victims who'd suffered extreme trauma. He didn't want to imagine how she'd been used by her drug-dealing father.

"You have siblings?" The sheriff slid a small notepad and pen from his pocket.

"I don't know." Tina's voice was flat. "The two boys close to my age were both shot before they turned thirteen, but I had an older brother, Aaron, who was still living when I left. I had a half sister too, but she and her mother disappeared. I don't know what happened to them."

"Your father murdered someone?" Morgan asked.

"I've no doubt my father murdered many people. But I personally witnessed him kill one man who worked for him. The man tried to skim money off Joe's cut. Stupid." Tina stared down at her hands again. "Joe and a couple of his other men took him into the basement. They beat him, and then they put two bullets into his head. I was in the basement when they came down. Joe didn't know I was there or he probably would have killed me too."

Shot in the head. Just like Paul. Just like the body the Redhaven police pulled from the Deer River.

"How old were you?" Morgan asked.

"Sixteen at the time of the murder." Tina rubbed her hands. "Eighteen by the time it went to trial."

"Why were you in the basement?"

Tina's mouth twisted into a crooked frown. "Ironically, I was hiding from Joe and his men."

The girls got worse.

"Did he threaten you?" the sheriff asked.

"Joe didn't have to threaten anyone." Tina stared back at him, her eyes wide. "Joe was a known drug dealer. The police had been trying to convict him for years. I'd been taken into the police station for questioning before. The cops would threaten me with prosecution of all sorts of crimes, but I knew what would happen if I told the police anything. He ruled the whole neighborhood with terror. It was commonly known how he treated those who betrayed him. Anyone who even thought about snitching on Joe was killed in a way that deterred anyone else from considering testifying. Being imprisoned for life was not nearly as terrifying as being beheaded with a chain saw or dismembered alive." She stopped and swallowed.

Lance's gut wrenched. It was no wonder Tina had a hard time trusting anyone.

"Could you please get Tina some water, Sheriff?" Morgan asked.

The sheriff got up and left the room, returning in a minute with water bottles. He passed them out.

"Yet you agreed to testify against him," the sheriff prompted as soon as he'd sat down.

With a single nod, Tina continued talking in a flat voice. "I was at a point in my life when the idea of dying seemed better than living." She paused to meet each one of their eyes for a second, almost in challenge. "When I was fifteen, Joe gave me to one of his lieutenants as a reward." Her entire body shuddered with revulsion. "Tyson had appetites. A year of being raped and beaten regularly had changed my perspective."

She stopped to drink water. She screwed the top back on the bottle and set it on the table with a solid thunk. "Joe's weakness was his ego. He was confident that I'd never turn on him. At the same time, he was sadistic and enjoyed hurting and humiliating people. He had no respect for women and focused on putting his sons to work in his business. He never considered that he'd made my life so miserable that I no longer feared death—or him. I testified. He went to prison."

"But he never threatened you directly?" the sheriff asked.

Tina shook her head. "You would not ask that question if you'd seen the look in his eyes as I testified. He would have loved nothing more than to strangle me with his own hands at that very moment. Several of his lieutenants were in the courtroom. One of them mouthed 'You're dead' over and over."

The sheriff's face was grim, but he didn't look shocked. How much of Tina's story had he known? "Where did you go after the trial?"

"When I was younger, I worked under the table when I could and put away as much cash as possible, although Tyson found one of my hidey-holes once and beat me for keeping the money from him. After that, he required me to hand over my pay each week, but I always held some back." Tina picked up the bottle and began to peel off the label. "After the trial, I took the money I'd hidden and ran. I used the cheapest forms of public transportation, mostly transit trains and buses, and paid cash for everything. This was before 9-11. Transportation security and rules were more relaxed back then. I spent the first month just running. Never staying in the same place more than one night. I didn't have enough money to take me a great distance away, but the rural nature of Grey's Hollow made it feel much farther from Newark than it really was. Still, I was looking over my shoulder for a long time."

Morgan folded her hands on the table. "Did the prosecutor's office try to get you into the witness protection program?"

Tina's snort was filled with disgust. "Like I would have trusted them with my life. They put me in a safe house before the trial and had to move me three times because my location was leaked. I was better off on my own."

"But you haven't heard from Joe since he was released?" Lance wanted Tina to be clear.

"No." Tina shook her head. "I hope he doesn't even know where I am, which is why I didn't want anyone asking questions back in Newark. I don't want anyone reminding Joe that I exist or telling him where I am."

But Lance bet Joe already knew. In today's world of the internet, cameras, and constant connectivity, it wasn't that hard to find someone if they weren't making a massive effort to stay hidden. Tina had put down roots.

The sheriff stood. "Thank you for coming in, Mrs. Knox. I'm sure I'll have more questions."

Morgan followed Tina around the table toward the door.

Lance hung back. "I'll meet you at the car." He handed Morgan the keys to his Jeep. He wanted to have a cop-to-former-cop chat with the sheriff. He leaned close to her ear. "There are questions Tina should probably not hear."

Nodding, Morgan took the keys. "We'll be out back."

After the women left, the sheriff crossed his arms over his chest and glared at Lance. "What do you want?"

"The truth." Lance went for it. "Is Evan your only suspect?"

"No, but he is on the list." The sheriff dropped back into his chair. "Mrs. Knox wants to downplay the friction between Evan and Paul, but the neighbor heard the yelling and saw the boy take a swing at Paul. I'd call that a fight, even if Evan was the aggressor."

"Mrs. Knox explained the incident."

"Which doesn't change the fact that the kid is a hothead with impulse control issues."

"He isn't normally," Lance argued.

"But he could have been Monday night."

It was times like this when Lance missed being on the police force. He didn't enjoy being locked out of an investigation, begging for scraps of evidence. "What can you tell me about the autopsy? Frank would have moved Paul to the top of the list."

The sheriff sighed. "I can't share the results of the medical examiner's preliminary report at this time. After we've made an arrest, the suspect's attorney will receive the autopsy information."

Frustration filled Lance. Colgate wasn't going to cooperate. But Lance would find Evan if he had to go over, around, or through the sheriff's roadblocks.

"Maybe the shooting was an accident," Colgate suggested. "Accidental shootings happen to experienced gun handlers. By Mrs. Knox's own admission, Evan is a beginner."

Lance pictured the position of Paul's body. The shot to his abdomen had to have come first. The heavy bleeding indicated that Paul's heart had been pumping after he'd been shot. He'd definitely been alive. The bullet to Paul's head had hardly bled at all. That had likely stopped Paul's heart. Plus, the centering of the shot indicated the killer was close. Lance envisioned the killer standing over Paul, watching him bleed, and firing the head shot at close range while Paul lay helpless. The belly shot could have been an accident, but there was no way the head shot was unintentional. That had been a cold act, one that put Lance in mind of an execution or a hired killer.

This had been nothing short of murder.

"Do you really think a sixteen-year-old kid could have shot Paul in the head?" Lance asked.

"I've seen worse."

Sadly, so had Lance.

The sheriff tapped the manila file folder with a finger. "Maybe Paul and Evan got into a fight when Evan missed curfew. He'd ignored Paul's texts and calls. He was angry with his father and transferred that anger to Paul. The Glock was out because Paul had been cleaning it. Evan picked it up and shot Paul. He has a history of impulsive behavior."

"But I know this kid. He didn't do this." Lance paced the length of the table and back.

"You're letting your personal feelings interfere with your objectivity. If you were one of my deputies, I'd pull you from the case. You can't ignore evidence." Colgate's voice was calm and reasonable, the exact opposite of the emotional turmoil in Lance's head.

But Lance's instincts were screaming that they were missing the biggest part of the case, and Colgate was focusing on the pieces of evidence that supported his narrative.

The sheriff continued. "Paul was killed with a 9mm bullet, which is the same caliber as his own Glock. Paul's weapon is still missing, so we don't know if he was shot with his own gun or simply another gun of the same caliber."

"9mm is a common caliber," Lance argued. "If there aren't two guns, then why is Evan bleeding too?"

"We don't know that Evan was shot. You saw the broken glass in the kitchen. Maybe Paul and Evan got into a physical fight. Evan could have no more than a bloody nose." The sheriff studied Lance for a few seconds. "Why do you think Mrs. Knox is holding back information? She didn't tell me about the fighting between Evan and Paul. She also forgot to mention her father is a recently released felon."

"She didn't think either one of those things was related to Evan's disappearance."

The sheriff's head-tilt and eyebrow-lift said he didn't believe Lance's answer. "Or she is worried that her son is guilty, which would also explain why she called you before she called the police when she found Paul's body."

Lance had no comment. Most people *would* have called 911 first.

"She knew you'd bring a criminal defense attorney."

"Tina had no way of knowing that when she called me," Lance said.

"It was a good bet. You and Ms. Dane live and work together. You always support each other." The sheriff gathered his papers, indicating their discussion was over. "Finding Evan would be a hell of a lot easier if Mrs. Knox didn't make me drag every bit of information out of her."

Lance left the conference room more frustrated than when he'd gone in. The sheriff was right on all counts. Evan was a natural suspect.

He'd been at the house at the time of death, which gave him opportunity. Paul's gun provided the means, and the argument with Paul was motive.

But Lance couldn't believe Evan capable of murdering Paul. The boy was an impulsive hothead, not a cool, cunning killer. Anything Evan did would have been unplanned and sloppily executed.

Which actually described the sheriff's theory of Paul's murder perfectly.

Chapter Thirteen

Sharp's feet hit the pavement in a sloppy rhythm. His stride felt slug-gish. He'd waited until the sun went down to run. Why the hell did he feel like he'd been run over by a bus?

The heat wasn't helping. Well into the evening, the temperature was still above eighty degrees, and humidity hovered somewhere around 1,000 percent. He felt like he was jogging through soup.

He passed the bank and turned right. His duplex sat in the business district of town. He loved the convenience and small-town ambience. Old houses lined the streets. Branches of mature trees arced overhead. Before he'd been injured back in March, he'd run a brisk five miles every day and hit the gym a few times a week for strength training.

But he'd been cleared for a short jog only a few weeks ago, and strength training was limited to his twice-weekly supervised sessions with his physical therapist. At first, the restrictions had irritated him, but now he was more concerned that he couldn't exceed them if he wanted to.

His strides slowed at the next intersection. From the corner, he could see Olivia Cruz's little white bungalow at the end of the block. Olivia had provided a few key pieces of information in their last case. In turn, Morgan had granted her an interview for the true crime novel

Olivia was writing about one of Morgan's previous clients, with the client's permission of course.

But the flow of information hadn't been even, and Sharp was in Olivia's debt.

Since he'd been given the go-ahead to jog, he'd jogged down her street every day. Before that, he'd driven past at every opportunity . . . like a teenager with a crush. He was a former cop. She was a *reporter*. The word rumbled through his head with the same distaste as *demon*.

There was something seriously wrong with him.

He put his perverse attraction aside and turned his feet in the opposite direction. Not because he didn't want to see Olivia—because he was an idiot and totally did—but because he didn't want her to see him in his current state of physical inadequacy.

By the time he'd slowed to a walk a block away from his place, sweat soaked his T-shirt and the humidity clogged his lungs. Two miles had seemed like seven. He climbed the steps to his second-story apartment and went inside, grateful for the air-conditioning. He filled a glass with water. A quick rush of fatigue hit him. Even alone, he was embarrassed that he had to sit down, drink the water, and wait for the weakness to pass.

Needing energy, he whipped up a high-calorie, nutrient-dense protein shake. He took the drink with him to the bathroom. Stripping off his wet clothes, he stepped under the spray. The ropey pink scar that wrapped around his belly itched when the water ran over it.

The calories in the shake gave him some pep, but he still wanted to take a nap more than go back to work. However, he dressed in jeans and a T-shirt, then filled a travel mug with green tea before heading out the door. He'd promised Lance he'd check on Jenny tonight. He'd be damned if he'd let Lance down. He'd been enough of a deadweight for the last three months. Lance had completely carried the business for the first two months, and even then, Sharp had returned part time for the next four weeks. The injury had kicked his ass much harder than he'd anticipated.

It was nine o'clock before Sharp knocked on Jenny Kruger's door, much later than he'd intended. He waited, the evening heat wrapping around him like a wet wool blanket.

Mental illness had kept Jenny in the same one-story house outside of town for more than twenty-five years, even though moving to town would have made life much easier for her son after her husband had disappeared when Lance was ten. Jenny's symptoms had worsened over the years. Now she left her home only for group therapy sessions and appointments with her psychiatrist.

Sharp waved at the security camera. A moment later, Jenny opened the door. She nervously glanced up and down the country road before stepping back and admitting Sharp to the house. She was thin and fragile looking, with shoulder-length white hair and a stooped posture that reflected her insecurities. Mental illness had worn on her, adding years to her physical age, and she looked much older than sixty.

He gave her a quick hug, noticing how her shoulder blades seemed more prominent. Then he handed her the strawberry shortcake he'd bought at the farm stand on the way to her house. Normally, he didn't approve of added sugar. But her illness and medications affected her appetite. She was a picky eater and needed calories any way she could get them.

When Lance's father had gone missing, Sharp had been the SFPD detective investigating the case. It hadn't taken long before he'd learned that Jenny wasn't capable of caring for her son without help. Sharp had looked after the boy, making sure he got to hockey practice and giving him a place to stay when Lance needed a break from his mother's illness or when Jenny was incapacitated. The timing had been fortuitous. Sharp had been at a bad place in his own personal life. They'd all needed each other. Now Jenny and Lance were the closest thing to family in Sharp's life.

"You look a little pale." Jenny studied him. "Are you feeling all right?"

"I'm fine," Sharp lied.

"I could make you some tea." She stocked his favorite organic green.

"I just had some, but thanks."

They walked down the hall into the kitchen. She stopped to reset the alarm system on the panel in the pantry. A short hallway led to the three bedrooms, one of which had been converted to an office. An L-shaped desk held a bank of monitors.

"I'm glad you stopped by." Jenny sat behind her desk.

Sharp settled into one of the two chairs facing her desk. "How's Kevin?"

"Very well, thank you." She clicked on her keyboard. She was currently engaged in a relationship with a man she'd met in group therapy. They saw each other once a week in person but video-conferenced every day. The relationship might seem odd to an outsider, but it made her happy.

Sharp had nothing but respect for Jenny. She'd been handed a raw deal, but she lived her life as best she could. In recent years, she'd worked hard to lessen her dependence on Lance.

"I was just about to call you," she said. "I verified Tina Knox's story and uncovered some additional information."

"I knew you would."

She smiled. "Before Tina's father was arrested for the murder, a young member of his organization confessed to the killing. At the trial, Tina stated that the boy had been instructed to take the hit for her father. The boy was thirteen. He would be tried as a juvenile. His penalty would be less. The murder weapon had been placed in his hand, so his fingerprints were on it. The boy was present at the execution, so he could describe the scene in detail. The organization promised to look after the boy's mother and younger siblings until he got out. Plus, if he refused, they would have killed him. They planned the false confession right after the murder. But Tina was a witness. She heard it all, and her testimony put her father in prison."

"Where did you get all this information?"

"Once I had Joe Martin's name, the details were easy to find. The case was big news at the time." Jenny's fingers flew across her keyboard. "There were numerous articles, but the best source was a *New York Times* piece with interviews of unnamed former drug dealers in Newark. I'll email you a copy. The *New York Times*'s website makes articles available as far back as 1851. It's fascinating."

Jenny's mental illness often took center stage. It was easy to forget that she was an unusually intelligent woman. She managed to make a good living without leaving her house. She taught online computer classes and ran her own business in website design, maintenance, and security. She also did much of the virtual legwork on their big cases. Sometimes Sharp forgot how much she needed to be useful.

She continued. "Joe Martin is linked to multiple businesses. Some seem legitimate. He owns a flooring company, a chain of pizza parlors, and a clothing manufacturer. There's a real estate holding company and at least a dozen shell companies through which he likely launders some of his drug money. Some of these businesses are now being run by Joe's son, Aaron Martin."

Jenny clicked her mouse. "Tina has kept a low profile since she moved to Grey's Hollow. She has no criminal record in New York State. She has been employed at the hospital for eleven years. Before that, she worked in a surgical center."

"What about her ex, Kirk Meade?"

"He's a piece of work." Jenny opened a new document. "Paroled a few months ago after serving three years for assault. Before that, he had a string of misdemeanors. Even before his incarceration, his employment history is spotty, with more gaps than actual working time. He currently works as a forklift operator for ABC Furniture."

"He's a lazy bum," Sharp muttered. "No wonder he's angry that Tina divorced him. He has to earn his own keep now."

"Next up, Paul Knox." Jenny's voice softened. "I found nothing. He lived in Grey's Hollow all his life. His twenty-five-year record with the sheriff's department is spotless. Paul was as clean as a bar of soap."

"But someone killed him. They must have had a reason."

"But that reason might not have been something Paul did," Jenny pointed out.

Did Paul have dirt on someone else?

"I have one more thing I want you to look into." Sharp pulled out his notes on Brian Springer and told Jenny what he needed. "The neighbor said the property is owned by a brother or brother-in-law and is on a lake. I know it seems like a needle-in-a-haystack situation, but it's all I have."

"I'll see what I can do." Jenny made a copy of his notes on the copier behind her desk. She handed the original back to him.

Jenny took her hands from the keyboard and leaned back in her chair. "I haven't started on Steve Duncan yet, but I'll tackle his records tomorrow morning after Brian Springer."

Duncan, Jake's quasi guardian, was at the bottom of Sharp's suspect list.

"Could you try and find any information on a man named Sam Jones who was arrested by the Randolph County Sheriff's Department between six and twelve months ago? He sued the county and Deputy Brian Springer for use of excessive force."

"Yes." Jenny made a note.

Sharp stood. "Thanks, Jenny. No one is as thorough and quick as you."

Jenny blushed. "I'm happy to help. I enjoy the work. I don't like to be idle."

"I'm sure we'll have additional names for you to run as the investigation proceeds."

Jenny followed him out of the room and walked him to the door. Once outside, he heard the dead bolt slide home.

Sharp texted Lance from the car, eager to share the news about Tina's father. Then he headed for the office. As he stepped out of his vehicle into the heat and humidity, another spot of fatigue washed over him. *What the hell?* He was almost tired enough to break into Morgan's coffee and donut stash.

Instead, he went inside, grabbed an orange from the kitchen, and took it to his desk. Jenny had emailed him detailed reports and photographs of everyone. He skimmed through them. Sometimes, a clue wasn't so obvious as a criminal history. But nothing jumped out at him.

He downloaded the *New York Times* article Jenny had sent him. It was a lengthy piece, part of the newspaper's expanded Sunday edition. His gaze dropped to the byline under the article headline and shock gave him a quick buzz of energy.

By Olivia Cruz

Excitement stirred in his gut. He tried to squash it and failed. He should not be looking forward to asking her for yet another favor.

But he was.

Chapter Fourteen

In the passenger seat of the Jeep, Morgan drummed her fingers on her thigh. One thought dominated her mind as she watched Lance walk across the sheriff station's parking lot toward the vehicle.

Tina keeps too many secrets.

Lance opened the driver's door and slid behind the wheel. Looking up, he frowned. "Is that Esposito?"

"Where?" Morgan's gaze darted back to the sheriff station.

A dark-haired man in a slick gray suit crossed the asphalt.

"That's him," she said.

In the back seat, Tina sat bolt upright. "Who is Esposito?"

Morgan answered, "Assistant District Attorney Anthony Esposito."

"Why would the ADA be at the sheriff station?" Lance asked.

His tone implied he did not think it was a coincidence that Esposito had been in the station while the sheriff was questioning Tina. Morgan glanced at Lance. He stared through the windshield, his eyes narrowed with suspicion.

"I don't know." Lance started the engine. "But I don't like it."

Lance didn't like Esposito. Period.

"He ran into a burning building with you," Morgan pointed out. On their last case, Esposito had backed them up when it had counted.

Lance shrugged. He was not convinced the ADA had good qualities.

"We don't know that his presence has anything to do with Evan's case." But Morgan was pretty sure it did. "He's the prosecutor. He could be here for any number of reasons."

Lance's snort was not in agreement.

Tina fastened her seat belt. "I don't trust the sheriff. He seems more interested in Evan and Paul's arguments than in finding who killed Paul."

Morgan twisted in the passenger seat to face her. "I don't like the sheriff focusing on Evan and Paul's arguments either."

Lance glanced in the rearview mirror. "Is there any other reason you didn't tell the sheriff about the arguments between Paul and Evan?"

"No." Tina's eyes shone with anger. "I didn't think they were important. There wasn't a huge rift between Evan and Paul. Twenty minutes after that argument, Paul and Evan had a heart-to-heart about it. Evan liked Paul. He was just upset that night."

Knowing Evan, Morgan thought Tina's explanation was plausible.

"What about your father?" Morgan asked. "Why did you keep that a secret?"

Tina's gaze dropped to her lap. "Because I don't want anyone contacting him. He hasn't come after me. Maybe he's just too old to care anymore. Whatever the reason, I'd like to keep it that way." Tina lifted her head. "Do you think they have other suspects? Or are they focusing only on Evan?"

Lance stopped at a traffic light. "The police can't rule anyone out in the initial phases of an investigation. I'd hoped Evan would be cleared quickly, but the initial evidence isn't helping. Honestly, if I didn't know Evan, *I'd* think he was guilty too."

"It's not fair." Tina shoved both hands through her hair. "Evan gets judged all the time, especially by cops, because of a couple of stupid mistakes he made when his father went to prison. Like vandalism and murder are anywhere close to the same thing." She pinched the bridge of her nose. "What am I going to do?"

"You're not alone," Morgan assured her.

"You're a lawyer, right?" Tina gnawed on a cuticle.

"Yes," Morgan said. "But if you want me to represent Evan, you have to answer all my questions honestly. No more holding back information."

Tina rolled her fingers into a fist. "If you're my lawyer, then everything I tell you is confidential, right?"

"Yes," Morgan answered.

Tina glanced at Lance.

"As my agent, Sharp Investigations is also bound by client confidentiality," Morgan explained.

"Then I want to officially hire you." Tina lowered her hand. "I need someone to protect Evan and me. I can give you a retainer. I have a little money put aside."

Morgan waved a hand. "We'll worry about payment later."

In a worst-case scenario, Morgan would defend the boy pro bono. She'd done it before. She would do it again. Her sense of justice didn't make her firm solvent, but money wouldn't stop her from helping someone she viewed as being wrongly accused.

"You left Newark after the trial. How did you get your nursing degree?" Morgan asked.

"The university was one of the reasons I chose Grey's Hollow," Tina said. "Lots of students meant cheap, flexible housing. No one asked questions if you didn't have any money. I found a job working in the university cafeteria and rented a room just off campus. I went to night school. I was pretty far behind, so getting my GED took years. But because I was a university employee, the tuition was free. Eventually, I applied to the nursing program and was accepted."

"You must have worked very hard," Morgan said with respect.

"The definition of *hard* is relative." Tina exhaled. "I had a roof over my head and a bed of my very own. Most days, I had something to eat. No one beat or raped me. Life was pretty good."

That Morgan believed.

"Are you sure you want to stay at the hotel?" Lance asked Tina. "Sharp has a guest room."

"I like the hotel." She rested her head on the back of the seat. "No one knows I'm there. The sheriff registered me under a different name."

"Let's stop for food on the way back to the hotel."

Tina pressed the heels of her hands to her eyes. "I couldn't."

Morgan doubted she'd eaten since she found Paul.

"You need to eat something," Morgan said. "Or you'll be ill. Does your room have a microwave?"

"Yes," Tina answered. "The room is a suite. There's a small kitchen."

"Then we'll stop for a few basics." Lance stopped at a convenience store and went inside. Morgan watched the parking lot the whole time he was in the store. He returned to the Jeep and set a bag on the center console.

"Are you sure there isn't a friend we can call for you?" Morgan hated to leave her alone.

Tina turned to the window. "There's no one."

She had no friends? She'd been close to no one except Paul? Tina had claimed that Paul had known about her criminal father, but had he? Morgan wanted to believe her. Tina had admitted she'd held back information. Had she lied as well?

Tina took her phone from her purse and checked it, shoving it back inside with frustration and disappointment. "I wish I could *do* something."

Morgan studied the woman's face. Bags gathered under her eyes. Her dark hair was limp. Tina looked as if she'd aged five years since she'd first called Lance for help.

"Did you get any rest today?" Morgan asked.

Tina sighed. "No. I drove around the lake, then town, like I'd see him on the street. It was stupid, but I couldn't sit still."

Morgan understood. Inaction created its own tension and stress. "I know it will be hard to sleep, but you should try to get some rest tonight. You will not help your son by getting sick. We'll touch base again in the morning."

"All right." Tina's sigh quivered. "But tomorrow, I'm going out looking for my son again."

Morgan would do the same. No one could keep her from searching for one of her kids.

Lance exited the interstate and parked in front of a chain residence-type hotel.

"What name are you booked under?" Morgan asked.

"Smith. The sheriff isn't very original." Tina climbed out of the car.

Lance and Morgan exchanged a knowing glance, both reaching for their door handles. Tina was a grown woman, and the choice to be alone was hers. But Morgan and Lance would make sure the hotel room was safe before leaving her.

"We'll walk you in," Lance said.

They bypassed the main lobby and went in a side door using Tina's card key.

"Wait here. Let me check the room first." Handing Morgan the grocery bag, Lance took the key and went in.

Morgan put her back to the wall and watched the hallway in both directions.

Lance returned in a minute. "It's clear."

They went inside. The room had a tiny kitchen and living area combined, with a separate bedroom and bath.

Tina wandered a few steps into the suite, looking lost. "I know you don't understand why I need to be alone. It's just my way. Paul didn't always understand either, but he let me be. I'm not a social person."

"You don't have to explain." Morgan would have hidden from the world after her husband died, but her family wouldn't let her completely isolate herself. "Everyone is different."

Tina nodded. She set her purse on the kitchen table. Her body stiffened.

"What is it?" Lance took two long steps and stood next to her.

"An envelope." Tina pointed to the table.

Morgan looked past Lance's shoulder. A letter-size white envelope sat in the middle of the table. It was addressed to *Mrs. Smith* with her room number and the hotel address. The letter had been postmarked in Scarlet Falls and dated the same day.

"Maybe it's from the sheriff." But as she said the words, Tina backed away from it.

"He would have told you if he'd sent you a letter," Morgan said. "And any written communication from the sheriff's department would be on official stationery."

Lance patted his pockets. "Do you have gloves?" he asked Morgan. She pulled a set from her tote and handed them to him.

He put them on before picking up the envelope. He went to the kitchen and took a knife from a top drawer. He used the blade to slit the flap. He pulled out a single piece of paper.

Blocky print spelled out I KNOW WHERE YOU ARE in all capital letters.

Tina flinched as if she'd been struck. "How? How did someone find me?"

"There are only a few hotels reasonably close to your house. It probably wasn't that hard." Lance snapped a picture of the note and the front of the envelope, then slid the paper back inside. "Let's go down to the lobby and see how that envelope got in here."

He led the way out of the room and down the hall. The registration clerk waved as they walked into the lobby. "Mrs. Smith. Your husband called for you."

Tina froze. Her eyes widened as she turned toward the desk. By the time she reached it, her face was the same color as the pale-gray tiles. Without any communication, Morgan and Lance separated to put Tina between them.

"He said he would be in later this evening," the clerk said in a chipper voice. "Would you like to leave a key for him here at the desk?"

"No!" Tina leaned both palms flat on the counter, as if she needed it to support herself. She took one long breath in and released it, visibly composing herself. "My husband is dead."

The clerk paled. "I'm s-sorry. Then how?" He looked from Tina to Morgan and Lance. "Maybe it was a mistake."

"Do you have more than one Mrs. Smith staying at the hotel?" Morgan asked.

The clerk typed on his computer and leaned closer to his screen. "No."

Morgan pointed out, "Then it wasn't a mistake."

With gloved hands, Lance raised the envelope. "How did this get in Mrs. Smith's room?"

"It came for her here at the hotel." The clerk adjusted his glasses. "I had housekeeping deliver it to her room."

"No one is supposed to know Mrs. Smith is at the hotel," Lance said.

"Hey, no one told me." The clerk focused on Tina. "What do you want me to do?"

"I don't know." Tina's words trembled.

"Did you give him any information?" Lance's voice was clipped.

"No, sir." A bead of sweat broke out on the clerk's upper lip. "That would be against company policy."

Morgan put an arm around Tina's shoulders and steered her away from the counter. "Let's go sit down. Lance will call Sheriff Colgate. He'll have to move you."

Lance walked a few feet away, his cell phone pressed to his ear.

"I need to get my things." Tina's body shook under Morgan's arm.

"Later." Morgan led her across the lobby, away from the door and windows to the tables where the hotel served a free breakfast buffet every morning and offered coffee and tea round the clock. Morgan picked a table in the corner. She steered Tina into a chair, then made her a cup of hot tea. She pressed it into Tina's shaking hands.

Tina wrapped her fingers around the cardboard cup. Morgan went back to the alcove and poured herself a cup of coffee.

Lance appeared next to their table. "He's sending a couple of deputies. They're going to take you to a new hotel, and you'll have a deputy with you 24/7."

Tears leaked from Tina's eyes. "But I want to be out looking for Evan."

"We'll take care of that," Lance assured her. "You stay safe. When we find him, he's going to need you. He's been through a lot."

She didn't look convinced.

Morgan pointed out the one thing that would get through to Tina. "If something happens to you, Kirk will get custody of Evan."

Tina's shoulders caved forward. "OK."

They stayed with her until the deputies arrived and took charge. They put the note in a plastic evidence bag.

Despite the coffee, Morgan was bone-weary as she climbed back into the Jeep. "Do you want to go back to the office?" she asked.

"No." Lance glanced at his watch. "It's past nine o'clock. Let's take a run by Scarlet Lake. Damn it. We already missed bedtime."

Morgan's house sat on the Scarlet River, which ran into Scarlet Lake, so the lake was close to home.

"It's all right. I checked in with the girls while you talked to the sheriff. Mia and Ava seem to be fully recovered from the virus. Gianna gave them their baths. Grandpa read them their bedtime story. They're not neglected by any means."

Lately, Lance was their choice to read bedtime stories, though they were happy enough when their great-grandfather took over.

"*I'm* the one who minds missing bedtime." Lance reached across the console and took her hand. "Before we started dating, I had no idea how attached I would get to the kids."

Three months ago, Lance had moved in with Morgan, and she'd accepted his marriage proposal. He'd become a part of their lives. He drove the girls to playdates and walked them to the bus stop in the morning.

Morgan smiled. "They do grow on you."

"I can't imagine going back to living alone."

"Good thing you don't have to."

Morgan thought of Tina and her absolute despair when she'd thought her son had died. At this moment, she was all alone in a hotel room, worrying about Evan, maybe afraid to hope that he was still alive. If he wasn't, she'd have to live through his death all over again.

"I'd really like to set a date for the wedding," Lance said.

Morgan sighed. She should be excited about getting married, but every time she started thinking about plans, memories of her first wedding intruded. John had died in Iraq more than three years ago, but she still saw him smiling at the altar in his uniform and holding each of the babies when they'd been born. Then she saw his flag-draped casket being unloaded from the plane. She loved Lance with all her heart. But she'd never stopped loving John either. His death had devastated her. *Damn it.*

How could she resolve feelings she didn't truly understand? "We have so much going on right now. Can we get through the renovations and then plan the wedding?"

"Grant says the kitchen reno will take three months. The addition at least another three."

"So nine months." That was a long time to put off setting a date.

"Three plus three equals six."

"Not in contractor time." Morgan shook her head. "Haven't you ever watched HGTV?"

"Do you want to wait that long?"

"You don't?"

"Not really." Lance frowned. "I was hoping we'd be married this year."

"It's already June." A tiny sliver of panic raced through Morgan's stomach. "Do you have any idea how long it takes to plan a wedding?"

"Apparently, I do not."

When they were halfway to the lake, rain began to fall on the windshield. A minute later, lightning flashed and thunder boomed. By the time they arrived, the rain had turned into a downpour, and the parking lot was empty.

Wedding details swirled in Morgan's head. "Let me call my sister and think about it. We don't need anything too fancy."

"If you want fancy, we'll do fancy." Lance released her hand to shift into park. "I can wait."

"Do you want fancy?" she asked. "You've never actually said where or how you'd like to get married."

He turned to face her. "I want you to have whatever you want for our wedding."

"That's not an answer." She sighed. Their wedding was *their* day, not *her* day.

Silence ticked by for a few seconds. She listened to the sound of rain beating on the roof of the car. After John had been killed, Morgan had sunk into a dark place for two years. She'd quit her job at the prosecutor's office in Albany. She'd moved back into her grandfather's house with her girls. She'd hidden from life for a very long time. But Lance had changed all that. She was living—and loving—again.

She was thrilled to be engaged to Lance, but she hadn't realized how many sad memories their engagement would bring back. Maybe she hadn't fully let go of John. How did one do that? She'd better figure it out or she'd ruin her second chance of happiness. Lance deserved better. He asked for so little from her and gave so much.

This was her issue, and she would have to deal with it.

"Let's get back to finding Evan," she said.

They climbed out of the car. Morgan opened an umbrella and held it over her head as they walked past the playground and picnic tables to the beach.

Lance ignored the rain. The downpour quickly plastered his hair to his head.

The sandy area spanned about a hundred feet of lakeshore. In the middle, smoke plumed from a pile of charred wood, the remnants of a very recent bonfire.

"We just missed whoever was partying out here." Lance kicked a branch. They could not catch a break.

Morgan stared out over the lake.

Evan, where are you?

Chapter Fifteen

Unable to sleep, Lance rolled onto his back and studied the dark ceiling. No matter how hard he tried to put Evan's face out of his mind, it didn't work. He checked the time on the nightstand clock. One a.m.

Evan had been missing for just over twenty-four hours.

Next to him, Morgan hogged three-quarters of the bed and blankets. She was not a nighttime cuddler but slept with her long limbs sprawled out on the queen-size bed.

Distant thunder cracked softly, but Morgan didn't stir. She had the unique ability to sleep through loud noises, but she woke up instantly at a single peep from one of the girls. It was as if she was tuned only to their frequency. He wouldn't wake her. She'd been exhausted from dealing with a week of sickness.

He turned over onto his side, but sleep wouldn't come. There was no point lying there. Useless. When he'd lived alone, he would have gotten up, poured a glass of whiskey, and played his piano to relax. But his piano had burned to ashes with his house when it had been set on fire three months before.

Needing to move, he eased out of bed. The dogs slept around Morgan's feet. Snoozer didn't budge. Rocket lifted one irritated eyelid, sighed, and closed it again. Lance grabbed dark pants, a T-shirt, and socks from a basket of clean laundry in the corner, then crept from the bedroom. As he passed the dining room, he snagged an energy bar and a bottle of water from the makeshift kitchen. His boots stood in the rubber tray by the front door. Carrying them, he let himself out of the house, being careful to lock up and reset the alarm system.

The downpour had slowed to a steady drizzle. The only remaining sign of the storm was the occasional flash of lightning and the quiet crack of thunder as the storm moved away. Water puddled on the ground and dripped from trees. He put on his boots and climbed into his Jeep. He needed a plan. He could cruise by the lake again, but there were no buildings at the beach. Evan was a smart kid. He would find somewhere to get out of the rain.

Where would Evan take shelter in the storm? If Evan were able, he'd contact one of his friends for help.

Jake? Or Rylee?

Lance thought of Steve Duncan's farm, with its big barn and numerous outbuildings. Lots of potential places for a teenage boy to hide there. Jake could come and go as he pleased. If Evan were hiding on the farm or somewhere else, Jake would visit him at nighttime. Lance couldn't see Jake going to Steve for help in hiding or feeding Evan. Hiding a runaway minor would be breaking the law, and Steve was a rule-following kind of guy. In fact, Jake would likely be afraid that Steve would kick him off the farm for such an infraction.

Lance decided to drive toward the farm. At the end of his and Morgan's road, the river had spilled over its banks and across the pavement. He had to backtrack and leave the neighborhood through the other exit. He made a note to check the crawl space for water. Morgan's house sat high above the riverbank, but the rain had been relentless for the past few weeks.

As he approached the farm, his headlights shone on a car parked alongside the road in the shadow of the overhanging branches of a large tree. Lance noted the vehicle's details in the brief second his headlights illuminated it. Dark four-door sedan. He couldn't tell what make or model. Shadow of a driver behind the wheel. But the car was angled to provide the driver a better view of the farm's driveway through its windshield, and Lance did not get a read on the license plate.

Cops drove unmarked four-door sedans. Could a county detective be watching Jake? The sheriff could have easily come to the same conclusion as Lance.

He drove past the vehicle without slowing. He continued driving for a half mile until the road curved enough that the sedan driver would not see him stop. Then he pulled the Jeep off the road, ironically tucking it into a shadow for concealment, just like the driver of the sedan had.

He killed the engine and turned off the dome light. The rain would help conceal him, but light would be too visible in the country. Lance reached behind the seat for the black watch cap he used to cover his bright-blond hair. He located his penlight in the center console, then got out of the vehicle. A large flashlight was useless when one wanted to remain invisible at night. He didn't bother with rain gear. Nylon was noisy and cumbersome.

He estimated the cleared land of the farm to be about fifty acres. Woods surrounded the fenced area. If Lance ran within the tree line, the sedan driver would not see him. He crossed the road and jogged through the trees in a huge arc. The humid air made the eighty-degree night feel much hotter. Rain and sweat soaked his T-shirt. When he emerged from the trees, he made sure the barn was between him and the sedan.

He stood in the shadows for a few minutes, scanning the area. Nothing moved. The pastures were empty. The barn doors were rolled halfway open, probably for ventilation in the summer heat. He could hear the steady patter of rain and the occasional snort of a horse from inside the barn.

Lance crept to the first building, a large shed. He cracked the door a few inches. The dusty smell of hay and straw hit his nose. He slipped inside, his boots scraping on the concrete slab. A few high windows provided scant light. He waited for his eyes to adjust to the dimness. Bales of hay and straw were stacked in neat rows. Wooden pallets kept the stacks off the floor. Something scurried in the darkness. Rats? Cats? Probably both. The bales were well organized, leaving no real spaces to hide. He used his penlight sparingly, taking care that its beam was always pointed toward the ground, and hoping it wasn't visible to the cop on the road.

He slipped back outside into the rain. A four-bay garage stood to his right. Crouching, Lance jogged across the muddy ground to the side entrance. A heavy-duty padlock secured the door. He tried one of the four overhead rolling doors, but it didn't budge. High windows were placed eight feet off the ground. They would provide light without compromising security. Lance walked under one, jumped, and caught the sill with his fingertips. Chinning himself, he looked inside. The space was dark, but he could make out the shape of a tractor, some other outdoor equipment, and a lot of empty concrete. What appeared to be large tools were hung on a wall, but this space was also ruthlessly organized. He saw nowhere to hide.

Lowering himself, he dropped to the ground. He picked his way across the mud to a long, rectangular building. The sliding door stood open. Lance glanced inside. Rain echoed on the metal roof. The space was open and the ceiling high. From the circular patterns of hoofprints in the soft soil, he assumed it was a small riding arena for inclement-weather training.

Which left the barn to be searched.

Lance peered around the doorframe. Horses snorted and shuffled in straw. He entered quietly. A cat wound around his ankles, purring. He walked down the aisle, pointing his penlight through the bars of each stall. The last space was an open wash stall, with a concrete floor, hoses with hot and cold taps, and a large drain. Lance went up the ladder and checked the loft, but all he saw were more bales of hay and straw. He came down and checked the stalls on the opposite side of the aisle. He saw two more cats and eleven horses but no teenage boy. He ducked into a feed room, using his penlight to look behind the bins. Empty. Then he went into a tack room. Saddles and bridles hung on racks. Two large chests stood against the opposite wall. Lance risked his penlight to check beneath the saddle racks. He turned, nearly bumping into a sink. Dark streaks in the bottom caught his eye. Was that blood?

He clicked on his penlight and was almost disappointed to see the stain was rust, not blood.

Something scuffed on the floor behind him. Lance pivoted. His hand went to his holster, his thumb sliding the safety straps out of the way. A dark shape whipped at his head. He turned and tried to block the blow. It struck him across the back of the head and shoulders. Pain ricocheted through his skull, his vision dimmed, and he pitched face-first toward the floor. The penlight flew from his hand. He landed on the wooden floor with a jaw-rattling impact that shook his gun free of the holster and sent it skittering across the floor. It disappeared under a large chest.

Lance blinked his vision clear. His attacker was standing next to him. He wore black athletic shoes and dark clothes. The darkness—and the NVGs strapped to his head so he could better see in the dark—concealed his face. Lance knew only two things. He needed to get his own night vision goggles, and his attacker wasn't a cop. Anyone with legal authority would have arrested him. He wasn't Steve either. The property owner would have called the police, not wrestled with him. Plus, even in the dark, Lance could see that this man wasn't big enough to be Steve Duncan. Lance looked for a weapon, but it was too dark to see if the man was carrying a gun. He held some sort of tool in one hand. The other hand appeared empty. If he were armed, Lance hoped he wouldn't want the sound of a gunshot to attract attention.

"Who are you?" the man asked in a low, harsh voice.

"Who are *you*?" Lance kicked the man's feet out from under his body. He went down hard and landed on the floor with a grunt. Lance rolled toward him, grabbing a pant leg and pulling the man toward him. The man kicked Lance's hand. Pain forced his fingers to release their grip.

The attacker rolled onto his hands and knees, then got to his feet. Lance levered a foot under his body. He stayed low, bending his knees, readying himself for his opponent's next attack. The man adjusted the NVGs on his face and circled to the left. Lance moved as well, toward the saddles. He spotted his penlight on the floor under the saddle rack.

Is this the man who killed Paul?

Is he now after Evan?

The man reached into his pocket and withdrew something. Lance squinted in the darkness. A knife? A soft click confirmed a switchblade, and an extra jolt of adrenaline shot into Lance's veins.

The attacker lunged, sweeping the blade toward Lance's belly. Lance jumped back, twisting his body just in time to avoid the flick of the knife. The man lunged again, the switchblade stabbing at Lance's face. Lance blocked, forearm to forearm. Pain zinged through his arm as their bones connected. His attacker fell back, then rallied.

Lance dove for the ground, and his fingers closed on the penlight. He rolled back to his feet just as the knife came at his belly. But Lance clicked the penlight on and shone it directly into his attacker's NVGs. The amplified light would be blinding. The man's lunge faltered, and he raised one hand to block the light.

Lance went for the knife hand with an outward sweep of his forearm. He continued to circle his hand, hooking it around and over the attacker's arm and trapping it against his own shoulder. Then he shoved the man's upper body backward and kicked his feet in the opposite direction. The assailant went down on his ass and lost his grip on the knife. It fell to the floor.

Lance moved toward him. The son of a bitch was his.

The man reached behind him and pulled a handgun from the small of his back. He pointed it at Lance's head. Lance froze, his hands rising in front of his body, palms facing his opponent. His attacker backed toward the exit, glancing behind him, then disappeared through the doorway. Lance stumbled into the aisle. But the man was gone. He heard the retreating slap of shoes in mud as the man ran away.

Lance's vision had begun to clear, but he was in no shape to give chase, especially not unarmed. He returned to the tack room. Kneeling on the floor, he swept a hand under the chest and retrieved his handgun. Sliding it into its holster, he contemplated his next move. If he called the sheriff, would he get arrested?

Possibly.

Would the sheriff even believe him?

Not likely.

The sheriff might be able to talk Steve Duncan into filing trespassing charges or Colgate would stick Lance in a holding cell for interfering with his case. Morgan could get Lance out, but all that would take time away from finding Evan.

Lance couldn't take the chance. He wouldn't be able to find Evan from a jail cell.

The sheriff had his own agenda, and he'd made it clear that it was the opposite of Lance's. Colgate wasn't a dirty cop, but his mind was made up. This time, Lance couldn't trust the sheriff to have his back.

Also, Lance did not want Jake to know he'd searched the farm. If the boy were helping Evan, Lance wanted him to feel safe doing so. Lance could follow him another day. Plus, he didn't want Jake to abandon helping Evan.

Lance made sure the tack room showed no sign of their struggle. Then he slipped out into the darkness. The trip back through the woods to his car seemed much longer than his initial approach. The rain had increased to a downpour. He slogged through the mud back to his Jeep.

It was four thirty when he climbed into his vehicle. Morgan would be up within the hour. He turned the Jeep toward home. Originally, he'd intended to slip back into the house so she wouldn't know he'd left. He doubted that could happen now. He touched the throbbing knot at the back of his head and felt a lump rising.

She was going to be pissed and rightfully so. He'd gone alone, nearly been stabbed, and possibly let the man who had killed Paul escape.

Chapter Sixteen

Morgan chugged her first cup of coffee standing in front of the pot and immediately poured another. At four forty-five in the morning, anger and worry had already cleared the sleep from her head.

Where was Lance?

When she'd woken in an empty bed a half hour before, she'd checked the house, then thought maybe he'd gone for a run. But his running shoes were in the bedroom closet. She'd texted him. When he didn't answer, she'd tried calling, but the call had immediately been sent to voice mail.

She turned and lowered herself into a dining room chair.

Where could he have gone in the middle of the night?

Dog tags jingled as Rocket and Snoozer lifted their heads from the carpet near her feet. Both dogs stood and trotted toward the front door. She heard the quiet chirp of the alarm as it was deactivated. She followed the dogs to the foyer. She exhaled as Lance came through the front door, tension rolling off her skin. He carried muddy boots in one hand. He was covered in mud and bits of organic debris.

But he was all right.

He set his boots in the rubber tray by the front door.

She wanted to kiss him, but she also wanted to shake him. Did he have any idea how worried she'd been for the last thirty minutes? She took two deep breaths, then walked closer and chose the kiss, because in the end, all that really mattered was that he was back, safe and sound. He looked surprised when her mouth left his.

"Where were you?" she asked.

"Jake O'Reilly's farm. Let me shower and change. Then I'll tell you everything."

"You can tell me *while* you shower and change." Morgan hooked a hand around the back of his neck to hold him in place.

Lance winced. She released him. Blood streaked her fingers. She took him by the hand and led him back to the bedroom. Steering him to take a seat on the closed toilet lid, she pushed his head down and examined the back of his skull. He didn't object. Parting his hair, she revealed a goose egg and a cut.

"You're lucky. I don't think this needs stitches." She reached into the shower and turned on the spray. "Get cleaned up, then I'll disinfect it. You'll need ice too."

He didn't argue but gave her a play-by-play of his night as he stripped down and stepped into the shower. Emotions swirled in Morgan's chest as she listened. She was simultaneously angry, frustrated, and grateful. As he finished washing, she took several deep breaths.

She had the first aid kit ready when he emerged. He wrapped the towel around his waist, bent his head, and let her clean the cut.

"It's almost stopped bleeding." She tossed the antiseptic-soaked cotton ball in the trash can. Her fingers brushed a large darkening splotch along the top of his shoulder. "You have bruises everywhere."

He shrugged. "They don't hurt."

She sat sideways on his lap and stared into his piercing blue eyes. Love for him expanded in her chest until it was almost painful. "Why didn't you tell me you were going?"

"I couldn't sleep, but there was no reason for both of us to be up all night. I wanted you to get some rest. You were awake most of last week."

"You need to sleep too."

"I'll sleep after I find Evan." Lance stood, forcing her to slide to her feet.

But Morgan wasn't done with him yet. She blocked his exit from the bathroom. "I thought we were a team, both on and off the job."

He broke eye contact. "We are. But we don't always work together. I stake out locations all the time by myself."

"In those cases, Sharp knows where you are." Conflicting emotions weighed heavily within Morgan's chest, love and fear of loss swirling inside her. "No one knew where you were tonight. What if you'd been shot? Or knocked unconscious? We wouldn't have known where to start looking for you." She cupped his jaw and turned his face toward her. "You can't leave in the middle of the night and not tell me."

"OK." He closed his fingers around her wrist. "I'm sorry."

She brushed her thumb along his jaw. She rose onto her toes and kissed him. Lowering back down to her bare feet, she rested her head on his chest for a few seconds. He wrapped his arms around her and held her close.

"I don't want to be clingy, but I also couldn't bear to lose you." She leaned back. "I love you."

"I love you too, and I'd like to promise I'll never be stupid again, but we both know sometimes I let my emotions get the best of me. I'm worried about Evan and frustrated with the direction of the sheriff's investigation."

"I know. Go get an ice pack for your head. I need to shower." Morgan shooed him out of the bathroom, dumped her pajamas in the hamper, and showered. When she came out, he was still wearing his towel, and he hadn't bothered to get an ice pack. The look in his eyes told her he didn't want to rest.

"Don't think sex will make up for what you did." But recognizing the need in him, she let him tug her toward him and wrap his arms around her. For a little while, they were both able to block out the world and all its harsh realities.

Afterward, she dressed and brought him an ice pack from the freezer. "Now, lie down and put this on your head for fifteen minutes."

"Yes, ma'am." He stretched out on the bed and settled the ice behind his head.

Morgan went to the dining room for more coffee.

Her grandfather shuffled into the room with his cane. "Good morning."

"Morning." Morgan surveyed the temporary kitchen. The toaster, coffee maker, and microwave were lined up on the sideboard. The table had been moved off center to make room for the refrigerator in the corner of the room. Packages of paper plates and bowls cluttered the table. "Remind me why we ripped out our kitchen?"

"Because we need a bigger, better one, and after the kitchen is finished, the contractor will start on the new addition," Grandpa said in a voice that was far too cheery for the early hour or the subject matter.

"Don't remind me." But Morgan was well aware that the old house on the river needed updating and enlarging to accommodate seven people. They were all on top of each other. A new master suite would give Morgan and Lance some much-needed privacy. They were also adding a bedroom and en suite bath for Gianna. Sophie, who suffered from night terrors, would move into Gianna's room. Without the youngest's nocturnal screams waking them, Ava and Mia might stop crawling into bed with Morgan and Lance. Nighttime was a game of musical beds.

"You look tired. Where's Lance?"

"Getting dressed." Morgan poured her grandfather a cup of coffee and set it on the table.

"Thanks." He hung his cane on the back of the chair and eased into the seat.

"You're not using your walker?"

"I hate that contraption with a ridiculous amount of passion." Grandpa had finally broken down and bought one of those walkers with the wheels, bike brakes, and a seat. He'd broken his leg protecting Morgan and her girls from an intruder the previous autumn. It was doubtful that he'd ever heal 100 percent.

"It enables you to be mobile." Morgan sat across from him. "You like to go places, right?"

"Yeah, but it makes me look old." He lifted a blue-veined hand. "I know. I am old."

"Old is a state of mind. You're wise, not old."

"I'm wise, all right. A wiseass." He chuckled at his own joke.

Morgan hated to see him aging. She refused to think about a day when he was no longer with her. Grandpa had raised her after her NYPD police officer father had been killed in the line of duty and her mother had died a short time later. After her husband had died in Iraq, Morgan and her three little girls had moved back home to live with Grandpa. She didn't know how she would have survived all three tragedies without him.

"I'll make breakfast." Morgan reached for the oatmeal, intending to nuke him a bowl.

"Don't make any of that slop for me." Grandpa drank his coffee. "I'll wait for Gianna to make waffles for the girls."

"Oatmeal is better for your blood pressure and cholesterol than toaster waffles and syrup." Morgan gave up with a single nag. He was going to do what he was going to do.

"Once you pass eighty, you get to eat whatever you want. It's a rule." Grandpa grinned. "From now on, I'm eating dessert first."

And with that, Morgan decided to stop for donuts on the way to the office.

"You worked late last night," Grandpa said. "Any ideas of where to look for the boy?"

"No." After getting home the previous night, she and Lance had phone-conferenced with Sharp. Then Morgan and Lance had reviewed Evan's cell phone records, email accounts, and online activity. "Evan didn't use much social media. He rarely posted anything except an occasional hockey game selfie. There was no unusual or new friend activity that we could find. His emails were school related, and he hadn't responded to most of those."

"Which says something about his general attitude toward school."

"Definitely. Evan recently changed schools. He wasn't happy about the move."

"It's rough to change schools at that age. What about his text history? Kids these days live on their cell phones." Grandpa hadn't forgotten anything about being a detective. His body might be failing, but his mind was still as sharp as his tongue.

"Texts back and forth from a very few friends, all ordinary stuff. There were some phone calls with a girlfriend his mother didn't know about. We tried to interview her. She wouldn't talk."

Grandpa scratched his chin. At six thirty in the morning, he'd already shaved and dressed in navy slacks and a pale-blue polo shirt. "It's not unusual for a boy to keep a relationship with a girl private for a while. Teenagers like to keep secrets. Makes them feel like they have some control over their lives. Most of the time, it's just stupid stuff. But you should definitely try to find a way to get the girlfriend to talk. I bet he told her things that he wouldn't tell his buddies."

Lance walked in, wearing his usual uniform of tactical cargos and a T-shirt.

Morgan kissed him on the mouth. "I was telling Grandpa about Evan's case."

He poured coffee and drank it black. He turned to Grandpa. "Any suggestions?"

But their conversation was cut short as Morgan's three little girls raced into the dining room. Ava, age six, was wide awake and already dressed. Five-year-old Mia hugged her blanket to her face, climbed up on Grandpa's lap, and leaned her sleepy head on his chest. Sophie bounded into the room in her purple kitten pajamas. As usual, the three-year-old's hair was an impressive mass of tangles. Morgan combed it thoroughly every night, but every morning, it looked like she'd slept in a tornado.

Sophie catapulted herself into Lance's arms. Expecting her affectionate attack, he caught her. She wrapped her arms and legs around him and kissed his cheek. "You smell good."

Morgan agreed.

Gianna, their nanny, was right behind the girls, and everyone settled into the chaotic but familiar morning routine. Fidgety as usual, Sophie picked at her toaster waffles. Morgan's wiry daughter seemed to exist on a forkful of food per meal.

After the girls were fed and dressed, Lance walked Ava and Mia to the bus stop while Morgan saw Grandpa, Sophie, and Gianna off. Since it was Wednesday, Grandpa would drive Sophie to preschool and drop Gianna at dialysis. Morgan returned to the bedroom to prepare to leave. She wound her hair into a neat bun, turning as Lance walked into the bedroom, his face grim.

Morgan shoved a hairpin into her bun. "What happened?"

"I just called Steve Duncan."

"You didn't tell him you searched his farm last night, did you?" Morgan did not want to bail Lance out of jail later.

"I left that part out of my story, but I did tell him I drove by the farm last night and saw someone watching the house. I told him he and Jake should be extra careful. Then I called Jake and told him the same. They needed to know."

"I hope they heed the warning." Morgan finished putting her hair up. Leaning close to the mirror over the dresser, she swiped mascara onto her lashes.

Lance's phone chimed with a reminder. "Grant will be here this morning to finish the demolition."

The dogs exploded in a frenzy of barking and raced for the front of the house, cutting off Morgan's response.

"That's probably him." Lance left the room.

Morgan put away her mascara and followed him. Instead of their contractor, her sister, Stella, walked in the front door. Stella and her boyfriend, Mac, lived close by. On her way to work as a Scarlet Falls police detective, Stella wore navy-blue slacks and a matching blazer. Her gun and badge were clipped to her belt, and her long dark hair was coiled into a utilitarian bun. She dropped to one knee to greet the dogs. Scratching behind Rocket's ear, she looked up at Morgan. "I have some information on the Evan Meade case. It's not good."

"Nothing about this case is good." Lance crossed his arms.

Stella rose to her feet and picked a few dog hairs off the knee of her slacks. "Even though Paul Knox had been retired for some time, the entire sheriff's department is treating his murder like a cop killing. SFPD might not be working the murder, but we're hearing plenty of chatter. Colgate's pride took a hard hit last spring when you solved the case and proved he was completely wrong. He's determined to prove he's right this time. He and all his men are gunning for Evan. I wanted to warn you."

"We're already getting resistance from Sheriff Colgate," Morgan admitted.

"Speaking of the sheriff." Lance checked his watch. "The press conference should be starting any minute." He went into the family room, turned on the TV, and selected a local channel. Stella and Morgan followed him, and they stood in front of the coffee table, staring at the TV.

Sheriff Colgate stood in front of the station, several of his deputies and ADA Esposito were at his side. To Morgan, the presence of the ADA was alarming.

The sheriff spoke into a cluster of microphones. "We are pursuing several leads in the investigation of Paul Knox's murder. At this time, an arrest warrant has been issued for the victim's stepson, Evan Meade."

Evan's picture flashed in the lower corner of the screen, and Morgan's heart clenched.

The sheriff continued. "Evan was last seen in a black T-shirt, jeans, and black Converse sneakers. He is six feet, three inches tall and weighs approximately one hundred ninety pounds. Anyone who sees Evan should call the sheriff's department immediately at the number on the bottom of the screen. Please be advised that Evan could be armed and is potentially dangerous."

Chapter Seventeen

Evan shivered so hard he could barely keep his grip on the paddle. The morning was already hot and humid, and he was covered in a layer of sweat. There was only one reason he could be so cold—he had a fever. His arm throbbed with its own heartbeat, and his entire body ached from his eyelids to his big toes.

His wound was infected.

He'd escaped drowning, barely, only to be taken out by the bacteria swimming in the river he'd been dumped into.

Tears filled his eyes. Where was his mom? Were the police watching her?

Luckily, he and the boat had been swept downstream together. He'd crawled out of the water and recovered the boat and paddle. Traveling on land would be much harder than paddling. But he needed medical supplies.

He positioned the small boat behind a tree. Scanning the riverbank, he spotted a house. This was the fourth home he'd seen. The first three had clearly been occupied. Could this one be empty?

The house was brown wood. A deck overlooked the river. Patio furniture was covered and stored beneath it. Dead leaves and debris were piled against the sliding glass door. Branches and other storm debris were scattered on the back lawn. No boats were tied to the short dock that extended over the water. Instead, in a stand of pines just above the dock, a canoe and a kayak were tied to tree trunks.

Wind gusted, chilling his bare back and chest, sending him into a shiver he couldn't stop. He looked up at the house again. He had to try.

He had no idea how far he'd gone.

Or how much blood he'd lost.

He had to hide the canoe. He would need it again. He tried to climb out, but his leg muscles had stiffened during the hours he'd spent on the river. He tripped and went down on his knees in the mud. The canoe slipped away.

No!

The last thing he wanted to do was go into the river again. With the humidity, the rain, and being tossed overboard, he'd been wet almost since he'd run. But he might need the boat, and he couldn't afford to have it discovered. The Camp Deer Lake emblem was too visible.

He splashed into the muddy river, the cold water rising to his waist. The shock rippled through him. His teeth chattered. Holding his arms high, he fought the current until he could grab hold of the boat. He towed it back to shore and used his last bit of strength to haul it, one-handed, up onto the bank.

Flopping on his back on the wet grass, he stared up, his energy depleted. Clouds shifted with the wind, exposing occasional bits of blue sky. He wanted to curl up and die. If it weren't for his mom, that's exactly what he would have done.

But he couldn't do that to her.

He rolled onto his one good hand and both knees. He reached into the canoe and retrieved the gun from the bottom. He stuck it into the waistband of his jeans. Then he stumbled toward the house in a crooked line. His wet jeans were stiff and plastered to his skin. His canvas sneakers felt like they'd soaked up ten pounds of water.

At the back of the house, he peered through a window into a big room. There were a few pieces of furniture and lots of empty space. A vacation house?

Hope gave him a little strength, but it didn't make him stupid. He walked the rear perimeter, looking for wires or cameras, but saw nothing that suggested the owner had installed a security system. Evan tried the back door. Locked. He went from window to window, testing each one. The sixth, on the side of the house, gave instantly. The latch seemed broken.

As much as he wanted to climb through, first he went back to the canoe. He dragged it up the bank and into the trees. The farther he got from the shore, the easier the boat became to pull. Closer to the house, dried pine needles covered the ground and the boat stopped leaving a track. When he'd reached the other boats tied to the trees, he turned his canoe so the Camp Deer Lake emblem faced away from the river. Then he tossed leaves and needles inside to make it appear as if it had been in the same place for a while.

Dragging the canoe had left a gully in the muddy riverbank, like a crocodile's slide. Evan used two downed branches to cover the boat's track. Satisfied that a casual glance wouldn't detect his exit from the river, he trudged back to the house. He fell more than climbed over the sill, banging his injured arm. Pain paralyzed him. He sat on the floor, cradling his arm to his chest and panting until the agony became bearable again.

Hugging his arm tightly, he staggered to his feet. He was in the middle of the family room. A faded blue couch and matching recliner faced a small TV. He stood still for at least three minutes, just listening. But he heard nothing. The house was weirdly silent.

Evan closed the window and crept from room to room until he was sure the place was vacant. It seemed to be partially cleared out. A formal living room at the front of the house was empty. He positioned himself out of sight behind a window frame. He looked around the blinds out the front window onto the porch and lawn. A FOR SALE sign had been driven into the lawn. Dead leaves piled on the front porch. It didn't look like anyone had opened the front door since before the big storm.

This was the best Evan could do, at least for now. He needed a couple of hours to get his shit together. He crossed his fingers that no one showed up.

He turned and walked to the back of the house. In the kitchen, he tried the faucet, relieved when water ran. He leaned over. Putting his mouth under the stream, he drank until the water felt cold and sloshy in his belly. Next to the kitchen was a laundry room and bath. He flipped the light switch. The room brightened. The electricity was on. He turned it off again. The house might not have any close neighbors, but it was visible from the river and road. No one could suspect he was inside.

Time to clean the wound. He needed a first aid kit.

Evan opened a cabinet under the sink, but all he found were cleaning supplies. He went through the kitchen cabinets and found dishes and canned goods. He opened the fridge. A single box of baking soda sat on a shelf. He opened the freezer. A bottle of Grey Goose vodka stared back at him. He grabbed it.

Upstairs, there were two bedrooms and a bathroom. One bedroom was completely empty. The other held a dresser and a bed. The dresser had some clothes in it. Evan grabbed a T-shirt, a flannel shirt, a pair of nylon sweatpants, and clean socks. The style looked like something an old man might wear, but they were clean. Goose bumps rose on his clammy skin.

In a narrow closet behind the bathroom door, he found a first aid kit, towels, and more cleaning supplies. Teeth chattering, he turned on the water in the shower and stepped out of his wet shoes and jeans. His shirt stuck to the wound. Tears welled in his eyes as he worked the fabric free.

He stuck his hand in the spray and almost cried when he felt the warm water. The only soap he could find was a dispenser of hand soap next to the sink. He took it into the shower with him. Under the spray, the water hit his arm like flames. Agony weakened his legs. Dizzy, he slid to the tile floor and rested his head on his knees until the light-headedness passed. Then Evan gritted his teeth and washed the wound. The edges were red, the surrounding skin hot and swollen.

It was definitely infected.

When he'd finished with the soap and water, he washed the rest of his body. Turning off the water, he reached outside the shower for the bottle of vodka he'd brought up with him.

Without letting himself think about it, he exhaled and dumped the liquid over his wound. It felt like someone had poured gasoline on his arm and set it on fire. Tears poured from his eyes, and he threw up all the water he'd drunk. Too weak to stand, he opened the shower door, grabbed the towel, and wrapped it around himself.

He didn't know how long he lay there, shivering and retching. Maybe he even passed out. But eventually, he was able to crawl out of the shower. Sitting on the bathroom floor, he slathered antibiotic oint- ment on both the entry and exit wound and covered them with gauze pads. Then he wrapped an ACE bandage around his arm to hold them in place.

Now he needed to get off the floor.

The house was for sale. Someone could show up at any moment. He needed to be ready to run.

Slowly, moving his arm as little as possible, he dressed in the sweat-pants and T-shirt. Pulling the socks on one-handed took time.

He needed to thoroughly search the house for useful items. He didn't like stealing, but he was desperate. On shaky legs, he went through the medicine cabinet. He'd been right about the house prob-ably belonging to an old dude. If the old guy had died, it would explain why half his shit was gone.

The shelves were filled with prescription bottles and over-the-counter meds. His mom talked about medical stuff all the time. He should have listened more. He didn't recognize any of the medications.

He wanted to call his mom. He needed to go to a hospital, but he couldn't risk it. The police would find out, and Paul's killer was a cop. He'd end up getting himself and his mom killed.

Fuck it. He grabbed the whole bottle of ibuprofen.

He found a nylon bag in the linen closet and filled it with supplies: the first aid kit, the meds, soap, and some small towels. Then he went back into the bedroom and took another set of clothes and a pair of slip-on old-man sneakers. They were a little tight, but his Converses were still wet. *And* they reeked. He zipped the bag closed and went downstairs.

In the kitchen pantry, he opened a can of chicken and ate it with a fork, swallowing four ibuprofen tablets as well. He found a second bag and filled it with a few cans of peaches and chicken, a box of crackers, and a can opener. Unfortunately, his ability to carry food and water was limited by its weight and his injured arm, but he found a few bottles of water in the garage and tossed them in the bag. What else could he use? He thought of his camping trip with Paul and the supplies they'd packed.

Paul.

Grief tightened Evan's chest. He shoved it down deep. When all of this was over, he could miss Paul and be sad. Now he had to figure out what he was going to do.

The house was warm and dry. Could he stay here for a while?

Did he have anywhere better to go?

The answer to that question was a big fat *no*.

He went back into the family room, set the two bags of stolen supplies under the window with the broken latch, and closed the blinds. He spotted a can of long matches on the mantel over the fireplace. On their one and only camping trip, Paul had taught him that fire could mean the difference between life and death. It could provide warmth and the ability to boil water to kill bacteria and parasites. Evan put the matches in his bag.

A fleece blanket was draped over the back of the couch. Evan sat and pulled the blanket around his shoulders. The ibuprofen was helping a little, but he still felt like shit.

He might not pay attention to everything his mother said, but he knew that an infection in a wound this deep was dangerous. If it spread, he could lose his arm or even die. Maybe he should consider calling her or the police.

If only he knew what was happening. His gaze lingered on the TV. He turned it on, surprised that whoever owned the house hadn't canceled the cable. He turned on a local news channel. A breaking news banner scrolled across the bottom of the screen: Sixteen-Year-Old Evan Meade Wanted in the Shooting Death of Stepfather.

Shock flashed through him like ice. As if a cop killing Paul and chasing Evan wasn't bad enough, now the police were going to try to pin Paul's murder on him.

He could never go for help. He had to run as far and as fast as he could. If the cops found him, he'd wind up in prison or dead.

The sound of a car door closing outside made Evan jump. He turned off the TV and hurried toward the living room. He peered around the edge of the blinds. A sheriff's department car was parked in the driveway.

Chapter Eighteen

Morgan drank from a Styrofoam cup in the conference room at the sheriff's office. Ten minutes after the press conference, the sheriff had called Tina, requesting she come down to the station for additional questioning. The timing could not be coincidental. The sheriff wanted something. Morgan schooled her face into a blank expression, but inside, her brain was scrambling. The sheriff had plenty of evidence against Evan, enough to convince a judge to sign off on an arrest warrant for Paul's murder.

The evidence required for an arrest warrant was lower than the *beyond a reasonable doubt* standard applied in the courtroom. In order to get an arrest warrant, the sheriff only had to establish that he had probable cause to believe Evan was guilty. Considering the evidence in the case so far, there was only one way to invalidate the warrant: find Paul's real killer.

Sitting on her left, Lance's posture was rigid in his chair, his arms crossed over his chest. He made no attempt to disguise the fact that he was seething. Tina huddled in the chair next to him.

"They're going to shoot him on sight." Tina chewed on her thumbnail. "I know it. They're setting up Evan so they can kill him. I was bullied by enough cops when I was a kid. I know how they operate."

Morgan doubted the police were intentionally setting up Evan to be shot. But listing him as an armed and dangerous suspect, rather than a missing person, definitely increased the risk.

She eyed the camera in the corner of the ceiling. The light was green. They were being recorded. She leaned close to Tina's ear and whispered, "Take a deep breath."

"But this isn't fair." Tina rubbed her hands together. She obviously hadn't slept the night before. The circles under her eyes were deep and dark. "Evan wouldn't hurt anyone. He's a victim."

The door opened. Morgan had expected Sheriff Colgate, but the appearance of ADA Esposito behind the sheriff was a surprise. Next to her, Lance stared. The sheriff closed the door. Esposito took the chair opposite Morgan. She and Esposito had faced off over several cases. So far, Morgan was well ahead, and Esposito was chafing for a win. The gleam in his nearly black eyes told Morgan he thought he'd scored big on this case.

Morgan didn't say a word as the sheriff and ADA settled into their chairs. Sheriff Colgate had a file, notepad, and pen. Esposito needed no props. He smoothed his suit jacket and tugged his French cuffs into place.

She waited, unmoving. They'd called for this meeting. They could open the discussion.

"You have the right to remain silent . . ." The sheriff read Tina her Miranda rights, then slid a piece of paper across the table. "Mrs. Knox, please sign that you understand your rights."

"Mrs. Knox is a suspect?" Morgan asked. She hadn't expected them to Mirandize Tina. It would be a conflict of interest for Morgan to represent both Tina and Evan if they were both charged in the same crime, but with no charges filed, she'd worry about that technicality if it ever materialized.

"That might depend on how she answers my questions," Colgate said.

He wasn't taking any chances with Tina's interview.

Lance's posture shifted. Morgan pressed her ankle against his. She needed him to let her handle the sheriff and ADA. He exhaled hard and settled back into the chair.

"But she was at the urgent care center when Paul was killed," Morgan said.

"She was," the sheriff agreed. "But that doesn't mean she wasn't involved in her husband's death."

Sheriff Colgate leaned forward, flattening both palms on the table. "Mrs. Knox, do you know where your son is?"

"No." Tina looked confused, but she signed the paper.

Sheriff Colgate slid it to his side of the table. "Has Evan tried to contact you?"

"No." Tina glanced at Morgan, then back to the sheriff. "This is ridiculous. You had an officer outside my hotel room door all night. How do you think he could have contacted me? Telepathy?"

Morgan bumped Tina's leg. Taking the hint, Tina clamped her mouth closed.

"What is this about?" Morgan asked.

The sheriff scratched the gray stubble on his face. "We think Mrs. Knox knows more than she's saying about her husband's murder and her son's location."

"Based on what evidence?" Morgan asked.

Sheriff Colgate glared at her. "The fact that Mrs. Knox withheld two very important pieces of information."

Morgan folded her hands in front of her. "Mrs. Knox provided a reasonable explanation."

"She forgot?" One of the sheriff's bushy white eyebrows lifted. "You call that reasonable?"

Morgan nodded. "Considering she had just found her husband's dead body? Yes."

"That makes no sense. If my father had served time for murder, he'd be the first person I'd think of if someone in my family were killed," the sheriff shot back. "And I think she kept the fight between Paul and Evan to herself because it made Evan look guilty."

Morgan didn't comment. Unfortunately, the sheriff's argument was stronger than hers, and they all knew it.

The sheriff tugged at the collar of his uniform and returned to his questions. "Mrs. Knox, did Evan kill your husband?"

"No!" Tina's brow lowered.

"How do you know?" the sheriff asked.

"Evan wouldn't hurt Paul." Tina enunciated each word distinctly.

"Evan once took a swing at Paul," the sheriff pointed out.

"That was different." Tina's eyes misted. "I already explained what happened."

He fired another question at her. "Did you delay calling the police to give Evan time to get away?"

"No." Her eyes narrowed, anger flashing.

The sheriff didn't pause for a breath. "Do you know or suspect where Evan might be hiding?"

"No." Tina's voice went flat.

"You left the hotel yesterday. Where did you go?" he asked.

"I was driving around, looking for Evan," Tina said.

"Are you sure you didn't meet him?"

"What's the meaning of this?" Morgan interrupted. "Tina is frightened for her son's safety. She has no idea where he is."

Sheriff Colgate sat back and studied Tina.

Esposito joined in. "I hope not. Because if you have any knowledge of where your son is or if you have helped him in any way, then you could be charged with aiding and abetting or conspiracy after the fact."

"Hold on." Morgan stood and turned to Tina. "Do not answer any more questions." Morgan faced Esposito. "You are out of line. If you want to charge Mrs. Knox, do it. You have zero evidence."

Esposito changed the topic. "We have plenty of evidence against Evan, though." He lifted his forefinger. "Paul Knox was shot with a 9mm bullet, the same caliber as his own weapon, which is missing. At the time of his death, Paul had been cleaning his gun. The weapon had been out of the safe and available to Evan. So the boy had the means to murder Paul.

"Next is opportunity." Esposito raised another finger. "There is no evidence of a break-in the night of the shooting. There is no sign that anyone else was in the house the night of the shooting. Paul was killed between midnight and one a.m. The teen was dropped off by a friend at the house at twelve thirty a.m., more than two hours past his curfew. We received the results of the expedited DNA tests on the blood on the fence and back door. The tests confirm that the blood is Evan's. So we know that Evan was at the house when Paul was killed."

Shit. Juries loved DNA.

"And finally, motive," Esposito said. "Two months prior to the shooting, the sheriff's department responded to a domestic disturbance at the Knox residence. A neighbor heard the teen and his stepfather fighting loudly. The teen took a swing at his stepfather, indicating a history of violent interactions between Paul and Evan. Evan has previous arrests for vandalism and destruction of property. He was also known to be angry about being forced to meet with his biological father. This anger could have been directed at Paul, who was the deputy who arrested Evan's father and put him in jail."

He paused for effect. Tina stared back at him, pure hatred in her eyes.

The ADA's body tilted forward, almost imperceptibly, his use of body language subtler—and more effective—than the sheriff's. "This is what we think happened. Evan came in late. Paul called him on it. They argued. They already had friction between them from other disagreements. The fight escalated and became physical. Evan sustained a cut or bloody nose. He picked up Paul's gun and shot him in the abdomen.

He panicked and shot Paul again." Esposito focused on Tina. "The real question is whether you helped him get away."

Lance hadn't moved since the interview began, but Morgan could sense the hostility emanating from him toward Esposito and Colgate.

"This interview is over. My client will not be answering any more questions."

"Think about Evan, Mrs. Knox." Sheriff Colgate got to his feet. He leaned his knuckles on the table. "Every law enforcement officer out there knows he is armed and dangerous. It would be easier and safer if he surrendered."

Chapter Nineteen

A new sense of urgency tightened Lance's chest as he gripped the steering wheel. The sheriff's department no longer considered Evan an innocent missing teenager.

He was wanted for murder.

They dropped Tina off at her hotel, with her deputy guard parked outside her door. At Morgan's request, Lance took a two-minute detour to pick up coffee and donuts via the bakery drive-through window. He parked outside Sharp Investigations, and Morgan carried the white bakery bag and her giant tote into the building. Lance grabbed the two tall cardboard cups of strong coffee from the Jeep's console and followed her inside. They settled in Morgan's office, now the case war room.

Side by side, Lance and Morgan leaned backward on the desk and faced the whiteboard. She offered him the white bag, and he took a chocolate cruller. With two nights of no sleep, he was running on pure adrenaline.

Sharp walked in, two protein shakes in hand. He gave one to Lance. "Drink this instead."

"I'll drink that as well." Lance popped the rest of the donut into his mouth, washed it down with coffee, then accepted the shake. Exhaustion weighed on his body and muddled his concentration. It was going to take caffeine, sugar, *and* Sharp's miracle concoction to get his neurons firing.

Sharp went back to his office for his laptop. "I want to update my case notes while we brainstorm. Mind if I use your desk?" he asked Morgan.

"Not at all." She took a second donut.

Shaking his head at her donut, Sharp opened his laptop and scanned the screen. "I don't even know where to start. Our primary objective was to find Evan, but finding Paul's killer now seems equally important. Do we have any more leads on Evan's possible location?"

"No. His friends deny having seen him. We've checked his favorite places. The sheriff's deputies have been trolling teen hangout spots. Every cop in the state is on the lookout for him. He must be holed up somewhere. He's not at Jake's farm." Lance told Sharp about his late-night reconnaissance.

"You're sure it wasn't a cop?" Sharp asked as he typed.

"A cop would have arrested me on the spot, not bashed me over the head." Lance drank more of his shake.

"Right." Sharp looked up. "An *honest* cop."

"I hadn't thought about dirty cops." The idea whirled in Lance's mind, generating new theories.

Sharp shrugged. "The sheriff's department has had its issues with corruption."

"If Paul knew something about one of the deputies he'd worked with . . ." Lance went to the board and wrote DIRTY COP? under MOTIVE.

"Could it have been Brian Springer?" Sharp asked.

Lance pictured the sedan in the shadows. "What does Brian drive?"

Morgan turned to the desk behind her, picked up her case file, and opened it. "A four-door black Ford Taurus."

"Is he a big guy?" Lance asked.

"Over six feet tall and in decent shape," Sharp said. "But he's not huge."

"It's possible then." Lance made a note next to Brian's name. A cop would be trained to fight.

Sharp got up and paced the space between Morgan's desk and her credenza. "As the victim, Paul is the center of all this."

Lance drank his coffee in the hope that the caffeine would kick in soon. "I have no doubt the sheriff's office is reviewing Paul's cases, looking for someone released from prison who held a grudge."

Sharp nodded. "We don't have access to his old case files, so we'll have to leave that task to the sheriff's department. I did an internet search but didn't come up with anything."

Morgan closed the file and set it on the desktop behind her. "The Knox front door was unlocked, and there were no signs of a break-in. If Paul let someone in that night, it would have been someone he knew and trusted."

"Like Brian." Lance underlined the words DIRTY COP on the board. "Would the boys have told you if he were corrupt?"

Sharp stopped pacing. His head tilted as he considered Lance's question. "They wouldn't lie to me. They know Evan is missing. But the answers I got were a little too vague for my comfort. Jimmy mentioned an excessive force complaint filed against Brian."

Did that mean Brian had a history of violent behavior or poor impulse control? The same argument used for Evan's motive could apply to someone else.

"Plus, it appeared as if Brian left his house in a hurry and took his desktop computer with him," Sharp said.

"Or someone stole it," Morgan suggested. "For the same reason that the police seize criminals' computers—to find out what they've been doing. Brian is a seasoned deputy. I'm sure he knows how to cover his tracks online. But no one sanitizes their actual machine every night. His hard drive would contain plenty of information about his recent activity."

Sharp returned to the chair behind the desk. "Jenny is looking for a property on a lake in Brian's family. We can't talk to him until we find him. Your mom is also trying to find any information on the excessive force complaint filed against Brian and the department by Sam Jones."

"Let's move on to other theories," Lance said.

Sharp leaned forward and pressed a key on his laptop to wake it.

"Have we ruled out robbery gone wrong as a possibility for his death?" Morgan pointed at the ROBBERY notation on the board. "As Lance pointed out to the sheriff, the fact that there was no obvious sign of a break-in does not rule out a robbery. Even quality locks can be picked by an experienced burglar."

"All true," Sharp agreed. "But since the killing was particularly cold-blooded, other motives come immediately to mind: revenge, elimination, and information."

"Don't forget anger." Morgan picked up her coffee. "That's how the sheriff is justifying Evan as the prime suspect."

"And with good reason." Sharp shifted backward in the chair and studied the board. "Evan has means, motive, and opportunity."

"I know, and I've struggled with that very question," Lance said. "But I can't see Evan hurting anyone but himself."

Shifting her coffee to her left hand, Morgan walked to the board and picked up a marker. She began to write notes in Evan's column. "If the weapon is recovered and ballistics proves Paul was killed with his own gun, that would be another hefty piece of physical evidence against Evan. He lived in the house and had access to the gun. His DNA and fingerprints will be all over everything. If he should be arrested, I'm sure the ADA will point out every damning occurrence, no matter how irrelevant or ridiculous."

"Even if you prove it's meaningless, the jury will have heard, and the damage will be done." Lance rubbed the bruised back of his neck. Three ibuprofen tablets had done nothing to alleviate the pain.

"What about Tina?" Morgan tapped the marker on the board under Tina's name. "Is Tina still on our list of suspects?"

"She's your client," Sharp snorted.

Morgan shrugged. "I promised to represent her to the best of my ability. That doesn't mean I trust her. Despite her excuses, she has to know that the information she withheld about her father could play into Paul's murder and Evan's disappearance. Yet she did not tell us until she was backed into a corner. I'm not as concerned about the friction between Paul and Evan. I can't see Evan as the killer. What would he have to gain by killing Paul? By all accounts, Paul was kind to him."

Lance scanned the names. Someone was guilty. Someone had killed Paul. "Tina was at work, in full view of a dozen people and security cameras. She couldn't come up with a better alibi if she tried."

Sharp rubbed his chin. "But she could have blackmailed or paid someone else to kill him."

"But what was her motive?" Morgan gestured toward the board with her coffee. "And why would she then come to us for help?"

"I don't know, but I don't like that she did not tell us about her father either," Sharp said. "That was a big-ass secret she was keeping."

"If Tina was behind Paul's murder, then where is Evan?" Morgan asked.

"Maybe Tina's plan didn't work out the way she wanted," Sharp argued.

Morgan shook her head. "But then wouldn't she suspect who had taken her son? That scenario doesn't work for me. Her father seems like a more likely suspect."

"I agree." Lance chugged more coffee, then swigged his shake, the combination waking his brain cells. "Her testimony put him in prison for twenty-five years. I'm sure that pissed him off. Joe Martin had a history of taking revenge. Killing Paul and destroying Tina's newfound happiness would be the perfect retaliation."

"He could have taken Evan too," Morgan agreed. "As additional payback or to convince her to come to him. Maybe he wants her to watch him kill Evan."

They were all quiet for a few seconds. Lance didn't like that scenario one bit, but it was all too plausible given Tina's story. "Can we verify any of the details Tina gave us on her background and her father?"

"Revenge is a great motive, but it wouldn't be very satisfying unless she knew it had been Joe who had done the deed," Sharp pointed out.

The printer on Morgan's credenza whirred and spit out a picture. Lance retrieved it.

"Your mother emailed this to me this morning," Sharp said. "That is Joe Martin when he went to prison twenty-five years ago. She is still looking for a current picture."

Lance positioned the photo on the board and labeled it.

Sharp said, "I have another lead on some info regarding Joe Martin and his gang. I'll follow up on that today."

"What lead?" Lance asked.

Sharp stared into his drink. "Twenty-five years ago, Olivia Cruz did an in-depth piece on gang violence in Newark, New Jersey. She covered Joe's trial and interviewed gang members."

"Olivia Cruz?" Lance grinned. "The same reporter who helped us out on our last big case?"

"Yes," Sharp said in an irritated tone.

"The same woman you owe a favor to?" Morgan asked, her mouth twitching with a small smile.

"Yes." Sharp jabbed a finger in the direction of the board. "Can we get back to the case?"

Sharp could deny it all he wanted, but he had a thing for Olivia Cruz. Considering that Sharp thought all reporters were the direct descendants of Satan, the attraction he was trying to fight was hilarious. If Lance weren't so worried about Evan, he would enjoy the hell out of Sharp's discomfort.

"Sure," Lance chuckled. "Evan's father, Kirk Meade, is next on my list. What do we know about him?"

"He has a supposed alibi at the group home, where he checked in for the night at seven thirty," Morgan said. "But when I asked the sheriff if anyone saw him after that time, he didn't answer."

"That's probably a *no*," Sharp said. "But we should talk to the supervisor and other residents of the group home."

"Morgan and I can do that this morning," Lance volunteered. "By all accounts, Kirk is a manipulative, lazy scumbag. Tina was his meal ticket. He was causing trouble for Tina and Paul, dragging Tina to court for visitation rights, charges of violating the court order, and parental alienation. All bullshit charges designed to make Tina's life difficult."

"Revenge for divorcing him," Morgan added. "How far would Kirk go to get even with Tina?"

"He blamed Paul because she wouldn't take him back," Lance said. "We need to talk to Kirk."

"Do we want to talk to Jake again?" Morgan asked.

"I don't see why. Lance already searched the farm." Sharp tapped his fingers together. "Evan wasn't there. When you questioned him, did it seem like he was lying?"

Morgan shook her head. "I didn't pick up on any lies."

"Me neither." Lance switched back to coffee. "But I'll bet the person who attacked me was looking for Evan there too."

"Do we have any other leads?" Sharp asked.

"Rylee Nelson, Evan's secret girlfriend." Morgan wrote her name on the board. "She was super defensive about her brother. Something is up there."

"My mother will research the family, but maybe we should drive by her house," Lance suggested. "Evan didn't want his family to know he was dating Rylee. Maybe the reason lies with her family, not his."

"Where shall we start?" Morgan scanned the board. "Are we agreed that our most likely suspects are Brian, Kirk, and Joe Martin?"

"Yes," Sharp said. "Let's focus on those three for now."

"Let's start with Kirk, then move on to Rylee." Lance picked up his empty cups. He'd finished the shake and the coffee and was feeling almost human. "Do we visit Kirk at the group home or furniture warehouse?"

"Group home first." Morgan turned away from the board. "Kirk is a parolee. His employer will be keeping a close eye on him. We shouldn't jeopardize his job. He can claim harassment. Besides, we want to talk to the group home supervisor anyway."

Lance glanced back at the board. They'd gathered information and generated leads, but their case still felt scattered. The lines of investigation bloomed across the white space like a spiderweb when what Lance wanted was a neat grid.

He tossed his cardboard coffee cup in the wastebasket. "Let's go poke some holes in Kirk's alibi."

Chapter Twenty

Standing on the doorstep of the group home, Morgan buttoned her blazer and pressed the doorbell. The door lock was an electronic card key entry system, with a slot to swipe a card and a keypad to enter a code.

She stepped back and scanned the street. A Hand Up Transitional Residence for Men occupied a huge brick-fronted Tudor-style house. The neighborhood was zoned for mixed use, with several of the large houses on the main street having been converted to professional offices. The group home sat between an accounting firm and a similar house that had been divided into apartments.

Next to her, Lance tapped an impatient boot on the cement. But they didn't have to wait long. A tall, thin man opened the door. Behind him, a chime echoed in the house.

"I'm Morgan Dane, and this is my associate Lance Kruger. We'd like to speak with the supervisor, Mr. Dougherty." Morgan offered him a business card. She had called ahead, so Dougherty should have been expecting them.

"I'm Stan Dougherty. Please come in." Mr. Dougherty moved back to allow them inside. "Welcome to A Hand Up."

"Thank you for seeing us." Morgan stepped into the foyer, well aware that Dougherty had no obligation to cooperate. Lance crossed the threshold to stand next to her.

"We're always happy to explain what we do." Dougherty closed the door. "We're very proud of our work in the community."

"How many men live in the house?" Morgan glanced around. On one side of the entry, a staircase led upstairs. On the left was a living room with couches, chairs, and a TV.

"We are at full capacity with twelve men in residence." Mr. Dougherty walked down a narrow hall. "I'm happy to say all but one of them are at work right now. And the one who is here is sleeping because he works the night shift. Employment is a requirement of residency."

Morgan followed him.

Lance brought up the rear. "What happens if a resident gets fired?"

"We provide mandatory counseling and job search assistance." Mr. Dougherty gestured to a small room tucked under the stairwell. "You would be surprised how many large corporations are willing to give convicted felons a second chance."

Morgan entered first. The office was tiny. There was barely enough room for two narrow wooden chairs in front of a small desk. She sat on the hard seat and set her tote at her feet.

"Excuse the small office. We've tried to utilize most of the space for living arrangements. Though the men are housed dormitory-style upstairs, we want the house to feel more like a home than an institution. We don't use the term *halfway house* anymore, but that's truly what we want to accomplish here, providing a halfway point between prison and normal life. Simply turning parolees out on the street with no support or transition doesn't serve them well." Mr. Dougherty sidled between the desk and the wall to take his seat. "We provide the closest thing to a real home as possible, but with some rules to ensure they don't fall right back into their old ways. They need to develop healthy work and life habits."

"How long do most residents stay?" Lance eased into the chair next to Morgan. His wide frame dwarfed the seat. He looked like a parent at a grammar school teacher conference.

"Sixty days is the average, although that can be extended if necessary. We work with parole officers to develop a reentry plan for each man, but all are required to submit to mandatory alcohol and drug testing, as well as abide by all the specific house rules." Mr. Dougherty leaned on his desk. "Now, how can I help you? You didn't come here to learn about transitional housing."

"We'd like to talk to you about Kirk Meade," Morgan said.

Dougherty stiffened. "Is he in trouble?"

Morgan answered, "No."

"Are you investigating Paul Knox's murder?" Dougherty asked before she could elaborate. "Because the sheriff was already here. He spoke to Kirk, and I answered all of the questions he asked me. The sheriff seemed satisfied."

"We represent Mr. Meade's ex-wife," Morgan clarified. "We're looking for their son, Evan."

"I saw the news this morning." Dougherty's tone was harsh. "Evan is wanted for Knox's murder."

"We believe that Evan is innocent. I can't imagine anything worse than an innocent sixteen-year-old being put in prison."

"That would be a terrible thing," Dougherty admitted in a reluctant voice.

"I knew you, above all people, would understand." Morgan gave his ego a subtle stroke. "We would like to double-check that Kirk was here that night, and we want to talk to Kirk in case he might have any idea where his son would have gone."

"You are not the police. I am not obligated to give you any information." Dougherty folded his arms on the desk. "I understand you want to protect your client. I need to do the same."

"Of course you do. But a teenager is missing," Morgan said in a soft voice. "Anything you can share would be appreciated."

But Dougherty wasn't buying her altruistic argument. He jabbed a finger at her in the air. "You can call him anything you want. That teenager is the prime suspect. The sheriff said he was armed and dangerous. But you're working for his mother. You want to pin the crime on Kirk. Well, you can get that idea out of your head. Kirk checked in at seven thirty that night. He didn't swipe out again until six a.m., when he went to work. Our residents are required to provide us with their weekly schedules. We know where they are at all times." He checked his watch. A frown creased his face. "In fact, he should be here any minute."

Dougherty looked concerned about the time. Was Kirk late?

"Does everyone have uniquely coded card keys?" Lance asked.

"Yes," Dougherty said.

The door chime sounded in the hall. Dougherty went to the doorway and peered into the hallway.

"Sorry I'm late," a deep voice said. "The alternator in my car went—"

"Kirk," Dougherty interrupted, "there's someone here to see you."

Footsteps approached, and a man stepped into view. One glance at Kirk Meade, and Morgan knew where Evan had inherited his size and athletic body. In tan chino pants and a red polo shirt bearing the ABC Furniture logo, Kirk was a few inches over six feet tall, broad shouldered, and well muscled. He'd clearly lifted weights in prison. He carried a shopping bag from an auto parts store.

Reaching across Lance, Morgan handed him a business card and introduced them. He took the card and read it in a glance.

"You don't have to talk to them," Dougherty warned.

"Thanks, Stan, but it's OK," Kirk said from the doorway. "I'll do whatever it takes to help find my boy. I'm worried to death about him."

"If I were you, I'd have my attorney present." Dougherty stepped into the hall to give Kirk room.

But Kirk didn't enter the tiny office. "I appreciate you looking out for me. But they aren't the police. They don't have any authority. My ex-wife hired them."

"Is there someplace where we can talk in private?" Morgan was surprised—and a little suspicious—that Kirk had agreed to speak with them so quickly. Did he have his own agenda?

"What about your room?" Lance asked, no doubt wanting a look at Kirk's private space.

Dougherty's phone rang. He excused himself and disappeared down the corridor.

"Not really," Kirk said. "My roommate works nights. He'll be upstairs sleeping now." Kirk raised the bag from the auto parts store. "Let's go outside. I'd like to get this alternator changed before it rains again."

He led them back down the hall to the foyer. The door chimed when he opened it. Morgan and Lance followed him outside.

Kirk went down the two concrete steps that led to a brick walkway. "That chime is obnoxious."

"Is the back door similarly equipped?" Morgan followed him down the steps.

"Yes," Kirk answered. "The whole place is wired, but the back door has a different sound, more of a buzzer."

"What's behind the house?" Morgan spotted a gate that led to a fenced rear yard.

"There's a back porch for guys who smoke, a barbecue, and a basketball hoop." Kirk walked down the driveway. "We're allowed to be outside until curfew, then they lock us in for the night."

"That sounds restrictive," Lance said.

"Better than prison," Kirk retorted. He shot Lance the side-eye. "But yeah," he admitted grudgingly. "No one gets in or out without everyone hearing the door open. They have my work and visitation schedules too. The supervisor on duty knows where I am at every minute. It's annoying, but I have to say, when the sheriff came to question me about Paul's death, I was fucking glad my whereabouts were accounted for. Everyone wants to pin a crime on the ex-con."

Morgan noted that for a man claiming to be worried about his son, he hadn't asked them a single question about their search for Evan.

The neighborhood was quiet. At one o'clock in the afternoon, children were in school, parents at work. A few cars were parked at the accounting firm next door.

Morgan did not like to interview people while walking. The side-by-side position did not allow her to read his eyes or body language. But the supervisor had been correct. Kirk was under no obligation to speak with them. She would have to accept whatever condition encouraged him to cooperate.

Kirk headed for the sidewalk. A dark-gray older-model Ford Crown Victoria sat at the curb. "I can't stand small spaces. I'll do anything to get outdoors."

"Understandable." Wanting to be a buffer between the two men, Morgan fell into step next to Kirk. Lance's temper ran hot on a good day. This was not a good day.

"I wish I could help search for Evan"—Kirk unlocked the car and popped the hood—"but my car is a piece of shit, I'm under curfew, and I've only just reconnected with my son after several years of not seeing him. Tina never brought him to see me while I was away. Not once." His voice grated on the last sentence.

"Did you ask her to bring him to visit you in prison?" Morgan asked.

"Many times," he said bitterly. "She claimed he refused to come, but I know she did nothing but bad-mouth me to him the whole time I was gone."

"Not seeing your son must have been very difficult for you." Morgan soft-pedaled her next question. "How did Evan act during your first visitation?"

"How do you think he acted?" Kirk's voice rose. "We hardly know each other. I hadn't seen him in years. He was sullen and hostile. The first thing he said was that he didn't want to be there."

"How sad." Morgan meant *sad for Evan*, but she didn't specify. She wanted Kirk to talk to her. She wanted him to feel safe and think he was running the interview.

"It was. A boy needs a father." Kirk opened the bag and removed what looked like a small ratchet.

Morgan pressed. "How was he when you saw him Sunday night?"

"The same. Still sullen. Still hostile." Kirk turned to the car. "He wouldn't put down his phone. He sat across from me in the booth and ignored me."

"That must have been frustrating." She wanted to see his face to gauge his honesty, but he kept his head bent over the engine.

"I couldn't believe the rudeness. I took the phone, put it aside, and told him how disrespectful he was acting." Kirk swapped tools for a shiny new wrench. "His mother obviously didn't teach him any manners."

"What did Evan do?" Morgan asked.

Kirk's lips pressed flat as he met her gaze. "He crossed his arms and said it wasn't his choice to come. That I could make him show up, but I couldn't make him talk."

"Teenagers can be emotional," Morgan said.

"He should still be respectful." A slight gleam of anger brightened Kirk's eyes. The wrench hit the palm of his hand with a solid smack.

He was furious that Evan had rejected him. "All I want to do is get to know my son better."

Lance jumped in. "Sunday night was the last time you saw him?"

Kirk nodded. "And he hasn't opened up enough for me to know anything about his life, so I wouldn't even know where to look for him."

"Well, we certainly appreciate your speaking with us," Morgan said.

Kirk turned back to the engine. "Like I said, I'll do anything to find Evan."

"I'm sure you would," Morgan lied.

"I wish I could have been more help." Kirk applied force to the wrench. Morgan couldn't help but think that the heavy tool would make an excellent weapon and could be legally carried in an automobile, even by an ex-convict. He went back to work.

A metallic scraping sound gave Morgan goose bumps. "Thank you for answering our questions."

Kirk acknowledged her statement with a wave of his wrench.

Morgan and Lance went back to the Jeep. Lance slid behind the wheel and slammed the door harder than necessary. "What a selfish little prick. Does he really think we'd fall for that woe-is-me story?"

"I think he does." Morgan fastened her seat belt. "Tina said he could be charming. He has the supervisor fooled."

Lance started the engine. "He was working hard to hide his anger with Tina."

"Yes, and he never asked what we were doing to find his son. Kirk was only thinking and talking about himself."

"He had no real concern for Evan." Lance tapped a finger on the steering wheel, his voice dripping with disgust. "His son was an afterthought."

"I agree," Morgan said. "But knowing he's a jerk doesn't help us find Evan. What did you think about the home's security?"

"I wasn't impressed. The system is dated." Lance checked the rearview mirror. "I could get in and out without anyone knowing."

"We didn't really learn anything from his interview."

"Sure, we did." Lance pulled away from the curb. "When he led us outside, he didn't swipe his card to exit the house."

Morgan replayed their exit. "You're right. The door opened without a swipe."

"It's against fire code to lock people into a structure," Lance said. "I'll bet swiping out is a requirement but not necessary to actually unlock the door. I'm not convinced his alibi is as strong as the sheriff thinks. Kirk is resourceful. I'll bet he could figure out a way to slip out of the house."

"But how would he get back in?" Morgan asked. "The door chime is loud."

"True." Lance glanced back at the house. "Maybe he didn't use the door at all. Maybe he went out through a window. Some of the upstairs windows opened onto the first-floor roof. If his roommate works the night shift, then Kirk would have been alone. From what I could see of the window contacts, they were standard magnetic sensors. Alarm systems are designed to keep people out, not in. Window magnets are mounted on the inside of the frame, and they can be fooled with a magnet."

"Do you think Kirk could have bypassed the window sensor, slipped out and killed Paul, then snuck back in to the group home with no one knowing?"

Lance nodded. "Exactly."

"That would also explain why Kirk didn't ask what we were doing to find Evan. Maybe he already knows where Evan is hiding."

"That's possible. Kirk feels like a good liar."

Chapter Twenty-One

Sharp drove to Olivia Cruz's address, pulled to the curb, and parked his Prius behind hers.

He had been inside her house once before. The quaint white bungalow seemed incongruous with Olivia's polished urban style, and yet she looked right at home in it. But then, Olivia Cruz was full of contradictions.

Not that he knew much about her. He hadn't allowed himself to investigate her background. He already had an unhealthy—maybe even unnatural—interest in her, like a male lion taking interest in a female tiger. It happened in the artificial environment created in zoos but never in the wild.

He found her attractive, and he didn't like it.

Not at all.

Nor did he like that she was going to see him looking like shit. Again. Her visit to the hospital the day after his surgery and been enough humiliation. But this was the situation fate had put him in, and sitting at the curb in front of her house was stupid.

He grabbed a jar of organic raw honey sitting in the console cup holder before getting out of his Prius. Though still overcast, the morning sky gleamed on solar panels mounted on the roof. Sharp walked through the opening in the picket fence that surrounded the property. Instead of a lawn, neat patches of herbs thrived on both sides of a brick walkway. He knew about the garden from his daily drive-by, but seeing and smelling an herb garden were two entirely different experiences. He inhaled. His nose detected basil, mint, and rosemary. Water bubbled from a small solar-powered stone fountain. Around it, the daisylike flowers of Roman chamomile bloomed. A patch of lavender rioted about a rain barrel in the corner.

He knocked on the front door. Footsteps approached and stopped, and he pictured her looking through the peephole. The door swung open.

"Lincoln, how nice to see you." The genuine smile on her face pleased him.

Olivia was in her midforties, with just a few crow's-feet around her deep-brown eyes. She wore faded jeans and a loose tank that showed off her tanned, toned arms. Her dark-brown hair was tied back in a long ponytail.

"I should have called ahead." But deep down, Sharp had been hoping to catch her in some activity or state that would make her less attractive.

Because you are an ass.

"It's fine." She stepped back and opened the door wide. "Please, come in."

He offered her the jar as he crossed her threshold, as if a little honey could put a ding in the debt he owed her. "I bought a case at the farmers market yesterday. I thought you might like some."

"Thank you."

Taking the jar, she led him down the bamboo-floored hall to the kitchen. A small porcelain teapot and a single mug sat on the recycled glass island. Above it, bunches of basil hung upside down, drying. The scents filled Sharp's nose, and he instantly craved Italian food.

"Your herb garden is impressive," he said.

"Thank you. I'd never gardened before my aunt left me the house. I was appalled to learn how many chemicals are required to grow a pretty lawn. The herb garden is low maintenance, and I like to use my own when possible. Then I'm sure it's organic." She nodded toward a kitchen window that looked out into a small yard. "I've branched out into vegetables this year. But I'm currently engaged in a hostile battle with a very clever groundhog."

Sharp wandered a circle around the center island. "How's the book?"

"Done and sent off to my agent." She sent him a wry smile.

"What will you do next?"

"Wait to hear from my agent, clean my garage, look for a new project." Setting the jar of honey on the counter, she frowned at him. "You look pale. I hope your recovery is going well."

Sharp felt the flush heat his face. "I'm fine."

Her elegant eyebrow arched. She didn't believe him. "You look exhausted."

"I shouldn't," he admitted. "I've done little but sleep, eat, and go to physical therapy for the past three months."

"You're obviously pushing yourself too hard." She stressed *obviously* like he was a moron. "It wasn't too long ago that you were mostly dead all day."

He couldn't help but smile at *The Princess Bride* reference. But today, he was too tired for the verbal sparring that he usually enjoyed with her. Not to mention the fact that he wasn't supposed to like her.

Her smile faded. "Seriously, you don't look good."

"Gee, thanks."

"Lincoln, give yourself a break. Not to be crude, but your insides were on the outside. You can't expect to recover as if you'd sprained your ankle."

She had a point. His hand went to the scar on his belly.

"Would you like some tea?" Before he answered, she was reaching into the cabinet for another mug.

"Sure, thanks." Sharp scratched his arm. The discomfort of asking for yet another favor spread over his skin like a rash.

"You're not here to discuss my herb garden." Pouring tea, she seemed almost disappointed at the realization.

Or maybe he was seeing what he wanted to see.

"No." Sharp got down to business. Murder was a much more comfortable topic of conversation. "I'm here to ask you about an article you wrote about twenty-five years ago."

He pulled out his phone and showed her the article. She reached for a pair of glasses on the counter and settled them on her nose.

Her brows shot up as she read the screen. "That was the piece that launched my career."

Sharp nodded. "I'm not surprised. It's a stunning bit of research."

The corner of her mouth turned up at the flattery. "But why are you asking about it now?"

"The name Joe Martin came up in an investigation we're working on. You wrote about his conviction in an article."

"That was a long time ago." She waited for more explanation.

Sharp sighed. "You've heard about Paul Knox's murder?"

"The retired deputy who was shot in his own home." She nodded. "The police suspect his stepson." Her eyes widened. "You're working for his mother."

Why was she always three steps ahead of him?

"How did you know?" Sharp drank his tea.

She lifted a shoulder. "His photo is all over the news, and Morgan would not be able to resist trying to save a teenager with evidence stacked against him."

"True," Sharp admitted. "Lance is the boy's hockey coach. He knows the boy very well and believes he's innocent."

Olivia's full lips pressed into a line. "Lance is prone to emotional decisions, and Morgan will support him regardless of her own opinion. Also, they are both far too sensitive when children and teenagers are involved. What do *you* think?"

Sharp snorted at her spot-on assessment of Lance and Morgan.

"Honestly, the evidence is rough," he said. "But I trust Lance's gut. He takes the time to get to know the kids he coaches. He takes mentoring them seriously. Plus, we've found some weaknesses in the sheriff's case."

"Now I'm intrigued."

"I was hoping you would be."

She smiled. "How is Joe Martin involved?"

"His daughter, Tina, is the missing boy's mother."

Olivia's mouth formed an O. "That certainly does make the case interesting, especially since Joe was released from prison recently."

"You know?"

"Yes." She crossed her arms and leaned on the counter. "So why are you here?"

"I want to talk to someone who knows where Joe Martin is and what he's doing now that he's out. I know it's been a long time, but I was hoping you might be able to point me in the right direction."

She snorted. "You can't be serious."

"Martin threatened his daughter. Now he's out of jail, and her husband was murdered and her son has gone missing. Do you still have any contacts that might help? I'm just looking for a lead here."

Olivia's crow's-feet deepened. "Twenty-five years is a long time in drug-dealer years. They don't have long life expectancies. I would bet most of the young men I interviewed for that article are dead. In fact, I know some of them are."

Disappointment filled Sharp. He set down the mug. "Thanks anyway."

"But I have kept in contact with people on the periphery of that life. If Martin returned to Newark, someone will know." She set her mug in the sink. "Let me make a few calls. I'll let you know if I'm successful."

"When will I hear from you?" Sharp pretended he was only anxious about the case, but he actually enjoyed her company. She was smart, confident, and had a quick sense of humor.

"Tomorrow morning at the latest. Give me tonight."

"Thank you." In the meantime, Sharp would return to the background files, murder board, and case reports. He could also stop and check on Jenny for Lance, letting him concentrate on the case.

She smiled, the upturn of her mouth just a little wicked as she walked him back to the front door. "You will owe me quite a few favors. Eventually, I'm going to ask for payback."

Sharp opened the door and glanced over his shoulder at her. "As you wish."

The last thing he heard as she closed the door was a burst of laughter.

Chapter Twenty-Two

The Nelson house was nothing like Morgan expected. Rylee's street could have been a Hollywood set for suburban America. The traditional two-story was well maintained, from its clean white siding to its freshly painted, deep-green shutters. The shrubs were trimmed, the lawn was mowed, and flowers lined the stone walkway that led to a wide front porch.

A gray minivan sat in the driveway, and the front door stood open.

Morgan could see through the screen into what appeared to be a living room. "Someone is here."

Lance parked in front of the house, and they got out of the Jeep. Morgan led the way to the front porch and knocked on the wooden edge of the screen door. A young man of about twenty came to the door.

He frowned. "Can I help you?" His tone suggested suspicion.

Morgan introduced them and offered him her card. "We'd like to ask you a few questions."

He ignored the card. "Questions about what?"

"We're looking for Evan Meade," she said.

"I don't know where Evan Meade is." He moved backward and reached for the wooden door as if to close it.

Lance stepped forward. "Does Rylee?"

The young man stopped and squinted at them through the screen. "Why would my sister know where Evan Meade is? We only know his name from the news."

"Rylee knows Evan." Morgan sensed deep distrust. "We're not the police. I'm a private attorney working for Evan's mother. She wants to find her son. She's terrified something has happened to him. Surely you can understand that."

The young man hesitated, then exhaled and nodded once. "OK." He glanced over his shoulder and scanned the room behind him before he opened the screen door.

"Thank you." Morgan stepped over the threshold into a painfully neat living room that smelled of fresh furniture polish. The furniture was old-fashioned and worn but clean. A soft blue sofa and flowered wing chair faced a TV in the corner of the room.

"I'm Rylee's brother, Trevor. Please sit down." Trevor gestured to the sofa.

Morgan perched on the edge. A spring poked her in the butt.

Lance sat next to her. "We were hoping to speak with Rylee's parents."

Trevor settled in the wing chair, his arms crossed over his body. "Our parents died in a car accident last year."

"We're so sorry for your loss," Morgan said.

Trevor's eyes misted. His throat shifted as he swallowed and regained control. "We're lucky. Mom and Dad were savers, not spenders. They had life insurance policies. We could stay in the house."

Morgan sensed there was much more to the story . . . and that Trevor was desperate. "But something else happened?"

His eyes filled with doubt, as well as the yearning to have someone on his side.

"The responsibility of your sister's well-being must seem overwhelming at times," she said. "And you must feel very much alone."

His shoulders sagged. "I'm a business major at the university, and I work part time as a cashier at the grocery store. Rylee picked up a job at the pizza place in town to help out. As long as we stick to our budget, we scrape by." Temper flared his nostrils. "But one of our neighbors called Child Protective Services, saying my sister is being neglected, which is a total lie. Now we have this social worker who shows up randomly to inspect the house. She'll drive by the house late at night, hoping to catch Rylee alone. I don't even know which one of the neighbors is calling."

Morgan knew that once a family got caught in the social services snare, it was all but impossible to escape it. "Does the neighbor have any specific concerns?"

"I don't know." Trevor's arms dropped to his thighs. "No one will tell me. The social worker keeps telling me if I don't fully cooperate, she can take my sister away. She talked to the school and interviewed my other neighbors. It's humiliating."

And frightening, no doubt.

"I'm sorry this is happening to you," Morgan said. "Does Rylee get into trouble at school?"

"No. Never. Her grades took a dive right after our parents died, but that's understandable. She worked hard this semester to bring her grades back up."

Trevor was at a distinct disadvantage if a social worker wanted to bully him. CPS would not tell him who made the report, and it was very difficult to prove one *hadn't* done something wrong.

"When did this start?" Morgan asked.

"About a month ago." Trevor leaned forward, resting his forearms on his knees. "I feel like we're being watched all the time."

"Do you have an attorney to protect your interests?" Morgan asked.

"I can't afford an attorney," he said.

"Would you allow me to contact social services on your behalf? You have rights, which I doubt they've made clear. They also have a limited amount of time to complete their investigation and declare the claim vindicated or unfounded."

Trevor shook his head. "I can't pay you."

"That's all right," Morgan said. "It will not take up much of my time."

Trevor licked his lips. He seemed to be making a decision. "I don't normally accept charity, but I'll take your offer. I can't let them take Rylee. I'm all she has."

And Morgan suspected the emotional dependence went both ways. Rylee was all Trevor had as well.

He got up and paced the area between the coffee table and the TV console. "The county sheriff left a message for me last night and another this morning. I haven't had the guts to call him back. I'm afraid of what he'll say. And when Rylee came home from work last night, she said a deputy had come to the pizza parlor looking for her in the afternoon. She hadn't started her shift yet. She was so scared, she hid in the bathroom, and the other workers told the deputy she wasn't there."

All of this explained why she had run from Morgan and Lance. No doubt, the sheriff had also tracked Rylee through Evan's cell phone records.

"He probably wants to talk to Rylee about Evan," Morgan said.

"It's not my neighbor's CPS complaint?"

"I don't think so." Morgan assumed Rylee had not mentioned their conversation in the pizza parlor parking lot but decided not to bring it up. She needed Trevor to trust her.

Trevor exhaled. "I can't tell you how much I appreciate your offer to help us. It bugs the hell out of me because I know the sooner I finish school, the better I'll be able to support my sister. If I continue as a full-time student, I'll graduate before Rylee starts college. I'll be able to help with her tuition. She's not athletic. She's smart and gets good grades but not the kind that are going to win her merit scholarships." He shook his head. "I'm not criticizing my sister. I'm not a genius or an athlete either. We're regular people. Our parents taught us that if we worked hard, we could get ahead, but I'm starting to feel like that's not true."

"I'll call CPS and see what I can do." Morgan suspected the report was unfounded, but she made no promises. The home appeared orderly and clean. Trevor seemed sincere, and Rylee had acted to protect her brother. But Morgan had learned many years ago that situations were not always as they seemed. There was a small chance that the neighbor was right, which was the reason CPS was required to investigate every claim. "But I'll be honest with you. Even if the accusation of neglect is declared unfounded, reports remain on file for years. Until she's eighteen, you'll have to be very careful."

Trevor dropped back into the chair. He pushed a hand through his short hair. "So I should call the sheriff?"

"Yes," Morgan said. "It's never good to ignore the sheriff. If I'm wrong, and the call is about the neglect complaint, tell the sheriff I'm your attorney, and we'll schedule an interview when we're all available."

The screen door opened, and Rylee walked in. She wore a frayed denim miniskirt and a black T-shirt. Her gaze landed on Lance and Morgan. Her face drained of color, and she spun, her hand reaching for the door as if to run through it.

"Wait!" Trevor called. "Ms. Dane is a lawyer. She's not with CPS. She's going to help us."

Rylee did a slow turn on the balls of her feet, her face still pale. She walked to her brother's side. He took her hand and squeezed it.

She looked down at Trevor. "Really?"

He nodded.

"We'll get to the bottom of the complaint," Morgan assured them.

Now that she'd seen the siblings together, she wanted to protect them even more. Rylee showed no fear or hesitation with her bother. They had a strong bond, and she clearly trusted him. Maybe the neighbor had been convincing. The CPS worker could be trying to do her best.

Social workers were just like any other group of people—a mix of good, bad, and lazy. Some were dedicated to protecting children. Some were average and simply showed up, and a few abused their power. Unfortunately, one bully in a position of authority could do irreparable harm.

"Ms. Dane and Mr. Kruger want to ask you about a boy named Evan," Trevor said to his sister.

She tried to move away, but he held on to her hand.

"Have you seen him?" he asked.

"No." Rylee didn't fidget or look away. Her posture had relaxed once she accepted that Morgan and Lance were on her side. A lock of short purple hair fell into her eyes, and she brushed it away.

"Why didn't you tell me about him?" Trevor asked.

"He's been arrested a few times." Her eyes brightened with anger. "I knew you wouldn't want me to see him."

"That's right!" Trevor's voice rose. "I can't have you dating a juvenile delinquent with all the CPS stuff going on."

"See?" Rylee jerked her hand from his grip.

Trevor jumped to his feet. "Rylee, this kid is wanted by the police for murder."

Her chin snapped up. "This is why I didn't tell you about him. I knew you'd be mad."

Trevor fought for control. "I'm not mad. I'm terrified."

"Evan is innocent." Rylee started to cry. "I'm sorry. I screw everything up."

Trevor put an arm around her shoulders. "It's OK. We'll deal with it."

She sobbed into his shirt.

"Rylee, I'm only trying to protect you." Frustration underscored Trevor's tone. "I'm trying to keep us together."

Tears wet her cheeks. "I'm sorry. I just—" Her breath hitched. "Most of the kids around here have perfect lives. They don't get what it's like to have your whole life disintegrate. Evan has his own shit to deal with. He understands. Mostly, we just talk."

"You can always talk to me." Trevor looked hurt.

"It's not the same." Rylee's purple hair swayed as she shook her head. "You act like a parent now."

Trevor couldn't win.

"It's important that we find Evan," Lance said. "He's been hurt, and he's in danger."

"We want to help him," Morgan added. "He's in a situation he can't manage by himself."

"I haven't seen him." Rylee chewed on her lip. "But I wish I had. I'm worried about him too." Her eyes turned angry. "The police are stupid. Evan would never have hurt Paul."

"You sound sure," Morgan said.

Rylee nodded. "I never met Paul, but I know that Evan liked him. His real father is a jerk. Evan knows the difference."

"Do you have any idea where Evan might go if he wanted to hide?" Morgan asked.

"No." Rylee shook her head.

Morgan's years as a prosecutor had made her adept at spotting a liar, except for the occasional sociopath. Rylee seemed to be telling the truth. So no one had seen Evan. Morgan wished the kids were lying. At least that would be a lead she and Lance could follow. But now they had nothing.

They left the house and returned to the Jeep.

"Now what?" Morgan asked. "We seem to have hit a wall. Evan has to be *somewhere*."

Lance's phone beeped. He pulled it from his pocket and answered the call. "Hi, Mom. You're on speaker. Morgan is here too."

"Hi, Jenny," Morgan said.

"Hello, Morgan dear," Jenny began.

"I'm sorry I haven't been over." Lance set the phone on the console. "I didn't want to give you the kids' germs. And now we're caught up in this case."

"Honey, you're doing exactly what you should be doing. I'm fine," Jenny assured him. "Now, I have some good news and some bad news for you."

"Tell us the bad news first," Morgan said.

"Sam Jones, the man who filed the excessive force complaint against Deputy Springer, was a transient. One of the reasons the complaint was dismissed was because Sam disappeared. I spoke to his lawyer. He has no idea where Sam might be."

Could Sam be holding a grudge?

"What's the good news?" Lance asked.

"I found a piece of land at Lake George owned by Robert Springer." Jenny gave them the details on the property.

"Thanks, Mom." Lance pulled away from the curb. "I'll be over to visit as soon as I can."

"Lance, you do what you need to do. I'm not going anywhere." Jenny ended the call.

"Could be Brian Springer's brother." Morgan plugged the address into the map app on her phone. "It's about thirty minutes away."

"Let's go." Lance stepped on the gas pedal, and the car accelerated.

Chapter Twenty-Three

Lance pulled over onto the shoulder of the road and studied the digital map on his phone. His Jeep was a blue dot on the single road that cut through a huge swath of green. "The GPS says we're here, but I don't see a house or a driveway."

Morgan turned her head to look behind the Jeep. "According to the information your mother sent, the property comprises two hundred acres and includes a stretch of waterfront. How far are we from the lake?"

Lance zoomed out on the map. The lake appeared as a huge blue area. He touched the screen. "Here."

"It's just on the other side of these woods." Morgan frowned at the map. "If you own lakefront property, you build your house both with a view of the water and access to the road. Keep crawling along. There must be a driveway or private road that cuts through to the lake."

He eased off the brake and let the Jeep roll forward. The trees were thick and green with summer foliage. Lance couldn't see very far into the woods.

A quarter of a mile down the road, Morgan tapped his shoulder and pointed to a gap in the trees. "What's that?"

Tree branches partially concealed a narrow dirt lane. Lance made the turn. The lane was rutted and muddy, and Lance kept the Jeep's speed slow. The narrow road ended in a clearing. A log cabin hunkered at the rear of the cleared space. Behind it, the lake stretched out as far as he could see. The day was still, and the overcast sky had turned the water into a mirror.

He turned the Jeep to face the lane in case they needed to make a quick exit.

"There's no vehicle here." Morgan scanned the clearing. "But I see tire tracks that look fairly recent."

"Someone has been here since Tuesday morning's storm." Lance took his flashlight and camera from the glove compartment and stuffed them into his cargo pants pockets. His phone took decent pictures, but it didn't have optical zoom or produce the same quality images as his digital 35mm. "Are you ready?"

Morgan changed into her boots. "Yes."

They stepped out of the Jeep. He could smell the pines and the mossy scent of the lake. Mud sucked at his feet as they crossed the clearing. He surveyed their surroundings. The storm had knocked small branches and leaves on the moss-covered ground in front of the cabin. The lot was heavily wooded, with dense foliage that would provide excellent cover should someone be watching them. A squirrel scurried up a nearby pine tree. Overhead, a hawk glided in a lazy circle.

They walked up three wooden steps to a rough porch. He stood behind the doorframe. Morgan did the same on the other side. He knocked. No one answered.

Moving to a window, Morgan cupped her hands over her eyes. "I don't see anyone inside."

Lance knocked again. Hearing nothing but forest sounds, he pulled a small leather case from his pocket and took out two small tools.

"You're breaking and entering into a cop's vacation cabin?" Morgan sighed.

"It's his brother's place, not his." Lance took a pair of gloves from his pocket and tugged them on. Then he dangled a second pair in front of Morgan's face. "If Evan's life weren't at stake, I wouldn't do this."

Probably.

"I know." She took the gloves.

Morgan had a black-and-white, right-versus-wrong sense of justice. Breaking the law bothered her. Lance's moral code was slightly more flexible. A simple B and E wouldn't keep him up at night.

He tried the knob. "The door is unlocked. So technically, we'll just be entering."

"We're not even sure this is the right place." She glanced at the driveway, then waved a gnat away from her face.

"We'll know soon." He pushed the door open and sniffed. "I don't smell a rotting corpse, but there's something in the air."

Morgan followed him in. "I smell mold, which isn't unusual for a waterfront property, but there's something else." She inhaled deeper, her nose wrinkling. "I don't know what it is, but it's unpleasant."

Lance sniffed. Under the must, the air smelled faintly like the locker room at the ice rink. Lance was always riding the team to clean their gear, but teenage boys being what they were . . .

"It's sweat."

"Yes, that's it," Morgan agreed.

The front door opened directly into a large great room. The kitchen was sized to accommodate large groups, with a generous center island and a table that seated eight. In the adjoining living area, a giant U-shaped sectional couch faced a wood-burning fireplace. The floors were wide-planked golden pine, and the walls were rough-hewn logs. Huge windows in both rooms faced the lake.

With Morgan at his left flank, Lance gave the house a thorough look-through to ensure they were alone. There were three bedrooms and two full baths on the first floor. A staircase in the back hall led to two additional bedrooms separated by a full bath. The upstairs bedrooms each held two sets of bunk beds. He crouched to check under beds and opened the closets. Morgan went into the Jack-and-Jill bath. Lance heard a door being opened and the scraping sound of a shower curtain being pushed aside.

She emerged a minute later and jerked her thumb over her shoulder at the bathroom. "The bath is stocked with rubber duckies and No More Tangles. Upstairs looks like kids' space."

"Agreed. Let's go back downstairs." Lance walked through the downstairs bedrooms, looking for anything that could belong to Brian—like a computer—but he found nothing personal. Towels and sheets were stacked in the linen closets. The bathrooms had plenty of soap and toothpaste.

"Maybe they rent out the cabin." Morgan led the way back to the front rooms. She went to the window in the living area and scanned the front yard. Seemingly satisfied that no one was coming, she wandered around the living room, opening drawers.

Lance poked through some envelopes and papers stacked on the counter. "These bills are addressed to Robert Springer, Brian's brother."

"Lance," Morgan called softly.

She stood in an empty spot in front of the TV. Her body was too still, her eyes cast down at the floor.

When Lance had first walked through the cabin, he'd been focused on looking for people. He'd glanced over the couch long enough to see that no one was hiding there. But now he registered details. The coffee table had been moved aside.

"What is it?" As he walked closer, he could see a wooden chair on its side in the middle of the space.

"Dark stains on the floor."

Lance crossed the floor to stand next to her. "Where?"

She pointed.

Lance squatted to examine the spots more closely. He pulled his penlight from his pocket and shone it on the floor. The stains were dark red on the honey-colored pine.

"Blood," Morgan said.

"That would be my guess." Though he couldn't be sure without a rapid stain ID kit.

"It looks like someone wiped up the liquid but didn't bother trying to clean the floor." Lance crouched. There were at least three stains on the wood. The police would likely find more with a spray of luminol and a black light. Lengths of rope were scattered around the chair, as if someone had been bound.

He stood. "Someone was tied to the chair."

"And tortured in some way," Morgan said. After a short pause, she added, "Paul was shot in the belly. Maybe that was torture as well."

"Maybe." Lance pictured the body in the morgue. "That teenage boy who was pulled from the lake was beaten before he was killed."

Morgan crossed her arms. "The killer wanted information. He's looking for something."

"Or someone." Lance stared at the bloodstains. "I don't like the odds of this victim still being alive."

"Paul was shot in the head. The boy in the morgue was shot in the head. If our killer is consistent, whoever was tortured here would have met the same fate." Morgan's head turned toward the kitchen window and its view of the lake. "He's already dumped one body in the water."

Lance photographed the bloodstain, then walked the rest of the room and found several more spots. Marks on the floor caught his attention. Faint scrapes formed two parallel lines. Heel marks. He followed them to the back door in the kitchen, snapping pictures all the way. "Someone dragged a body through the kitchen. I'm going outside to see if I can find tracks. See if you can find any more blood inside."

Morgan opened her tote bag and produced a flashlight. She shone it on the floor and began moving the beam in a grid pattern across the room.

Lance went out onto a large deck. The deck was well worn, and at the base of the steps, he found matching drag marks in the mud. He followed them as they sloped to the lake and traveled onto the dock that extended over the water. At the end of the dock, where a loose rope suggested a boat had been tied, was a long dark stain.

Blood.

It stained the bottom of a piling and cleat, as if someone had tried to grab the dock to keep from being dragged onto a boat. Lance looked out over the water. The cabin was on the south shore. From this viewpoint, the water seemed endless. He'd been to Lake George to hike, camp, and a few years ago, to compete in a triathlon. Long and narrow, the lake was over thirty miles long and up to two miles wide. Its maximum depth was two hundred feet. The killer could have tossed the victim overboard anywhere. They didn't even know if the person was alive or dead. If a body was weighted down and dumped somewhere in the lake, it would be damned hard to find.

As he backtracked to the cabin, he took pictures of the drag trail.

Alarm prickled when he didn't see Morgan in the kitchen or living room. "Morgan?"

"Here." Her head appeared above the couch. "I found something."

"What is it?" Lance walked closer.

Morgan was crouched low, her flashlight pointing under an end table. Her head tilted. Her breath caught, and the color drained from her face. "Oh, my God. It's a finger."

Lance hurried closer. Her skin grayed. She rocked back on her heels and covered her mouth. He moved her aside and took her place. The finger lay on its side. "The severed end looks neatly clipped off. He used something sharp."

Morgan shuddered and got to her feet. "I'm going outside for a minute."

Lance took pictures of the bloodstains and finger. The flash went off, illuminating another finger next to the leg of the sofa. It looked like a pinkie. He examined the first finger a second time. Slightly longer than the pinkie, it was probably a ring finger. Lance checked under the rest of the furniture, then stood.

He joined Morgan on the porch. She was staring at the woods.

"There was another finger under the couch," he said.

Still pale, she closed her eyes and swallowed. "We have to call Sheriff Colgate and the local police."

"We'll be spending the rest of the evening being drilled by the local cops." What did it matter? Lance had no idea where to look for Evan. But he wanted to be back in Scarlet Falls in case they found a clue.

"There's no avoiding that." Morgan's arms were folded over her waist. She clutched her phone in her hand. The tips of her fingers trembled.

They'd both seen dead bodies before, but Lance had to admit, body parts freaked him out too. He pictured a man tied to a chair, and someone snipping off his fingers one by one.

"We are missing something big in this case, something that would drive a person to kidnap, torture, and murder someone."

"Maybe two someones." Morgan dialed 911 on her phone. "There's a very good chance that someone was killed here today."

"But who? Did Brian lose two fingers, or did he remove someone else's?"

"That's the big question, right? Is Brian a victim? Or did he kill Paul?" Morgan turned away to speak to the emergency dispatcher.

Lance prayed the fingers didn't belong to Evan.

He paced the porch. He felt trapped, useless. Their investigation was one dead end after another, and he couldn't help but feel like Evan's time was running out. He glanced back at the cabin. The killer was getting desperate.

Chapter Twenty-Four

Evan paddled. Luckily, the current was still strong, and he really only had to steer. He needed to put as much distance between himself and the house he'd broken into as possible.

He'd managed to get himself and his bags of stolen goods out the window and into the canoe. He'd also successfully launched the boat without getting wet. But how did the police know he'd been there?

He must have been seen. He would have to be more careful and stick to the woods. His arm throbbed as he worked the paddle with his good hand. The wound burned now, and he felt hot all over. He ate a few crackers, opened another water bottle, and drank, swallowing down some more ibuprofen. But camouflaging the pain wasn't enough. He needed antibiotics. Bacteria was holding a rager inside his body.

He wished he could contact his mom. She would know what to do, and she deserved to know he was still alive. She flipped out if he was more than fifteen minutes past curfew.

I'm a nurse. Every time you're late, I picture you on a gurney covered in blood.

She must be losing it by now.

Guilt compounded his misery. *I'm sorry, Mom.* He didn't know how he could have handled the situation differently, but he still felt like he'd fucked up.

The canoe slid through the water. Gnats buzzed around his face, and he waved them away. Though the current was strong, there were no big rocks or piles of debris in this stretch. The water seemed to be deeper here. Woods thickened on both sides. The seclusion was comforting, but he wished something around him looked familiar.

Would the police know he'd been in the house? If they did, they'd come after him. He needed to get off the river. But how could he find a place to hide if he didn't even know where he was?

The sound of rushing water floated across the forest. Evan lifted his paddle and listened. The rush grew to a roar. He used the paddle to guide the canoe to the bank. Grabbing a low-hanging branch to steady the boat, he tried to get his bearings.

The roar seemed louder than the rapids he'd encountered the day before. There was only one body of water that made that much noise. He must be near Scarlet Falls, which meant he'd traveled the whole Deer River because that's where it ended. The falls spilled into big rocky pools and eventually ran into Scarlet Lake.

He worked the canoe closer to the riverbank. If he were truly at the falls, he wouldn't be able to go farther by canoe, not unless he was willing to drag the boat over land for a significant distance. Even if he were willing, he wasn't able.

He and Rylee sometimes hung out at the Scarlet Falls lookout. It was close to the beach on Scarlet Lake where all the kids went. Could he get help there? The only people he could trust were Jake and Rylee. Jake was his best friend, and Rylee . . . they'd never even kissed. So she wasn't exactly his girlfriend, but he wanted her to be. All that mattered was that he knew he could trust her.

What if the police knew he'd left the house by boat? They'd follow him downriver. They'd end up here. They'd bring dogs. They'd find him.

He had to hide the boat, so they couldn't be sure where he'd left the river. He released the branch and let the canoe drift farther. The roar of water grew louder. A few minutes later, Evan could see the jagged boulders that marked the end of the Deer River. The water was deeper here. Engorged from recent rain, the river poured over the edge.

He couldn't risk getting any closer. He snagged another branch and worked the canoe to the rocky riverbank. He removed his bags of supplies and set them on the shore. Then he climbed out of the canoe. He hated to part with the boat, but he absolutely had to prevent anyone from finding it.

He began tossing rocks into its hull. Large, small, it didn't matter; they added up. Exhaustion weighed on him as much as the rocks weighed down the canoe. It seemed to take forever. But he shouldn't have worried. It was all a matter of physics and water displacement. Eventually, the canoe floated lower. Water rose up its sides and began to pour over the edges. As soon as the water filled the canoe, it sank. Evan watched it disappear.

Grabbing his supplies in one hand, he stumbled along the riverbank, sticking to the rocks to avoid leaving tracks. The old-man sneakers he'd stolen had decent traction, but Evan's body was weakening. Sinking the canoe had sapped his strength. His head spun, and his thigh muscles felt soft and rubbery.

The sun was starting to dip toward the trees as the day faded toward evening. On the horizon, dark clouds approached. He didn't know exactly what time it was, but the thought of spending the night outside in the rain made his eyes fill. His stomach clenched with hunger pangs. He sat down on a rock and fished into the nylon bag for a can of peaches and the can opener. He ate every section of sweet fruit with his fingers, then drank the juice from the can, making sure to get every last drop. Fluid was precious, and his supplies were running low already.

He rinsed the can in the river. If he could find a safe, concealed place to start a fire, he could filter water through a T-shirt and boil it in the can the way Paul had showed him. It might not taste great, but it would be safe to drink.

Opening one of the stolen water bottles, he washed down the peaches. His mouth and throat were still dry. The ibuprofen was taking the edge off his fever, but between the heat, the humidity, and his elevated body temperature, he could not stay hydrated. He ran his tongue over his lips. They felt chapped and dry.

He picked up his bags again, hoisted them over his good shoulder, and started walking. The rocky trail was rough. Normally, he and Rylee hung out at the overlook on the other side of the ravine from the falls. He had no idea how to get down on this side. The trail twisted and became steep. He rounded a bend. The trail opened and gave him a view of the waterfall from the opposite side. He was at the top of the ravine.

Sitting on his haunches, he caught his breath and stared at the falls. White water rushed off a rock ledge into a deep pool forty feet below. The pool at the bottom was circular, maybe fifty feet in diameter, and was surrounded by sheer rock walls on three sides. The fourth side opened up to rocky ledges and holes where the water would eventually make its way to the lake. The water looked deep, even though the force of the falls churned up the sediment and turned the entire basin murky. Foam floated on the surface.

Gray-and-black clouds hung low on the horizon, and the air was heavy with a coming storm. He needed to find shelter. On the other side of the ravine, there was an observation deck at the top of the falls. It had wooden steps that led down to a second lower deck and finally to the ground. From there, you could walk to the lake, which was about two hundred yards away. The water from the falls flowed from the pool over a wide section of shallow white water filled with big rocks and narrow pools before it turned and circled around to dump into the lake. The water was fenced off from the public area and several signs proclaimed it DANGEROUS and warned visitors to KEEP OFF THE ROCKS.

But there were no such accommodations on this side of the ravine. He'd have to climb down, cross the white water using the boulders that stuck out of it as stepping-stones, and climb over the safety fence.

He scanned the trail below him. The last twenty feet of the descent were very steep. Could he slide down on his ass? He could use the rope he'd stolen. But once he'd climbed down, how would he get back up if he needed to make a quick escape? He wouldn't. Rope climbing wasn't possible with one hand.

He made his way down the first ten feet and looked over the edge. Now that he was closer, he could see that the descent wasn't as impossible as he'd first thought. The walls of the ravine weren't completely vertical. They were made up of large sheared-off slabs of rock. Small ledges formed irregular, narrow steps. Weeds sprouted between the rocks. At the bottom, small trees grew in crevices. He tied the rope to a nearby tree trunk and used it as a backup safety measure, winding it loosely around his waist and holding it in his good hand in case he lost his footing. He began his descent, moving painstakingly from foothold to foothold. Ten feet from the bottom, his foot caught in a vine. It snapped under the weight of his body, and he slid down the rock face eighteen inches until he hit the end of the rope. The jolt sent pain shooting through his arm.

He unwound the rope, righted his body, and finished the descent. His weak knees gave out, and he landed in a patch of waist-high weeds. His tailbone rang on impact, but he'd survived. He stood on shaky legs and stared into a small cave.

The cave had been formed by two giant flat-sided rocks leaning on each other. The opening hadn't been visible from above, but his fall had flattened weeds and dislodged a section of intertwined vines and moss to reveal the entrance. It wasn't much wider than Evan's arm span, if he could have held both arms out. He tied the rope to a tree trunk. The tan color blended in with the rocks.

He stuck his head inside the cave. Empty and dry, it extended about ten feet to the base of the rocks. The ground rose slightly in elevation toward the rear. Daylight shone through the top, where the two boulders met. He crawled all the way to the back. Here, the cave ceiling was about four feet high. No one would be able to see him from the outside. When the thunderstorm broke tonight, at least Evan would be able to stay mostly dry. The last thing he needed was another soaking-wet night.

He wanted to lie down and sleep, but instead of resting, he stowed his meager supplies in the cave and took the nylon bag with him as he went looking for firewood.

He had matches. Maybe he could risk a small fire tonight. He didn't want to be spotted, but the opening at the top of the cave would draw the smoke up like a chimney, and the spray and mist that rose from the waterfall would conceal the smoke as it escaped.

He left the cave, shivering as he passed through the mist. In order to reach the trees, he navigated a series of jagged wet rocks. Water swirled and eddied around them. He moved slowly, placing each foot with extreme care. He had to make several trips across. He filled the nylon bag with dried pine needles and small pieces of bark. He cradled larger logs one by one with his uninjured arm. By the time he'd accumulated a decent stockpile of dry wood, he was exhausted, and it was dark. He finished the bottled water, but it wasn't enough to quench his thirst. His vision blurred, and he squeezed his eyes closed a few times to clear it. He was dehydrated.

Without some help, Evan doubted he'd survive. The need for water drove him to risk the treacherous trip to the lake in the dark.

Please let Rylee or Jake be at the lake tonight.

Either one of them would surely bring him supplies.

He crossed the water with painstaking care and started down the trail that led to the lake, moving carefully and stopping to listen every few minutes. As he drew closer, voices carried from the beach. He could see the lake. Under the overcast sky, it lay as black and shimmery as an oil slick.

The faint smell of smoke scented the air. More than anything, Evan wanted to go back to the days when getting caught setting an illegal bonfire at the lake was the worst of his worries. His arm burned, and mosquitoes swarmed around him as he crouched behind a fallen tree and scanned the beach. Twenty teenagers sat on the sand, smoking cigarettes in groups and talking. The cops were always chasing the kids off the beach when the kids weren't doing anything wrong. Why was it illegal to be on the beach after dark?

Evan scanned the gravel parking area. His heart leaped when he saw Rylee's old car. She was here. She would help him. At least she would bring him water and blankets. He looked for her on the beach and spotted her sitting in the sand. She was hugging her knees and staring into the fire. Kids clustered in small groups around her.

How could he contact her without showing himself to any of the other kids? His gaze swung back to her old Buick. The door lock on the driver's side was broken, so she never bothered to lock any of the doors, not that anyone would want to steal her POS. The car barely ran.

Crouching, Evan ran toward her car. The effort of the short sprint winded him. He popped his head up to make sure no one was around, then opened the rear door. The dome light seemed as bright as a floodlight as he climbed into the back seat. The door made a squeaking sound as he gently pulled it closed, trying not to make too much noise. The dome light didn't go out. Panic wormed through his belly. The heavy door hadn't closed completely. Someone was going to see the light. He quickly opened the door and pulled harder. It shut with a noise that sounded deafening.

Praying that no one on the beach heard or saw him get into the car, Evan huddled in the dark behind the driver's seat. Minutes passed. Sweat dripped down his back, followed by a cold shiver. His fever was rising again.

Footsteps crunched on gravel. Evan's pulse spiked. The driver's door opened with the familiar rusty squeal. He peered around the headrest. *Rylee!* Relief weakened his muscles.

"Hey," he whispered.

Rylee startled. Raising her hands in a defensive posture, she turned and stared at him for a second. "Holy shit. You scared me to death."

He cleared his throat. There was no need to whisper. No one could hear them. "Sorry."

"Oh, my God, Evan. Are you OK? Where have you been? Everyone is looking for you."

"I know." He glanced around. The parking area still looked clear. "No one can find me. But I need help."

Voices approached.

"Get down out of sight." Rylee faced forward and lifted her phone, pretending to send a text.

Evan ducked behind the seat.

"OK. It's cool. They're gone." Rylee glanced back at him, her eyebrows scrunched with worry. "You look like shit. Are you hurt? On the news, they said you could have been shot."

"I was. In the arm. It's bad." Somehow, talking about his wound made it hurt more. More dry tears pressured his eyes. "I need help."

"OK." Rylee's jaw tightened. "What can I do?"

"I need water and a blanket."

"I can get those." Rylee nodded.

"I'm pretty sure my arm is infected. Do you have any antibiotics at your house?"

"I don't know," Rylee said. "I don't think so, but I'll look."

"Thanks." Evan couldn't conceal his disappointment.

Rylee turned to stare between the seats at him. "Seriously, you look bad. Do you want me to contact your mom? She'll know what to do."

Evan knew he wouldn't survive much longer on his own. For a minute, he balanced his own life with placing his mother in potential danger. She'd always told Evan that he was her world.

"You'll have to be careful." He gave Rylee his mom's cell phone number. "I'm sure the police are watching her. They think I killed Paul."

"I'll make sure no one is listening before I tell her anything," Rylee assured him.

Evan leaned his face on the back of the seat. The vinyl was cool against his cheek. "Aren't you even gonna ask me if I did it?"

"No." Rylee's lips curled in anger. "I know you wouldn't shoot Paul. Anyone who thinks you did is an idiot."

"Thanks." Sadness and despair built in Evan's chest. "I really liked Paul." The hitch in his voice embarrassed him.

Her expression softened. "I know you did. What I don't understand is why they think you're guilty."

"Because it was a cop who did it. A detective. He had a badge on his belt."

"Shit. No wonder you don't want to be found."

Rylee checked the time on her phone. "I have to get home. My brother has been a real hard-ass about curfew because some asshole neighbor keeps calling CPS for no reason." She reached for her door handle. "But my brother did set me up with an emergency road kit in my trunk. Let me see what's in there."

Evan closed his eyes. Just talking to her made him feel better. Someone believed him. Someone was on his side. Someone he could trust.

She got out of the car and went around to open the trunk. A minute later, she returned with a small black duffel bag in her hand. Closing the car door, she handed the bag over the seat. "There's a few bottles of water, a space blanket, and a couple of protein bars. If that will get you through the night, I can bring you more supplies tomorrow evening.

If I try and sneak out later tonight, my brother will get suspicious. I'll have to come while he's at work."

"Thanks. I knew I could count on you."

"Dude, you'd do the same for me."

Evan nodded.

Rylee looked up. "Shit. There's a cop here. Not a regular police car but an unmarked one. That's weird."

Evan lifted his chin to peer over the seat. A dark sedan had stopped at the entrance to the lot. It looked like the same car that he'd seen the night of Paul's murder. It must be the killer's car. Terror clenched his throat. "I have to get away."

Rylee leaned on her steering wheel, her face scrunched in confusion. "He's just sitting there. Why isn't he running everyone off the beach?"

"Because he's looking for me." Evan's breathing quickened. "I can't let him find me."

"Where are you going to be?"

"There's a small cave in the ravine on the other side of the falls. It's hard to see from the top. I'm going to hide there. If you go to the overlook and whistle real loud, I'll hear you."

"OK." Rylee stared through the windshield. "Hold on. A man in a suit just got out of the car. I'll tell you when he's not looking." She popped the plastic cover off the dome light and unscrewed the bulb. "Kids are scattering."

Evan eased himself onto the seat, bending double to stay out of sight.

"Now," Rylee said.

Evan slipped out of the car, duffel bag in hand. Adrenaline gave him an energy boost as he weaved his way through the parked cars. Dozens of kids were scattering on the beach. Evan went the other direction, toward the woods. He stumbled into the trees. Hiding behind the trunk of a big pine, he peered around it. The cop was busy asking questions.

He squinted at the man. Was that the man who had killed Paul? He was too far away, and it was too dark to tell. He was too afraid to get any closer, especially since it seemed that he'd gotten away without being seen.

Turning around, he lugged the bag back to the falls. At the crossing, he slung the handles of the duffel bag over his good shoulder and began placing each foot with extreme care. He tested the placement of each foot before transferring his weight. On the third boulder, water gushed over the top. He lost his footing and slipped. He threw his hands forward. His wound went white-hot with agony. He went down on one knee, pain exploding through the bone as it landed on solid rock.

He breathed through the pain. Next to the rock he knelt on, a swirling eddy made a sucking sound, and he was grateful he hadn't slipped into it.

Evan made the rest of the crossing without incident. When he reached the safety of the cave, he crawled to the rear and curled up in a fetal position. As the blackness took over, he closed his eyes and hoped he didn't die overnight.

Chapter Twenty-Five

Morgan faced the sheriff over his messy desk, a cup of cold coffee in her hand. "Does the finger belong to Brian Springer?"

At her side, Lance fidgeted, clearly annoyed at being called to Colgate's office. It was late, and they'd missed bedtime with the kids. Again. Morgan was equally as irritated.

They'd already spent several hours being questioned by the Warren County sheriff, who'd insisted on a summary of their whole case. He'd threatened to lock them up on trespassing charges if they didn't cooperate. Morgan had argued them out of a breaking and entering charge, but the trespassing was harder. Since they'd discovered body parts, it seemed wiser and more expedient to comply. Neither she nor Lance wanted to spend the evening sitting in a holding cell. Now Colgate wanted them to rehash the entire case.

She was running out of patience. She and Lance were, once again, making up for the inadequacies of his department. The sheriff's department was understaffed, and Colgate didn't have the mental or physical energy for an investigation of this magnitude. He looked thoroughly worn out. Unfortunately, Stella had been right about his stubbornness and his pride. His chin was up, and his posture was stiff.

He would never admit his investigation was lacking. Instead, he'd get angry that they'd found a lead in his case.

The sheriff's chair squeaked as he shifted forward and slammed two fists onto the desk. A giant stack of pink message slips fluttered. "You're both lucky the Warren County sheriff didn't lock you both up for breaking and entering."

"We didn't break and enter," Morgan said. "The door was unlocked."

"Trespassing then." The sheriff picked up a pen and pointed it at Lance. "Why the hell were you up there anyway? If you had evidence that something happened to Brian, and you didn't share it with me . . ."

"We had no evidence," Morgan clarified. "Just a hunch."

"We were concerned about Deputy Springer." Lance crossed his arms over his chest.

"The neighbors said Brian talked about going fishing." Morgan was a terrible liar. So she stuck with the truth and omitted what she didn't want to share. "But he normally left them a key to feed the cat and bring in the mail. He didn't do either of those things. Yet no one has seen him."

The sheriff huffed. "That's thin. Lots of men like to go camping, fishing, or hunting and get off the radar. Not everyone wants to be available or have a phone attached to his ass 24/7. Brian planned his vacation months ago."

"Which is exactly why we didn't call you." Morgan sipped from the cup. "We didn't want to waste your time."

The sheriff tapped his pen on the blotter. "You haven't explained why you went inside the cabin."

Technically, their transgression was in the Warren County sheriff's jurisdiction, and he had eventually accepted their explanation. On the other hand, Brian's disappearance was Colgate's business.

Lance answered, his voice flat from repeating the same story multiple times. "We went to the cabin. There was no car parked outside, but we knocked on the door anyway. No one answered. The drag marks I found out back concerned me very much. When I discovered the front door was open, I decided to go in to see if Brian was in any trouble."

While waiting for the Warren County Sheriff's Department to respond to their call, Morgan and Lance had agreed on which details they needed to omit from their statement. Morgan might be a terrible liar, but as a trial lawyer, she had mad fact-manipulation-and-omission skills.

"We saw the bloodstains, the overturned chair, and the severed fingers. We called the Warren County sheriff and you." Morgan lowered her cup. "Frankly, you should be grateful. If we hadn't entered the cabin, no one would know someone had been tortured there."

Colgate scowled, then his expression shifted into resignation. "The fingers belong to Brian. We were able to match his prints."

Lance sat back. "Shit."

So Brian had been the victim. Could both Paul and Brian have known about another corrupt deputy? Was there another person involved they hadn't even identified yet? On the bright side, the discovery of Brian Springer's fingers made Evan look less like Paul's killer.

"Have you found criminals Paul arrested who might want revenge?" Morgan asked.

"No." The sheriff shook his head.

"What about Sam Jones?" Morgan asked.

The sheriff stared at her. "How did you find out about him?"

She didn't answer. "Did Brian beat Mr. Jones? Did Mr. Jones hold a grudge?"

"The case was minor." The sheriff exhaled loudly. "Jones disappeared as soon as he was released. I doubt very much he came back to take his revenge."

But Morgan didn't let it go. "How badly was he injured?"

The sheriff waved off her question. "It was minor. Mr. Jones was just a drunk."

A few heartbeats of silence passed.

The sheriff dropped the pen and scrubbed a hand down his face. "Warren County is putting divers in the water, using sonar, and dragging parts of the lake, but that water is damned deep. If a body was properly weighted, it might not turn up for a very long time."

"Have they found the boat?" Lance asked.

The sheriff nodded. "Yes. Sonar picked it up. It's sunk about two hundred feet offshore. It'll take a while to salvage it. They sent a diver down. There was no body on board."

Lance said, "This killer is *CSI*-savvy. He didn't leave prints or DNA behind at Paul's murder scene. This one will be no different."

"Why didn't he make any effort to cover up his activities?" Morgan asked. "He didn't scrub the floor. He didn't bother to look for the fingers."

"It wasn't his DNA," Lance speculated. "He wasn't concerned about it."

"Maybe he didn't have time," the sheriff added. "I have one more piece of news for you."

Morgan held back a smart comment. Had the sheriff decided to share with them again? She didn't fully trust him now.

"The teenage boy in the morgue has been identified as Dylan James. He's nineteen and lived with his parents near Deer Lake. His parents reported him missing Tuesday. He was supposed to be staying over at his girlfriend's house, which is about a mile from home. But they got into a fight, and he decided to walk home. His girlfriend had picked him up, so he didn't have his car. The girlfriend isn't sure what time he left her house, but he never made it home."

"Superficially, he looked like Evan," Lance said, his voice quiet.

The sheriff nodded, grim. "They were both dressed in jeans, sneakers, and black T-shirts."

"That's the standard teenage uniform." Morgan blinked hard, trying to clear her tired eyes.

Colgate shuffled a few file folders on his desk and removed two photographs. One was of Evan. The second was another older teen with the same coloring and similar features.

Lance glanced at the photos and sighed, his chest heaving once.

Morgan scanned the images. "They would be easily confused in the rain and dark."

"Or it was a coincidental accident," the sheriff said.

"You can't still believe Evan killed Paul?" Morgan asked. "Not after we found Brian's severed fingers?"

The sheriff's face flushed deep pink. "We have no evidence that Brian's situation is related to Paul's murder. Coincidences happen." The sheriff folded his arms.

"Two of them?" Lance's voice rose.

Morgan was too damned tired to argue with the bullheaded sheriff. She sat straighter and dropped her empty coffee cup in the trash can next to his desk. "If you don't have any more questions tonight, we'd like to go home and get some sleep."

"Go." The sheriff waved them off. "But if you find any more information, I want a call immediately."

Morgan nodded once, but she was careful not to make any verbal promises. They left the sheriff's office and went out into the sticky evening air. Morgan lifted the neck of her blouse away from her body. "Could it get more humid?"

"Not without the air being liquid." Lance glanced at the sky. "There's another thunderstorm coming."

"Maybe it will break the heat." Morgan hopped into the Jeep.

Lance slid behind the wheel. "Home?"

"Yes. We both need sleep. We can't function if we keep going at this pace." Morgan glanced at Lance. Would he be able to sleep? "I know you're worried."

"We are running out of leads. Maybe some sleep will help." Lance turned the Jeep toward home.

"One thing I've been thinking about," Morgan said. "If the fingers belonged to Brian, then he's not our killer. But that doesn't necessarily mean it isn't a cop, maybe another deputy, either active or retired."

"That would explain how the killer gained entry to Paul's house."

"Paul let him in." Morgan rubbed the back of her neck. "Would Paul have let Kirk in?"

"Maybe." Lance steered the Jeep through an intersection. "Kirk is Evan's father. Tina said that Paul liked to take care of her. Maybe he thought he could talk Kirk out of being an asshole."

"I think that's a permanent affliction." Morgan smiled.

"Seems like."

Twenty minutes later, thunder rumbled and rain began to fall as they parked in front of the house. Morgan whipped a travel umbrella out of her bag. Opening the car door a few inches, she stuck it through the gap and pressed the button.

Lance shook his head. "Is there anything you don't keep in that bag? You're like Mary Poppins."

They'd watched the movie four times when the kids had been sick.

"I like to be prepared." Morgan stepped out of the Jeep. Shoving the door closed with her foot, she jogged to the front porch and unlocked the door. Lance followed her inside.

The house was dark. She'd called home hours before to let everyone know they'd be late. Morgan set her umbrella by the door and removed her shoes. Lance left his wet boots by the front door too. They walked with quiet steps down the hall. She opened the girls' bedroom door and poked her head into the room. All three kids were asleep. Morgan eased the door closed and continued to the bedroom that she now shared with Lance.

She washed up, put on her pajamas, and crawled into bed. Lance had changed into his pajama bottoms and doubled his pillows. Bare chested, he reclined against the headboard, looking at his phone.

Morgan slid into bed. "Anything important?"

"No." Lance plugged the charging cord into his phone.

Morgan did the same. "I'm sorry. I know you're worried."

He leaned over and kissed her. "Let's sleep now. We'll worry tomorrow."

Morgan knew he was saying that for her benefit. She was the one who slept when she was depressed or stressed. Lance was the opposite. But she was too tired to argue. She rolled closer and closed her eyes. Remembering his vanishing act the previous night, she threw a leg over one of his to make sure he didn't disappear.

Chapter Twenty-Six

Lance cracked one eyelid. He felt like he'd just closed his eyes. What was that smell?

"I frew up," a tiny voice said in the darkness. Sophie stood next to the bed, her face teary. The unmistakable odor of vomit wafted from her.

"Poor baby." Morgan climbed out of bed on the other side. "Let's get you cleaned up. Where did you get sick?"

"In my bed." Sophie sniffed.

Morgan took her by the hand and led her to the bathroom.

The mattress shifted as Lance stood. "Got it."

He left the bedroom and headed down the hall toward the girls' bedroom. The stench turned his stomach. How were the other two kids sleeping through this? He stripped the bed and carried the dirty sheets and mattress protector to the washing machine. After tossing them in, he returned to the girls' room, sprayed the mattress with Lysol, and found a pair of clean pajamas. He knocked on the bathroom door. Morgan opened it, and they made the exchange. They'd performed the same ritual a dozen times the previous week.

He'd learned many things in the past three months. Teamwork was essential in parenting. With three kids and two adults, he and Morgan were down a man. If their family were a hockey team, they would be trapped in a never-ending power play in the kids' favor.

When the washer was running, he returned to the bedroom and donned a T-shirt, intent on giving Sophie his spot in the bed and sleeping on the couch.

Sophie and Morgan emerged from the bathroom, the normally happy, rambunctious child sedate and miserable enough to break his heart.

Instead of climbing in bed with her mother, Sophie leaned on his legs and wrapped her arms around his thigh. "Can I sleep with you and Mommy?"

He lifted her into their bed and put her between them. "Of course."

Her face was flushed, and she seemed much too small to be that sick.

He touched her forehead. Her skin felt hot. "Fever?" he asked Morgan.

"Yes." She went to the bathroom for a cool, wet cloth and the thermometer. "I don't want to give her anything for it just now."

"Right." Lance had learned the hard way not to give a vomiting child anything to drink unless you were sure they were done vomiting. Children's purple liquid medicine was nearly impossible to scrub out of a beige carpet.

Morgan ran the thermometer across Sophie's forehead. "One hundred two." She fetched a stainless steel mixing bowl from the kitchen and tucked it next to Sophie. "Just in case."

They barely dozed for the rest of the night. Sophie was sick several more times. When dawn filtered through the blinds, Lance scanned her face. She was sleeping, but except for the unnatural flush of her cheeks, her face was so, so pale. The hollows around her eyes looked sunken.

He nudged Morgan, who had dozed off sitting up against the headboard. "I don't like the way she looks."

Morgan roused instantly. She reached for the thermometer on the nightstand and took the child's temperature. "One hundred four."

"She's too listless." Lance's chest tightened. Worry knotted in his gut. This was his first bout with a seriously ill child. Neither Mia nor Ava had been this sick. "This isn't normal, is it?"

Morgan was already out of bed. She tossed her pajamas into the corner and slipped into jeans. "No. We're taking her to the ER."

Lance exchanged his pajama bottoms for a pair of pants lying on the chair. He jammed his bare feet into his running shoes and scooped Sophie into his arms.

"I'll tell Grandpa." Morgan stepped into her dog-walking sneakers and hurried from the room.

"We'll be in the car." Lance headed for the hallway.

Sophie stirred in his arms and murmured, "I want my bwankie." She was not the type of child who lugged any special object around. Normally, she was too busy to be bothered.

"OK, sweetheart." Lance ducked into the girls' bedroom and grabbed the kitten blanket off the floor. Luckily, she had not puked on it.

He tucked it around her, gave Mia and Ava a quick scan to make sure they were all right, and left the house. Morgan flew out the front door as he buckled Sophie into her car seat in the minivan. Lance saw Morgan's grandfather standing at the storm door, leaning on his cane, wearing his bathrobe.

Morgan got into the back seat with Sophie. Lance drove the minivan like a patrol car and had them at the entrance of the ER in under fifteen minutes. He pulled up in front of the sliding glass door. Morgan carried Sophie inside, and he parked the car. He jogged across the parking lot, dread gearing up inside him.

He rushed inside and spotted Morgan at the desk, talking to a nurse. Her tote hung from the crook of her arm, and Sophie was draped over her shoulder. Lance hurried over. The second Sophie saw him, she leaned away from her mother and held both arms out to him. He took her in his arms and held her close. Her body felt light and small, and he could feel the heat her body generated through her thin cotton pajamas.

Lance rubbed her back while Morgan talked with the nurse and filled out forms.

"Come right back." The nurse led them through the double doors and into a small room. More nurses arrived. Lance moved to place her on the gurney, but she clung tightly to him. He tried to gently pry her loose.

"It's OK, Dad," the nurse said. "She can sit on your lap."

Lance's heart skipped at the word *Dad*, but he didn't correct her. He sat on the gurney with Sophie in his arms while the nurse took her vital signs.

The pediatrician who bustled into the room was a young, slender woman with a warm smile. She wasted no time and examined Sophie in a few minutes while Morgan detailed her symptoms.

"There's a stomach virus going around," the doctor said. "It's been brutal on the littlest kids and babies." The doctor turned to the nurse next to her. "Go find Laurel. Tell her I need her."

The nurse nodded and left the room. Morgan's face was almost as pale as Sophie's. With the vision of a big needle and a screaming child in his head, Lance hugged the little girl tighter. While they waited, the doctor opened a laptop computer mounted to the wall and typed some notes.

A few minutes later, the nurse returned and began gathering supplies. "Laurel will be here in two minutes."

"She's dehydrated, so we're going to start an IV." The doctor looked up from her typing at Morgan, then Lance. "Do either of you have games on your phone? Something colorful and possibly noisy would be best."

Neither Lance nor Morgan did.

"Then while we wait, one of you should download a game. *Candy Crush* will do nicely."

Lance pulled out his phone, started the download, and set it aside.

The doctor crouched to Sophie's level. "Sophie, do you know which hand is your left one?"

Sophie lifted her left hand.

"Wow. You are smart. Not many three-year-olds know that." The doctor turned Sophie's hand over and traced a finger along a vein. She straightened. "OK. I have a plan to make you feel better. Do you want to hear it?"

Sophie gave her a tiny nod.

"We're going to give you something called an IV, so we can give you medicine without you having to drink it." The doctor's tone was soothing, but she did not talk down to the child. "You're going to have to be just a little bit brave, though. An IV is a needle."

Sophie cringed away from the doctor.

"I know it's scary, but I promise the medicine will make you feel a whole lot better, and as soon as your tummy settles, you can have a Popsicle."

"A gwape one?" Sophie asked in a tiny voice.

"We have grape and orange and cherry flavored," the doctor said. "Do you think you can be brave?"

Sophie hesitated, then her chin dipped once, but her lower lip quivered. Lance tightened his arms around her.

Another nurse walked into the room. She wore pink scrubs with puppies and kittens all over the top.

The doctor gestured to the newcomer. "Sophie, this is my friend Laurel. She is the very best at giving kids IVs."

"Do you need me to move?" Lance asked.

"No." The doctor shook her head. "She can stay right where she is."

Lance picked up his phone and showed Sophie how the game was played. The bright colors and jingling sounds proved a solid distraction. The tech numbed Sophie's hand, raised a vein, and inserted the

IV. Sophie whimpered and pulled at her arm as the needle slid under her skin.

"Hold still for one more minute, sweetie." The tech worked fast, testing the line and hooking up the ports. She taped a clear covering over the site and used plenty of tape to secure it. "All done."

"That hurt." Sophie laid her head on Lance's chest.

"I know, sweetheart." He stroked her hair. "You were very brave."

And too weak to put up much of a struggle.

The nurse hung bags of fluid from the IV stand and connected the lines to the IV. She spoke softly to Morgan. "We're giving her fluids and medication for the fever and nausea."

Morgan nodded. Her face was tight, and she clutched her tote bag in her lap as if it were a child.

Lance felt a pang of guilt. "Do you want to hold her?"

Morgan smiled and shook her head. "She wants you."

Sophie sighed, and her body relaxed. Lance leaned against the elevated head of the gurney, put up his feet, and arranged the child so they were both more comfortable. The way the nurse hovered suggested she too was very worried, which did not ease Lance's anxiety.

The minutes ticked by. Sophie fell asleep, and Lance spent the next hour watching her breathe, afraid to blink.

Morgan rose and touched Sophie's forehead. "She feels a little bit cooler."

"Finally."

She nodded. "You're really good with her."

"I was afraid of seizures from the fever."

"I'm impressed. I didn't know about febrile seizures until I had kids."

"I've been reading that parenting book you left on the family room table." Lance's face flushed with heat. "I'm taking this stepdad thing very seriously. I often feel very clueless."

"You have nothing to worry about." Staring down at her daughter, Morgan gave a small smile. "You're a natural. You love them, and that's what really matters. You love them enough to read a book on parenting."

"I have a lot of catching up to do. Jumping into parenting with no experience and three kids is taking the fish-out-of-water metaphor to a whole new level."

Morgan brushed Sophie's hair out of her eyes. "Sophie clearly thinks you've got this, and so do I."

All Lance wanted was for Sophie to be all right.

Chapter Twenty-Seven

Sharp tapped his foot and waited for Olivia to spill her news. Her call had been cryptic, with a summons to her house he'd obeyed far too quickly.

Olivia lowered her mug of tea from her lips and placed it on the kitchen counter. "I have the most interesting news."

Sharp didn't like Olivia's emphasis on the word *interesting*. "Go on."

"While in the midst of his inquiries, my contact received a request from Joe Martin. He wants to meet with us directly."

"How did Joe know we were asking about him?" Sharp knew the answer before the question left his lips. *Joe knows everything.* Sharp brushed goose bumps off his forearm. This whole situation was going to give him hives.

Olivia lifted a bare shoulder, reinforcing his assessment. She wore dark jeans, a sleeveless blouse, and yet another pair of skinny-heeled sandals. What was it with this woman and the impractical shoes?

Her phone vibrated, shimmying on the countertop.

"Excuse me. I need to take this call." Picking up her cell, she walked toward the patio door. "Make yourself at home," she called over her shoulder. "There's some black bean and sweet potato stew in the fridge if you're hungry. We'll likely miss dinner."

He watched her out the window. She paced the length of a brick patio, her phone pressed to her ear. Her free hand moved as she spoke, the gestures becoming more animated as her conversation continued. The sky beyond was brewing another storm.

He opened the refrigerator and found the stew in a large glass container. Bowls were easy to find in a glass-fronted cabinet over the dishwasher. He scooped stew and ate it cold.

Olivia walked back into the kitchen. "You didn't even heat it up."

"It was good. Thank you." Sharp rinsed his bowl in the sink, then faced her. "Did you learn anything?"

"I did."

"Are you going to tell me?"

"Give me ten minutes."

"For what?"

"We're taking a drive."

We?

"I was only looking for information," he protested. "Not to involve you in the case."

She propped both hands on her hips. "If you don't want to work together, I can go alone. I'd have much better luck without you. You still look like a police officer."

"This is dangerous."

"You wanted to pique my interest. You were successful." She turned toward a hallway that presumably led to her bedroom. "I'm taking a drive. You can come with me or not. It's up to you."

She disappeared down the corridor. Sharp heard a door close. This was not how he had envisioned their conversation going. But then, Olivia rarely cooperated with his expectations.

While he waited, Sharp paced her kitchen, trying to think of a good argument to keep her at home. Then he gave up. Saying it was too dangerous for her was not only condescending but senseless. She was the one who had already interviewed the dealers. Olivia had the contacts.

When she returned to the kitchen, she still wore the jeans and sleeveless shirt, but she'd let her hair down. It hung in loose, shiny waves down her back.

His gaze dropped to her leather sandals. "How do you not break an ankle in those skinny heels?"

"Practice." She smiled. "Are you ready?"

"I am." Sharp followed her to the front door. They went outside, and she locked up.

"I'll drive." She set off for her white Prius without waiting for him to respond.

Sharp hustled to keep up. "I prefer to drive."

What he meant was that he liked to be in control.

"Too bad." She pulled a pair of huge sunglasses from a boxy bright-blue purse. "You don't know where we're going." She climbed into her car.

Resigned to letting her boss him around, Sharp slid into the passenger seat. Olivia started the engine and pulled away from the house.

"You're not going to tell me where we're going?" he asked.

She considered his question with a twist of her lips. Her eyes narrowed as if she didn't trust him. "So you can figure out a way to leave me out? I don't think so. This is my contact and my professional reputation on the line. Also, you would go alone, which would not be a good decision."

Sharp almost denied the accusation, except that it was true. He would have tried to do exactly that. He didn't like taking her into a hazardous situation.

"I'll tell you when we're closer. For now, there's nothing to do while I drive. Why don't you close your eyes? I'll wake you when we get there." She glanced over at him. "You still look tired. You were right when you said this would be dangerous. I'll need you to be alert to watch my back."

"OK," Sharp grumbled. Then he must have dozed off because he startled awake, blinking. It took him a moment to remember that he was in the car with Olivia. The traffic was bumper to bumper. "Where are we?"

"I-87," Olivia said from the driver's seat. "There was an accident. Traffic is slow, so I let you sleep."

"Thanks." Sharp rubbed his eyes.

"We're almost there." Olivia smiled.

"And where is that? I-87 runs into New York City, not Newark." Sharp looked for landmarks.

"Joe is not in Newark. He is in Albany."

"Albany?" Sharp was surprised. Albany was barely an hour from Scarlet Falls. Joe was very close to Tina. Sharp texted Lance to let him know where he was headed.

"Yes. I had a call while you were sleeping. My contact gave me some disturbing details about Joe Martin. People are still very much afraid of him, even though he's in his sixties. He was always known for his brutality, and his time in prison didn't change that. My contact said it was as if Joe's power could reach right out of prison and grab you by the throat."

"Wonderful," Sharp said. "Let's hope he isn't in a bad mood tonight."

"There are rumors about Joe ordering hits from prison. He'd have a body left in the middle of the street with the face peeled off or the arms and legs hacked off with an ax. Sometimes they were the competition or someone who had crossed Joe in some way."

"He relies on sheer brutality and terror to keep people in line."

"Yes. A few months after Joe's conviction, two of the detectives on the narcotics task force that led the investigation against him were found in the county dump. Both had been beaten and beheaded."

"Executed."

"Yes," she agreed. "Money went missing when Joe was arrested and his house searched. There were rumors that the two cops were corrupt and had helped themselves. It seems Joe holds a grudge against those who go against him."

"Great." Sharp rolled his head from shoulder to shoulder, and his neck cracked. The sleep had helped. His head was clearer. "Where are we going?"

Olivia plugged an address into her phone. "I don't know yet. The arrangements were made through an associate through another associate. We're spinning this as a follow-up to my story on his conviction—that I want his reaction to being released, how prison changed him, his plans, et cetera. Admittedly, I don't know exactly how this will work."

"Can you tell me your contact's name?"

"No." She drove for about ten minutes, the traffic restricting her speed. "The suburbs have become a hotbed of drug activity. Serious drug dealers are leaving the cities. They don't want to deal with territorial gang wars. These are real businessmen. They deal in shopping center parking lots and offer heroin delivery services. Most of the legwork is done on cell phones now."

"Drug dealers have become regular entrepreneurs." Sharp watched the landscape roll by. Trees, strip malls, and medical centers lined the road. They drove past another residential development.

"The area is low crime, with a large customer base. Mexican heroin is the current trend. It's cheaper than prescription pain pills." She spoke with an unusual venom.

"You sound like your hatred is personal."

The veins in her forearms corded as she gripped the wheel. "One of my cousins overdosed in high school, and two years ago, my nephew died of a heroin overdose. My sister will never be the same."

"I'm sorry." Sharp suspected Olivia had changed as well.

With a curt nod, she said, "My cousin's death prompted me to do the *New York Times* piece after college."

Olivia turned into an office complex. The businesses looked closed, with dark windows and empty parking slots. She parked in the back of the lot under a streetlamp. Leaning over, she jammed her cell phone in the glove compartment. "You'll want to lock your phone and gun in the car."

Sharp touched his Glock. Going into a gang-infested bar unarmed seemed wrong. "Why?"

"We'll be searched before we'll be allowed to see Joe. Wires, phones, cameras, and weapons will be taken at the door. Your things are safer in my car."

Sharp removed his holster from his belt and placed his weapon in the glove box. He sent Lance another quick text letting him know what was happening before setting his phone on top of his gun. Olivia locked the compartment with her key.

A black sedan pulled up next to her Prius. Sharp couldn't see inside. The rear windows were tinted Florida-dark.

Sharp's cop-senses tingled. He was fairly sure this was a very bad idea.

"You're sure this is safe?" He reached for the Prius's door handle. They were both unarmed. He had no idea if she could defend herself.

Olivia's shrug did not ease his fears.

"We don't have to do this," he said. "I'll find another way to determine if Joe Martin is involved in Paul's death."

"Such as?" Olivia asked, returning her sunglasses to their holder.

"Shit. I don't know right off the top of my head."

Two young men got out of the sedan. In jeans, T-shirts, and expensive sneakers, they could have worked at the university or a local tech company.

She hid her purse under a towel in the back seat. "Joe requested the meeting. There's no reason for him to harm us, and why would he risk going right back into prison? If he didn't want to talk to me, he wouldn't have agreed to the interview."

All good points, but unease crawled over Sharp's skin like spiders as he climbed out of the car. Maybe Joe wanted the interview so he could eliminate two people who were asking questions about him.

A humid wind gusted, sending an empty water bottle tumbling across the hot asphalt. Sharp smelled rain competing with the scent of garbage that had been lying around too long in the summer heat.

The driver wore aviator-style sunglasses. Tattoos covered one arm in a full sleeve.

Sweat gathered under Sharp's arms. It would take all of two seconds for these men to kill him and Olivia. Her car would be driven to the local chop shop. Their bodies would be dumped somewhere. Just another business day for this bunch.

He'd gone into dangerous situations in the past but never without backup handy. Lance was an hour away. What was Olivia thinking? What had *he* been thinking?

"Is your contact nearby?" he whispered to Olivia.

"Maybe," she said.

Not reassuring.

"You were informed of the rules?" the driver asked. "No cameras, no phones, no wires."

"Yes," Olivia said.

The driver raised a hand and made a circle in the air. "Turn around. Hands in the air."

Olivia obeyed. Sharp did too.

The second man went to Olivia. She lifted her arms and let him run his hands along her sides. The way he took his time made Sharp want to shoot him. But at the same time, he didn't want to die. Also, his gun was locked in the car. So he bit his tongue as the guard felt around Olivia's bra line, clearly looking for a wire, but the hostile smirk on his face said he was enjoying the process.

Olivia didn't cower or cringe. Instead, she bore an expression he'd never seen before, but then, he had never witnessed her being manhandled by a thug. She was pissed but also cool and collected.

When it was Sharp's turn, he lifted the hem of his T-shirt. The guard ran his hands down the outside of Sharp's legs and felt around his ankles. The whole pat down took five seconds. Sharp was glad he wasn't wearing a clinch piece.

"All good?" Sharp asked without turning around.

"Get in." The driver opened the rear door.

Sharp slid onto the leather seat. Olivia entered the vehicle on the other side. The two men got in.

The passenger handed two pieces of fabric over the seat. "Put these on."

Olivia took them and gave one to Sharp. He held it up. A black hood. With an apprehensive blink, she tugged hers over her head.

"Is this really necessary?" Sharp asked.

The driver met his eyes in the rearview mirror.

Sharp put on the hood. The engine started. A minute later, the sedan lurched into motion.

Sweat rolled down Sharp's back. What had they gotten themselves into?

Chapter Twenty-Eight

The vehicle came to a stop, but Sharp had lost track of how long the vehicle had been in motion. It felt as if they'd been driving in circles.

The hood was snatched from Sharp's face. Overhead lights blinded him.

Next to him, Olivia squirmed. Her hood had also been removed, and her hair was tousled around her face.

The driver and passenger climbed out of the vehicle and opened the rear door. "Let's go. Out of the car."

Olivia stepped out. She wobbled, then caught her balance.

Sharp climbed out and stood next to her, blinking as his eyes adjusted to the bright light. The car had been driven into a small, empty warehouse. The overhead doors were down. There were no windows or signs to indicate where they were. A second black sedan was angled next to theirs. The sound of the car door shutting echoed in the two-story space.

The building was narrow, with a pallet of boxes in the center stacked six high. Sharp wondered what was inside them. Four men sat in chairs or leaned against the wall. Most were dressed in well-fitted jeans and T-shirts, like young professionals at work on casual Friday. Despite their lounging postures, they were focused much too intensely on Olivia and Sharp. He saw no guns but didn't doubt that they had weapons handy.

The look in their eyes sent a chill through Sharp's belly. They were dark and cold and filled with a vicious malice that Sharp had seen only a few times in his long police career. Every one of these men was extremely dangerous. Each would kill without blinking.

Hell, these men would kill if there wasn't anything good to watch on Netflix.

Sharp automatically put his body between the men and Olivia, not that it would matter. If these men wanted to hurt her, there would be nothing Sharp could do to protect her. He was outnumbered six to one. One of the men sneered at Sharp's chivalrous gesture.

They all knew it was an empty act.

Offices lined one wall. A man came out of one of the doors. In jeans and a polo shirt, he was whipcord-lean. Sharp pictured the photos on the whiteboard. This man looked exactly like Joe Martin had twenty-five years before.

"Aaron, bring them in," a voice commanded from the room.

Clearly Aaron, Tina's half brother, was still involved in his father's business.

Aaron waved them forward. The door was guarded by a man the size of a refrigerator. The guard's head was shaved, and the biceps that bulged out below his shirtsleeves were as big around as Sharp's head.

Aaron stepped aside and gestured toward the open door. "After you."

Sharp went in first. A rectangular table and eight chairs were set up like a conference room. Smoke filled the room. An older man sat at the head of the table. A cane was hooked on the table at his side. Sharp didn't need an introduction to know this was Joe Martin, although he'd aged significantly since the photo on the whiteboard back at the office was taken. He looked much older than sixty. Prison had ruined him. He was twenty pounds underweight, and his skin was an unhealthy white. He wore gray slacks and a black long-sleeve button-down shirt with a dark-gray sport coat. Yet, despite his physical weakness, he radiated power.

When Joe walked into a room, everyone knew it. He had that same vicious look in his eyes as the men in the warehouse but amplified to the one hundredth power. Joe's eyes also gleamed with acute intelligence.

The end of his cigarette flared as he dragged on it. "Have they been searched?" he asked Aaron.

Aaron nodded. "Yes."

"Were they carrying weapons?" Joe flicked the end of his cigarette into an ashtray.

"No," Aaron said.

Joe turned to Sharp and Olivia and gestured toward two chairs to the left of him. "Please, sit."

Olivia eased into the seat next to Joe. Sharp sat next to her. Aaron backed to the wall and leaned on it. Sharp did not like having Aaron outside his direct view. He shifted his position until he could see them both.

"I apologize for the drama," Joe said. "My son takes no chances with my safety. I've been betrayed many times. In the end, only family can be trusted."

Sharp's gaze darted between Joe and his son. Aaron stiffened, his posture angry. Was he mad because others had betrayed his father? Or for some other reason? Maybe pissed-off was just Aaron's normal state of being.

Joe continued. "I survived my sentence. Plenty of people want to kill me. I couldn't have you see where we are. Nor could I have anyone see you come in here. The parole board turned down every one of my petitions. I served my whole sentence. I am not required to report to anyone. No one knows where I am, and I intend to keep it that way."

Sharp nodded. "We understand."

"Then you'll also understand if I ask you not to make any sudden movements." Joe set his cigarette in the ashtray and produced a long, thin knife from somewhere.

Sharp had not seen him pull the weapon, which disturbed him.

Joe twirled the knife in his hand—not in a showy manner but alternating between a forward and reverse grip. "I am no longer a young healthy man."

Yet Sharp did not want to fuck with him. Joe kept his eyes on Sharp while the knife smoothly snapped forward and back, his grip secure, strong, and experienced enough that he could handle the knife deftly without looking at it. Sharp had no interest in learning how fast Joe could put that knife to use.

"You wanted information about me," Joe said, his voice low and chilling.

"How does it feel to be released from prison after all these years?" Olivia began.

Joe's chin lifted, and he met her gaze with a long, hard stare, the knife still in a reverse grip. "Why don't you ask me what you really want to know? Why you really came here?"

The hairs on the back of Sharp's neck lifted. He did not like the direction the conversation had taken. It felt as if Joe were interviewing them instead of the other way around.

Showing the first crack in her confidence, Olivia swallowed. Her lovely throat shifted, looking as delicate and breakable as a swan's. Smoke rose in a skinny plume from the lit cigarette to the ceiling.

"Why do you think I'm here?" She tossed the question back at him.

Joe's murky eyes narrowed to cruel slits. "To find out if I am responsible for the murder of my daughter's husband."

Olivia didn't miss a beat. "Are you?"

The woman had a brass set.

The old man clearly thought so too. He snorted with amusement. "No."

"How do you know that's why we came here?" she asked.

"I know everything," Joe said slowly, pausing to let that fact sink in. "I know where you live, and I know where Tina lives. I follow the news in Randolph County. Her husband's murder was a big story."

Sharp figured the pretense was over, so he jumped in. "How long have you known where she was?"

"I tried to find her for the first year after she disappeared. I was angry with her, as you might imagine." Joe stabbed the table with the knife. Leaving it quivering, he picked up his cigarette and took a drag. The embers burned close to the filter. "She was very good at hiding and kept a low profile for a very long time. After I'd been released, I found that technology was very much my friend. Changing her name was clever. Those records are not as readily available as marriage and birth certificates. But it was only a matter of time and persistence until I found her. Once my agent discovered her new identity, her recent marriage and home purchase made tracing her very simple. Marriages and real estate transactions are public record. Most are accessible on the internet. It is much harder to stay hidden these days, isn't it?"

A sudden chill flashed through Sharp's bones. Had Joe been watching Tina since he was released?

As if he could read minds, Joe stubbed out the cigarette and said, "If I had wanted to hurt her, I could have done so many times."

The fact that he'd been incarcerated had not affected his ability to communicate with his men and give orders. Criminals thrived in prison. There was a profitable drug trade behind bars. In fact, some experts considered prison to be a form of higher education for aspiring young criminals.

"Why didn't you?" Sharp asked.

Joe considered the question for a few seconds before exhaling loudly through his nose. "If I had found her immediately, I would have made a different decision. I was angry, and I had plenty of time to imagine the ways I could take revenge. She was not the only one to turn on me. But the others were not smart enough to get away, and they paid for their betrayal." Cruelty twisted his mouth.

Who else had Joe killed around the time of his trial? The detectives who had stolen his money? Had they been working with Joe and double-crossed him?

"But you didn't find Tina," Olivia said.

"No." Joe's voice filled with reluctant respect. "I made a mistake. I didn't pay enough attention to her. She was only a girl. She barely spoke and spent most of her time cowering in the corners. But I should have expected her to be smart. She *is* my daughter."

"But when you finally learned where she was . . . ," Sharp prompted.

"I decided to leave her alone." He frowned as if he didn't truly understand why. "I grew very sick with diabetes. Such a disease is not easily managed in prison. Much damage was done." He pointed to his foot. "I lost some toes. My sight is fading. My life will not be a long one." He pried the knife loose and touched the point.

Complete and total bullshit.

Sharp couldn't believe the man who had given his daughter to his lieutenants to use for sex had suddenly turned into a doting parent. Joe thought of only Joe. Sharp's face must have shown his disbelief.

"Do not think I let her go because I forgave her. I have not. But she is cunning like me. I respect that." Joe's head inclined slightly. "Also, she has a son. I have only one other living relative." He gestured to Aaron, still leaning on the wall, still staring at Sharp as if he'd like nothing more than to peel the skin from his face.

Sharp's belly cramped. He liked his skin *on* his face.

"So far, Aaron has no sons." Joe cast an accusatory glance at Aaron. "Evan is the reason she still lives. He carries my blood. He can ensure that our bloodline survives."

"Evan is missing." Sharp watched him carefully for a reaction.

There wasn't one. Joe let the knife dangle from between two fingertips. Joe didn't care about Evan. Joe cared about Joe's legacy, his DNA.

"I know," Joe said. "But he carries my blood. He is a smart boy. He will not be found until he wants to be found. Why do you think he runs?"

Sharp added, "The police consider him a suspect in his stepfather's murder."

Joe dropped the knife. It pierced the table and stood upright. "Did the stepfather need killing?"

"I don't think so," Sharp answered. "But the police think Evan is the murderer. They might just shoot the boy."

"If he gets caught that easily, then he doesn't carry enough of my genes," Joe said, his voice emotionless. "Is he guilty?"

"No," Sharp said.

Joe seemed almost disappointed. "I have not seen his mother since her husband was killed. I assume the police are hiding her."

Sharp didn't respond.

Something glimmered in Joe's eyes. There was something he wasn't saying. Sharp couldn't shake the feeling that Joe wasn't ignoring Evan's plight. But it was very hard to read the face of a sociopath.

And that's exactly what Joe was. He had no conscience. No empathy.

Pushing on the cane, Joe stood. He pulled the knife out of the table, and it disappeared under his sport coat. "And now I must go. I have business to attend to." He glanced from Olivia to Sharp. "Unfortunately, you'll have to leave the same way you came."

Sharp and Olivia stood as he shuffled past. He opened the door and left the room.

Olivia shrugged. She and Sharp stood and walked to the door.

Aaron stopped them with a hand on Sharp's chest. "Wait."

Aaron barely blinked as they waited. Finally, he received a message on his phone and stood aside. Olivia exited the room first, but Sharp stayed close. Aaron herded them across the concrete floor.

Nerves formed a cold ball in Sharp's gut. The threat felt huge and looming as they walked toward the sedan. The four extra men and the second car—and presumably Joe—were all gone. Only Aaron and his two thugs remained in the warehouse.

Sharp breathed. This would all be over soon. They'd climb into the car, put on the hoods, and be delivered to Olivia's Prius.

Keep your cool.

With the additional men missing, the warehouse felt too silent. The only sound was the click of Olivia's heels on the floor. They approached the car.

Aaron gestured to the car. Sharp turned to open the rear door. Something smacked him in the head. A hood slammed down on his face, and his hands were bound with plastic ties.

Over the ringing in his ears, he heard a feminine gasp.

Olivia.

He heard the sound of a trunk opening and barely had time to think, *Shit*, before a solid kick to his back sent him sprawling forward. His thighs hit the lip of the trunk. He put his bound hands in front of him to catch himself. But someone shoved him inside, scooped up his legs, and tossed them in. Sharp's face burned as it slid on the carpet.

A soft weight landed on top of him.

"See that no one finds their bodies," Aaron said, just before the trunk slammed closed.

Chapter Twenty-Nine

Lance's arm fell asleep, but he didn't move it. Sophie's long eyelashes fluttered as she woke. She lifted her head and pushed off Lance's chest. Her color had improved, her face had plumped up, and her eyes were no longer sunken. Her pajamas and his T-shirt were soaked with her fever-breaking sweat.

"Can I have a Popsicle?" she asked.

Lance kissed her temple. "You sure can."

Morgan called a nurse into the room.

"Well, don't you look better." The nurse ran the thermometer over Sophie's forehead and smiled. "Ninety-nine point six. Excellent. How does your tummy feel?"

"OK." Sophie picked up Lance's phone. "Can I play that game again?"

"Sure." Lance thought this would be a good time for her to ask for her own phone or a car. At that moment, he would have given her anything she wanted.

He woke his phone and handed it to her. She played the game and ate her grape Popsicle.

By lunchtime, Sophie was sitting up and chatting as if she'd never been ill. Morgan looked as if she were barely keeping her eyes open, and Lance felt like he'd been run over by a preschooler-size bus.

When Sophie had successfully kept down Popsicles and crackers, the doctor decided she was well enough to go home. By the time the discharge paperwork was processed and they had driven back to the house, it was late afternoon. Gianna and Grandpa greeted Sophie with relieved hugs. Under Grandpa's watchful eye, Morgan, Lance, and Sophie sprawled on the couch in front of cartoons. As if the dogs knew she was sick, they couldn't get close enough to the little girl. They curled up on the sofa next to her. Snoozer kept one paw on her at all times.

Lance had no memory of falling asleep, but he jolted awake at the jab of something sharp into his sternum. He opened his eyes. The something sharp was Sophie's kneecap.

She sat on his stomach. "I'm hungwy. Can I have waffles?"

"I can make that happen." Lance rubbed his eyes.

"Shh." The little girl put her finger over her lips. "Mommy is sweeping."

Lance lowered his voice. "Then let's not wake her."

Morgan's grandfather had also dozed off and was snoring in his recliner.

Lance touched Sophie's forehead, but her face felt cool. He held out both hands to carry her into the dining room, but she skipped away from him, seemingly fully recovered from her hospital experience. Lance felt like he was scarred for life. He followed Sophie and the smell of food to the dining room. Gianna stood at the sideboard, stirring something in a slow cooker.

"Someone wants waffles," Lance said.

"I'll get them." Gianna smiled. "I made soup."

"Thank you." Lance rolled a kink out of his shoulder.

"Mia and Ava are home from school. They're playing in their room."

But they must have heard Lance's voice. The two little girls raced into the dining room and hugged him. Morgan appeared, looking rumpled, beautiful, and better for the nap. Grandpa wandered in, and they settled down for dinner. Afterward, Sophie followed her sisters into their room to play.

Lance showered. Morgan joined him in the bedroom as he dressed in ancient cargo pants and a T-shirt.

"I feel almost human again," she said as she tossed her clothes into the hamper.

"How is Sophie's fever?" Lance asked.

"I gave her some Tylenol, but she seems perfectly fine."

"I can't believe the way she bounced back."

"Kids." Morgan stepped into the shower.

Lance scooped his clothes from the bathroom floor. His phone fell out of his pocket. He picked it up and glanced at the screen. Sharp had texted, and the sheriff had called. Lance hadn't checked his phone for hours. He didn't even know what time it was.

Six p.m.? He glanced out the window. Thick clouds blotted out the sky. A storm was coming, and darkness would fall early.

He hadn't thought about Evan or the case or the sheriff since the night before. Worry for Sophie had totally consumed him. It struck him like a rock to the head. The nurse had been right. He was going to be a dad to Morgan's girls. *Stepdad* might be the technical term, but in Lance's heart, the DNA didn't matter. Love was stronger than blood. Look how close he was to Sharp. Lance's terror for Sophie had been bone deep. He would have traded places with her in an instant if it had been possible.

Morgan stepped out of the shower and wrapped herself in a towel. She coiled her hair into a messy knot on top of her head.

"The sheriff called." Lance checked the time of the incoming call. "Three hours ago." While he'd been sleeping.

"Do you know what he wanted?" Morgan dressed in faded jeans and a T-shirt.

"No. I haven't called him back yet." Lance glanced at the closed door. "I feel like I neglected Evan's case, but I couldn't have chosen differently."

He was shocked at how quickly he'd put everything else aside. As worried as he was about Evan, the case had never entered his mind while Sophie had been ill.

He had never thought about balancing parenthood and work, especially work that was so often urgent. His already healthy respect for Morgan quadrupled. She'd been juggling kids and work and grief for years. She was the strongest person he knew.

Morgan took his hand and squeezed it. "See? You're already great at this dad thing. But Sophie is fine now. My sister just arrived. Gianna and Grandpa are going to spoil her rotten for the rest of the evening. We should call the sheriff back. It could be important."

Lance dialed the phone.

Had something terrible happened to Evan?

The sheriff answered on the third ring. "About time you called me back." Colgate's voice was snippy.

Lance had no patience left for the sheriff's attitude. "Sorry. We were at the hospital with Morgan's three-year-old daughter."

"Oh, I apologize." Colgate's tone became polite. "I hope the child is all right."

"She is now, thank you. Why did you call?"

The sheriff said, "We had a sighting of Evan Meade."

Chapter Thirty

"Put the sheriff on speakerphone." Anxious to hear the sheriff's report, Morgan hurried to Lance's side.

The sheriff continued. "A statement has already been given to the media. In case you missed it with your medical emergency, we held another press conference late this afternoon."

Lance tensed. "Where was Evan seen?"

"We had a report of a squatter in a vacant home on Deer Lake this afternoon," the sheriff said. "A neighbor was kayaking and saw someone in the kitchen through the window. The homeowner is deceased, and his children live several hours away. No one should be in the home except a real estate agent. By the time the deputies arrived, the intruder had gone. But they found blood in the bathroom."

Evan was still bleeding. He must be seriously hurt.

"Are you sure it was Evan?" Lance asked.

"Yes," Colgate answered, his voice testy. "The fingerprints matched."

"I thought his prints were unavailable in AFIS," Lance pointed out.

"We located his original fingerprint card," the sheriff said.

The sheriff's department had recently upgraded to digital fingerprinting. Their budget was ridiculously small.

Morgan went to her nightstand and pulled out a notebook and pen. "You said the house was on Deer Lake?"

"Yes." The sheriff read off an address. "We also found a gully in the riverbank that suggests someone launched a canoe or kayak. We suspect Evan is still traveling on the river, which would explain why he's been hard to find. I'm sending patrol units after him now, and a K-9 team and patrol boat will go out at first light. We'll find him."

Not if we can find him first.

Lance frowned. "What time did all of this happen?"

"This call about the intruder came in at eleven o'clock yesterday morning, but we just matched the fingerprints today." But when he'd been speaking with them the previous evening, he'd known about the possibility that Evan had been seen. And he'd kept it to himself.

Unfortunately, until Evan was caught and formally charged, Colgate had no legal obligation to provide Morgan with evidence regarding the case. If he gave them information, it was either a courtesy or for his own benefit.

Lance went to his nightstand and took his iPad from the drawer.

Evan was resourceful, Morgan would give him that. The sheriff hadn't been able to find him despite the sighting.

"I'll let Ms. Dane know once he's in custody," Colgate said. The line went dead.

Lance pulled up a map app on his iPad and entered the address. He pointed to a red dot on the screen. "Here is the house."

On the digital map, Morgan followed the river from the campground at Deer Lake to the red dot. "He's traveled quite a distance."

"The river is high. I'm sure the current is giving him a good push, which is why they haven't caught up with him."

Morgan continued to trace the course of the river. "He's a smart kid. He'll stay on the river as long as possible. He'll know it's the best way to put distance between him and the deputies."

"But now that they know he's on the river, they'll pursue on foot, by boat, and by vehicle. At least we know he's still alive." Lance paced in front of the bed. "I want to go out and look for him."

"I know, but where? We don't have the resources to follow him three different ways." Morgan's finger stopped. "Look. He'll have to stop here."

"At Scarlet Falls." Lance leaned over the iPad. "Technically, the Deer River continues right into Scarlet Lake, but the part between the falls and the lake isn't navigable by boat. That section of waterway is all eddies and boulders."

Morgan moved her fingertip across a patch of green. "And the falls are a forty-foot drop."

Lance tapped on the big blue blotch that represented Scarlet Lake. "He'd have to carry or drag the canoe at least two hundred yards to reach the lake. If he can do that, then he can't be injured too badly. Otherwise, he'll have to walk from here."

"Or steal another boat," Morgan suggested. "He's already proven he's clever."

"Then we'll never catch up to him." Lance clasped his hands around the back of his neck.

"We're lucky the sheriff waited until the fingerprint match came in to try and head him off."

"Colgate has manpower issues, budget, and procedure to consider. I'm sure his men have been logging overtime on this case. He can't afford to chase every lead until it's verified." Lance straightened. "But we can move on a hunch."

Morgan scanned the map. "He could have gotten off the river anywhere along here." She glanced out the window. Rain beat on the glass. "It's dark already."

Lightning flashed. The storm was approaching.

If only they'd gotten the sheriff's message earlier. *No.* Morgan would not regret putting her own child first. Sometimes parenting required hard choices. Not that she or Lance had made a conscious decision. Their response had been instinctual.

But if Evan suffered because of their choice, they would both have to live with the guilt.

Morgan's phone vibrated on the nightstand. She reached for it but didn't recognize the number on the display. She answered the call. "Morgan Dane."

"Hi. Um. This is Rylee. Rylee Nelson."

"Hello, Rylee." Morgan waggled her fingers at Lance. Then she tilted the phone so that he could hear.

"I didn't know who else to call." Rylee sounded out of breath and her voice quivered.

"What's wrong?" Morgan asked.

"It's Evan." The girl hesitated.

"Rylee, I can't help unless you talk to me."

Rylee breathed for a few seconds. "After you left our house, I went to the lake last night, just to sit in the dark and think. Evan was there."

Lance jerked straight.

"Was he OK?" Morgan asked.

"No," Rylee said. "He looked awful. I think he had a fever. I gave him some emergency supplies from my car: a blanket, water, protein bars . . ."

Lance folded his hands and clenched them together until his knuckles whitened.

Morgan touched his forearm. "How badly is he injured?"

"He was shot in the arm." Rylee's voice hitched. "He's in really bad shape."

Next to Morgan, Lance grabbed socks from a laundry basket.

Once Rylee started spilling her secret, the words poured out at rapid speed. "I don't know if he can climb out of the cave. Evan asked me to call his mom. He gave me her number. He doesn't trust anyone else, but his mom said she was being watched by a deputy. She didn't know how long it would take her to sneak out. She asked me to call you. She doesn't trust the cops either. She's afraid they're going to shoot Evan."

Morgan didn't believe the police would shoot a teenager on sight, but tension and adrenaline were factors. Local law enforcement was convinced that Evan was an armed killer. They would respond with that in the forefront of their minds.

"I promised I wouldn't call the cops, but I'm afraid he's gonna die."

"Where is he?" Morgan cradled the phone between her shoulder and neck. She went to her dresser for socks and grabbed her boots from the closet. Lance retrieved their handguns from the gun safe.

"He's at the falls," Rylee said.

They'd been right. And no doubt, the sheriff would be there in the morning.

"We're going to go get him right now, Rylee." Morgan shoved her feet into her boots. "Where are you?"

"On the observation deck. Evan is hiding in a little cave at the bottom of the falls, but I couldn't get any cell reception there. I had to climb higher."

"Well done, Rylee. We're on our way."

"OK. Please hurry."

Morgan reached for a waterproof jacket and turned to Lance. "You heard all that?"

"Yes." He headed for the door. "You don't have to come. If you want to stay with Sophie, I'll be all right on my own."

"You can't go alone." Morgan held up a hand. "That's not up for discussion. Have you heard back from Sharp?"

"He sent me a text. I haven't had a chance to read it." Lance read his screen. "He's in Albany with Olivia Cruz. They're going to meet with Joe Martin. Actually, he sent this text hours ago. The meeting might be over by now."

"Joe Martin is in Albany?" That was too close for comfort.

"That's what the text says." Lance pressed a button on his phone to return his boss's call. "Sharp isn't answering."

"I'm not worried that Evan is going to shoot us. Are you?"

"No," Lance agreed. "Can we call your sister? I trust her and her partner, Brody."

Morgan dialed. "She isn't answering her phone. I know she was working tonight, and Mac is still on a search and rescue in the Adirondacks. You're stuck with me. Let's go get Evan before this storm gets any worse."

"I wouldn't call it *stuck*. There's no one I trust more." Lance kissed her. "But I'd like us to have backup."

"I know." Morgan walked to him and put her hands on his biceps. "But Evan needs us now. He can't wait. Besides, we're just going to pick him up."

"We'll go alone and assess the situation. If it's too dangerous, we'll call for assistance. But I'd like to get him out of that cave to ensure he is unarmed. It would be safer for Evan if he voluntarily gave himself up."

"Agreed."

They checked in with Gianna and the kids, who were eating cookies in the dining room. Grandpa drank a mug of tea. Sophie sat on his knee.

Morgan quickly explained that they had to run out for a while.

From Grandpa's grave expression, he clearly sensed the importance of their mission. He waved a hand. "Don't worry about Sophie. Gianna and I won't take our eyes off her. Go do what you have to do."

Gianna nodded and reached out a hand to touch Sophie's cheek, her affection for the child palpable. Gianna had become one of the family in every way.

Lance put on his boots on the way out the door. Morgan pulled up her hood and tucked in her hair as they ran out to the Jeep. The lake and falls were only a short drive from the house. Rain poured onto the windshield. The wipers could not move fast enough to keep the glass clear. Lance leaned over the wheel and squinted, his face tight with concentration.

An emergency weather alert appeared on Morgan's phone screen. "The entire area is on a flash flood watch. People in low-lying areas are being encouraged to go to shelters." She was glad her house was on high ground.

"Oh, no." He stopped the Jeep. The Scarlet River coursed over the bridge that led out to the main road. "It's too deep to drive through." Hooking one arm behind the passenger seat, he backed up and turned the vehicle around. The Jeep surged forward.

Morgan grabbed the armrest. Water sprayed from the tires as the Jeep roared through a puddle.

Lance turned on the defroster to clear fog from the inside of the windshield. "I've been to the falls dozens of times. I didn't know there was a cave there."

"Me either," said Morgan, though she had not been there in some years. Steep stairs and sheer rock drop-offs were not child friendly. Railings couldn't be high enough to safely contain Sophie.

Lance looped through the neighborhood and left via the back exit. Morgan held her breath as they approached the second bridge, but it had been built higher. Water lapped at the edges, but the swell was still several feet below the road as they drove across. The trees on both sides of the road swayed. The ground was saturated from the recent heavy rains. Trees would go down tonight, hopefully not on them.

"There's the lake." But Morgan hardly recognized the normally placid water. Wind gusts had whipped its surface into white caps. "Oh, my God. The lake is everywhere."

Four inches of water covered the parking lot.

"That's not the lake." Lance drove past the lake toward the falls, where the ground was higher. "That's the Deer River."

The parking area for the Scarlet Falls overlook was on high ground. Lance drove up the gravel road and parked the Jeep at the top. There were a few dozen cars in the lot, but they all looked empty. "People must have moved their cars here in case of flooding. It's the highest elevation in the township."

Morgan recognized Rylee's old sedan and squinted out the Jeep's windows. "Rylee is here."

"Let's go find her. Are you ready?" Lance stuffed a flashlight into a cargo pocket on his pants. "Do you want to wait in the Jeep?"

"No." She tugged her waterproof jacket over her Glock. "It's only rain, right?"

But as she stepped out of the vehicle, the fierceness of the driving torrent hit her full in the face. She leaned into the wind. The first observation deck wasn't visible from the parking area. Foliage and trees blocked the view. Six wooden steps led to a wooden walkway, which made a sharp right turn around a stand of mature trees and ended at the first observation deck. On the other side of the platform, staircases that descended to the ground-level deck had been built to follow the natural contours of the rocks.

Lightning streaked across the sky. The crack of thunder followed right on its heels. The storm was on top of them.

On the third step, Lance leaned back and shouted over the storm. "Rylee said the cave was at the bottom of the falls. We'll have to take the steps down. I hope he's on this side of the water."

Morgan kept one hand on the railing as they went up the steps to the walkway. She glanced over the edge and got her first view of the falls.

The waterfall was spewing twice its normal volume. Her gaze dropped to the ravine below. Large boulders filled the center of the ravine. Normally, the water flowed and eddied around them. But the water had risen so high that only the very tops of the boulders were visible. She scanned the bottom for a cave and saw a small opening at the base of the ravine wall, on the other side of the water. If the flooding continued at the current rate, it wouldn't take long for it to rise above the cave's entrance.

Anyone inside would drown.

Water slicked the wooden treads, and the wind whipped branches in her face. She slipped. By the time she caught her balance, the more athletic, better-coordinated Lance had moved a half dozen strides ahead of her. She rushed up the last few steps onto the landing, to be stopped by Lance's hand.

Tina and Rylee stood in the far corner of the observation deck, drenched from the rain, eyes wide with terror as a man pointed a gun in their faces.

Chapter Thirty-One

Evan woke to the sound of thunder echoing in the small ravine. Rylee had brought him a real blanket. He pulled it up to his chin, but his teeth continued to chatter and the shiver that ran through him rattled his bones. His mouth and lips were dry, his skin was hot, and his arm throbbed. His fever was spiking again.

He reached for his water bottle. How long had it been since Rylee was here? The rain seemed to be going on forever, and the sky had been overcast all day. He had no idea what time it was or how much time had passed since she'd left.

Opening a protein bar, he forced himself to eat it, even though chewing nauseated him. But the protein would help him heal, as if that were possible. Once the food was in his belly, he swallowed more ibuprofen tablets.

A noise outside caught his attention. Had he heard voices? He tried to sit up, but dizziness forced him right back down to the ground.

Shit.

He should have taken the ibuprofen earlier. He waited a few more minutes for his head to stop spinning. Then he drained the bottle of water and opened a new one. He sipped every few minutes. He'd learned the hard way not to chug the water. Slow and steady worked best.

Another voice carried into the cave's entrance. Was that Rylee and his mom? Evan didn't want to get his hopes up. The noise could have been the wind. When it gusted through the narrow canyon, sometimes it made a weird whistling sound.

But he had to know.

Afraid he'd fall and smack his head if he stood, he crawled on his knees and one hand toward the cave's entrance.

The storm had picked up in intensity. Wind and water lashed sideways across the cave opening.

Another voice drifted down into the canyon. Someone was here. Someone could help him.

Evan dragged himself forward another foot, until he could see the falls on one side of the ravine and the observation deck on the other. Two people stood on the deck. They were facing away from him.

Hope unfurled inside him. His mom!

His ordeal was almost over. He was in the cave's shadow. He needed to drag himself forward a few more feet so his mom could see him. Before he could move, another figure appeared on the deck. A man. And he was pointing a gun at his mom.

No!

It was probably the same man who had killed Paul. Fear gave Evan a burst of strength. He had to help his mom. He crawled to the ledge in front of the cave, only to be brought up short. He rocked back on his heels. The water had risen. The huge boulders he'd used to cross to the other side were barely visible. Evan watched, horror spreading like ice through his veins, as a small wave crashed over the ledge. Water lapped over his legs and formed a puddle in the cave's entrance.

He couldn't get out now. He was trapped.

Chapter Thirty-Two

"Come out where I can see you!" the armed man shouted at Lance.

Rain hammered on the nylon hood of Lance's rain jacket. Wind pushed the rain sideways, pelting his face and blurring his vision. He took one more step forward, until he was under the protective overhang of thick branches. He wiped the rainwater from his face and met the gaze of a killer.

"Stop right there or I will shoot one of them in the face. Hands up!" About twelve feet away, the armed man had cornered Rylee and Tina against the observation deck railing. All three were soaking wet, their hair plastered to their heads. The man changed the angle of his body to keep Lance and Rylee and Tina in his line of sight.

In his peripheral vision, Lance saw Morgan, at his flank, lift both hands, palms out.

Lance raised his hands in front of his body and studied the man. He looked familiar. The photo of Joe Martin stuck to the whiteboard back at the office ran through Lance's mind. The man's identity clicked into place. Aaron Martin, Tina's half brother, looked very much like his father had two and a half decades ago.

"Is he your rescuer, Tina? Did you call him to get you out of this mess?" Aaron snarled. "When he dies, remember it's your fault.

Everything is your fault, including your husband's death. That's what you get for being a greedy, backstabbing bitch."

"What do you want?" Lance yelled into the wind.

"I want my fucking money." Aaron shook the gun in Tina's face. Tina didn't look as terrified as she should have. Her gaze kept dropping to the water and the cave below. She was more afraid for Evan than for herself.

"What money?" Lance kept his gaze on Aaron, but his brain scrambled for options. He needed to get Aaron away from Rylee and Tina. How could he draw the man away?

"The money this bitch stole from our father." Aaron gestured with the gun. His eyes went to his half sister.

The second Aaron shifted his eyes, Lance took a step forward. "What are you talking about?"

Ignoring Lance, Aaron turned back to Tina. "Where is the fucking money? And don't you dare try to tell me you don't have it. Joe still thinks those two cops he had in his back pocket took it. That's why he ordered me to kill them. But that's not what happened, is it? Those cops were dirty, but they didn't take the hundred grand. I've tortured enough people to know that no one could have kept a secret after what I did to them. Everyone breaks. They didn't know where the money went. The only other person who could have taken it was you."

Tina's eyes were flat, emotionless, but Lance could see her brain working.

"The money is in a safe place," she said.

"Fuck. I should just kill you now." Aaron clipped her on the side of the head with the butt of the gun. "I am not playing games."

Tina fell back a half step. Her hand cupped behind her ear. "I didn't know you wanted it."

Under the coating of rainwater, his face reddened. "I sent you a letter. But you sent your husband and his cop buddy to meet me instead of coming yourself. Stupid bitch."

Tina's mouth dropped open. "I never got any letter."

They stared at each other for a few seconds.

"Doesn't matter," Aaron said. "I want that money. I know you. Always hoarding cash here and there. Always squirreling it away. You still have the money. Where is it?"

"In the trunk of my car in the parking lot." Tina glanced over the railing again. Next to her, Rylee cowered and clutched the wooden railing as if it were the only thing holding her upright. "I was going to use it to take my son away from here."

Aaron thought about her statement, then seemed to decide it sounded plausible. He switched his aim from Tina to Rylee. "How do you propose we get it?"

Lance kept quiet. If Aaron went with Tina, maybe Morgan could get Rylee to safety.

"I'll get it for you," Tina said. "I don't even care about it anymore. Just take it and go."

"No fucking way. This girl is my insurance." Aaron looked over the railing. "Better think fast. The water is rising. You're going to lose your son."

"OK. I'll take you to the money." Tina started to move.

"Hold on." Aaron reached into his pocket and pulled out two zip ties. He handed them to Tina and motioned toward Lance and Morgan. "Tie their hands behind their backs. Don't do anything stupid. I will shoot this little bitch's face right off." He waved the gun at Rylee's nose.

Tina took the ties and walked toward Lance. Aaron grabbed Rylee by the hair and hauled her in front of his body. He pressed the muzzle of the gun into her temple. Lance couldn't tell if it was rain or tears running down Rylee's face.

He tried to catch Tina's gaze, but her eyes were cold and determined as she refused to make eye contact. She glanced one more time at the water rushing across the bottom of the ravine. She would do anything to save her son. Anything. Lance, Morgan, and Rylee could be collateral damage. She was creating distance between them without taking a step.

And there wasn't a damned thing Lance could do about it. He was too far away to even consider trying to disarm Aaron.

She moved behind Lance. He cooperated, putting his hands behind his back. He made two fists and pressed the heels of his palms together as she tightened the strap. She moved on to tie Morgan's hands the same way.

"Turn around," Aaron yelled. He examined Lance's binds and seemed satisfied. "Take his gun and slide it toward me."

"I'm sorry." Tina lifted Lance's handgun from his holster, placed it on the wooden deck, and pushed it toward Aaron.

"It's OK." Lance would have done it himself to keep Aaron from shooting Rylee.

The gun stopped a few feet short of Aaron's feet.

"Check her for a weapon too," Aaron ordered.

Tina lifted the hem of Morgan's jacket and removed her weapon from its holster. She slid it across to join Lance's Glock.

Aaron tried to reach the weapons with his foot but couldn't. He stooped, dividing his attention between Lance, Tina, and Rylee. He looked down and grabbed Lance's gun.

The gun pointed at Rylee's temple shifted, its barrel dropping toward the deck. The instant the muzzle pointed away from her face, Rylee attacked Aaron. She slammed her head backward into his, then grabbed for his gun arm with both hands.

Lance bent at the waist and raised his bound hands. The plastic dug into his skin. He slammed his hands down onto his lower back as hard as he could. The tie didn't give. He tried again, this time using more force and pulling his hands apart as his forearms hit his body. The zip tie snapped.

He was free.

A gunshot boomed. Red bloomed across Rylee's thigh. She froze and looked down.

"Stupid bitch." Aaron punched her in the head.

Using the distraction, Lance launched himself at Aaron, catching him in a full tackle. They went down on the deck, slid across the water-slicked wood, and tumbled down a short flight of steps. Lance was on the bottom when they came to a stop on the first landing. Out from under the branches, he could barely see. Torrential rain beat down on his face.

Aaron must have dropped his gun. Straddling Lance's chest, Aaron wrapped both hands around Lance's neck and squeezed. Lance gagged as two thumbs pressed on his windpipe. He raised his arms, folded them so his forearms overlapped, and used them as a lever to press down on the insides of Aaron's elbows. Aaron's arms bent, and Lance pinned his attacker's hands down. The pressure on Lance's throat eased.

He dragged in a breath, the oxygen reviving him.

With Aaron's hands and wrists pinned to his chest, Lance bent one leg and hooked his foot around Aaron's ankle. Then Lance bridged over his own shoulder. With his foot trapped against Lance's thigh, Aaron could not extend his leg sideways for balance. The maneuver should have flipped them over and positioned Lance on top, but they rolled down the next flight of steps.

Lance fell sideways, his shoulder slamming into step after step as he slid across the treads on his side. His descent was stopped by the safety railing on the lower observation deck. He slammed into the wooden rungs, the impact knocking the wind out of his lungs.

Aaron was on his feet, coming at Lance. Something shiny gleamed in his hand.

A knife.

Adrenaline surged through Lance's blood like twenty espressos. He scrambled to his feet. Aaron lunged. The blade swiped at Lance's belly. Lance jumped backward, turning his gut away from the track of the weapon. Aaron came at him again, stabbing at his midsection. Lance dodged the blade again.

Lance maneuvered away from the confines of the railing. He backed off the deck onto open ground. He needed room to move. Aaron followed, waving the knife back and forth in the air. Lance feinted left. Aaron countered. Then Aaron attacked, making a hard line for Lance's face. Lance ducked, turned, and grabbed Aaron's wrist with both hands. He bent Aaron's hand backward, applied pressure, and twisted until he felt the bone snap. The knife fell to the ground.

With an angry roar, Aaron ran at Lance. He caught him around the waist, and they careened toward the swollen water. They went over the edge of the bank and fell into the freezing river. Lance hit a boulder, slid off, and was sucked into a deep eddy. The last thing he saw as the water closed over his head was the storm raging above him.

Chapter Thirty-Three

"Do you have a phone?" Morgan shouted to Tina.

"Yes," Tina yelled back.

"Call 911! Then help Rylee." Morgan ordered over her shoulder as she raced down the wooden steps. She couldn't make a call with her hands tied behind her back.

Behind her, Tina was at Rylee's side.

"OK!" Tina answered.

She'd left Tina and Rylee on the upper deck, with Tina trying to stanch the bleeding of Rylee's bullet wound. Morgan hit the lower deck, turned, and raced across the boards to the wet ground.

Where is Lance?

She tracked a line of footprints in the mud. They led right into the river. Morgan ran to the riverbank, scanning the water. A head broke the surface. Was that Lance? A second head popped above the water. The two men struggled, fighting the white water and each other as the current swept them away.

Morgan ran along the bank, keeping pace with them, feeling helpless.

The men shot between huge boulders and disappeared as they were sucked down into a dark pool of water.

Morgan stared over the water, her heart clenching as Lance disappeared, refusing to blink in case she missed some sign of him. But nothing happened. Seconds ticked past as dread eddied and pooled behind her solar plexus.

He couldn't drown. Not after everything they'd been through together. Morgan moved to the water's edge, her eyes scanning the surface. Rain pummeled the river and her face.

Where are you?

A head broke the surface. But it was Aaron. Clutching one hand to his chest, he used his other to grab her ankle and try to pull her into the water. With no hands and no way to reach her gun, Morgan pulled her free leg back and kicked him in the head as hard as her precarious balance would allow.

Her boot connected solidly with his face. Blood spurted from his nose, and Aaron's head snapped backward. She fell on her ass in the weeds, but he kept his grip on her foot, grunting and pulling her toward the rapids. His eyes lit with desperate cruelty.

Morgan's body slid a few inches in the slick mud. She kicked at his hands, but he held on, his mouth set in grim determination to drag her into the water.

Lance's head popped up. He grabbed Aaron by the hair. Morgan sent one final kick into Aaron's face as Lance dragged him away. Both men went under. Morgan couldn't see any bubbles. The water was too turbulent.

Desperate, she held her breath and searched the surface.

Where are you?

A head broke the water. *Lance!* Relief pushed the air from her lungs. He shook the water from his hair and swam to the bank. Morgan rushed forward as Lance climbed out of the water.

They both collapsed for two breaths. Rain pounded Morgan's face as she kept one eye on the surface of the water in case Aaron came for them again. "Is he . . ."

Lance sat up. His eyes narrowed. "You don't have to worry about him. He's not coming up again."

"Good." Morgan had no pity for the man. He'd killed Paul. He'd shot two innocent teenagers.

Nodding, but clearly still out of breath, Lance stood.

With her hands still bound behind her back, Morgan kicked out, using momentum to rock onto her knees. Lance helped her to her feet.

"I couldn't break the zip tie," she said as they hurried across the muddy ground.

"It takes practice." Lance dug into his pocket and pulled out his keys. "Turn around."

She did. The plastic dug deeper into her wrists, but he released the tie in a few seconds. Morgan rubbed her wrists and stared at the falls. A fresh burst of alarm shot through her. The water had risen significantly since they'd arrived, and the rain showed no sign of letting up.

She gasped. "The river is almost at the entrance to the cave."

"Did you call 911?"

"Tina did."

"But there's no telling how long it will take them to get here. The roads are flooded, and I'm sure they're inundated with emergency calls." Lance sprinted to the edge of the water across from the cave. He cupped his hands around his mouth and shouted, "Evan!"

There was no response.

Panting, Morgan stopped next to him. She assessed the swirling, raging water. How would they get across? "What are you thinking?"

"I don't know." Lance's body was still, but she knew he was trying to come up with a plan. "I could probably swim to the cave, but I don't know how I'd get Evan back across."

"Do we have rope?" she asked. "You can string a line across as a guide."

"In the Jeep." He turned and ran up the steps. Morgan followed. She reached the higher deck just a few seconds behind him.

Rylee lay flat on her back, with her leg elevated on the deck railing. Tina had tied her jacket around Rylee's leg. The girl was bone white and trembling, and the pant leg of her jeans was completely saturated with blood from midthigh down.

Tina glanced over the edge of the deck. "I have to save my son."

But how? Neither Tina nor Morgan was physically strong enough to cross the river or move someone the size of Evan.

"It's going to take some muscle," Lance said. "If you look after Rylee, I'll get Evan."

"I don't want Rylee to move." Tina stood. "If you carry her down to the parking lot, I have additional first aid supplies in my car."

While Tina held Rylee's leg still, Lance scooped the girl into his arms, being careful not to jostle her. He carried her across the walkway and down the short flight of steps to the parking area.

Tina went to a vehicle parked a few spaces away from the Jeep and opened the trunk.

Morgan slid her hand into Lance's pocket, took his keys, and opened the cargo hatch. She removed Lance's Go Bag.

Lance set Rylee in the cargo area of the Jeep. Morgan kept Rylee's leg as stable as possible, elevated on the back of the rear seat.

Leaving the girl in Tina's care, Lance grabbed his Go Bag. He and Morgan ran back toward the river.

"What's your plan?" she asked as thunder shook the ravine.

"I don't have many options." Lance opened his bag and removed a skein of yellow paracord. He tied one end of the rope to a tree trunk and the other around his waist. "I don't know how helpless Evan is going to be, but we have to get him out of that cave fast." He glanced at the water, then back toward the Jeep.

Morgan nodded and turned toward the river. Water lapped at the cave's entrance.

It was now or never.

Chapter Thirty-Four

Lance had a rough plan in mind, *rough* being the operative word. But he had no choice.

A branch careened over the falls and crashed to the turbulent pool at the bottom in a spectacular splash. Getting Evan out alone was going to be treacherous. But if he waited any longer, the boy was sure to drown. The water was rising too quickly. He couldn't wait for help to arrive. He took his body armor from his bag and put it on for some protection against blunt impact with rocks. He held up Morgan's vest but decided it wouldn't fit around Evan's muscular chest. She was tall, but Lance had had the armor specially made to fit her slender body. He stuffed a few carabiners, D-shaped metal clips, in his pocket.

He turned to Morgan and gave her a quick kiss. "I'm going across."

She grabbed his arm and kissed him back. "I love you."

"Love you back."

Looping the excess rope over his shoulder, Lance walked into the water. The first half of the trip would be the hardest because the water was deeper. It rose to his knees, then to midthigh. He let out the line as he walked, keeping some tension in the connection to help stabilize him. But the current pulled at his feet and legs. He dodged debris, mostly tree branches, as it swept by him.

Instead of fighting the current, he crossed on a diagonal, going with the flow as much as possible. Rain continued to pour from the sky, obscuring his vision. In the middle of the river, he clambered onto the top of a boulder to catch his breath. A wave crashed over the rock, sweeping him off. He went down. A large branch struck him across the ribs. His vest dispersed some of the impact, and he was damned glad he'd worn it.

Lance fought his way back onto the rock, then waded into a shallower section. The water pushed and pulled and threatened to sweep him off his feet, but he pressed forward. By the time he made it across, he was fifty feet downriver from where he'd started. He climbed onto the narrow, rocky ledge on the other side. Pressing his belly against the rock wall, he sidled along the ledge until he reached the cave's plateau.

Lance saw a tan nylon rope anchored to a tree trunk and extending to the top of the ravine. Evan must have used it to climb down from the top. Unfortunately, pulling Evan out from above was a two- or three-man job. Lance couldn't do it alone.

He untied the rope from around his waist and tied it to the trunk, pulling it as taut as possible. This would serve as their guide across the river. Then he used hand- and footholds to scale the rock wall and retrieve the second rope.

Water splashed over his ankles. The water level had risen several inches since he'd started across. It flowed into the cave. Lance wasted no time. Ignoring his heaving lungs, he crouched and ducked into the opening.

Evan lay at the back, curled on his side, facing Lance, but the boy's eyes were closed. The bottom of the cave dipped slightly, and the gully was filled with water.

"Evan?" Lance called as he splashed across.

The boy stirred and opened his eyes. "Lance?"

Rylee hadn't been exaggerating. The boy looked like death. Except for an unnatural, spotty flush, his skin was pale and pasty. His eyes appeared sunken, like Sophie's had when she'd been dehydrated and running a high fever. Lance placed a hand on the teen's forehead. He was burning hot. An ACE bandage was tied around his upper arm.

"Is my mom OK?" Evan asked. "I saw a guy pointing a gun at her. I couldn't do anything about it."

How like the boy to be worried about his mom when his own life was in danger.

"Your mom is all right." Lance didn't take the time to assess Evan's wound. "We need to get you out of here right now. Can you walk?"

"Honestly, I don't know. I can crawl, though."

"I'll take that for now." Lance removed his vest. "You need this more than I do. It won't help you swim, but it will protect you against rocks and debris." Lance worked it onto the boy's injured arm first. Sweat poured from the teen's brow, and his jaw tightened as he fought the obvious agony generated by the movement. Then Lance fashioned a harness with the second rope and secured it around Evan's body. Lance coiled up the extra thirty feet of leftover rope and slung it over his shoulder. He could toss it to Morgan at the halfway point. She and Tina could help Lance get Evan across the deeper half of the river.

"Let's go." Lance kept hold of the harness as they moved into the water at the front of the cave, now more than a foot deep. The water level had risen above the top of the opening. Only three feet of air space remained in the cave. Evan shivered as the water splashed over his legs. He rolled onto his knees. His crawl was painstakingly slow with only one good hand.

Lance barked out rapid commands as the water level continued to move higher. "I'll get you through the opening. Take a deep breath. One. Two. Three."

The boy sucked in air. Lance submerged them both and pulled the teen out of the cave. As they surfaced, Lance grabbed for the taut rope connecting them to the other side of the river. He used a carabiner to fasten Evan's harness to the yellow paracord. The metal would slide along the rope. Then Lance clipped a second carabiner to his belt and Evan's harness. Now Evan's body was suspended just above his.

The guide rope would help him combat the current. As long as it held, they wouldn't get swept away. But it didn't allow them to move with the flow of the water. Lance would have to fight it with brute strength. But there was no way that Lance could fireman-carry Evan across the water. Evan was not a small kid. He weighed almost as much as Lance did. Yet Lance had to get him out without help.

Who knew when the rain would end or when responders would arrive? The flood could eventually submerge the rope.

On the other side, he saw Morgan and Tina waiting.

Lance began the treacherous crossing, his arms straining to pull Evan's weight and his against the powerful current. Evan could do nothing to help. He was deadweight. Lance's biceps burned as he hauled them through the shallower section and onto the center boulder. Evan landed on Lance's legs. He could feel the boy's body shaking with pain, but he didn't cry out. Lance paused to breathe. His arms felt rubbery from the exertion and cold water.

"You all right?" Lance shouted in Evan's ear.

"Yes." The boy's words trembled. His lips were blue, and the fever flush had drained from his face. He needed a hospital—quickly. He was going to end up with hypothermia on top of an infected wound.

Lance met Morgan's gaze across the twenty-five feet of rough water that separated them. Almost there. But the water was deeper and the current stronger in the next section. He would need help pulling Evan across.

He cupped his hand around his mouth and shouted, "I'm going to throw you the rope."

Morgan moved to the bank, ready and waiting. Lance uncoiled the second half of the harness rope. He dug his flashlight out of the cargo pocket of his pants and tied the wrist strap to the rope. Then he let out some line and began circling the flashlight over his head, letting out the rope as the circle widened. When he let go, the flashlight soared across the water, but fell a few feet short of the bank.

Lance hauled it in and moved a few feet into the water. Bracing a foot against a boulder, he tried again. The flashlight soared, struck the bank, and bounced off. Morgan dove on it, snatching it from the shallow water at the river's edge. She held the end and backed up to take up the tension in the line. Tina joined her, clearly waiting for a few more feet of rope so that she could get hold of it.

Lance summoned his strength. "Let's go," he shouted to the boy.

Evan curled around himself as they moved back into the water. Lance pulled them both along the line. The force of the water made him struggle for every inch. Twenty feet.

Come on. Pull harder.

Lance gritted his teeth against his aching arms. He pushed off a rock with a foot, using his legs to gain another foot on the rope.

Fifteen feet.

Almost.

On the bank, Morgan and Tina leaned into the effort. Using their legs to pull, they inched backward.

Something crashed upriver. Lance's head swiveled around. A small tree shot toward them, riding on the swift water. He grabbed Evan and pulled him toward the shore. The tree struck the guideline on the cave end. The rope snapped. The release of tension sent Lance and Evan flailing into the current. Lance hung on to the rope. But the nylon was slippery and his strength was flagging.

They dangled in the current. Lance kicked, but he couldn't get his feet back under his body. He could barely hold on.

On the bank, Tina and Morgan strained, but the combined weight of the men and the strength of the river was working against them. They were not physically strong enough.

The yellow paracord was the only thing keeping them from being washed away.

Chapter Thirty-Five

In the darkness of the trunk, Sharp felt the car moving and the body next to him trembling.

"Olivia?" Sharp said softly.

Her body jerked, then stilled. "Lincoln?" Her voice shook.

He could hear her teeth rattling.

"Are you all right?"

"Physically, yes." But her body trembled hard.

Sharp could sense a big fat *but* on its way. He began feeling around for something he could use to cut their zip ties. He and Lance sometimes practiced breaking them, but he had no room to maneuver.

Her breathing came hard and fast. "I'm claustrophobic. I have to admit, I'm freaking out right now."

"Is your head covered?" Sharp tugged at his hood. It was secured around his neck with a thin piece of nylon. He had to work at the knot for a few minutes, but he eventually loosened it. He pulled the hood off. The trunk was dark and the air stale, but he could breathe a little better.

"Yes." Her tone rose, as if she were going to cry. The vulnerability in her voice was unexpected. "I can't get it off. It's getting tighter."

The fabric over Sharp's head had been stifling. He couldn't imagine how Olivia felt.

"Let me try." He reached for her head, but his hands tangled in her masses of thick hair. He brushed it aside and found the nylon cord with his fingers. She'd pulled at it, tightening the knot.

He worked at the knot until it loosened. Then he eased the hood off her head. "There."

Her gulps for air were audible. "Thank you."

"I can give you more room too." Sharp held his hands tight against his chest. There seemed to be an inch or two of space behind him.

The trunk was large as trunks went, but it was still a tight squeeze. Sharp wriggled backward. His legs were bent, and his body was curled into a C. But he managed to ease out from under her. She slid to the carpet. "Is that better?"

She was smaller and fit into the curve of his body. "Yes. No. I don't know."

"Keep—"

"Do *not* tell me to keep calm."

"I won't." Sharp would rather her temper flare than her fear. "I was going to say *Try and keep your breathing slow and even.* Close your eyes."

"I can't breathe at all." She choked. "There's no air in here."

"Trunks aren't completely airtight. If we control our breathing, we'll be fine." *For a while.* Sharp kept that last part to himself.

"Do you see a trunk release lever?" he asked.

"No," she answered.

Sharp wasn't surprised. Men who transported bodies in trunks no doubt made alterations to suit their needs, like removing the emergency trunk release.

The car hit a bump, and they both bounced. His body position was awkward. His shoulder was pressed into the floor by his body weight. Pain sang from his wrist to his shoulder. If they were kept in the trunk for a while, his whole arm would be numb.

He was unarmed. He didn't have his cell phone. And he had no freaking idea where they were going. He didn't even know the lay of the land to guess. What was he going to do when the car stopped?

He needed to free his hands. He went back to searching the carpet with his fingers. He needed a nail or a paper clip.

Would the two thugs drag them out of the car to shoot them? Probably. They wouldn't want to get blood in the trunk. Sharp would have to assess the situation as it happened.

But there was no point thinking of that right now.

Olivia trembled against him. Her breaths hitched.

"Breathe with me. In . . ." Sharp inhaled loudly, then blew out the air in two long slow words. "And out."

Olivia mimicked him. Even in the dark, cramped space, Sharp could feel the tension radiating from her and respected her herculean effort to keep her shit together.

"Again." He repeated the breaths, this time counting to four on the inhale and again on the exhale. They got a rhythm going, and Sharp turned his attention to listening. The road noise under the car's tires sounded like a paved surface, and the car had picked up speed. They were on a highway or empty rural road. He listened harder, but heard no traffic other than the vehicle they were in.

"I'm sorry," Olivia said. "This was not how this was supposed to go."

"I know."

The car came to a stop, paused for a few heartbeats, then started up again. Sharp rolled a little as the vehicle made a turn. His weight hit the wallet in his back pocket. His lockpick was in his wallet. He could use the pick to open their zip ties. He tried to get his hands around his body to reach, but he wasn't flexible enough.

"Are your hands bound in front of you or behind your back?" Sharp asked.

"In front," she said.

"I have a tool in my wallet I might be able to use to spring these zip ties. My wallet is in my back pocket, but my hands are bound in front of my body. Do you think you can somehow get it out? We'll both have to roll over."

"I'm small. I can do it."

"I'll give you as much room as I can." Sharp flattened himself against the back of the trunk.

"Here goes." Olivia began to squirm. Thankfully, criminals preferred vehicles with large trunks. "Can you slide up a bit?"

Sharp was game. Any action was better than simply waiting for their fate as if it were inevitable. He mapped out the trunk space in his head. Sharp began to inch along the carpet.

Olivia continued to move. Some part of her jammed Sharp in the groin. If he hadn't been pinned, the pain would have doubled him over.

"I'm sorry," she said.

"It's OK," he hissed and breathed. It had been a light blow, and the pain ebbed quickly.

"I'm over," she breathed. Her hands grasped his.

He gave hers a return squeeze. "We can do this."

"OK. I'm wiggling backward." She shifted away from him.

He released her hands, then started to move. He was taller and could move only an inch or so at a time. But eventually, he was facing the back of the trunk.

He felt fingers in his pocket and his wallet slid out. A few totally inappropriate thoughts skittered through his mind.

You're an idiot.

"I have it." Olivia sounded triumphant. "I'll drop it in front of you?"

"Yes."

"Then how will you open the ties?"

Sharp snorted. Without being able to see, it wouldn't be easy. "It might take a while."

"If you roll back over, I could do it for you."

"That makes sense." Sharp went through the reverse motions of turning onto his other side. He was out of breath and sweating by the time he faced her. Their legs were tangled, and he could feel the heat of her breath on his face. He slid the pick from his wallet and pushed it into her fingers. "You need to work the pick between the locking mechanism and the teeth."

"All right."

The zip tie moved, biting deeper into Sharp's skin as she worked with it.

"Do you think Joe gave the order to kill us?" she asked.

Sharp rewound the meeting in his head. He'd been focused mostly on Joe, not Aaron, but there had been definite anger in the son's face. "I'm thinking that Aaron is staging a coup. He didn't seem all that happy that his papa was back from prison."

"I think so too. Aaron didn't give the order for us to be killed until his father was gone," Olivia noted. "Aaron has been running the business for twenty-five years. He might resent having to give up control now because his father's been released."

"It has to be a kick to Aaron's ego to have his weak old father giving *him* and *his* men orders after he spent more than two decades at the helm."

"Do you think Joe or Aaron had Paul killed?" Olivia asked.

"Aaron," Sharp said, almost surprised at how quickly the answer came to him. "If Joe had done it, *he* would have had us killed. Or he wouldn't have asked to meet us in the first place."

"I'm not sure why Joe wanted to meet with us anyway."

"He wanted information from us about Paul's murder." Sharp replayed the conversation in his head. "He was bluffing when he said he knew everything."

"And he was hoping we'd fill him in," Olivia said.

"Yes." Sharp replayed the interview again. He hadn't told Joe anything that wasn't public information. What had Joe been hoping to learn?

Did he want to find Tina? Or Evan?

Sharp couldn't shake the feeling that he was missing a huge piece of the puzzle.

The car rumbled on and on. Sharp tried to keep Olivia's mind engaged and off their dire situation.

"I'm sorry this is taking me so long," Olivia said. "I suspect we've gone farther than back to the office complex."

"It might just seem that way," Sharp lied. He was betting on a very isolated secondary location, with no witnesses and adequate open space for two shallow graves. But Olivia was already scared. She didn't need his ideas in her head along with her own fears.

"They will want to take us somewhere very private." She was too smart.

The sound of tires on pavement became a flat and monotonous track of white noise. Sharp realized the car hadn't stopped or changed speed for a long time. They were on a long road that didn't require them to stop for lights or intersections. He'd felt the slight force of the car speeding through curves in the road, but that was all.

"I've got it," Olivia said, her voice excited.

Sharp heard the sound of the plastic teeth moving through the lock. A few seconds later, his hands were free.

He rubbed his wrists, then took the pick from her hands and went to work on hers. He had the lock open in a few minutes. "There you are."

"Oh, thank you."

"You're welcome." Sharp slid the lockpick into his pocket. "Move your hands and feet. Tighten and release all your muscles to keep them from going to sleep. If I can disable or distract the men, I want you able to run."

Sharp flexed his fingers and rolled his ankles, tying to keep the blood flowing into his limbs as best he could.

"If I can turn around," Olivia said, "I can try to break a taillight. Maybe I can signal someone."

"Good idea." But Sharp suspected they were in the middle of nowhere. He doubted there would be anyone to signal.

The car began to bounce up and down. Sharp wrapped his arms around Olivia to protect her from the jarring. Had they left the road? Dread pooled like acid in his belly.

Olivia tensed. "We're stopping."

"Maybe. Position your hands as if they are still joined."

"I thought I wanted to get out of this trunk more than anything else, but now I'm afraid of that too. They're going to kill us." She was bracing herself.

"They're going to try."

The brakes made a soft squeal as the car came to a complete stop. When the vehicle remained motionless, Sharp waited. He'd have preferred to be between Olivia and the opening, but the limited space in the trunk did not allow for them to switch positions.

The trunk popped open. The night was dark, and rain fell on Sharp's face. Thunder crackled as someone reached into the trunk and hauled Olivia out.

Sharp was next.

"You got the hoods off. Now you can watch each other die." The driver pointed a gun at Sharp. "Get out."

Sharp pressed his wrists together, pretending his hands were still bound. The driver became impatient and half dragged him over the lip of the trunk. Sharp landed on his knees in the mud.

He got his bearings. The sedan was parked in the middle of a field. There was no road in sight. The passenger had Olivia over his shoulder like a rolled carpet. Her feet kicked, and her body flailed.

"You bitch." The passenger dropped Olivia to the muddy ground.

She fell to her knees, lifting her chin and staring up at him with a fierce look.

He touched his cheek, pulled his hand away from his face, and looked at it. "You scratched me."

He slapped her across the face, knocking her to the ground. Pressing a hand to her cheek, Olivia started picking herself up. She was plastered in mud from head to toe.

Anger and fear pulsed in Sharp's veins. He needed to save himself before he could save her.

Closing in on Sharp, the driver chuckled, his voice radiating arrogance. "If you can't handle the woman, I'll get her next."

Sharp got one foot under his body and repositioned his weight. He needed to be able to act in an instant should an opening arise. The driver whipped out his gun and pointed it six inches from Sharp's forehead. Sharp had a split second of time before he would be dead.

"Fuck!" the passenger yelled.

In Sharp's peripheral vision, he saw Olivia launch herself at the passenger. Wrapping her arms around him, she drove a knee toward his groin.

"Fucking get off me!" The passenger twisted away from her driving knee and pulled at her arms, but Olivia held on.

The driver's gaze wavered at the distraction.

And that was the split second that Sharp needed. In one quick movement, he slipped his head to the left, out of the line of fire, while grabbing the slide of the gun and redirecting the weapon's aim to the right. At the same time, he used his right hand to strike the inside of the driver's wrist, then grabbed the gun and twisted it out of the driver's grip. Sharp shot him three times in the chest, then spun toward Olivia.

The passenger had shaken her off and was reaching behind him. He brought his gun around his body. On her knees, Olivia flung a handful of mud in his face. Sharp fired. His first bullet hit the man in the neck. The second and third were body shots. The passenger jerked twice, stared down at his chest for a second, then his legs folded and he collapsed.

And just like that, it was over.

Adrenaline rushed through Sharp's blood like a subway train. His heart hammered, and his vision blurred.

Olivia crawled over to him. Her mouth was moving, but all he could hear was the echo of his own heartbeat.

He held up one finger and motioned for her to stay behind him.

Staggering to his feet, Sharp walked closer to the driver. With the gun still pointed, he kicked the man's legs. The body moved limply. Sharp checked both bodies to make sure they were good and dead. Then he pocketed their weapons and cell phones.

He stumbled a few feet away and leaned on the bumper of the car.

Steady rain pattered on the vehicle and splashed in puddles in the muddy weeds at his feet. Lightning rushed across the sky, brightening the landscape with three flashes of light.

Relief—and exhaustion—flooded Sharp. They were alive. He almost couldn't believe it.

Olivia was still on her knees, catching her breath.

"Are you all right?" he yelled over the sound of the storm.

She nodded, then felt around in the mud and pulled a sandal out of the muck. She held it up to the sky like a trophy. Then she climbed to her feet and walked over to him, her gait lopsided in one shoe and one bare foot.

She was a piece of work.

Olivia joined him at the car and turned her face up to the rain. The rain washed away some of the mud. Neither of them moved for a few seconds, as if they couldn't believe they were still breathing.

Sharp broke the silence. "You were supposed to run."

She brushed a streak of mud off her face. "Fuck that."

Leaning over, she tried to put on her sandal, but the strap was broken. A stream of Spanish flowed from her lips.

Sharp spoke a little Spanish, mostly profanity from his years on the police force. When you're arresting someone, they generally don't say nice things to you. Even with the Cuban flair she put on the language, he recognized most of the words and was impressed with her creativity.

"Let's get out of the rain." Sharp opened the driver's side door and slid behind the wheel. Olivia got into the passenger seat.

He started the engine, turned on the heater, and offered her a cell phone. "We should probably call a cop."

Chapter Thirty-Six

Morgan's feet slid in the mud. She and Tina were losing ground. The current was too strong. She glanced at a tree next to her. Before she lost the play in the rope, she wrapped it around the tree to help anchor it.

The rain began to slow, but no one told the river.

"I'm going to get the Jeep," she shouted. "We can't pull them in ourselves."

"I'll keep trying." Tina braced her foot against a boulder on the riverbank.

Morgan tied off the rope and ran for the stairs to the observation decks. Her lungs cried as she jogged up the wooden steps, and for the fiftieth time in the past year, she regretted not being in better physical condition.

A little regular cardio wouldn't kill you, Morgan.

She raced across the first deck and took the next set of steps to the second. Panting, lungs burning, she reached the upper parking lot. Her thigh muscles were on fire as she ran for the Jeep.

She hoped this would work. The mud was deep. The Jeep could easily get stuck. But what were her options? There was no way she and Tina could pull Lance and Evan to safety, and Lance wouldn't be able to hang on long.

Morgan slid to a stop behind the vehicle. She'd forgotten Rylee was in the back.

Rylee lay in the cargo area with her leg elevated and the hatch raised. A silver emergency blanket covered her torso. Blood dripped from the bandage Tina had wrapped around the girl's thigh. The tight gauze had slowed but not completely stopped the flow of blood. A wide-mouthed duffel bag filled with medical supplies was open next to her.

"I have to close this door," Morgan said. "Hold on and try to stay still."

Rylee nodded. Pain and shock glazed her eyes. She needed a hospital. How long would it take for the police to get here?

In the vehicle, Morgan started the engine, her hands shaking from the cold and the rush of adrenaline through her blood. She drove across the muddy ground to the riverbank and turned the Jeep around so that its bumper faced the river. She backed the vehicle until it was as close as possible to Tina and the tree that tethered Lance and Evan to the shore.

Setting the brake, she jumped out.

Before Morgan untied the rope, Tina anchored it as best she could, wrapping it under her butt and sitting low.

"Ready?" Morgan yelled.

Tina nodded.

Morgan unwound the rope from the tree. Instantly, Tina's feet began to slide forward in the mud as Lance and Evan's combined weight pulled at the rope. They drifted a foot farther out into the water. Morgan tied the end of the rope to the hitch on the rear of the Jeep. Once it was secured, Tina fell back, gasping.

Morgan jumped back into the vehicle and inched it forward. The wheels spun. Mud flew from under the tires as they dug into the slippery ground. Morgan braked, then tapped the gas, rocking the vehicle out of the ruts they'd created. The tires rolled over the top edge of the furrow, gained traction, and began to move forward.

Morgan eased the gas pedal down with steady pressure, not letting the tires stop rolling for fear that they would become bogged down again. She kept the tension steady. She didn't want to break the rope. She checked the rearview mirror. Lance and Evan still dangled in the current. A wave crashed over Lance's head.

Hold on. Another minute.

Foot by foot, she pulled Lance and Evan to the side of the river. Once they reached the bank, she set the brake again, tumbled out of the driver's seat, and ran toward Lance.

Tina waded into the water to help them ashore. She wound her arms around her son as if she hadn't really expected to see him alive again. Lance collapsed on the bank. Morgan dropped to her knees beside him. She touched his face, but she couldn't form words. His blue eyes fixed on hers, and she realized she didn't need to.

The wind eased, and the rain decreased to a steady drizzle.

Lying on his back, Lance unclipped his belt from Evan's rope harness. Tina tried to untie the knots of the harness, but the rope was twisted. When she released the rope, it was smeared with blood. Her hands were raw from the tug-of-war with the river.

Morgan looked down at her own hands. They too were raw and bloody, with rope burns and pieces of missing skin. She wiped them on her thighs. They were the least of her problems.

Kneeling in the wet weeds, she fished in Lance's bag for a utility tool. She used it to cut the harness off Evan and to cut the rope attaching the men to the Jeep. She tossed the rope aside. Then she found a Mylar emergency blanket and wrapped it around Evan.

The boy was white and limp, his eyes closed.

Tina placed two shaking fingers against her son's neck. Her body sagged with relief. "He's just unconscious."

Lance staggered to his feet. "How long did the dispatcher tell you it would take for the emergency response?"

Tina didn't answer. Instead she opened the back of the Jeep and dug through her duffel bag for a fleece blanket. She checked on Rylee's bandage and gave the girl a pat on the arm. Rylee shivered. Morgan had left the Jeep running and the heat on, but the girl's teeth were chattering.

"I'll close this door in a minute, and it'll get warmer in here," Tina said to Rylee.

"Yes, ma'am." Rylee nodded. Her wound was nasty, but she was awake and alert.

Tina removed her bag from the Jeep, closed the rear hatch, and brought the medical supplies to Evan. "Are there any more blankets?"

Morgan looked through Lance's kit. "No."

"Would you bring my car down here?" Tina brushed raindrops from her forehead. "We can put him in the back seat and run the heater. I have blankets and some additional medical supplies in the trunk."

Morgan ran up to the parking lot and drove Tina's car down. She parked it next to the Jeep. When she climbed out of the car, Tina was preparing to start an IV.

Morgan took in the volume of supplies: gauze, antiseptic and other wound-cleaning and dressing materials, bags of saline, vials of drugs. Tina's bag was no normal first aid kit. She'd stocked it with her son's injury in mind.

"Where did you get all this?" Morgan asked.

"Rylee described Evan's wounds when she called, so I stopped at the urgent care on the way here." Tina leaned over Evan. She straightened one arm and tied a rubber tourniquet above his elbow. She tapped on the skin, clearly looking for a suitable vein. "He's dehydrated. I need some light."

Lance retrieved an umbrella and flashlight from the Jeep's glove compartment. He held the umbrella over Evan and shone the flashlight on his arm.

Tina cleaned her bloody hands with sanitizer, donned a pair of gloves, then began opening packages. She used an alcohol prep pad on

Evan's arm, then inserted a needle. Swearing, she tried again. On her third attempt, she had successfully placed the IV. She taped it down, attached a bag of saline, and held it high. "Let's get him in the back seat of my car. I can hang the saline drip from the headrest."

Lance hesitated. His clothes and hair were plastered down. He was bleeding from several shallow lacerations and abrasions, and he looked not quite steady on his feet. His muscles were likely weak from the massive exertion of getting Evan to shore. Yet the eye contact with Morgan made his face go even grimmer, which shouldn't have been possible. His gaze locked on Tina's medical bag, then met Morgan's eyes. She followed his line of sight and knew exactly what he was thinking.

That was no first aid kit that Tina had brought in her trunk. Her bag was stuffed with a week's worth of medical supplies. She'd planned to do more than save Evan.

She'd planned to run.

"Tina, you didn't call 911, did you." The words came out of Morgan's mouth as a statement, not a question.

"No." Tina looked up at Morgan. "I can't trust the police. They have a warrant out for Evan's arrest. I'm taking my son and leaving here. You can't stop me."

"Evan needs to go to the hospital." Morgan glanced at the boy. His pallor was alarming. If Tina took him away, Morgan feared Evan might not survive.

But Tina was riding on her own wave of fear.

"All Evan needs is me. We're better off on our own." Without any more explanation, Tina reached into her waistband at her back and produced Lance's gun. She pointed it at Lance and spoke, her voice cool. "Please put Evan into the back seat of my car."

Chapter Thirty-Seven

"No." Lance met Tina's gaze without flinching. He could not believe that she would shoot him.

"Do it!" Tina gestured with the gun.

At the increase in danger, Lance looked instinctively for Morgan. She had her phone out and was inching behind the tree. Calling 911, no doubt.

He had to stall for time.

Every inch of Lance's body ached. He'd almost drowned and had been beaten, kicked, and slammed into rocks. He'd risked his life to save Evan multiple times. From the looks of the boy, the job wasn't done yet. Lance would be damned if he'd let Tina's refusal to trust anyone kill her son.

"I'm taking both kids to the hospital," he said simply. "We both know Evan needs more than a few bags of saline."

"I have antibiotic injections," Tina said.

Lance's gaze cut pointedly to the teen, lying far too still on the ground, his face a mask of sickness. "That wound has been festering for days. It's been submerged in bacteria-laden floodwater. He needs an ICU and probably surgery."

Frustrated, Tina raised her voice. "I know what he needs."

"Do you?" Lance accused. "What about Rylee? Are you going to shoot her too?"

"Of course not!" Tina shot back. "I can't hurt a child, and Rylee is no threat to Evan."

"And you think *I'm* a threat to you or Evan?" Anger gave Lance's freezing body a shot of heat. "I almost died at least six times today for your son."

"And I thank you for that." Tina's expression softened for a few seconds. Her eyes pleaded with him.

"You can't get him into the car without me." Lance crossed his arms over his chest. "He's not even conscious now."

Panic lit Tina's eyes.

"I don't want to hurt you or Morgan," she said. "All you have to do is cooperate. Put Evan in my car, and we'll be on our way. You can take Rylee to the hospital. She needs surgery or she is going to bleed out. The tourniquet on her leg should only be used temporarily."

"No." Lance shook his head. "I will not be a party to you killing your kid."

Tina stared back at him in disbelief.

Morgan slid out from behind the tree. A small nod confirmed that she'd called for help.

Tina swung her arm around so that the weapon pointed at Morgan. "I said, put Evan in my car."

Morgan shook her head. "That's not going to happen."

Shit!

Lance was OK with risking his own neck, but he didn't like Morgan doing the same. But he didn't interfere. She was damned good at reading people, and she didn't think Tina was going to shoot either. But his heart still skipped a few beats as Tina's gun hand trembled.

"I'll handle the sheriff and the prosecutor," Morgan said. "We know who killed Paul. It might take some time to prove it, but once Aaron's body is dragged from the river, the case against Evan will be dropped. You don't have to fear the police now."

"You can trust Morgan to handle Evan's legal needs, and while those legal issues are sorted out, Evan will be getting the medical assistance he desperately needs." Lance scanned the teen. "You can't run from the law, and there's no reason for you to try. Especially when you know he needs major medical intervention."

"It's not the law I'm afraid of," Tina said. "It's Joe. You cannot keep us safe from him. He found us once. He will do so again."

"You might be right, but you need to prioritize the threats." Lance was done with the conversation. "You need to put the gun down and let us finish saving your son's life. Then you can worry about Joe."

Tina's brows lowered. She was trying to think of a way to force him to comply without shooting him. She should have been crying. She should have been emotional. Instead, she was thinking. But behind the mental exercise, he saw fear.

Pure fear.

She'd been planning to run for some time, as soon as she'd realized that Joe might have found her. She was desperate. She'd do anything to save her son, no matter how crazy. Lance's experience in the ER with Sophie had given him fresh insight into the parent-child bond and the primal instinct to protect one's young. She was fixated on her father and the terrible things he'd done in the past, the ways she and others had suffered at his hands. She saw him now as he'd been in her childhood. And the vision terrified her.

Lance couldn't threaten or bully her. He needed to appeal to the one thing that would break through the fear.

Her son.

"We can't wait. Have you checked his vitals? He looks worse." Lance moved toward Evan.

"Don't touch him!" Tina turned her body so the gun aimed squarely at Lance's chest. "I will shoot you."

Unfortunately, he'd given Evan his body armor. "You're going to have to."

He moved smoothly and slowly, faking confidence. Despite the cold, despite being soaking wet, despite being almost sure that Tina wouldn't shoot him, Lance poured sweat and held his breath.

He dropped to one knee next to Evan. "Morgan, would you open the back seat of the Jeep?"

She rushed to the vehicle and opened the rear doors on both sides.

Evan was no lightweight, and Lance's muscles were already taxed from the water rescue. He wasn't sure he could pick the boy up.

"I can't do this alone. I need help." Lance looked straight down the barrel of the gun at Tina. "You can keep pointing that gun at me, or you and Morgan can lift Evan's legs so we can get your son to the hospital."

Tina lowered the weapon. Morgan rushed in and disarmed her, quickly sweeping her hands along Tina's sides. Morgan pulled her own gun from the pocket of Tina's rain jacket. Tina had been smart enough to collect both guns from the observation deck.

Before Lance could attempt to transfer Evan to the car, the sound of sirens approached.

Tears poured from Tina's eyes. Morgan holstered her own weapon and handed Lance's to him.

Lance squinted. The rain had stopped, but he was so wet, he hadn't noticed.

He put a hand on Tina's arm. "No one will know what just happened."

She nodded once, then returned to her son to check the bag of saline to his IV line.

The sirens grew louder, and Lance saw the swirl of red and blue lights in the distance.

Tina adjusted the flow of fluids.

"I'll handle the sheriff," Morgan said. "Don't answer any questions at all unless I'm there. I will let the sheriff know not to question Evan either, unless I am present."

Tina nodded. "As I said before, it isn't the sheriff that I fear."

Lance turned toward Morgan, who had opened the cargo hatch of the Jeep and was sitting on the tailgate, holding Rylee's hand. He heard a banging sound. He tilted his head and shook some water out of his ear. The banging repeated, three quick taps, three with longer pauses between them, then another three fast taps.

SOS?

"Did you hear that?" he asked Morgan.

She nodded and started to rise.

"Stay with Rylee." Lance followed the noise. It was coming from above them. The parking lot? He took the steps two at a time, crossed the higher elevation deck, and emerged in the parking lot. The banging led him to the back of a dark-blue four-door sedan.

Someone was in the trunk.

Lance walked around the vehicle. The driver's door was unlocked. He used the hem of his shirt to open it, reached in, and pressed the trunk release button.

The trunk popped up a few inches. Lance opened it all the way. A bound and gagged Brian Springer blinked up at him. Lance untied the gag from around his mouth.

"You're alive." Lance was surprised. He'd assumed Brian was fish food.

"Thanks," Brian croaked. Bruises and swelling mottled his face. His lips were cracked, and a bloody bandage encircled his left hand. A zip tie bound his wrists.

"I have to get something to cut that plastic." Lance pointed toward the lower level. "The police are here. I'll be right back."

Brian nodded and closed his eyes in relief.

The sirens were loud enough that Lance knew the first responders had arrived. Discovering Brian had energized him. He jogged back down to the lower level. A paramedic unit and two ambulances were parked next to his Jeep. Sheriff's department and Scarlet Falls PD vehicles were approaching.

Lance was not surprised to see Sheriff Colgate park his vehicle. Lance rushed over as the sheriff hauled himself out of the driver's seat.

"What's going on here?"

"Long story. We'll jump to the end for now. One, down here we have two seriously injured teenagers, including Evan." Lance pointed toward the upper parking lot. "Two, I just found Brian Springer in the trunk of a car up there. He looks beaten up, but he's alert. Lastly, the body of Paul's killer, Aaron Martin, washed downriver. Someone will need to retrieve it."

The sheriff's mouth snapped shut. He spun and began barking orders. Uniforms scattered. Two men jumped back in their patrol vehicles and drove toward the upper lot.

Lance walked over to Morgan. She had backed away from Rylee, giving the paramedic room to work. The second paramedic leaned over Evan. Tina rocked back on her heels, pressed her hands together prayer-style, and rested the tips of her fingers on her lips. Her eyes never left her son as the paramedic assessed him.

Rylee and Evan were loaded into ambulances. The ambulances drove off. Tina followed the ambulances in her car.

The sheriff returned. "Aaron Martin beat the hell out of Brian, but he's grateful to be alive. A deputy is transporting him to the hospital."

"Could have been worse," Lance said. Not that being badly beaten and having his fingers snipped off were trivial injuries. But Brian could have been tethered to a few cinder blocks under a hundred feet of lake water.

The sheriff braced both hands on his belt and nodded.

A dark-blue sedan pulled in. Stella and her partner, Brody, jumped out. Stella checked her sister for injuries, then hugged her.

Morgan hugged her back. "I'm fine. Just wet."

Stella turned to Lance. "You look like you went ten rounds with a prizefighter, underwater."

"That's how I feel too," Lance admitted. Now that his adrenaline high was fading, every inch of his body hurt.

"We should go with the kids," Morgan said.

"Not just yet," the sheriff said.

Morgan turned to him. "I'm taking Lance to the ER. He's covered in cuts and bruises, and he's been swimming in floodwater. You can talk to him after he's been treated."

Colgate propped both hands on his hips. "You both need to be questioned."

"Do not cross me right now." She jabbed a finger at Colgate's chest. Her eyes narrowed to fierce slits, and two bright spots colored her pale cheeks. "Lance almost died doing *your* job." She waved a hand toward the road. "If we hadn't gotten involved, both of those kids would have died today because you were too damned stubborn to listen."

The sheriff leaned back, his face grim and maybe a little pale. Lance doubted anyone had called him out in a long time.

"As I already said, we'll answer your questions *after* Lance has been treated." Morgan's nostrils flared. Lance had never seen her this angry. She was the articulate and tactful member of their team, the one he could count on to keep a clear head and use her brain under duress. She didn't rail on people—that was his territory. But tonight, he was too exhausted to care about the sheriff at all. Colgate's entire department needed to be rebuilt. They were running on half staff with no real leadership. They all knew it.

The sheriff backed away just a few inches. "All right, but your vehicle is evidence."

"I'll give you a ride." Stella stepped between Morgan and the sheriff. She took her sister's arm and steered her toward her unmarked police vehicle.

Her partner waved and said, "Go ahead. I'll catch up later."

"Come on, Lance." Stella wrapped her free arm around Lance's waist. "You're a mess. Neither one of you should be driving anyway."

"Don't you want to stay and work the case?" Lance asked.

"Not really." Stella opened the rear door of her car. "The case is solved, right? This is going to be nothing more than a messy cleanup of the sheriff's screwup. Oh, joy."

"You have a point." Lance slid into the vehicle and rested his head on the back of the seat. He felt like he could sleep for a week.

Morgan sat up front with her sister. He heard them talking quietly. He was glad Morgan had stalled the sheriff on their questioning. He and Morgan needed to talk to Tina. There was something not adding up in Lance's head.

"Where do you want to go?" Stella started the car.

"The ER," Morgan said.

Lance stirred. "I don't need—"

Morgan glanced over the seat. She was wearing her *do not give me any trouble* face.

Lance closed his eyes. All he really needed was a shower, a hot meal, and some sleep, but there were times in a relationship when arguing was not the best course of action. This was clearly one of those times.

Two hours later, he and Morgan found Tina in the surgical waiting room. An SFPD officer stood just outside the door. Stella had requested a guard for Tina, at least until Aaron's body was recovered.

"Any word?" he asked.

Tina shook her head.

The hospital had let both Lance and Morgan shower, and they'd changed into fresh clothes Stella had brought them. Stella had supplied them a pizza as well, and they inhaled it while waiting for his discharge papers.

Lance's multitude of small cuts and abrasions had been thoroughly disinfected and bandaged, as had Morgan's hands. He hadn't broken any bones, but from the feel of his body, he was going to be black and blue tomorrow.

A deputy had come and taken their statements. They kept their stories brief and basic. Morgan and Lance had fielded a shocking call from Sharp too. Since the call had ended, Lance's brain had been sorting through the details Sharp had relayed about his meeting with Joe and Aaron's comments on the observation deck. Sharp believed that Joe had nothing to do with Paul's death. Aaron had acted alone, possibly in an attempt to stage a takeover of the organization he'd been running for twenty-five years. The missing money had been vital to his plan. But how had Brian gotten involved, and *why* had Aaron killed Paul? There were still too many missing pieces in the puzzle.

Did Tina have the answers? And even if she did, could Lance trust her answers?

Tina wore dry scrubs, likely provided by someone at the hospital. She looked frail and lost, sitting in the corner chair, her knees drawn up into a fetal position.

Morgan beelined for the coffee maker. Lance crossed the room and sat next to Tina. He didn't say anything, just leaned his head back on the wall.

Morgan brought Tina a cup of tea. "Can I get you something to eat?"

Tina shook her head. Morgan produced a small package of shortbread cookies from the kangaroo pocket of her sweatshirt.

"Sharp called," Lance began. "He's on his way back to Scarlet Falls. It seems Aaron was in Albany earlier. He tried to have Sharp and a reporter killed."

Tina wrapped her arms around her knees.

Lance continued. "Then Aaron headed up here. Sharp also learned something interesting. Right after Joe was convicted, two cops were murdered. It seems the cops were dirty, and Joe thought they stole a hundred grand from him. He had Aaron execute them."

Tina rested her face on her knees.

"But the cops didn't steal that money, did they?" Lance asked. Aaron had seemed certain it had been Tina.

Tina lifted her head and looked from Lance to Morgan. "Whatever I say to you is confidential. You can't tell anyone."

"That's right." Morgan opened the package of cookies.

"Joe had been bribing those cops forever," Tina began. "When the money went missing, everyone assumed they took it."

"But you stole the money?" Morgan asked.

"I don't know anything about the money," Tina lied. She didn't show any of the classic body language of a liar, but Lance had come to recognize that her lack of expression was its own tell.

"Where is it?" Lance asked.

Tina met his gaze squarely, her eyes vacant of any emotion, her face deadpan. No doubt she had learned to lie smoothly as a survival tactic early in her life.

"You still don't trust us." Lance suspected Tina was too damaged to ever trust anyone. Except maybe her son.

"Once Evan is well, we won't be able to stay here. Joe will come after us." Tina had the money. Lance was certain of it, and she was determined to keep it.

"Sharp didn't think it was Joe who ordered this. He thinks Aaron either wanted to oust Joe from the organization, or Aaron was going to fund his own retirement. Aaron thought you had the money and wanted to get it back from you. Sharp's theory is that Aaron didn't like handing the business back and taking orders from his father after he had been in charge for the last twenty-five years."

"Aaron was always a greedy bastard, just like his father." Tina lifted her chin. "But I will never feel safe as long as Joe is alive, and I still don't understand why Aaron killed Paul."

"To pressure you to give him the money?" Morgan suggested.

"That would only work if I knew that he wanted it." Tina didn't admit to having the cash. But she had it.

Lance could see it in her eyes. If he hadn't been so tired, he would have realized it immediately. "It really *is* in the trunk of your car, isn't it?" At the time, Lance had assumed she was just trying to keep Aaron from shooting anyone. The idea of her carrying a large sum of cash in her trunk had seemed absurd. But it all made sense.

Her surprised glance was all the answer he needed.

"You collected medical supplies, but you couldn't have run without the money," he continued.

The muscles of her jaw tightened. She would admit nothing, and he wouldn't make her. There was no point. Lance didn't care about Joe's drug money, and having it was Tina's safety net.

"We'll be glad to help however we can," Lance said.

He understood. Tina had been abused and betrayed from birth. The only person she'd ever been able to count on was herself. And who was to say she was wrong about Joe? She knew him best. Maybe he *would* come after her.

"There is something you can do." Tina's face creased. "I need to speak with Joe. I need to look him in the eye and ask him if he has any intention of coming after me or Evan. It's the only way I'll ever be able to sleep again. Can you arrange a meeting?"

"I can try." Lance didn't like the idea, but he understood. She needed to literally face her fear.

"Thank you," Tina said.

"Let's get through tonight." Morgan stood. "I'm going to go find Rylee's brother."

Rylee's surgery had been short and successful. When Lance and Morgan had checked an hour before, she'd been in recovery and doing well.

Morgan disappeared.

Thirty minutes later, a doctor in green scrubs came in.

Tina jerked straight.

"So far, so good," the doctor said. "The wound didn't look as bad as I expected. We're keeping him in the ICU. We'll see how his body reacts to the antibiotics. We should know more in the morning. But he's a tough kid. I'm more hopeful now than I was before the surgery. I'll send a nurse in when you can see him."

The pressure in Lance's chest eased. He was almost afraid to be relieved.

Tina nodded, close to tears.

The doctor left.

"Are you staying here tonight?" Lance asked.

"Yes," Tina answered. "There's a sleep chair in Evan's room."

"OK." Lance stood. "I'll be back to check on him tomorrow."

Tina met his eyes. "Thank you."

"You're welcome." Lance left the room and went looking for Morgan. He found her in the hallway, headed back to see him.

He turned her around and relayed the update on Evan's condition.

"Let's go home and get some sleep," Lance said.

Now that he'd had some good news about Evan, adrenaline seemed to be draining from Lance's body. He slung an arm over Morgan's shoulders and pretended he didn't want to lean on her.

"What about Tina?" Morgan wrapped her arm around his waist, as if she knew he could use the support. But then, she always knew what he needed.

"As long as Evan is here, Tina isn't going anywhere. And they should both be safe enough in the ICU with a cop outside the door."

Morgan put her head on his shoulder.

Tonight, Lance needed to recharge his batteries with his own family.

Chapter Thirty-Eight

Morgan woke to the gray of predawn. She'd slept poorly. Every time she closed her eyes, she saw Lance fighting Aaron, going under in the river, and being swept into boulders. She rolled over and watched him sleep for a few minutes. One arm was flung over his head. Gauze and tape covered a large abrasion on his forearm.

He was still sleeping off the sheer physical exertion of the previous night's water rescue. She did not want him disturbed. His battered body needed rest.

There was no other man like him. How did she get so lucky?

Morgan slipped out of bed and into her favorite worn pair of jeans and a tank top. She stopped in the bathroom to brush her teeth and put her hair in a ponytail. Sliding her phone into her pocket, she tiptoed around the bed and turned off Lance's ringer. A sound from the hallway caught her attention. She left the room, closing the door behind her.

Sophie stood in the hallway. Morgan greeted her with a kiss on the forehead, which was beautifully cool.

Sophie frowned at the closed door. "Is Wance still in bed?"

Nodding, Morgan pressed her finger to her lips. "He was up late. Let's let him sleep a while longer, OK?"

Sophie considered the question for a second, then tilted her head. "Can I stay home from pweschool today?"

Was she trying to make a deal or was her question unrelated to allowing Lance to sleep? Considering how sick her youngest had been, Morgan had had no intention of sending her to school anyway. A preschool was basically a giant brick petri dish, and Sophie's immune system would be weakened.

"Yes." Morgan scooped her up, settled her on her hip, and carried her toward the dining room. They walked past the plastic sheeting that covered the opening to the gutted kitchen.

Sophie rested her head on Morgan's shoulder. "I miss our kitchen."

"Me too." Morgan turned into the dining room.

"I like waffles." Sophie sighed. "But I miss pancakes."

Morgan noted Sophie's correct pronunciation of the *L* in *like*. Was Sophie growing out of her lisp? That shouldn't make Morgan sad, but there was a tiny part of her that didn't want her children to grow up so quickly.

"Me too," said Grandpa. Dressed in slacks and a blue polo shirt, he sat at the table, reading the news on his electronic tablet. He pointed toward the coffee maker. "The pot's full."

"Thank you." Morgan set her daughter on the chair next to Grandpa and poured a cup of coffee. She lifted the mug awkwardly, the bandages on her hands getting in the way.

"How is Lance?" Grandpa asked.

"Exhausted. Sleeping."

"It's no wonder." Grandpa pointed to his tablet. "There's an article on the rescue. I don't know how he did it."

"Me either, and I watched." She shuddered, another vision of Lance and Evan in the water flashing in her mind. Lance had succeeded with his intelligence, strength, willpower, and luck in equal measures.

"I'm sure you did more than watch." Grandpa moved his tablet aside. He studied her for a few seconds. "Why haven't you two set a date?"

"We've been busy." Surprised by the change in topic, Morgan sipped her coffee.

Grandpa rolled his eyes. "Try feeding that lame excuse to someone who hasn't interrogated a thousand suspects."

"I've never been able to fool you." Morgan stared into her cup, searching for the words to express an emotion she didn't understand. "Every time I think about a church and a fancy dress, I think of John. It's like wedding details and my memories of him are tied together."

"That's understandable. You two didn't drift apart. He was taken from you." Grandpa sighed. "Do you still want to get married?"

"I do," Morgan answered, with no hesitation.

"Then make new and different memories with Lance. Who says you have to get married in a church? Fly to Vegas. Wear jeans. Rent a food truck. I can think of a hundred ways to get married that don't involve a church or a fancy dress."

"That's all well and good for me, but Lance has never been married. He's been talking about a big traditional wedding."

"Have you *asked* him if that's what he wants?"

"He says he doesn't care, but I worry that he's just saying that to make me happy."

"What's wrong with that?" Grandpa caught her eyes. "Lance is a straight shooter. I'm going to bet he doesn't give two hoots about *how* you get married."

Morgan smiled, warmth spreading through her. Was the answer that simple? Had she been overcomplicating everything? "Maybe you're right."

"Of course I'm right," Grandpa huffed.

The rest of the family trickled into the room, and the morning shifted into gear. Morgan walked Ava and Mia to the bus stop, and

Grandpa drove Gianna to dialysis. Grant arrived to take some measurements in the kitchen. The activity seemed too normal, and Morgan felt disoriented.

She took a fresh cup of coffee to the family room. In the middle of the floor, Sophie was hosting a tea party for Snoozer and Rocket. Both dogs sat companionably with the little girl, listening to her chatter and sniffing at the plastic teacups she set in front of them. Sophie rounded out the party with a few stuffed animals. She seemed content to entertain herself, so Morgan watched and enjoyed every moment.

The dogs lifted their heads and turned toward the front door in unison. Rocket shot across the carpet, upending a teddy bear and spilling imaginary tea. Morgan went to the door, grabbing the dog's collar as she started barking.

"Shh," she said. But Rocket was having none of it.

There was a man on the doorstep. Morgan looked out the window. Surprise drew her back.

Esposito?

The ADA was impeccably dressed in a dark-gray suit and white shirt. Morgan opened the door, using her foot to hold the dog back.

Esposito glanced at the dog and frowned. "I need to speak with you."

"Please, come in." Morgan stepped back.

Snoozer went back to the tea party. Rocket growled. Esposito crouched and held his hand out to the dog. She sniffed his fingers, wagged the stub of her docked tail, and let him scratch behind her ears.

"You like dogs?" Morgan closed the door.

"What's not to like?" Esposito stood. He took in the house in one quick glance.

It was a mess, Morgan realized, without caring.

Sophie ran to Morgan, grabbed her hand, and tugged on it. Morgan leaned down. Sophie cupped her ear and said, in the loudest whisper ever, "Who is he?"

Morgan picked her up and straightened. "Sophie, this is Mr. Esposito."

To her surprise, Esposito held out his hand. "It's nice to meet you, Miss Sophie."

Sophie shook his hand, then giggled and threw her body backward over Morgan's arm. Grandpa came through the front door, and Morgan introduced him.

"Sophie and I are going to have a tea party." Grandpa took her tiny hand. "Why don't you take coffee out onto the deck?"

"Coffee?" she offered Esposito.

"Sure," he answered.

She pointed to the glass doors. "I'll bring it right out."

When she brought out the two mugs, Esposito was standing at the railing. The deck overlooked the Scarlet River. The river was still high and the current choppy, but the sun shone on the water, and the air felt cooler than it had in weeks.

Below the deck, a fence surrounded the yard and kept the children away from the water.

"Pretty view." Esposito took the coffee mug. "Your kid is cute."

"Thank you." Morgan leaned on the railing next to him. "I admit, your visit was not anticipated. I expected the sheriff to contact me this morning."

"Colgate quit."

"What?" Morgan shouldn't have been surprised. He'd been ill suited to the job from the moment he stepped into it. But he'd shown no indication of leaving office when she'd last spoken with him.

"Well, not exactly quit." Esposito turned to face her. "He's retiring and taking accrued vacation time until the paperwork is complete. He also might have been encouraged to step down by the powers that be. Not everyone is OK with looking like a chump."

Esposito would never say it, but Morgan interpreted *powers that be* as his boss, the district attorney. Technically, only the voters or the governor could remove a duly elected sheriff from office, but Colgate had inherited the job. Supervision over him was murky. Not that it mattered. The current DA was a very persuasive man, and lack of support from his office could make the job of sheriff all but impossible. The DA had backed up Colgate on the last two important cases—his reputation had suffered when the sheriff's investigations had gone sour. The prosecutor would not make that mistake a third time.

"Who will handle the investigation?" Morgan asked.

"Deputy Todd Harvey has just been promoted to chief deputy. He'll be cleaning up the case, with some help from the SFPD and the state police. Harvey will be in touch."

Morgan studied him. "Why are you really here? You could have told me that Colgate quit in a phone call."

"To relay a message."

"Also from the *powers that be*?"

"Maybe." Esposito lifted a shoulder. "Randolph County needs a sheriff. Someone smart. Someone who can whip that department into shape."

Shock dropped Morgan's jaw. "You can't be serious. I have no policing experience."

"You don't need any. Sheriff is an elected office. You would be required to take a training course prior to taking the oath of office." Esposito's dark eyes glittered. "The DA's office would back you in the election. You'd win."

Morgan considered the offer. Every decision made by the DA was a chess move. There was a reason he wanted her to run for sheriff. Since she'd opened her defense firm, she'd gone head-to-head with the prosecutor's office several times and come out on top. Did the DA want to eliminate her as his opponent? It didn't matter. Morgan had no desire to be a politician.

"Well, thank you for your support," she said. "But I'm not interested. I like what I'm doing, and I very much enjoy being my own boss."

Esposito acknowledged her answer with a slight incline of his head.

The sliding door opened, and Lance stepped out. He wore a pair of faded jeans and a gray T-shirt. A bruise had darkened on his jaw, and his arms were covered in small cuts and abrasions. He shifted his coffee to his left hand and shook Esposito's hand.

"Colgate quit." Morgan brought Lance up to speed on the case. They'd talk about Esposito's weird proposal later.

"I heard Morgan told him off at the scene last night." Esposito chuckled.

Warmth flushed into her cheeks. But she didn't offer apologies for her behavior. She'd meant what she'd said.

Esposito set his cup on the railing. "Don't feel bad. He wasn't a very good sheriff. You were just the only one with the balls to tell him."

"Have you pulled the arrest warrant for Evan?" Morgan asked.

Esposito exhaled hard through his nose. "Yes. The homeowner he stole from is not pressing charges, and we've decided not to pursue a charge of fleeing the scene at this time."

Morgan's temper spiked. She was too drained, physically and emotionally, to play games with Esposito. "If you pursue any charges against Evan, I will eviscerate you."

His nostrils flared, but he didn't respond.

She stepped closer. "I expect a press conference to be held today clearing Evan of all charges. Or I will hold one of my own, and I assure you, my words will not be flattering to the sheriff's office or yours."

"That'll be up to Chief Deputy Harvey."

Morgan rubbed the bridge of her nose. What was it with Esposito? It felt like he wanted to be decent, but he couldn't do it unless she made him. Is that what he wanted? For her to force him to do the right thing? Or maybe he needed to use her as an excuse so that he didn't ruin his tough-guy reputation.

She needed more coffee.

Esposito walked toward the sliding glass door. "One last thing. The urgent care center is not pressing charges against Tina." Esposito sighed with disappointment. "Her boss said he understands the highly unusual and desperate nature of her situation. She isn't even going to lose her job."

"She took some supplies to save her son," Morgan argued. "Her boss sounds like a reasonable person who doesn't want to lose a valuable employee."

"He's a chump. She stole from the company." Esposito didn't roll his eyes, but she could tell he wanted to. He shook his head in disgust as they walked back through the house. Lance wasted no time showing him to the door.

After he'd left, Lance said, "I told you he was still an asshole."

Morgan snorted. "I know Esposito is mostly difficult, but he's done us a few good turns."

She wondered what Esposito would do if he knew that Tina was probably hiding a large chunk of stolen drug money. It would be best if he never found out.

"He wanted the urgent care to press theft charges against Tina," Lance said.

"OK. Esposito is still an ass, but he's no longer the devil incarnate. Agreed?"

"I guess," Lance huffed.

Sophie ran out of the family room. "What's an asshole?"

Of course, she pronounced that *L* perfectly.

Chapter Thirty-Nine

That afternoon, Lance walked into the ICU, afraid of what he might find. His hand reached for Morgan's. Walking next to him, she squeezed his fingers.

Tina started to rise from the bedside chair.

"Don't get up. How is he?" Lance asked, stopping by the bed.

The teen was breathing on his own, and his color looked better than it had the night before.

"Better." Tina smiled. "The doctors were afraid of sepsis, but the infection seems to be localized." Tina scanned the blinking and beeping monitors. "His vital signs improved a little during the night. The antibiotics seem to be working."

"That's good." Lance's throat tightened.

"Thank goodness." Morgan breathed and gripped his hand tighter.

"Yes." Tina touched her son's hand, then looked up. Her eyes went from Morgan to Lance. "Thank you both for saving my son and for making me see the truth. If you hadn't, Evan might not be here. He did need much more medical support than I could have given him."

"You would have made the right choice in the end." Lance tried to sound more certain than he was.

Tina brushed her son's face with her knuckle. "I don't know about that. Fear is a terrible thing. It blinds you." She smoothed the blanket over Evan's chest. "But it won't happen again."

Tension eased inside of Lance's chest. "You can call us anytime. Don't think you're all alone."

"Thank you." Tina nodded, but she didn't make any promises.

There was nothing Lance could do to change her. "Would you let me know when he's awake? The team will want to see him." Lance would too, but nothing would cheer Evan up like his buddies.

"I will," Tina said.

Lance and Morgan left the ICU through the double doors. They went to Rylee Nelson's room in the surgical wing. Her brother stood next to her bed. Tension lines on his face made him look much older than the last time they'd seen him. Rylee was awake. Her leg was wrapped, elevated, and supported on pillows. Her face was as pale as the pillowcase.

A woman in a dark suit turned as Morgan and Lance entered the room.

Trevor's face brightened with relief. "This is Mrs. White, the social worker I told you about."

Morgan's face split into a Cheshire-cat smile. "My name is Morgan Dane. I'm the Nelsons' attorney. Why are you here?"

Mrs. White frowned, the skin around her mouth puckering as if she were smelling something foul. "I'm talking to Rylee. I will be filing a report about this incident." She gestured toward Rylee. "Ms. Nelson was gravely injured. She could have been killed."

"Indeed." Lance was not going to let this miserable woman use Rylee's courage against her. "Rylee was extremely brave. She saved her friend's life. She was quite the hero. It wouldn't surprise me if the mayor recognized her courage with some sort of civic award."

Mrs. White's mouth opened, but no words came out.

Morgan pulled a business card from her bag. "From now on, all correspondence should be conducted through my office."

Mrs. White took the card, shoved it into her pocket, and hurried from the room.

"Wow." Trevor stared at the doorway. "Thank you. She's never retreated like that before."

"She's never had to deal with Morgan before," Lance said with pride.

"As I told you before, this isn't over," Morgan said. "Your CPS file will likely remain open until Rylee turns eighteen, but it will be easier on you if I handle Mrs. White." Morgan smiled at Rylee. "How is your leg?"

"It's OK." Rylee smiled. "The nurse said as soon as Evan wakes up, she'll take me down to see him."

"That's wonderful." Morgan turned to Trevor. "Please let me know if you need anything."

"We will." He gripped his sister's hand. "But I think we're going to be all right."

Morgan and Lance left Rylee's room and took the elevator to Brian Springer's floor.

"Is everyone we know in this hospital?" Lance asked.

"It certainly seems that way." Morgan led the way out of the elevator. "We should be grateful. It could have ended much worse."

"You are so right." Lance knocked on Brian's doorframe.

"Come in," a voice said.

They entered the room. Brian was alone. His hand was wrapped in thick gauze and propped on a pillow. Bruises mottled his face. "I can't thank you enough for saving me."

Lance didn't tell him it had been an accident. "How did you get involved?"

"It all started when Paul unintentionally opened a letter addressed to Tina. I have a picture of the letter on my phone, but I read it enough to remember it word for word. 'This is a blast from your past. You've done well for yourself, bitch. But I want the money. Give it to me, and I won't have to destroy your new life.' There was a time and place where Tina was supposed to go. Paul wanted to find out what the hell was going on. He was pissed about the letter. He called me. He wanted my opinion. The postmark was local, and he thought it was probably from Kirk, trying to scare her. The ex was bitter and had been looking for a handout from Tina. He was especially pissed that his application for alimony had been denied."

Tina had said that Paul liked to take care of her.

Brian took a breath and sipped his water. "There was no way Paul was going to let Tina go to the meeting. He and I went instead."

"Where was it?" Morgan was taking notes.

"In the parking lot of a vacant office complex. Tina was supposed to go there at nine o'clock the following night. Paul and I took separate cars. I parked in a shadow at one end where I could see him. He went to the meeting site."

"But no one came," Lance said.

"No." Brian shook his head. "Paul still thought it was Kirk's prank. But it wasn't Kirk who grabbed me at my house."

"Did he break in?" Morgan asked.

"No. He didn't have to. I'd been out mowing the lawn. I wanted to get it done before I went fishing. When I went inside after I finished, he was waiting for me. He had a gun. I'd left the door unlocked while I was working in the yard, and I didn't hear anything over the sound of the mower."

Morgan looked up from her notebook. "How did he get you out of the house without your neighbors seeing?"

"He tied me up and put his car in the garage. Once he forced me into the trunk, he was clever enough to tie a wire noose around my neck and connect it to my hands and feet. I couldn't move without garroting myself. This was clearly not his first kidnapping."

"How did he know you were involved?" None of this made any sense to Lance.

Brian shrugged. "I guess he got my license plate number when I was in the parking lot. It's the only thing I can think of. In hindsight, we should have taken more precautions. But Paul really was convinced that Kirk was behind the note."

"What did he want from you?" Morgan asked.

"He wanted to know where Evan would hide. He also said Tina had money that was his. He thought I would know where it was. I didn't know what he was talking about." Brian's voice faltered. "I didn't even know *who* he was. He didn't believe me. He kept punching me. Then he brought out the shears—" His voice faded as he stared at his bandaged hand, pain and horror crossing his face. "If I had known anything, I would have told him. I would have said anything to get him to stop. I even tried making some shit up, but I didn't know enough to tell a plausible lie. I'm lucky he didn't kill me. He kept me alive as emergency leverage. If he had found Evan, he would have put a bullet in my head."

"Why did Paul call you? I thought you two had a falling-out right before he retired?" Lance asked.

Brian frowned. "We did. It was my fault. I lost my patience with a suspect. I listened to my lawyer and denied the whole thing. I said I didn't know where he got the bruises on his ribs. He could have had them before we arrested him. It was the suspect's word against mine. Paul backed me up, but he wasn't happy about it. Paul had a clear sense of right and wrong. He felt compromised."

Brian's head fell back on the pillow. "I shouldn't have asked him to cover for me. It was wrong of me to put him in that situation. I should have owned up to my mistake like a man. A few weeks ago, I called Paul and apologized." His eyes misted. "He accepted without missing a breath. Paul was a great guy."

Lance couldn't think of any more questions for Brian. Two off-duty deputies arrived to see him, and Morgan and Lance left.

Lance's phone vibrated. "It's the sheriff's department."

He answered the call.

"Hey, Lance. Todd Harvey here. I'd like to talk to you, Morgan, and Sharp. Can I drop by the office?"

"We're at the hospital now," Lance said. "We can meet you in about twenty minutes."

When they arrived, Harvey was in Sharp's office. A small voice recorder sat on the desk.

Harvey stood and shook Lance's hand. He was gentle with Morgan's bandaged fingers. "I've taken Sharp's statement. I'd like to get both of yours individually, and then I can fill you all in on what we've learned so far."

Lance and Morgan both kept their statements brief. They might have omitted a few details about Tina's attempt to take Evan and run. When they had finished, the four of them gathered in Sharp's office. Morgan took the chair next to Harvey. Lance leaned on the wall behind Sharp's desk.

Todd consulted his notepad. "We found Aaron Martin's body at the dam above Scarlet Lake. The ME has already positively identified him from fingerprints. The dark-blue sedan that Brian was locked in was registered to Aaron. In the glove compartment was a Newark police badge stolen from a murdered cop twenty-five years ago. He also had a big map of Randolph County and Paul's handgun. A 9mm handgun was recovered from the ground below the Scarlet Falls observation deck. Prints on the weapon matched Aaron's. We are running ballistics tests to confirm that it was the weapon used to kill Paul. Also, Brian positively identified Aaron as the man who kidnapped him."

"So Aaron was pretending to be a cop," Lance said as the last pieces of the puzzle fell into place. "I assumed the officer Brian's neighbors mentioned was a county detective, but I was wrong."

"Yes," Harvey agreed. "Brian's neighbors picked Aaron's picture out of a photo array. He was definitely impersonating a police officer. Sheriff

Colgate never sent anyone to talk to Brian's neighbors. He wasn't convinced that Brian's disappearance was related to Paul's murder."

It had likely been Aaron who'd been watching Jake's farm and who had attacked Lance, but Harvey didn't need every single detail, especially not the ones that could get Lance's PI license revoked.

Harvey continued. "Aaron also had a list of locations in the car. Some were checked off. It appears he'd been looking all over the county for the boy. The vacant house where Evan was seen was circled. There was a line drawn to the lake." He looked up from his notes. "I spoke with Rylee Nelson this morning. She told me that she saw Evan at the lake Wednesday night and that an unmarked police car showed up. The sheriff's department didn't have a vehicle in the area at that time. We checked with the SFPD. It wasn't one of their cars either."

"Aaron was looking for Evan," Morgan said.

"That's what we think." Harvey clicked his pen closed. "The arrest warrant for Evan has been pulled, and I've scheduled a press conference for this evening to make a public announcement. Evan has been completely cleared."

"Thank you." Morgan smiled. "Do you know if Joe Martin was involved or was the whole plan concocted by Aaron?"

Harvey shrugged. "The Albany cops interviewed Joe. He denied knowing anything about Paul's murder, and we haven't run across any evidence that implicates him. For the moment, we believe Aaron acted alone." Harvey nodded at Sharp. "Sharp suggested that Aaron might have been unhappy that his father was released and took back control of the company."

"I doubt you'll find proof either way," Morgan said. "Joe must have an army of lawyers to hide his businesses behind shell companies."

"I'm sure he does." Harvey stood and stretched. "Thank you for your time."

Lance walked him to the door. "Are you going to run for sheriff?"

"Hell no. The department is a mess. Colgate's office and files are complete chaos." Harvey jammed his hat on his head. "At this point, the county will be hard-pressed to find anyone willing to run for the office in November." He pointed to Lance. "You could run."

"Hell no." Horrified at the thought, Lance echoed Todd's response. "I do not have the patience for bureaucratic bullshit."

"I hear you." Harvey adjusted the brim of his hat and left.

Lance closed the door and returned to Sharp's office.

"I'm starving." He rubbed his empty stomach. They'd missed lunch.

"Pizza?" Morgan's voice lifted in hope. "We can take it home and eat an early dinner with the kids."

"Sounds good." Lance had a few missed meals and bedtimes to make up for. He wanted to spend the rest of the day binge-watching cartoons and cuddling with the girls.

"Do you want to come home to eat with us?" she asked Sharp.

"No, but thanks. I promised Olivia I'd drive her down to Albany to pick up her car."

"You seem happy about that." Morgan's smile widened.

Sharp actually blushed. "Yeah. Well, she's all right."

Lance thought about teasing him, then reconsidered. Sharp deserved some happiness. His boss had not had a special woman in his life for a very long time, and Olivia seemed perfect for him. Sharp left Morgan and Lance to lock up the office. They were leaving through the front door when Lance's phone rang. "It's my mom."

He answered the call. "Hey, Mom. Morgan and I were going to stop and see you on our way home."

"Now, that's silly," his mom said. "After all you've been through, you should both go home and get some rest. I am fine."

"I haven't seen you in a week." As busy as he'd been, Lance missed her.

"You've called me every day," his mom pointed out. "Go home to your family. Spend time with Morgan and the girls. Do something fun. That's an order."

"Yes, ma'am." Lance ended the call and relayed the conversation to Morgan. "Sometimes I forget that under her mental illness is a smart, tough woman. She's a survivor. I need to remember that."

Morgan took his hand. "Well, it seems she will be more than happy to remind you."

Chapter Forty

"After we pick up my car, you have to follow me."

"Why?" Sharp glanced at Olivia, who sat in the passenger seat of his Prius. She'd covered up the bruise on her cheek like a pro, but its presence still bothered him.

"I'm taking you to dinner."

"Shouldn't I be taking you to dinner?" he protested. "I got you into this mess. I almost got you killed."

"Nothing was your fault," she shot back. "I'm a big girl. I walked into the situation knowing the score."

"Neither one of us really knew the score." He exited the interstate and made his way to the parking lot where her Prius still sat. The night before, they'd spent hours being questioned at the local police station. Neither one of them had been in any shape to drive. A cop had taken them home.

"Thanks for setting up the meeting for Joe and Tina." Sharp was headed there later that evening. He didn't trust Joe one bit, and he would not let Morgan and Lance meet him without backup.

"You're welcome," Olivia said. "I hope it brings Tina some closure."

"I suppose I owe you another favor."

Her smile was just a little wicked. "I'll add it to the list."

He dropped her at her car, then followed the white Prius.

She drove through the streets as if she were used to them. Ten minutes later, she drove into a neighborhood of tiny, nearly identical one-story houses. She parked in front of a white house with red shutters. Olivia opened her car door and stepped out of the vehicle.

Sharp met her on the sidewalk.

"This is my parents' house."

"Oh." Surprised, Sharp brushed a hand through his hair. He hadn't met a woman's parents in . . . more years than he wanted to count.

"There is no way I can drive to Albany a second time without stopping to see my parents," she said. "On the bright side, you will love my parents, and there will be food."

"But your mother won't be prepared for dinner guests."

"I have two brothers and a sister. When I was growing up, friends ate at my house all the time. My mother's cooking is legendary. Even though my parents moved into this senior community a few years ago, my mother has never adjusted to cooking for two. She is always prepared for dinner guests. There will be enough food for at least ten people. Do you have family?" she asked.

He shook his head. "I was an only child, and my parents have been gone for more than ten years."

"I'm sorry."

"Thank you, but it's been a long time." He followed her up a cracked concrete walkway to cracked concrete steps.

She opened the door and walked inside without knocking, calling, "Mami! Papi!"

"Olivia!" Her mother was short and trim, with a head of curls dyed dark brown. She greeted her daughter with a hug and kiss on the cheek. Releasing her, Mrs. Cruz eyed Sharp. "And who is this?"

"Lincoln Sharp." Olivia hesitated. "An associate."

Her mother raised a drawn-on eyebrow at *associate*.

"It's nice to meet you, Mrs. Cruz." Sharp offered his hand.

Mrs. Cruz used it to pull him closer and kiss his cheek. Afterward, she didn't let go but tugged him down a short hallway. "Come in. Come in. You're in luck. I've been cooking all day."

Olivia leaned over Sharp's shoulder and whispered in his ear, "She cooks all day every day."

The kitchen was small but modern. Black granite counters topped white cabinets. Baking pans sat steaming on the stovetop.

An older man drank beer from a tall glass at the head of a table set for two. He stood when they entered the room. He was lean and dark, with gray hair shorn close to his head. Olivia introduced them. "Papi, this is Lincoln Sharp."

Mrs. Cruz released Sharp, allowing him to shake hands. Then she steered him to a chair. "Sit."

Mr. Cruz lifted his bottle. "Beer?"

"No, thank you," Sharp said.

Olivia set two extra places and brought Sharp a glass of water.

"You're so thin." Mrs. Cruz heaped food on his plate: black beans and rice, some sort of shredded meat, and a couple of fried items. "Ham *croquetas*, and the empanadas are filled with chicken."

"I thought you were a vegetarian?" Sharp whispered to Olivia.

"I love seafood, so I'm more of a pescatarian. But at Mami's house, I eat what I'm told." Olivia flashed him a wry grin. "I have interviewed drug dealers, gang leaders, and convicted murderers, but I am not brave enough to refuse my mother's cooking."

"What brings you home?" Mr. Cruz asked his daughter.

"We're here to do an interview." Olivia passed a platter of shredded beef and onions. "Lincoln is an investigator."

Mr. Cruz nodded.

They ate, and Mrs. Cruz caught Olivia up on the activities of what seemed to be dozens of nieces, nephews, and cousins. Sharp worked hard not to overstuff himself, which wasn't easy with Mrs. Cruz continually refilling his plate. He had no idea what he ate, but it was all good.

"Coffee?" Mrs. Cruz asked.

"No, thank you," Sharp said. "I don't drink coffee, and I'm stuffed."

"You haven't had dessert," Mrs. Cruz said as if that were a crime.

"I couldn't possibly eat any more. Thank you for dinner." Sharp shook Mr. Cruz's hand and accepted a kiss on the cheek from Mrs. Cruz. He followed Olivia down the hall toward the front door.

"Wait!" Mrs. Cruz's call was not a request but a demand that brought Sharp and Olivia both to a halt.

Her mother hurried into the hallway with a white bakery box. "I made *pastelitos* yesterday. You will take some with you."

"Gracias, Mami." Olivia took the box.

The sun slanted over the tightly packed houses as they walked to the cars parked at the curb.

"What's in the box?" Sharp tapped the lid.

"*Pastelitos de guayaba.*" The way the Spanish rolled off Olivia's tongue was hot. "Pastries filled with cream cheese and guava."

"Well, that sounds low in calories."

"Are you watching your weight?" Olivia took her sunglasses from her purse and set them on her face. "You need to lighten up and enjoy yourself a little, Lincoln, and you could use a couple of pounds. Life is short."

Sharp had been recently reminded that life could be cut even shorter at any time. "I haven't eaten that much meat in ten years."

Olivia raised her sunglasses and eyed him. "Your color looks better." She held the box in front of his face and waved it tauntingly. The pastries smelled amazing. "If you come to my house for brunch tomorrow, I'll share these with you."

"All right." He rubbed his gut, which ironically did seem happy with the high-fat, carnivorous meal.

"And I'll know you survived the meeting with Joe." Her words were light, but she didn't smile. "Be careful tonight."

"I will." He watched her fish for her keys—not a hair out of place, her petite frame fitted out with fashionable clothes. His gaze dropped to her feet. She was wearing a pair of those dainty, pointy-heeled, completely impractical sandals she loved. Her fingernails and toenails were painted fiery orange. Did her nail polish match her purse?

Yes. Yes, it did.

But underneath all that fancy window dressing, she was tough. She'd had his back when he'd needed it. Not only hadn't she run from the fight, she'd fought dirty and owned it. On top of that, she was smart. She had class and integrity. She took zero shit from anyone.

He was going to have to face facts. He liked her—even if she was a reporter.

And he was totally fine with that.

Chapter Forty-One

The bell on the glass door of the diner jingled. Lance spotted Joe Martin and two goons entering the lobby. Under his breath, Lance spoke to Morgan, who sat next to him. "There he is."

Joe walked with a cane, his posture stooped. Despite the limp and physical frailty, the two men who flanked him gave him complete deference.

Sharp and Tina sat at a table in the back. Sharp and Tina had both selected seats that put their backs toward the rear wall of the restaurant. As backup, Morgan and Lance had taken a table across the aisle. Morgan swirled the straw in her chocolate milkshake. Lance picked at a plate of fries on the table between them.

Sharp set down his water glass and stood. He covered his mouth and coughed. "I'll tell him to lose the muscle."

A few patrons sat at the counter, but at ten o'clock at night, most of the tables were empty. Sharp crossed the room and planted himself in front of Joe, blocking his path. Joe frowned. He glanced over at the table where Tina sat. He didn't hesitate but waved his men toward the door.

Sharp led Joe to the table and pointed to the chair opposite Tina. Joe sank into it.

Lance kept his eyes on his fries, but his ears were wide open.

"Tina." Joe's voice held no trace of warmth.

"Joe." Tina's answer was glacial. "Let's dispense with the pleasantries."

"All right," Joe agreed.

"Aaron killed my husband."

"Yes," Joe said. "He did that without my knowledge or consent."

"How do I know you're telling the truth? I assumed you wanted me dead." Tina's voice held no trace of fear. Lance risked a quick glance at her face. She wore her emotionless mask. His gaze shifted to Joe. He wore the same impassive expression.

"If I wanted you dead, you'd be dead. Unlike Aaron, I don't fuck around." Joe sounded like he meant it.

"Don't come anywhere near me or my son." Tina lowered her voice to a near whisper. "I have an excellent memory. I've made notes. Names, dates, places . . . crimes." She paused. "My notes are in a safe place, but if anything happens to me, they will automatically be forwarded to the district attorney. You would go back to prison." She rested her joined hands on the table. "I don't fuck around either."

Joe shifted back. "You are much smarter than Aaron."

There was no sign of grief on his face. His son had meant nothing to him. Aaron had been a pawn to be used.

"I'm waiting," Tina said.

Lance knew she was terrified. She'd been shaking during the entire drive to the diner. But as soon as they'd gotten out of the car, she'd wiped all traces of fear from her face.

Joe reached for his cane. "As I said before, I have no desire to kill you."

Tina's gaze didn't waver. She didn't believe him for a second. "I mean it. You stay far away from me and Evan or you'll be back in jail before you can blink."

"All right." Joe used his cane to struggle to his feet.

Lance didn't trust him. This felt too easy. Did Joe know Tina had the money? Lance couldn't tell. Tina could give up nursing and play professional poker, but Lance suspected Joe's lack of emotion wasn't an act. Father and daughter were not the same. Tina had learned to conceal her emotions as a coping mechanism. Joe didn't have any.

Joe limped out of the diner. The bell on the glass door jingled as it swung back into place. Through the plate-glass windows, Lance watched the goons escort Joe to a town car. The car drove away.

"Do you think Joe knows you have the money?" Sharp asked Tina.

"Probably," Tina said. "But he's hard to read."

No shit.

Lance rose to his feet and turned to Tina. "He won't come looking for it?"

She shook her head. "I don't think so. He knows I have the upper hand. He looks pretty sick. I assume he doesn't want to spend his remaining years in a cell."

Morgan pushed her empty milkshake glass aside and collected her bag from the floor. "Do you really have dirt on Joe?"

Tina's mask faded, and fire filled her eyes. "You do not bluff with men like Joe. They can smell it. They must know you will follow through with every threat."

Sharp pushed his chair under the table. "In short, you don't fuck around."

Chapter Forty-Two

Three days later

In the backyard, Morgan leaned on the fence and watched Ava and Mia blow bubbles. Sophie and the dogs raced in circles, trying to catch the bubbles before they drifted over the fence. The sun shone on the river, and the yard had finally dried out.

The gate squeaked as Lance came into the yard. Morgan greeted him with a kiss, happy to note that his bruises were fading. He wrapped his arms around her, clasping his hands at her lower back.

"How did it go?" she asked.

"Very well." He smiled down at her. "Evan was awake and joking with the team for a solid thirty minutes. He's beginning to grieve Paul's death, and he has some tough times ahead, but I think he's going to make it. Tina talked about selling the house and moving. Evan convinced her to stay here. He wants to move back to their apartment in Scarlet Falls."

"Do you think she'll stay, long term?"

"I don't know." He sighed. "I don't think she's ready to make any long-term plans."

Morgan turned to check on the girls. "If she does need to leave town, she has the means."

"Not that she will admit it to us."

"No." Morgan tried to understand. Tina's distrust ran back to her birth.

Lance tightened his grip around her waist, pulling their hips closer together. He was definitely fully recovered. "Now, tell me why the thought of planning our wedding always makes you sad."

"Grandpa helped me work it out." Morgan took a deep breath and began. "John and I had a formal church wedding. It doesn't feel right for us to have the same."

"Then we won't."

"You don't mind doing something small and less traditional, maybe even fun? This is your first and hopefully only wedding."

"I want to marry you. I'm not particular about how it happens, and I'm all for fun." He kissed her again. "I have two people to invite, and there's a very good chance one of them will attend via Skype."

"We still need a location. With the house under construction, we can't have it here." Morgan's mind whirled with possibilities.

"Is anything else bothering you?" He leaned back and studied her face.

"No." Her mood felt lighter at the thought of planning a fun event.

"Promise that you'll talk to me immediately if you're sad again? Your grandfather is an awesome source of advice, but I want you to feel like you can tell me anything."

"I will." She nodded. But now she was looking forward to the planning. "What do you think about September?"

"I love September." He kissed her again.

A squeal caught their attention. Sophie was racing across the grass to Lance.

Lance released Morgan and caught the leaping child in his arms.

"You're always kissing Mommy," Sophie said with just a hint of disgust.

"Yes, I am." Lance leaned sideways and kissed Morgan again. Ava and Mia ran toward them. Panting and breathless, they hugged Lance around the legs.

Morgan smiled wide. "We should get married at Scarlet Lake. We could have a picnic on the beach."

"That sounds perfect," Lance said.

Excitement bubbled up in Morgan's chest. "I'll have to check with the parks department to see if we need a permit, but I doubt it will be a problem. I know other people have held private events at the lake."

"My friend Emily had her birthday at the lake. She had a bouncy castle," said Ava. "Can we get a bouncy castle?"

Mia clapped her hands. "Bouncy castle!"

"I wike ponies." Sophie took Lance's face in both hands and turned him to face her. "But no clowns. I don't wike clowns."

And Sophie's lisp was back. She'd outgrow it eventually. But for now, Morgan was going to enjoy it.

Lance nodded. "I promise. There will be no clowns."

Sophie nodded solemnly.

Morgan grinned. "It sounds like we're going to have more of a carnival than a wedding."

"I like carnivals." Lance set Sophie down and tugged Morgan back into his embrace. "And as long as I get to marry you, I will be a happy man."

Acknowledgments

It truly takes a team to publish a book. As always, credit goes to my agent, Jill Marsal, for nine years of unwavering support and great advice. I'm thankful for the entire team at Montlake Romance, especially my managing editor, Anh Schluep, and my developmental editor, Charlotte Herscher. Special thanks to Rayna Vause, Leanne Sparks, and Adriana Herrera for help with various technical details, and to Kendra Elliot, for helping me push through those days when I need to write but don't want to.

About the Author

Photo © 2016 Jared Gruenwald Photography

#1 Amazon Charts and *Wall Street Journal* bestselling author Melinda Leigh is a fully recovered banker. A lifelong lover of books, she started writing as a way to preserve her sanity when her youngest child entered first grade. During the next few years, she joined Romance Writers of America, learned a few things about writing a novel, and decided the process was way more fun than analyzing financial statements. Melinda's debut novel, *She Can Run*, was nominated for Best First Novel by the International Thriller Writers. She's also garnered Golden Leaf and Silver Falchion Awards, along with two nominations for a RITA and three Daphne du Maurier Awards. Her other novels include *She Can Tell*, *She Can Scream*, *She Can Hide*, *She Can Kill*, *Midnight Exposure*, *Midnight Sacrifice*, *Midnight Betrayal*, *Midnight Obsession*, *Hour of Need*, *Minutes to Kill*, *Seconds to Live*, *Say You're Sorry*, *Her Last Goodbye*, *Bones Don't Lie*, and *What I've Done*. She holds a second-degree black belt in Kenpo karate; teaches women's self-defense; and lives in a messy house with her husband, two teenagers, a couple of dogs, and two rescue cats.